Behind Closed Doors

Also by Betina Krahn

A Good Day to Marry a Duke

Three Nights With the Princess

The Girl With the Sweetest Secret

Published by Kensington Publishing Corporation

Behind Closed Doors

BETINA KRAHN

ZEBRA BOOKS
KENSINGTON PUBLISHING CORP.
www.kensingtonbooks.com

ZEBRA BOOKS are published by

Kensington Publishing Corp.
119 West 40th Street
New York, NY 10018

All Kensington titles, imprints, and distributed lines are available at special quantity discounts for bulk purchases for sales promotion, premiums, fund-raising, educational, or institutional use.

Special book excerpts or customized printings can also be created to fit specific needs. For details, write or phone the office of the Kensington Sales Manager: Attn.: Sales Department. Kensington Publishing Corp., 119 West 40th Street, New York, NY 10018. Phone: 1-800-221-2647.

Zebra and the Z logo Reg. U.S. Pat. & TM Off.

First Zebra Books Mass-Market Paperback Printing: November 2019
ISBN-13: 978-1-4201-4356-0
ISBN-10: 1-4201-4356-5

ISBN-13: 978-1-4201-4359-1 (eBook)
ISBN-10: 1-4201-4359-X (eBook)

10 9 8 7 6 5 4 3 2 1

Printed in the United States of America

For my dear friends.
Pamela Muehlbauer
Charlie and L'Myra Hoogland
and
Thea Devine

Prologue

The golden rays of the midsummer sun had scarcely left the horizon when they returned, reclaiming the sky and the land. The shortest night of the year was past, and with it the great revels that accompanied the yearly Midsummer festivities, a celebration of warmth and light in a land that saw much cold and darkness.

Around the vaulted, oak-paneled hall of the Count of Aelthar lay the remains of a great celebration: guests lying limp in puddles of ale and draped over the banquettes that lined the walls, snoring servants curled on benches, scattered pitchers and tankards, and tattered streamers hanging from the wrought-iron torch frame overhead. Two male figures sat amidst the ruins, nursing dwindling tankards at the great oaken table in the center of the hall. Tall, blond Rugar Kalisson, the Count of Aelthar, and his friend, Baron Torgne Sigurd, had long since discarded their swords and starched ruffs, and their velvet doublets were half unbuttoned. Their strong, angular faces were drink-reddened, and their long, Norse frames were sprawled over the heavy estate chairs.

"He's sending you to England?" Torgne Sigurd stared blearily at his friend. The only thing sober about Torgne was his coloring: subdued brown hair and gray eyes. "Y-you can't be thinking of going. . . ."

Rugar Kalisson's Nordic blue eyes glinted in the fading glow of the torches, and his wide, sensual mouth drew up in a mischievous smile. "Damme, Torgne," his deep voice rumbled silkily, "you do get notions. Why can't I think of going?"

Torgne's jaw dropped. "Well, you *hate* England." When his declaration had no impact, he offered up evidence: "The women are all whores, you said."

"I?" Rugar leaned forward in his chair and quaffed the dregs of his tankard. His grin grew wine-warmed and wicked. "You have mistaken me. I believe I said the women are all *wonderful*."

Torgne's jaw snapped shut, and his drink-reddened eyes narrowed. "The men are all drunken cowards, you said. I heard you!"

"*Tsk* . . . Torgne," Rugar chided with a look of pained indulgence. "Sometimes I think you half listen to me. I am wounded." His muscular hand massaged the creamy white velvet of his doublet, above his heart. "Surely I said the men are *devout* and *courageous*. You must pay me closer heed if you're to be part of my delegation to London."

"Me?" Torgne's lean face blanked briefly. "Me? Go to London with you?" He sounded so horrified that Rugar chuckled.

"Who else? I will need you to help me set a proper, dignified tone as I carry the king's greetings to England's august court and glorious queen."

"Glor—" Torgne, caught with his nose in his tankard, swallowed and coughed and turned on Rugar with confused heat. "Glorious queen? She's a great walloping trollop! You named her Old Henry's loudest and smelliest fart—I heard you with my own two ears!" He pushed himself to his feet as if to leave, swayed, then sank back into his chair. His legs were grape-shot, and his wits were increasingly fuddled by this rare overindulgence in strong French wine.

Rugar's laughter exploded about the hall, a rich, full-timbred sound that seemed to warm the entire chamber. "I said that? *Gud*—I must have been drunk as a brewer's pizzle!"

"Dammit, Rugar, don't toy with me," Torgne said testily, trying to resist being drawn into Rugar's seductive good humor. "For years you've railed about what a vile stinkhole England is . . . and suddenly you sing its praises? Why would the king send you to England, knowing how you loathe the place?" His scowl darkened. "And why in hell would you agree to go?"

Rugar let out a deep breath and settled a beguiling grin on his lanky friend. "King Johan wishes to create 'good will' toward Sweden in the English court; to make them receptive to improved trade and a possible military alliance. He needs someone familiar with the court's ways and wiles. Who knows them better than me? And he needs someone who can set forth an impressive appearance for Sweden." He shrugged matter-of-factly. "Who in Stockholm has better skills at arms or more mastery of the courtly graces?"

That much was certainly true. No man in Sweden could match Rugar Kalisson's skill as a warrior and courtier. He was a paragon of Swedish manhood, the very pinnacle of Swedish nobility. Over the past ten years, he had relentlessly honed his strength and agility on training fields all over the Continent. And when not acquiring martial skills, he had cultivated courtly graces as he represented the king in royal Presence Chambers and refined his natural charm in ladies' bedchambers throughout the glittering courts of Europe. If it was King Johan's desire to impress, he had chosen the perfect man for the task.

"It's true I have no love for England," Rugar admitted, squelching Torgne's next protest before it formed. "But it is a great honor the king does me in sending me as his personal representative, his special ambassador to the powerful English court. He has been good to me; I owe him much. I will not fail him."

"Special ambassador?" Torgne whistled. That explained a great deal. Rugar was invited to follow in his father's footsteps as the king's personal envoy to the powerful English queen. It was indeed an honor, one which Rugar would be hard put to refuse.

"It is also a golden opportunity, Tor." Rugar's tone warmed. "Think on it. When we return home, our mission a success; there will be laurels and advancement for us at court. Successful diplomatic service is one of the surest routes to the enlargement of a man's estates." His eyes took on a telling light as he weighed his next words carefully. "And it is the perfect opportunity to teach the cursed English a lesson in respect for things Swedish."

The wine-sogged gears of reason finally produced a spark of comprehension in Torgne. Rugar Kalisson had carried an English "thorn" in his side for as long as Torgne had known him. He had been to England with his ambassador father when he was a boy, and though he never spoke of it directly, Torgne knew that his days at the young Elizabeth's court had bred in him a ripe loathing for things English. It began to make a sort of sense. King Johan and Rugar both wanted to "impress" the English . . . though apparently for very different reasons.

"W-well, how do we create this 'good will'?" Torgne

propped an elbow on the table to brace his head up. All this thinking after so much drinking was purely exhausting.

"We don't." Rugar beamed at Torgne's unwitting use of "we," thinking that his friend already had one foot aboard the ship and didn't even know it. With a roguish grin he explained, "It is not humanly possible for a Swede to create good will in an Englishman's stony heart. The English believe we are barbarians . . . crude, graceless, and uncivilized. I have tasted firsthand their contempt for our king, our language, and our ways. They will never love us." His patrician features tightened. "But we can make them respect us. It is high time someone taught them an appreciation for Swedish manhood." His voice roughened. "And I'm of a mind to do some teaching."

A moment later Rugar's natural charm emerged once more as he settled his broad shoulders back against the chair and considered his longtime friend.

"England isn't entirely wretched and bleak, Tor. In fact, you may find some aspects quite agreeable. The women, for example. You'll love them, Tor." His hands moved to suggest a woman's voluptuous contours and the tantalizing heft of a rosy breast. "They all wear those scanty little Italian bodices." His cupped fingers wiggled suggestively. "The ones that make you think they'll slide straight out of them with their next breath." His face filled with wistful lust. "And, *Gud,* they have the boldest eyes of any women on earth. They can strip you naked with one glance and damn near devour you with two." His grin tightened in response to some distant memory. "They're just like cats, Englishwomen. They rub themselves against you every chance they get." His voice lowered to a sensual growl. "And when you rub them back . . . they purr."

Torgne's eyes narrowed to slits as he pronounced his judgment. "Whores."

"Yes, indeed." Rugar chuckled and leaned forward, snatching up his friend's tankard and finishing it with a flourish. "Shameless tarts . . . the lot of them." Torgne's stern, Lutheran views on the morals of "court women" were well known. Rugar simply couldn't resist giving his friend's righteousness a prod. "Who knows, Tor? Perhaps we'll find you a hot-tailed English wench . . ."

With a snort of contempt Torgne shut his eyes against Rugar's insinuating leer . . . which allowed the wine and darkness to claim him. As Torgne slid toward oblivion, drink and the late hour began to affect Rugar as well, lowering his guard and his discretion. Talk of England had stirred long-buried memories in him.

"Did I ever tell you that I had my first woman in England . . . at the English court?" From the corner of a half-closed eye, Rugar witnessed the barely perceptible shake of Torgne's head. "Or rather, she had me. I was twelve years." He spoke in a whisper, an echo of memory. "She was dark and sloe-eyed. And very thorough. And I . . . I was scared witless." Deep in his fathomless blue eyes a glint appeared, the light of a flame long hidden. His voice deepened. His jaw hardened. "I went to England an innocent . . . and I came back . . ."

Torgne's head slid down his arm and landed on the table with a soft thud, pulling Rugar's thoughts back to the present. He shook off the pall of memory and watched Torgne settle into a creditable snore. Final protests and persuasions would have to wait; the rigors and revels of the year's shortest night had taken their toll. He settled back in his chair and let drink-weighted languor seep through him, claiming all but the enigmatic smile on his handsome mouth.

Through his mind came a slow, sensual procession of pouty lips and sly, questing fingers, fashionably bared breasts and dark, hungry eyes. The jaded ladies of the English court . . . the queen's own women worst among them. They had the morals of alley cats and loyalties to match. And he intended to claim them all . . . one after another.

Chapter One

North of London
June 1576

"B-but . . . *bosoms* are in fashion!" The Earl of Straffen settled his fists upon the waist of his peascod doublet and summoned yet another desperate objection.

"My dearest Jack. Bosoms have *always* been in fashion." The Countess of Straffen looked up from her stitchery to cast a half-amused, half-flirtatious glance at her tall, handsome husband. She let her eyes roam his elegant, broad-shouldered figure as he turned to stare out the leaded window into the side court below Straffen Hall. His shoulders had lost none of their commanding width to aging; his jaw was still as square and stubborn as it had been. His hair was just as dark—except for intriguing silver wings at his temples that bespoke his years and experience. "At least they've always been popular with *you.*"

The earl reddened and turned on his heel to stare at his lovely wife. There was a knowing sparkle in the deep, velvety blue of her eyes. He knew that look and what it betokened. She was being reasonable, so damnably reasonable.

"I mean, they wear them open . . . with no partlets, no in-filling for decency," he insisted. "All laced and lashed up so that they bulge out, Italian-style. . . 'neath scanty little ruffs. Lord-love-it, Merrie . . . I was at court last spring and saw for myself!" He stalked across the great bedchamber and towered above her, his arms dangling at his sides. Horror crept into his voice, constricting it. "Merrie," he whispered hoarsely, "they rouge their bubbies. Prop them straight out and dab them up like cherries!"

The fatherly worry visible beneath his indignation brought a rueful smile to the countess's lips and sent a sympathetic quiver through her heart. He was frantic to keep his precious jewel of a daughter at home, away from the worldly intrigues and debauchery of London's glittering but jaded court. And for the past two days, he'd been conjuring excuses, reasons, and rationales to bolster his refusal to let her go.

"And just how would you know how they rouge their bubbies, Jack?" she asked with a look askance.

The earl straightened as if stung and reddened prodigiously. "I . . . I . . . looked. Dammit, Merrie, I *looked*." He shoved his arms behind his back and locked one wrist fiercely in the other hand, bracing.

There was no gasp of outrage, no explosion of righteous anger. Instead, the countess let her gaze slide pointedly down his exquisite velvet doublet until it came to rest on his handsomely embroidered codpiece. She lowered her hoop of needlework and gave his manly accoutrement a penetrating stare.

"Well, as long as you only looked," she said dryly. Then she dragged her eyes up with a smile. "I trow that's what most men at court do . . . look. And I suspect there are precious few of the queen's waiting ladies that rouge anything a'tall."

"God's Nightshirt!"

"Jack, lower your voice—there are guests everywhere." she reminded him in a firm whisper.

"That's yet another thing I despise"—he bristled, lowering his voice—"being saddled with half of the queen's wretched hangers-on, just because our lands border hers." His arms flew out at his sides, palms up, in exasperation. "Elizabeth pauses at her own estates, on her summer 'progress' through the countryside but sends us more than half of her retinue to house. We're swarmed by her feckless hounds— strutting hedgecocks, pretentious strumpets, and gouty old croats—each demanding food, attendance, and entertainment. We'll be paupered for months to come. Now she wants our daughter as well!"

He strode back to the open window to stare hotly at the goings-on around his bustling estate. "Lord, look at them." He gestured to the courtiers teeming on the grounds below. "Crammed into every nook and cranny— I can't go to the damned privy without half the court taking note. Things have come to a fine pass in England when a man cannot have a satisfying squat or utter a decent oath in his own abode without dread of giving offense! And it's a dark day indeed when a man has to retreat to his bloody bedchamber to manage a close word with his wife."

But even in the privacy of the vaulted and paneled master bedchamber of Straffen Manor, the earl and the countess were not totally proof against prying eyes and ears. At that very moment, they were being observed through the crack of the partly opened door that led into the servants' passage on the far side of the great master bed.

A pair of jade-green eyes blinked, then withdrew from that opening during the lull in the earl's tirade.

Rouge? Corrie Huntington stood in the dim hallway, frowning, puzzled. She looked down at her own plain, modestly buttoned bodice and pressed first one, then the other of her breasts experimentally. Why on earth, she wondered, would court ladies apply rouge to their bubbies? Her mouth pursed thoughtfully. Why rouge them up if they were just going to be stuffed out of the way in a body stitchet? And why should the fact that the ladies did it outrage her father so?

She closed her eyes briefly, imagining the way a gentleman's eyes might drift over what a court lady's sparingly cut bodice revealed . . . *looking*, as her father admittedly had looked. A spark of insight was struck in her stunning eyes as they suddenly opened and refocused. Men sometimes *looked* at what women bore beneath their garments . . . and women must sometimes *let* them, else there'd be no need for rouge!

For a moment she was perfectly stunned. Color flooded her face in a rush, and a sudden chill raised gooseflesh all over her demurely covered shoulders. She sagged against the doorframe.

Pitch and dunk, she groaned silently. She'd never learn anything about the world if she didn't keep her ear to the ground and her nose to a door crack. She was going to be stuck with tutors and books and stuffy old music masters until she was ninety, she knew it . . . while the rest of the whole, wide, fascinating world rumbled on, around and past her. Her head tilted so that her temple rested against the doorframe, and a wistful expression crept over her features.

Outside the circumscribed borders of Straffen Manor lay all manner of wonders. There were great cities, vast oceans, and exotic lands . . . places so cold that the snow never melted, and places so hot that the peoples were burned brown and went as naked as Adam and Eve in the Garden of Eden. There were teeming bazaars and lofty pagan temples and exotic forests filled with strange and marvelous beasts . . . some as big as mountains with snakelike snouts and some like deer with ten-foot-long necks! Out in the wide world were fearsome armies, noble courts, universities filled with erudite scholars, and cathedrals so vast and beautiful they made one weep. And there were sages so wise that they knew the secrets of turning lead into gold, and monks so holy that they had actually beheld the fluttering tips of angels' wings.

Then there were the marvelous inner mysteries of mankind that beckoned to her; the intricacies of human nature, emotion, and experience . . . most especially love.

Courtly love, holy Christian love, love of sovereign and country. But the one that intrigued her the most was the unfathomable and irresistible love between a man and a woman, which found expression in the lofty pinnacles of art and music and poetry. More and more she found herself thinking about it, watching her parents, and wondering about this hallowed but elusive force, this *love* that seemed to bind a man and woman together in mysterious ways.

She sighed heavily. There was a huge world outside Straffen, just waiting to be experienced. And until a week ago, she'd glimpsed it only in the tantalizing text, tale, and verse of her studies. Then the queen's miles-long retinue of courtiers and servants had descended like a storm, catching her up in its dizzying swirl of spectacle and revel. Suddenly the first lords and ladies of the realm were stacked three abed and six-deep at table all over the manor. It was the grandest of Corrie's imaginings come to life; England's glittering court had journeyed to her very doorstep.

Then the great Elizabeth herself had come. Her majestic eye had paused, then fixed upon Corrie. Corrie was stunned that their sovereign lady talked with her at length and even invited her to games of chess. At her parents' request, Corrie had played the virginal and performed recitations in Latin from the writings of Seneca, known to be the queen's favorites. She had been invited to dine at Elizabeth's side and to meet her closest ladies. For Corrie, it had been like beholding the face of the sun itself to experience the queen's sharp wit and prodigious learning. And it was a thrill beyond measure to have the Queen of England praise her modest accomplishment.

Then, inexplicably, Corrie's father had restricted her to the tiny, isolated garret beneath the roof gables, where she had slept since surrendering her own chamber to several of their lady guests. It was wholly infuriating!

All her life, she'd been encouraged to seek and to search, to think and to question. It simply wasn't possible to stanch the tide of her curiosity now, even to please her beloved father. In desperation she'd begun to sneak and to snoop.

A rattling came at the main bedchamber door, jarring Corrie back to attention, and she again applied her eye to the slit in the doorframe. A veritable tide of humanity surged into the great bedchamber: guardsmen, waiting ladies, pages, and at last, when it seemed there was no more room, Elizabeth herself. She paused in the doorway, drawing all eyes upon her while surveying the chamber and its occupants.

She was resplendent in a gold velvet gown, a large, lace-rimmed ruff, and slashed and picked sleeves set with pearls and crusted with blackwork embroidery. Her thinning red-gold hair was mostly concealed by her demi-wig, and her mannish, short-brimmed hat was cocked at a rakish angle. A riding quirt in her gloved hand tapped restlessly at her skirts, as if venting the energy trapped in her tall, slender body. Her piercing brown eyes seemed to capture and catalog everything and everyone in a single sweep.

"Leave us. I would speak with my earl and countess privately." She waved a dismissing hand at her entourage. In moments the wave of humanity that always surrounded her imperial presence withdrew, and she strolled purposefully about the chamber, coming to stand before an ancient wardrobe with a ghost of a smile.

"You are fortunate indeed to have so fine a house . . . and family." The angular hauteur of her pale, faintly lined face faded. "What a pearl you have cultivated in your bosom, here. Corinna is a gell of exceptional learning and accomplishment. She gives such a twist to a Latin phrase! Your doing, I trow," she said, looking at Merrie, who flushed with embarrassed pleasure. "I cannot wait to present her to my old friend and tutor, Roger Ascham, when she gets to court, to see what he will make of her." The glint in her eye said she knew that she presumed—and that she fully intended to get by with it.

"Your scholar, Ascham, may have a long wait." Jack stepped forward stiffly, searching the determination in her face while deciding how much of his own to reveal. "Regrettably, we must decline your kind offer to take Corinna to court as a lady of your chamber. She is far too young and tender to leave her home."

"Ye gods, Straffen, she's eighteen years." Elizabeth exploded with a sardonic laugh. "Most gells are long wedded and well on toward childbed by eighteen." The crinkles at her eyes and the lines at her mouth deepened, turning her genial expression into flint. "You've ignored her future quite long enough to keep her near you," she declared bluntly. "It's time someone else took up her interest. And who better than her sovereign queen?"

Jack winced inwardly and glanced at Merrie, whose face was draining of color. They had indeed dissuaded matrimonial overtures toward Corrie, and in truth, not solely to spare her the hazards of childbed until she was older. She had been their only child for ten years, until their twin daughters were born almost nine years ago, and they were loath to part with her on any account.

In the servants' passage, Corrie stood frozen, shocked witless by what she'd heard. She? Invited to court . . . to join Elizabeth's own ladies? Oh, precious thought—*court!* And at Elizabeth's side—Lud!—in her circle of intimates! Her thoughts went spiraling off into vistas of magnificent

chambers and elegant clothes, discussions amongst sage
and learned councillors, and spectacles of ambassadors
from exotic lands come to pay homage to England's sovereign lady. The whole world came to England's court, and
she was being invited to witness—

Wait! Her father was *declining* it. Her eyes flew wide
with horror. How could he do such a thing to her?

"—to have a home and children about her someday," her
father was saying. "I shall find her a worthy husb—"

"God's Death!" Elizabeth swore, spreading her feet and
setting beringed hands at her waist. Her combative pose
warned of royal prerogative about to be unleashed. "There
are brood mares aplenty for England's noble houses!

"Corinna is no ordinary gell—she has a wit and a way
about her that fit her for something beyond the common
burdens of womanhood . . . for something rare and splendid. You did not teach her the orations of Cicero and the
dialogues of Plato so that she might recite them while
trapped, bare-arsed, beneath some fat nobleman's heaving,
pussley gut!"

Merrie blanched and Jack's jaw slackened at their queen's
bawdy and venomous reproach, which was intended to leave
a horribly vivid image in both their minds—and succeeded.
Their shock was so profound that Elizabeth reined her ire
slightly and lifted her chin. "Corinna deserves a better fate
than disposal in a barter of flesh and property."

"She deserves better than the moral corruption and disillusionment she'll find at court," Jack insisted. "Being
pawed by every randy young blood and horny old croat—"

"She will be a maid of honor of the Privy Chambers,
under my personal protection," Elizabeth countered with
regal heat, jabbing an imperious finger at him. "No man
would dare approach or molest a maid of my chambers . . .
unless he be afflicted with a perverse loathing for his own
neck. Corinna would be as safe as in a nunnery . . . sharing

my personal guard and guaranteed safe conduct, day and night."

Jack's smile came perilously close to a smirk. "Forgive me, but I've seen how loosely the rear doors to the ladies' apartments are guarded, Your Grace. I know full well how easily the sanctity of the queen's attendants may be breached."

"Mayhap in the *old* queen's time." She burned fiercely at his bold male challenge, knowing that he spoke from personal experience. "But never in *mine*."

Merrie watched the confrontation with mounting alarm. Corrie's future—perhaps all their futures—hung in the balance between her strident queen and her stubborn husband. Conflict boiled up in her loyalty to both her husband and her sovereign queen, and concern for Corrie's welfare.

"Perhaps we should send for Corrie," Merrie offered in a small, choked voice, "to determine her wishes."

Both Elizabeth and Jack turned on her in an instant, one in disbelief, one in delight. "By all means!" Elizabeth's mood lifted instantly. "The gell has a finely wizened head on her shoulders. Let her hear and state her wishes."

"She's a mere gell," Jack protested, "bedazzled by all—" *"Send for her."*

Jack swallowed hard against the hot words rising in his throat. His shoulders sloped as he stepped to the door and ordered a houseboy to fetch his daughter.

In the servants' passage, Corrie whirled from the door, shaking her hands and groaning silently. A heartbeat later, she snatched up her skirts and flew down the narrow hall to the servants' stairs, which led upward toward the garret.

In the master chamber, Elizabeth studied the conflict evident on Merrie's face. "We have weathered much together, Straffens, in perilous days gone by." Her voice lost much of its brittleness, and the depth of the need in her eyes stopped Merrie's breath. "The cares of the Crown are many, and they bear heavily upon me. Alas, there are few I can trust and fewer still who give me pleasure and peace of mind in companionship. Your Corinna is one such. Her freshness and buoyant spirit, her learning and the delightful facility of her mind—she renews me, just by her presence."

Elizabeth seated herself in one of the large chairs by the cold hearth. Her tautly held body relaxed, as though briefly released by the reins of power and obligation that held her even as she held them. Her sharp features softened, taking on a grave and wistful look that revealed Elizabeth was indeed a woman underneath, with a woman's heart and a woman's need for comfort and companionship. "I would not ask," she said quietly, "if I did not need her."

There was a scrape of hurried footsteps on the gallery outside, and the chamber door was flung open. Corinna lurched into the arched doorway and stopped on her toes, settling back on her heels to a more ladylike decorum.

Three pairs of eyes fixed on her as she curtseyed and stood waiting to hear the reason for their summons. Her hip-length hair was black as midnight and given to a slight curl, so that it seemed to caress her shoulders and waist as it flowed from beneath her pearl-rimmed cap. Her exquisite ivory skin was blushed with rosy excitement, and that same emotion sent golden sparks into the deep, jewellike green of her thickly lashed eyes.

The vivid contrast of her coloring was what first beckoned to the eyes, but it was the features of her heart-shaped face that bade them linger in admiration. Her satiny skin was molded over high cheekbones, a straight, slightly upturned nose, and a delicate chin that flared to a determined jaw. Her mouth was the only part of her face that could not have been described as delicate, and the only acceptable term for it was lush.

Yet for all her classic beauty, there was an air of sweet

impetuosity about her which threatened to overtake her at any moment. The velvet bow of her lips seemed continually on the verge of curling into an enchanting curve of pleasure, and the demure set of her shoulders poised continually on the edge of melting into seductive movement. Corinna Huntington was no remote, untouchable lovely; she was warm and accessible, temptingly alive and caressable. It was precisely that inviting, sensual quality about her that had given her worldly father sleepless nights of late.

"Corinna." Jack motioned his daughter forward. "I would know your mind on a matter touching you." He drew a ragged breath, struggling with the heaviness in his heart. "Her Grace has invited you to court, as one of her maids of honor."

"Oh! Oh, Your Grace . . ." She turned to Elizabeth, then back to her father, her eyes alight. Excitement boiled up in her, causing her tightly clasped hands to tremble. Her whole being was coming alive with the buoyant spirit that Elizabeth had just laid sovereign claim to.

"Oh, I would do as our sovereign lady would have me do," Corrie said in a breathless rush. Then, seeing the darkness in her father's expression, she amended it dutifully. "Of—of course, with my father's blessing."

"Court is a difficult place at best, Corinna," Jack admonished, his distress overlaid by sternness. Corrie's smile faded as she sought a rebuttal. Her chance to go to court now hinged on the suppleness of her wits.

"But a smooth sea never made a skillful mariner," she declared, hope rising. "We often learn best through adversity."

Her father's brow knitted at her pithy response, and he tried again. "At court, manners are all in all, Corinna. You have not been schooled in such strict disciplines and protocols."

"*Experientia docet stoltos,*" she countered earnestly. At

his irritable glare, she translated contritely: "Experience teaches even fools."

Jack's jaw clenched as a soft chuckle came from Elizabeth. He drew a long breath for one last try. "I see I am forced to speak bluntly. The morals at court are, alas, far from exemplary, Corinna. Men and women behave in depraved ways toward one another . . . using deceits to satisfy their foul urges for lust and power. I would spare you the sorrow that comes with encountering such wickedness."

"Do not the Scriptures teach that every man carries within his breast the seeds of both good and evil?" She came closer, her eyes bright with the artless sagacity her parents had cultivated in her. "May not morals fail and hearts be broken in cottages as well as in palaces? Is there any place on earth, no matter how grand or humble, which is proof against wrong and hurt and sickness?" She stood before her father, entreating irresistibly. "Has there never been a deceit or a wrong done here, upon Straffen land?"

Jack drew his chin back abruptly, and his ruddy color deepened. He had no answer to her weighty questions and no justification for further refusal—except her oddly wizened innocence and his own experience in the wicked ways of the world. He glanced at Merrie, whose eyes held the ache of remembrance, and he recalled the wrongs that had been perpetrated against her innocence, many years ago, in this very place.

He felt Elizabeth's hard gaze burn into his back as he turned to his daughter. There was an aching void in his chest. "It will pauper me to wardrobe you for court," he said thickly, announcing the only decision left to him. "And it will take some time. You cannot possibly go before autumn."

Corrie squealed and abandoned every grave and goodly manner she'd been taught to throw her arms about her father's neck. She hugged her mother tightly, then knelt before her queen and benefactor, to press the hand that was offered against her forehead.

She was flushed, dizzy, and trembling with excitement. She wasn't just going to London, she was going to *life!* She'd learn about far lands and cultures and languages . . . and perhaps someday the mysteries of love. From now on—the realization left her speechless—the world itself would be her tutor!

Elizabeth rose, smiling broadly, and raised Corrie by the hand to lead her to the door. She had won, as always, with her characteristic blend of cajolery, brute force, and disarming candor. And she was disposed to be magnanimous in victory. "I shall see to her welfare, Straffens. You needn't fear."

Chapter Two

Corrie learned literally hundreds of things in her first days at Whitehall with the queen: to always keep a fragrant pomander near her nose, that the sprawling red brick palace was a veritable rabbit warren of courtyards and corridors, that courtiers were a cool and clannish lot—but most especially, that to keep up with her royal mistress required the stamina of a regiment of horseguards.

From the moment of her arrival at court, she had scarcely stopped to catch her breath. Early mornings were spent in private with the queen and her closest ladies, and the strongest daylight was spent in scholarly endeavor: reading and translating, searching the marvelous old texts assembled in the queen's library. Late afternoons were filled with the queen's audiences or rides in the great park which lay just outside the palace. Each evening there was the ritual of the queen's dining, vespers, and finally dancing or other court amusements to attend. Through those long and sometimes hectic days, Corrie was frequently called to the queen's side to recite, ride, play the virginal, or simply watch her mistress at the work of statecraft.

Corrie's favorite times, by far, were the spectacles of the grand audiences, in which the world presented itself before England's sovereign lady. The French Ambassador,

Monsieur Pasquier, introduced a delegation of legal scholars from the Seine, who made the queen a gift of a copy of their revised codex of laws for her library. A delegation of Spaniards—with their elegant black velvets, sculptured beards, and dramatic posturing—came seeking redress against a broken marriage contract. An envoy arrived bearing gifts from the powerful Medicis of Florence, and a pair of dashing sea captains reported on a lucrative voyage chartered by the queen and presented her with her share of the profit. It was exotic, exciting—purely marvelous for Corrie to behold.

Occasionally, Elizabeth paused in the proceedings and turned to Corrie to discuss a translation, an opinion, or to share some juicy tidbit. Once, the queen recognized an emissary from Scotland and halted his prepared speech in midstream. She turned pointedly to Corrie.

"Be so good as to offer an opinion, Lady Corinna. How accountable should a man be held for the thoughts he expresses . . . and publishes?" The long-bearded Scot sputtered, but a severe look from Elizabeth silenced him.

Corrie swallowed hard and glanced about her at the many faces turned her way.

"I believe it is as the proverb says: 'An ox is bound by ropes and a man by his words.'" When the queen settled back in her chair, looking pleased by the response, Corrie ventured more. "A spoken word will die away, but a written word—a published word—has many lives; it is reborn in the mind of every person who reads it. A man should always be careful in what he speaks, but he should be fourfold cautious in that which he writes. It is a sobering lesson from the ages past that a man's words, committed to parchment, often outlive him." She all but melted with relief when Elizabeth beamed approval and turned to the Scot.

"I am of like mind, Sir Edmund. John Knox should be

bound by his words . . . preferably bound and gagged!"
Bold laughter erupted around the chamber, and Corrie's
face flamed as she realized the queen had wielded her
opinion against the fiery Scottish religious reformer, John
Knox. "His cursed pamphlet, *First Blast of the Trumpet
Against the Monstrous Regiment of Women*, declared the
rule of women to be unnatural and repugnant."

"B-but that was long ago," the ruddy-faced Scot protested,
squirming under her fierce regard. "He has since written
that Your Grace is the exception to the principle of female
unfitness—exempted by God's mercy, given the facility
to rule—"

"Unlike John Knox, I am one to honor my words,"
Elizabeth intoned regally. "I once declared he would not set
foot within the sovereign borders of this realm so long as I
am queen. His request to enter England and travel to Cam-
bridge is once again denied." As Sir Edmund withdrew, she
gave Corrie a conspiratorial smile.

The moments Corrie spent away from her royal benefac-
tress were usually claimed by Lady Blanche Parry, one of
the great ladies of the Privy Chamber, who had undertaken
to introduce Corrie and teach her the protocols of court and
her duties as a maid of honor.

There were scores of personages, great and small, who
each held a place in the Privy Chambers: Elizabeth's "great
ladies" and the dozen other maids of honor; members of
the Privy Council; Elizabeth's renowned Secretary, William
Cecil, now Lord Burghley; and a legion of undersecretaries,
envoys, and advisors. Old Lady Blanche seemed determined that Corrie learn them all.

Her head buzzing, Corrie seized her first free afternoon
in a fortnight to explore the expansive Privy Garden. The
setting sun found her on a stone bench in an isolated bower,
gazing dreamily upward, watching nighthawks soar above,

silhouetted against gilded clouds. An unseasonably warm evening breeze lulled her fatigued wits and overworked senses, so that she forgot the time altogether.

Rousing with a start, she cradled to her bosom the precious, velvet-bound book she'd been reading and hurried down one path, then another, trying to recall the way back to the Privy Chambers. Two left turns, then the statue of the painted lion. Or was that supposed to be a unicorn?

As she turned a corner, she spied two elegantly dressed gentlemen of the court, strolling and conversing. Recognizing one of them as a gentleman she'd been introduced to by old Lady Blanche, she approached to ask directions. Sir Christopher Leighton seemed to recognize her and, upon hearing her difficulty, brusquely demanded to know where her attendants were. When she confessed that she had ventured into the gardens alone, he insisted on escorting her back to the Privy Gallery straightaway.

As Sir Christopher joined her on the path, she glanced up at him, examining the way his fashionably trimmed beard complimented his regular features. He caught her in the act of looking at him and stiffened, turning his face away as if she'd offended him. She lowered her eyes, her cheeks reddening. She'd seen him in the Presence Chamber for the past several nights, during the evening revels and dancing. His handsome smiles came readily for the other ladies . . . which made his aloofness toward her all the more disheartening.

They walked, unspeaking, until they reached the great Stone Gallery, where servants were lighting torches and placing them in the iron brackets which hung high upon the stone walls. The silence worked on Corrie's pride, and she grew determined to make him speak to her. She slowed and paused, drawing him to a reluctant halt, but when she opened her mouth to speak, the tolling of distant bells, vibrating through the long, leaded windows and echoing down the gallery, drowned out her voice.

Evening bells . . . calling to vespers. Her eyes flew wide. She glanced down at the velvet-bound book clasped against her breast . . . the queen's prayer book. She had lent it to Corrie so that Corrie might read and contemplate the notations that it was her habit to make in the margins.

"I'm missing vespers," she whispered, "and likely causing the queen to miss them as well." She raised the small volume to Sir Christopher. "I have her prayer book."

"God's Teeth!" Sir Christopher grabbed her wrist and pulled her along behind him as he began to run. They flew down a bewildering labyrinth of corridors and stairs, past clusters of gawking courtiers and household officers. They ran at breakneck speed through the edge of the empty Privy Gallery, across a small paved court, then through yet another set of apartments and hallways. When they arrived, breathless, at the chapel entrance, he shoved her ahead of him through the heavy doors. She halted inside, clutching the book and straining to control her breathing.

The creaking of the massive doors, the swish of her silk underskirts, and the patter of her slippers on the smooth stone floor caused heads to turn as she hurried toward the front of the chapel. Soon the wave of murmurs reached the queen, who knelt upon her prayer bench at the very front of the worshipers.

Corrie knelt and approached the queen on her knees, her eyes downcast, holding the prayer book out to her. Elizabeth's smile was brittle as she accepted the missal and turned pointedly to search the rear of the chapel. She caught a clear glimpse of the scarlet-faced Sir Christopher slipping in amongst the worshipers at the rear. She motioned Corrie's head up and nodded forgiveness for the tardiness that had delayed her royal vespers. Corrie breathed

a heartfelt sigh of gratitude and took her place on her knees
at one corner of the queen's long train.

All through the service, Corrie could feel the stares of
the courtiers arranged in ranks behind her. They didn't
seem to like her very much, these noble lords and ladies.
They were standoffish and excessively polite, just as Sir
Christopher had been. There were not more than half a
dozen gentlemen, most of them doddering old fellows, who
would even nod to her in passing. And the noble ladies,
while usually polite enough to greet her, never included her
in their conversation or showed any interest in making
her acquaintance.

It didn't take more than a thimbleful of wits to guess why.

They thought her a dull country mouse. She sighed
quietly, shifting from one prayer bone to another on the
stone floor. Their sidelong glances and whispered comments made plain their opinion: she was a graceless, untu-
tored bumpkin . . . a silly, mannerless maups of a gell. And
worse, she dressed like a novice penitent from a severe religious order. Corrie popped one eye open, keeping her
head bowed, and stared irritably at her stark white velvet
gown. Her wardrobe had to bear much of the blame for her
cool reception at court, she was convinced.

Her father had hired a renowned seamstress to wardrobe
Corrie for court, then had proceeded to ignore the woman's
advice and dictate every detail of her clothing himself. Drat
and blast him! Everything she owned was now either stark
white or pitch black, and all her gowns were made with
severe, high-necked bodices, wanting only a wimple to
make her into the veriest nun in England. Her ruffs were
small and of plain linen, and her skirts were cut so modestly
that she couldn't wedge a respectable Spanish farthingale
beneath them without looking like an overstuffed partridge.
The most she could manage under the petticoats was a

small bum roll that was flattened in the front, and she'd had to plead to be allowed even that.

In a court presided over by a queen enamored of ostentatious finery, England's nobility had come to gauge worthiness by the extravagance and originality of an individual's wardrobe. It was little wonder, Corrie believed, that the courtiers, in their rich velvets and cloth-of-gold sleeves, in their billowing skirts and great ruffs and jewel-crusted doublets, thought her a sad country cousin.

Her father hadn't been able to prevent her coming to court, she mused darkly, but he had managed to see that she'd never be truly accepted here. Who wanted to consort with a maid who appeared to have given up life itself for a perpetual Lent? Whoever invited a drab little "nun" for a walk in the gardens, a scholarly discussion, or a spirited ride?

Nobody. She sighed. Except the queen. And for the queen's fond regard she should be eternally grateful. Elizabeth was a marvel, a wonder of mankind . . . fluent in seven languages and learned of all the great classics, the Scriptures, and law and literature and philosophy. Her personal greatness eclipsed her overdressed courtiers as the brilliant sun outshone the pale moon. And she had chosen Corrie as a companion of her thoughts. It was enough, Corrie told herself wanly. To desire more was surely vanity.

When the service ended and Elizabeth passed out of the chapel, she handed Corrie her prayer book once again and bade her ferry it to the royal bedside, before joining them in the Presence Chamber for the evening's diversions. Corrie saw her pause by the door to have a quiet word with Sir Christopher Leighton, at which he reddened, made an exceptionally deep bow, and strode out by a side door.

It was not until sometime later, when Corrie was seated on cushions by Elizabeth's feet in the Presence Chamber, that it occurred to her to wonder what the queen had said to

Sir Christopher. She looked about the Great Hall, hoping to
see him amongst the dancers, but he was missing.

The music was lively, and the colorful gowns and doublets glinted richly as the dancers whirled and leaped in the
golden glow of torch and taper. She soon forgot Sir Christopher in the wondrous spectacle. All around her were
famous persons: Ambrose Dudley, earl of Pembroke; the
handsome and worldly Edward de Vere, earl of Oxford;
the dignified Countess of Main; and the extravagant Lady
Devonrie and Lady Beatrice Smallwood in their daring Italian bodices. Corrie found herself squinting, trying to detect
traces of rouge.

A line soon formed near the dais containing Elizabeth's
great chair: gentlemen removing their short swords and
smoothing their doublets, jostling like cocks in a cage for
the honor of partnering Elizabeth in a dance. Several went
despondently on their way before tall, dark Christopher
Hatton arrived at her feet. Elizabeth flushed like a young
girl, placing her hand in his and allowing him to lead her
out for a graceful pavan.

Corrie smoothed her excrutiatingly plain white velvet
and sighed . . . dancing with them in her heart of hearts.

The next evening after vespers, Corrie looked up from a
game of "tables" with one of the queen's other maids, to
find her mistress bearing down upon her with a gaggle of
curious onlookers in tow. Corrie rose to her feet as gracefully as she could, her cheeks heating as she felt their eyes
upon her lackluster garb.

"Lady Corinna, we have someone for you to meet."
Elizabeth extended a heavily jeweled hand, calling forward
a stunning young woman arrayed in exquisite Bristol red
velvet inset with gingerline brocade and overlaid with gold-
wire embroidery. "Anne—Baroness Bosworth—has just

returned to our side from her late husband's estates in Sussex," she intoned. She chuckled at the polite but uncomprehending look on Corrie's face. "You've never met your cousin, Anne Huntington, now Baroness Bosworth. How delightful that you'll have a chance to know one another at last, brought together in our service."

Corrie fastened her attention on the lush features of the enchanting, hazel-eyed blonde before her. Her cousin? The daughter of her dour and righteous Uncle Henry, Baron Huntington?

She extended both her hands to her cousin, and her gesture was accepted in kind. "How wonderful to learn I have a kinswoman at court. I have heard my father speak of your father . . . and your husband." She halted, with the discomfitting feeling that her pretty cousin was measuring her like a tailor from beneath her perfect smile.

The courtiers crushed around them and watched, between, the two lovelies: one in red, as silky and sophisticated as the richest claret; the other in pristine white, as fresh and delectable as risen cream. Their commonalities—oval faces, prominent cheekbones, and lush, expressive mouths—bespoke an unmistakable Huntington ancestry. But the difference in their coloring suggested the great disparity in their experience of the world, and in their natures.

"How delightful to meet my little cousin at last," Anne of Bosworth said, releasing Corrie's hands abruptly. "We shall have to talk . . . someday." Cocking her head coquettishly, she listened as the music began afresh. "Is that a coranto I hear? My feet positively itch for a dance." The beautiful Anne Bosworth was instantly besieged by offers and was quickly spirited off.

Elizabeth watched Corrie staring after Anne. "It is difficult for minds to meet under such public scrutiny." She gave Corrie's hand a pat. "Come, sit a hand of primero with me and tell me what you think of Heywood's new play."

It was sometime later, after several hands of cards, that Corrie looked up from watching the queen dance and found her cousin bearing down on her with a tight smile on her lips and a fleck of red in her tawny eyes.

"I hope you're pleased with yourself," she said as she bent near Corrie's ear. "Chris Leighton's been sent packing. You've just managed to rid the court of the most virile stud around—and deprived me of a long-awaited jogging on my first night back at court."

Corrie's jaw dropped as Anne straightened and sailed smoothly on to greet several of Elizabeth's great ladies. Corrie blinked and looked about the grand chamber, profoundly shocked and thinking she must have imagined the words. Then she caught sight of Anne of Bosworth's sweetly duplicitous gaze upon her and knew she'd heard right. Sir Christopher Leighton sent from court . . . and she was being blamed?

An instant later she was summoning a footman with a tray of wine cups, then making her way to Anne's side, her thoughts narrowing and senses humming. She caught Anne's eye and spoke in hushed tones.

"What do you mean I rid the court of Sir Christopher?"

Anne turned to her with a determined smile that Corrie realized was meant for those who might be looking on. "It was your stupid little tryst last evening. The queen got wind of it and sent him packing back to Bristol for a cooling-off."

"A tryst?" Corrie flushed, suddenly realizing what Anne meant. "But it was nothing of the sort. I was in the Privy Garden when darkness overtook me, and I became lost. Sir Christopher was good enough to show me the way."

"I trow he did show you the way . . . to paradise." Anne raked her with narrowed, catlike eyes, then snatched the cup from Corrie's hand and took a deep draught of the watered wine. "Damme, I get the itch just thinking about his—I ought to throttle you!"

Paradise? The itch? Corrie's blush deepened. It was clear that Cousin Anne didn't have the Garden of Eden in mind, and it didn't take a sage to divine what sort of "itch" she had intended Sir Christopher to scratch. Lusts. Cousin Anne was caught hard in the grip of carnal lusts . . . and was brazen enough to chide Corrie for interfering with them! Her frozen jaw hinge finally thawed.

"It wasn't like that at all. He was simply kind enough to escort me, I swear it."

Anne of Bosworth stared hard at her cousin with the luxurious jet-black mane and the eyes like emeralds and the skin like Flemish satin . . . and felt an unprecedented stab of jealousy. For the last full day, since the moment of her return to court, all she'd heard about was Lady Corinna Huntington, and she was prepared to ripely loathe her famous little cousin on sight. Lady Corinna knew Latin and French *and* Italian, they said. Lady Corinna played the virginal like an angel. Lady Corinna could best Elizabeth at chess and recited classical masters by heart. Worse yet, Lady Corinna was a raven-haired beauty with skin as delicate as rose petals . . . so unsullied and virginal, so perfectly modest and admirable of temperament. And now Anne could see for herself: it was all true! *Dammit!*

There was an air of genuineness and—ugh!—a sweetness about the chit that were utterly disarming. She had a country-bred air of innocence, but without a vapid underpinning of country-bred ignorance. There was a liveliness of curiosity and a spark of wit in her gaze. Anne was torn between hating her very liver and wanting to discover what was behind those beguiling eyes. It grudgingly occurred to Anne that if this Corinna was the innocent she appeared, then perhaps she didn't know about Chris Leighton . . . or the way of things with regard to Elizabeth's ladies.

"Look here, Cousin." Anne put her arm through Corrie's, turning her so that they faced the gaiety of the great Presence Chamber together. "I see I must explain a few of the facts of life in the 'Privies.'" She waved a disdainful hand toward the dais. "You see those gells?"

"The maids of honor . . . yes." Corrie frowned.

"Well, they're giddy tits, the lot of them," Anne declared. "It's not their fault, however. And it's nothing that couldn't be cured by seven consecutive nights of vigorous rump-bumping" Corrie's eyes bulged, and Anne flashed a wicked smile. "You know: a good rogering, a bit of the old 'spread and spike me.' You lettered sorts probably know it better as 'fornication.'"

"It's true!" Anne scowled down Corrie's shocked protest. "Look at them: pouty, snappish, nerves on edge, and flighty as pullets. Ready to scratch eyes at the drop of a hair ribbon. Do they still have nightly pillow fights in the coffer chamber, where you sleep?"

Corrie nodded, her mind awhirl. The rational sense of it seized her, and her finely honed curiosities overrode her girlish sensibilities. There was a major discovery to be made here!

"A hot bit of screwing would work all that puss and vinegar straight out of them," Anne insisted nastily. Her eyes narrowed with challenge. "It always did me. Made me docile and loving as a lamb . . . for a whole day or two . . . until I felt the randy itch coming on again."

"Are you saying that women have lustful urges, too?" Corrie asked, more as scholar than as maid. "And that if they're not satisfied, they cause women to go all cross-grained and out of sorts?" Corrie turned to probe Anne's face, sorting both the truth and the motivation for her shocking revelations. Deep in Anne's eyes she glimpsed a hoard of anger, which she realized had to do with Anne's own thwarted urges.

Anne noted Corrie's earnestness, the curiosity and lack of moral outrage in her countenance. Hadn't she managed to shock the chit at all? "God. You do learn fast." She pulled away to bury her nose in the wine cup again.

Corrie chewed her lip, deep in thought. She could feel Anne watching her from the corner of her eye and turned back with a judicious look. "Well, there's a long-standing remedy for torturesome passions. St. Paul says it is better to marry than to burn. If they are so miserable, why do they not find husbands?"

Anne's glare was scorching. "There's not a sane or honorable man at court who would come near them, that's why. Bess is possessive of her maids, and even her great ladies, to the point of perversity. She'll not allow any lady in her chambers to court decently or marry. She guards her maids' virtue more jealously than she ever guarded her own, the great old tart. Whenever a man dares come too near one of us, he's quietly shuffled off to some netherland of randy swains, banished from court until he's done proper penance and learned to keep both his seed and his plowshare to himself. Bess is a bitch in heat, with no hope of easing it— so she insists the rest of us burn right along with her."

Corrie pulled back in astonishment. "How can you speak that way about our sovereign lady?"

"I'll tell you how," Anne said, biting out each word. "I came to court two years ago, after mourning my good husband, intending to make another honorable match. I was twenty-two and eager to plunge back into life. Then Bess laid exclusive claim to me as one of her ladies and began to banish or humiliate every man who came too near or admired me too openly."

"Why? Why would she wish to keep you from marrying?"

"God knows. Jealousy? Her looks are fading, and she's

fiercely aware of it. Miser's greed? We're all her chattel, her possessions, to be used or disposed of at will. Perhaps it is the pleasure she gets from wielding such power over others' lives. Who knows? She has a convoluted mind, that woman. It's said she has an unholy fear of marriage, learned at her ruthless father's knee . . ." Anne began to realize how dangerously she spoke and stopped, tossing her head, forcing herself to become calm.

The cold fury in her cousin's lovely face jolted Corrie. A woman didn't come to such deep anger without cause, whether the cause be true and just or not. She studied Anne, weighing her unthinkable charges against the queen.

"Do you talk to everyone like this?"

Anne had the grace to redden, suddenly appalled by her own garrulousness with a cousin she'd only just met—one who happened to be Bess's new pet. She must be drunk as a sow!

"No, only to you, Cousin. You're so blessed untouched and virginal . . . it's damned annoying. Brings out the claws in me." She lifted her chin and gave a sniff of superiority. "Do my bluntness and vulgarity offend you?" Her look said she hoped they did. Corrie was determined to disappoint her.

"I'm not sure. I shall have to think on it," Corrie responded stubbornly.

"Plow and plant me!" Anne slammed the empty wine cup on the nearby sideboard. "By all means—before you decide—be certain to consult whatever your wretched Greek masters might have to say about wasp-tongued widows deprived of all hope of a decent bit of fornication!" She stalked off, straight into the middle of a clutch of handsome gentlemen, who preened like cocks at the sight of her.

Corrie watched Anne throughout the rest of the evening, thinking hard about her shocking revelations. She now observed the gaiety of the lords and ladies through a new perspective, wondering with broadening insight what secrets, intrigues, and passions the rest of them carried in their elegantly clad breasts. And she perceived the frantic quality of their frivolity . . . and contemplated the difference between that vain and clamorous spirit and what she knew of "happiness."

At that moment, she felt the brilliant lights of court dim slightly in her curious, searching soul. And she knew that it was true, what the sages said: "Beware of seeking wisdom, for you may someday find it."

Chapter Three

Two days later, Corrie sat by Elizabeth's feet in the queen's gilded private closet, trying to concentrate on a communique from the French urging the relaxation of England's sumptuary laws. Her mind kept drifting from silk quotas and the burgeoning trend of the "lessers" trying to garb themselves like their "betters." Finally she lifted her face to Elizabeth and asked the question that had been plaguing her.

"Am I to blame for Sir Christopher being sent away from court?"

"What?" The queen turned restively in her chair and put down the document she was reading to frown at Corrie. "Whatever gave you that idea?"

Corrie stiffened her spine and summoned all her nerve. "It's said that you felt he had behaved improperly toward me that night when I was late to chapel, and that you sent him from court because of it. Please, I must know if it is true, so that I may set a great wrong to rights. I was sitting in the Privy Garden and lost track of the hour. He graciously offered to escort me to the chapel. He did me a simple Christian kindness, Your Grace, and I would not have anyone believe ill of him because of it."

Elizabeth's taut face smoothed with a reassuring smile.

"Ease your mind, Corinna. I sent Leighton to Bristol with urgent dispatches for my shipbuilders. I know Leighton for what he is." Her eyes glinted as she watched Corrie's troubled features and cursed Leighton for an impudent pup . . . approaching, attempting her Corinna. "His loyalty and gallantry have never been in doubt. Where in Heaven's Name did you hear such foul rumblings?"

"It is whispered all over court."

Elizabeth stared straight into Corrie's eyes, burning to know which vicious, wagging tongues had lashed her innocent ears. First Leighton and now someone else had the temerity to meddle with her pet—when she'd made it known that all were to keep their distance from her. How dared they try to poison her Corinna against her! Growing agitated, she rose to her feet and began to pace, her wide skirts sweeping the floor as her heels came down harder and harder.

"Corinna," she said, "this court is constantly atilt with some scandal or other. Rumors rage, and malice and jealousy stir tempests great and small. It is enough to buffet the wisest and steadiest of heads, betimes. You must not let such foul nets ensnare you. You are too precious to me." Her rigid stance eased, and she smiled wanly, a weary expression that tugged at Corrie's heart. Then she returned to her chair and reached for Corrie's hands.

"From the moment I saw you, Corinna, I cherished you. You are like a part of me, the tender, womanly side of me I may show to no more than a handful of souls on this earth. You are the innocence that the condition of my birth and my destiny never permitted me. In you I am reminded of the world dawning anew each day, full of wonders."

There was some truth, Elizabeth knew, to what was being said in the court about them: Lady Corinna was the queen's very image, turned inside out. Elizabeth was tough-minded and polished, an unassailable fortress . . . with what unknowable softness on the inside? And Lady Corinna was tolerant and generous of nature, a supple, yielding tree . . . with what unknown strength inside her?

"You must not believe anything you hear, Corinna, and only half of what you see. At court, away from the constancy and substance of land and labor, appearance and impression become all-powerful. Then who can say when impression becomes illusion?"

Corrie smiled wistfully. She was learning some of the most unexpected things at court. "'What once appeared as vices now appear as manners.' Then what appear as manners . . . may be vices in disguise?"

Elizabeth laughed, recognizing her beloved Seneca, paraphrased. "What a quick little thing you are, Corinna Huntington. Take care you do not grow too wise too fast."

The next afternoon, Elizabeth was closeted with a clot of privy councillors, and Corrie was free to stroll about the ladies' apartments. She came across Anne Bosworth sitting in a sunlit window seat in the ladies' private solar, working on a hoop of embroidery.

Corrie couldn't believe Anne's charges against the queen; nor could she dismiss the depth of Anne's resentment. It was a puzzle. And Corrie Huntington could never resist a puzzle, no matter how intricate or unpromising. But then Anne herself was something of a riddle. There was something intriguing, even appealing, about the toughness she affected. She had been married and widowed; those bare facts bespoke her experience in life. There were things to be learned from Anne Bosworth. And Corrie could think of no greater attraction that anyone could hold for her than the ability to *teach* her.

She approached and stood quietly for a moment before

speaking. "The queen didn't send Sir Christopher away because of me."

Anne looked up, seeming surprised by Corrie's presence. "And how would you know?"

"I asked her."

"Good God." Anne's jaw dropped and her eyes jolted wide. Several emotions flared in her expression—anger, confusion, excitement, fear—before she managed to find her tongue. "And I suppose you told her every wretched word I said the other night!"

"You would hardly be here, speaking to me, if I had," Corrie said with sudden heat. "I have very strict standards about such things, Anne Bosworth. I would never tell you the queen's confidences . . . and I won't tell her yours." She plopped down hard on the window seat and glared at Anne, feeling pleased that she'd managed to shock her worldly cousin. "I would have you know I am utterly trustworthy."

Anne stared at the determination in Corrie's enchanting face and scrambled mentally, rethinking her cousin. And, as was characteristic of her, she came right out with her new assessment.

"I'll bet you are, damn you. Probably keep secrets and always tell the truth and say your prayers every morning and evening without fail." She heaved a huge, disgusted breath and shook her head. "Leave it to Uncle Jack to sire a saint . . . while my pious prig of a father sires a strumpet." She scowled, horror dawning afresh. "Think what a horse-laugh it will be on me when the court learns I've taken up with a bloody 'nun.'"

Corrie began to smile. Anne was going to take up with her. They were going to be friends! Her smile grew to a laugh. "That's life for you," she declared impishly. "Unfair all around."

* * *

In the days that followed, Corrie spent her hours of freedom, as she was coming to think of them, with Anne. Life in Cousin Anne's company took an invigorating turn. Anne showed her which of the merchants who came to the palace with their wares were honest and which combatants to lay modest wagers on in the weekly tilt at the Tilt Yard. Under Anne's tart-tongued tutoring, she learned how to spot a cheat at cards, how to finagle oranges and sweetmeats from the palace kitchens, and how to see that her "smalls" were given priority in the palace laundry. But most importantly, it was at Anne's prodding that she approached the queen with a request for a separate sleeping chamber of her own, away from the noise and commotion of the other honor maids. It was graciously granted. Then, in the privacy of Corrie's modest new chamber, they experimented with ways to make the most of Corrie's luxurious hair and restricted wardrobe.

"Who chooses your gowns . . . Mother Mary Penitent?" Anne asked, wincing as she held up a stark black velvet bodice.

Corrie erupted in giggles. "Worse. My father."

Anne laughed, too, infected by Corrie's wonderful sense of the absurd and her oddly shockproof innocence. She'd never met anyone as paradoxically learned and ignorant, or as innately curious, as Corrie Huntington. And she understood exactly what worldly Uncle Jack had been about in sending his irresistible daughter off to court in such nunlike trappings. It had worked . . . and it hadn't. The elegant simplicity of Corrie's clothing had indeed set her apart from the glut of color and ostentation. But it had also highlighted her blooming womanliness and the lushness of her dark-light coloring. Half the men at court were covertly aching to give little Lady Corinna a sample of their heated admiration.

"You know what you need?" Anne mused, as though to

make up for her sin of omission in not enlightening Corrie as to her sensual appeal. "You need to air the dairy a bit."

"Air the dairy?" Corrie frowned, then backed a step as Anne advanced on her, brandishing a pair of shears snatched from a nearby sewing basket.

"The *dairy,* gell. Come on, you're not that slow. Flash the flesh . . . bare the bubbies . . . give the gents a peek at the twin pearls of pleasure." Corrie gasped and tried to escape, but it was already too late. She stood, stunned, watching Anne cut a hank of fabric from the top of her bodice. "With a facing and lace, another snip and a tuck . . ." Anne finished cutting, stuffed the raw edges into Corrie's corset, then stepped back to eye her brazen handiwork. "There! You're perfectly ravishing."

Corrie stared in disbelief at her pale, rounded breasts, which were now exposed almost to their very tips. She felt positively naked! How could she ever walk about like this, with her bubbies bared? Never mind that the other ladies, Anne included, did it all the time. Her hands splayed protectively across her breasts. What would her father say?

The thought sent a bolt of pure rebellion through her, and her eyes narrowed fiercely. Her father indeed. It would serve him right if she hacked up the fronts of all her bodices!

Still, when Anne gleefully made to modify her other garments in similar fashion, Corrie stayed her eager shears, consenting to make "Italians" of only two of her bodices until she grew more accustomed to the style. And, using the excuse that her tiring woman would have to finish and trim the alterations properly, she put off wearing them for a time yet.

Anne seemed determined to make a true "court lady" of her, and Corrie wasn't sure how she felt about that. But her delight in her cousin's incurably irreverent company was indisputable. Anne seemed to have a tidbit, a tale, or a ribald jest about everyone at court. And what she didn't know, she endeavored to find out often through devious means. More than once, Anne dragged Corrie discreetly from the court's evening diversions to follow some unsuspecting young blood to an amorous tryst, to discover the identity of his partner. And it was in Anne's dauntless company that she first spied on an all-male gambling rout and glimpsed a scantily clad gypsy dancer in heated performance, albeit from a distance.

Thus, Corrie's courtly education occasionally took unplanned, unscholarly, and even risky turns. None of what Anne pulled her into was unlawful or even immoral, but Corrie sensed the queen would be shocked, even angered, to learn of their clandestine forays. As much as she loved Elizabeth, she discovered she loved *learning* even more.

Sneaking and skulking again, Corrie sighed. Just like home.

The queen was seen to bed each evening in a formal court ceremony, amidst a cloud of perfume and the angelic voices of boy choirsters bidding her good night and God's bountiful rest. The royal garments were removed and kissed reverently by her ladies, then handed off to the queen's wardrobers. Elizabeth then lifted her hands to offer a prayer; and dismissed the courtiers to their private amusements.

It was in those enfranchised hours that license and mischief ran amok amongst Elizabeth's courtiers. The sternly reproved and restricted maids of honor clamored rowdily in their chamber, such that the household officers, whose chambers were nearby, complained of the noise. Gambling took a serious turn, promises of licentious liaisons were kept, and wholesale assaults were made on the palace wine cellars. Drunkenness, intrigue, and debauchery went on all around Corrie, leaving her untouched and unaware—until Anne Bosworth determined it was time to further her education yet again.

Late one night, a week before the Queen's Day celebration in mid-November, Anne appeared in Corrie's chamber to pull her from her warm bed.

"W-where are you taking me?" Corrie stammered, clutching her dressing robe about her as she stumbled along.

"An orgy," Anne whispered, flashing a grin as she hurried Corrie down cold, darkened corridors. "Your first, I trow."

"An *org*—"

Anne clamped a hand over her mouth, dragging her into a shadow and casting a frantic look around the empty corridor. "Look, Bess has her crown and scepter to cuddle up with at night, and the adoration of her courtly swains to compensate for her juiceless existence. But what have her ladies got? A bellyful of bowing and scraping, and a lot of itches that can't be scratched. So we take our pleasures as we can—in the odd orgy here and there." She pulled Corrie along, then paused long enough to add, "Oh, and not a word about this to anyone, or we could all bloody well lose our heads!"

Anne soon dragged her through a door and down a set of steps that led into a long, stone-walled chamber. The place was brightly lit with torches, the floor rimmed with straw and mounds of pillows. Tables laden with delicacies from the royal kitchens were laid out at one end.

Corrie stopped dead on the steps, staring at bare smocks and bare shoulders and bare legs. The guests were all in some state of disarray . . . and they were all *women!*

Someone thrust a great tankard of brandy-laced wine into Corrie's hands, and Anne tilted it up so that she had to either quaff or drown in the stuff. She came up sputtering, eyes watering, throat afire. A crown of wine-warmed faces were suddenly pressed around her, laughing at her reaction and raising their own cups in salute. Lud! There was old Lady Cobham . . . and the Countess Olivia of Barreton . . . the dignified Lady Lennox, Lady Devonrie, the Countess of Main, and even the elegant Beatrice Smallwood, all in varying stages of undress! Corrie was staggered.

They drank prodigiously and stuffed themselves with fried pasties and drippy fruit tarts, sugared almonds and fig dainties, while all around them flowed the music of the lute, recorder, and tabor drum. In the cleared area of the floor, a few scantily clad ladies swirled into wild, spontaneous motion, dancing as the urge struck them. Their whirls and leaps were utterly unlike the strained steps that were performed under the court's expert eye.

Anne caught Corrie by the arm and pulled her to the ring of ladies forming loosely around the open floor for a wild rendition of a country ring dance, where each of them took a turn dancing in the middle while all kept time with their hands. It was astonishing to witness some of the great ladies of court gamboling about like giddy country lasses.

At length, the music wheezed to a halt, and the ladies refilled their cups and stuffed their mouths full of sweetmeats. Some toddled off to collapse upon cushions, while others milled about the tables, laughing and carousing. Suddenly the haughty Bess of Hardwick picked up a silver dish cover and plopped it upon her head, striking an arrogant pose. "My train, you dolts!" she bellowed in a voice that was purposefully—*recognizably*—shrill. "I must have a train!" The ladies scrambled and ranged over the cellar to find something . . . and soon presented her with two horse blankets, tied together, which they fastened on her shoulders between fits of laughter.

"I am 'Bumptious Bess,' your queen!" Bess of Hardwick declared, swaggering up and down, parodying the *other* Bess's strident manner and mannish graces. Corrie didn't know whether to be offended on her lady queen's behalf or not. But one look at Anne's laughing face, and she burst into helpless giggles.

"Oh, Your Benevolent Bawdiness!" Several maids and ladies went running to "Bumptious Bess," complimenting her elegant train, bouncing figure, and vulgar crown. With each outlandish compliment, she preened wickedly and the ladies roared, demanding more. In truth, Corrie realized, they only said those things which were said to Elizabeth in earnest flattery: the stars winked from embarrassment that they were not as bright as her eyes; she was the fairest maiden in Christendom. . . .

"Yea; verily I am that!" the pretender-Bess cooed raucously. Then she giggled and whirled, kicking her train about in a raging parody of Elizabeth's famous mannerism, and demanded that someone find her a throne. Corrie watched, weak from laughter, as an old barrel was rolled out and Bess of Hardwick waggled her bottom and made a comical display of mounting and settling herself upon her "throne."

This must be what drunkenness is like, Corrie thought helplessly. She couldn't seem to control herself; she was seized by the same contagions of laughter as the rest of the ladies. The release was heady and exhilarating. Her sides ached, her cheeks hurt, and still she laughed.

It was indeed an orgy, she thought. A bacchanal of lewd wit, which purged feelings that were never allowed to show in the rigid confines of the daily court.

Bess downed a goblet of brandied wine, then surveyed her kingdom with exaggerated gravity. "Wait!" she shouted. "You!" She pointed a finger straight at Corrie, standing not far away. "Who in hell's blistered hump is that? Bring me yonder tart!"

Corrie was seized by the arms and trundled forward, to

stand before Bess-of-the-Barrel. "Who the devil is this creature? And how dare she invade my court?"

"Oh, Your Magnificence . . ." Laughter threatened to erupt through Anne's ceremonious tone. "She is, regrettably, an innocent. Dare I say it? An *unlicked cub*, still wet behind the ears."

"An *unlicked cub*, you say?" Bess shouted, seeming horrified. "Then, by God, I'll lick her! Hold her steady—"

Corrie was too weak with laughter to struggle as Bess grabbed her head and gave her face a great slurpy lick from her chin all the way to her forehead while the ladies pealed with laughter.

"A tasty tart!" Bess roared above the merry chaos, licking her lips and rolling her eyes as Corrie sputtered and swiped at her soupy face. "She'll make some man a savory mouthful! Come . . . dance, you lazy strumpets! I shall have dancing!"

The ladies obliged in suitably raucous style. Everyone danced—even Corrie—in rowdy rings or in pairs, heedless of the beat of the music. Then someone handed Bess a broom handle for a scepter and she pounded it vigorously in time to the music while calling out appraisals and insults to the dancers, just as Elizabeth was wont to do.

When the dance ended, Mary Talbot, Bess of Hardwick's daughter, snatched up a great two-foot sausage from the food table and brandished it brazenly, drawing howls and rude hoots from the ladies.

"Lud, I'd know that sausage anywhere!" Bumptious Bess exclaimed. "It's"—the ladies all shouted with her— "*Dudley!*"

Corrie watched in puzzlement as the cellar rang with laughter. That great sausage was supposed to be Robert Dudley, earl of Leicester, the queen's long-standing favorite, who'd lived for years in heated expectation of marriage with her? But why would they deem him a saus—

"You've kept me *dangling* for years, my bouncing Bessie!" Mary Talbot roared, waggling the sausage suggestively. "But, by thunder—I'm *dangling* no longer!" The laughter increased to peals and howls as she pranced and strutted about with the sausage, then chased Bess up and down the room with it—removing all doubt as to which part of Robert Dudley it was meant to represent. Then Bess trapped that sausage between two rounds of bread, and the ladies howled as Mary and Bess began to struggle and heave.

Corrie could scarcely breathe, her sides hurt so much. She staggered to the nearby cushions and plopped down, holding her ribs. The sight of the sausage and the implication of the way Mary had wielded it were scored into her fertile mind. All she could think was that now she had a hint of what was involved in the act of passion. Like buns and sausages, it was . . . heaving and puffing, groaning and stuffing . . . it was purely shocking. And it was that unprecedented shock that Anne Bosworth encountered when she sought Corrie out later and collapsed beside her. She grabbed Corrie's chin to stare at her.

"Lud, you're not going to be sick, are you?" she demanded.

Corrie shook her head, her eyes still somewhat unfocused. "Is that what they're really like . . . men?"

It took Anne a moment to be sure she'd heard properly, then she rolled back on the cushions, cackling with glee. Corrie's face caught flame as Anne uncrumpled herself and lurched to her feet, calling to their fellow debauchees: "Our 'unlicked cub' is in dire need of education. Come help me enlighten her and these other young maids on the arts of love!"

Amidst rowdy laughter the ladies began to collect on the cushions around them, with full wine cups and heated faces. Corrie was stunned by their frank good nature and their intent to discourse on so unthinkable a topic for the "cub."

From the start there was little agreement on the details of what they revealed of the amorous arts. It was best, Lady Beatrice opined, to be deflowered while lying upon one's back. When that met with mixed response, she declared she ought to know, since she'd been deflowered *thrice*—once by each of her first two lovers, then by her first husband! They howled, and aging Lady Cobham took it up, declaring that she'd always regretted not getting "rogered" first on a chair, which would have prevented her from being squashed witless beneath her swag-bellied husband. On hands and knees, side to side, standing, kneeling, spoon-fashion, against a wall, atop a table, astride or astridden; the possibilities, they vowed, were endless—even to hanging by the toes. All stopped and stared at sweetfaced Lady Lucy Montague, who had contributed this last. She blushed and swore it was possible, and somebody bashed her with a pillow.

Seeing Corrie's eyes glazing over, Anne handed her a full wine cup and took up the task, declaring that the process invariably started with kissing. The ladies agreed unanimously that a man often tried to get by with just a few dry pecks, instead of the deep, lubricious penetrations a lady needed to get herself primed for an enjoyable bout of "leather stretching." Some well-intentioned jade at the back cautioned everyone against kissing Lord Settlesby. "Old thunder-tongue!" numerous others shouted in recognition. The warning came too late. "Soft and sinuous" was the preferred kissing motion, they agreed.

Corrie drank frantically from her cup, her tongue squirming against her teeth as she shuddered at the idea of a man invading her mouth so. How could these ladies possibly think such a thing was pleasurable? But since they obviously did . . . how must it *feel?*

To caresses and sweet nibbles they progressed, with side

steps into the merits of "disrobing" versus "being peeled."
Names were boldly bandied again; the handsome Earl of
Oxford was a master of the licentious nibble, while the
Earl of Essex was a toothy grunter who all but devoured
a gell and left marks. Very bad form, leaving marks. Nippies,
all agreed, were to be teased delicately, palmed and rolled
and laved with the tongue.

Corrie was close to swooning. Her bubbies were tingling
alarmingly, and she was feeling twiddly in places she didn't
want to scratch. She looked at Anne with eyes wide with
discovery. It *was* like an itch!

Then came the main business of lovemaking . . . the
movement of eyes and hands, and the positioning and blend-
ing, and the glorious friction of heated bodies. And the
climax. It was shooting stars. It was rainbows bursting. It
was a great splintering shock that ripped through a woman
like a lightning bolt. Everyone present had a different way
of describing it. To Corrie it sounded a bit frightening and
confusing, but she drank in every word.

Faces reddened all around as the ladies slid further into
their cups. Then, as things became increasingly quiet, one
small, somewhat slurred voice was raised. "De Vere's the
best bum-tickler in the entire court."

That brought them back to their senses instantly, and a
hue and cry of dissent was raised as candidates were put
forward for that salacious honor. Shortly the manly at-
tributes of the lords and knights and younger sons—even
the councillors themselves—were being cataloged. Lord
Grundy was too soss-bellied and didn't bother to use his
elbows; Lord Greville's rootle was too long and thin for
much satisfaction—shorter and thicker being universally
preferred. Hatton was right well equipped, but seldom in
the market; the queen kept him on too tight a leash. Sir
Christopher Leighton was magnificently provided and

marvelously skilled. He'd been known to make a woman see stars just by diddling her ducks!

One by one, amorous judgment was passed upon the males of court: de Vere was ever one for a quick "dive in the dark"; weasel-beaked Suffington usually fell asleep halfway through; anyone from the French ambassador's party was "a good frisk" or "a worthy tumble"; Lord Winter did a unique and delicious grinding motion; and young, whey-faced Lord Latimer still suckled a lot and called it "stable my naggie." Corrie began to see England's noble manhood prancing before her bleary eyes in a lusty line . . . dangling, jiggling, and writhing. She shook her head vigorously, then finished her wine in one breath-holding chug.

Things really began to swim in Corrie's head. Her eyes closed of their own accord. Her shoulders slumped. Voices and vision dimmed, and she slid into warm, welcoming blackness . . . right down the shoulder of the Countess of Main, who was sprawled beside her.

"The cub has snuffed it, Bosworth," the countess said, laughing as she lowered Corrie's limp body to the cushions. Anne smiled tipsily down at her cousin.

"I trow she heard enough. She is a quick little thing."

The next day Corrie awakened to find herself safe and snug in her own bed, suffering no more physical ill effects than a furry mouth and a thundering head. Her mental and emotional states, however, had been more drastically affected by her first night of debauchery. There was now a raging fire in her already heated imagination and, worse, an insatiable itch of curiosity in the rest of her.

All evening long, and indeed for several days to follow, wherever she went she encountered gentlemen of the court whose sundry parts and privities had been explicitly detailed to her. She saw waddling sausages where mere codpieces used to nestle and found herself peering at their mouths and hands, trying to recall which had been identified as "slow and sinuous" and which were "squeezers" and "tweakers." Her secret knowledge of them made it impossible to meet their eyes and sent chills racing up her arms whenever any of them took her hand in greeting.

It seemed that all of her formidible curiosity had congealed about one topic and had somehow sunk through her body to rest disconcertingly in her bubbies and loins. Lovemaking, passion, and the mysteries of men were suddenly all she could think about!

Almost as shocking was seeing her fellows in debauchery as they appeared once more in ladylike guise. Lady Cobham was again the firm and dignified matron, and Bess of Hardwick was every bit as contained as before. Mary Talbot appeared as plain and pious as ever, and Lady Beatrice still seemed a glowing, untouchable beauty . . . except that now Corrie knew she was "touched" after all, and frequently. Only the merest glimmer of an eye as they traded demure smiles indicated that anything had gone on at all. Even Anne never spoke of it, except to call Corrie "Cub" in private.

It was that extreme discretion and the smarting of her own scholar's pride that kept Corrie from approaching Anne with the million curiosities that her night of revel had provoked.

One thing had been settled in her mind, however. Anne was not the only lady at court with a grudge against Corrie's beloved queen. There were a number of women who chafed at the limits that Elizabeth imposed on them. Corrie had to believe that there was some basis for their resentment. But she also believed, after the evidence of her own eyes and ears, that Elizabeth had reason to disapprove of and limit their behavior.

Day after day, she had seen the queen as few others saw her; wrestling with her moods, grappling with affairs of state, bowing to the intolerable restrictions of her personal being in the service of her crown.

Corrie would be loyal to Elizabeth, she vowed, whatever befell. For the queen, above all women, needed a true friend.

Chapter Four

A week later, Corrie sat in the main gallery of the palace Tilt Yard, her eyes alight with fascination at the color and pageantry unfolding around her. Excitement shivered through her as the far-off sounds of clashing metal and the whinnying and tromping of nervous horses combined with the beat of drums and the blare of trumpets. Banners and flowers decorated the edges of the tilt floor, and the great bar which divided the arena was freshly whitewashed and wrapped by great lengths of red ribbon which matched the splendid red uniforms of the queen's guardsmen, posted around the arena. Above the crowded stands that ringed the field of combat, Corrie glimpsed the tops of tents blazoned with brilliantly colored pennants, glowing jewellike in the strong morning sun.

In those tents a society of "knights" prepared themselves, their armor, and their steeds for ritual battle in the queen's honor. It was Queen's Day, the yearly celebration commemorating Elizabeth's accession to the throne, and it marked the start of a three-day tournament.

Corrie and Anne were seated with the queen and her ladies and nobles, beneath the cover of a massive green velvet canopy draped with garlands of fresh evergreen, ivy, and autumn flowers. Elizabeth was dazzling in a jewel-encrusted gown of gold cloth and a fanciful conical headdress draped with shimmering veils. The great ladies, seated around her, wore more subdued but still lavish gowns, and the first gentlemen of the realm yielded nothing to the ladies in the richness of their gilded garments and plumed hats. But none of those richly garbed nobles, not even the queen herself, drew more notice today than Corrie.

She sat demurely at Elizabeth's side, wearing her customary white velvets, which had been daringly recut to bare the tantalizing bounty of her bosom and were now adorned with rivulets of blackwork embroidery. She had forgone a cap, wearing only a circlet of gold on her raven hair, and about her throat nestled a small ruff.

The heated stares, shocked whispers, and speculative glances turned her way made her sit straighter and lift her chin. She felt exposed under the courtiers' bald scrutiny, and oddly guilty under the queen's tellingly silent regard. But for once, she told herself firmly, she looked more like a refined young woman than a graceless maups of a gell who knew naught about life.

Suddenly the trumpets blared a great fanfare and the drums rolled. Excitement rushed through the crowd, and all craned their necks toward the far end of the field to witness the entrance of a column of twenty-four mounted knights. Great colored plumes trailed from gleaming helms, and both breastplates and saddles were draped with rich brocades emblazoned with the heraldry of the knights' ancestral houses. On each knight's shoulder piece, the hammered silver initials ER, the queen's personal monogram, marked them as her devoted vassals.

The column thundered once around the great yard with lances posted in stirrups, then came to a halt by the dais, where Elizabeth tied her shimmering veils on the lances of Sir Henry Lee and the dashing Earl of Oxford, designating them her champions. Corrie turned to Anne, seated behind her. "Five gold sovereigns against your silver brooch that the Red Hawk unseats the Silver Dragon," she proposed.

Anne squinted, studying the combatants, then straightened. "So be it!"

It was thrilling combat. Two by two, the contestants lowered their visors and lances, set their heels, and charged. The blue knight against the green, the Silver Dragon against the Red Hawk; they clashed with ferocious intensity. Even so, the combatants were evenly matched, and it often took several passes before one of the two knights was unseated. "Splendid sport!" the queen shouted, and all roared approval with her.

By midafternoon, the number of knights had been reduced by half, and Corrie was the new owner of a worked-silver brooch. The queen's champions entered the lists for the first time, issuing a ringing ritual challenge to all comers.

Soon the number of combatants had dwindled to six.

As the six made a ceremonial sweep of the yard before the final rounds, another knight appeared at the gate that led onto the tilt floor, a new contender, unseen until this moment. A ripple of confusion spread through the galleries. A new challenger, so late in the contest? They searched his imposing figure for some sign of his identity and found none. All fell to a hush, during which Oxford and Sir Henry turned and rode forward to confront this unknown threat.

"State your intentions, Sir Knight!" the earl called.

"I've come to do battle!" His deep, resonant voice rang out through the silent yard. "You have sworn to take all challengers in the queen's name." Banners whipping in the wind were the only sound as the queen's champions and her court took his measure.

It was difficult to see him clearly, for his armor and the silver-trimmed white of his trappings were so bright in the afternoon sun. The great plume of his helm, his breastplate banner, his lance, and his saddle hangings were all pure white, woven with silver, so that he seemed to shimmer before their eyes. His massive warhorse, a pure white Normandy, arched its neck with anticipation and pawed the ground as if eager for the spur. The knight seemed to dwarf the queen's champions.

"Then declare yourself and the house for which you ride!" Sir Henry Lee demanded.

"I ride for God and my master, whose name will not be revealed until I am victorious!" the knight thundered.

Corrie glanced up at Elizabeth's fierce scowl of concentration, then at Anne, whose eyes were alight with the same excitement she herself was feeling. Corrie looked back in time to see Oxford turn to Elizabeth for a sign. She raised a queenly hand, admitting the challenger, and the mysterious white knight dropped his visor and spurred his mount, which exploded into motion beneath him.

Pandemonium broke loose in the galleries. The unknown challenger was claiming the far end of the field as his stand! Elizabeth's six knights turned to face him, their anger blatant in the curt reining in of their horses. Then, as one man, they lowered their lances . . . six challenges, made as one. All watched breathlessly as the huge white knight lowered his lance . . . six times in succession.

He was going to fight them all!

Corrie's heart began to beat in her throat. All around her she heard reckless wagering and expressions of mingled anger and admiration. She turned to watch the challenger, filtering the dazzling sight of him through her dark lashes. She was the queen's loyal servant, but something in the beauty and daring of the mysterious knight enticed her heart into his camp. He was grace and power, courage and strength: the knightly virtues personified. And in the first pass of his first bout, he was also victorious.

Corrie and the rest of the queen's gallery came to their

feet as Sir Harold Cottrell toppled into the churned earth along the tilt bar. Cheers and hoots quickly faded as the courtiers settled on their seats again, like uneasy birds at roost. They flew up again when the second knight was unseated. By the third, they remained on their feet, shouting encouragement to Elizabeth's beleaguered champions.

He was effortless in his movements, this white knight. He handled his lance as if it were a mere sword and shifted his armor-clad body in the saddle as gracefully as if taking a step in a dance. He took one glancing blow to the shoulder from his fourth opponent. Corrie's gasp was swallowed up in vengeful cheers from the galleries. The hit only seemed to spur him on, for he dispensed with his opponent on the very next pass. Suddenly there were only the queen's two champions left between him and the victor's laurels.

It was unthinkable that anyone should actually try to best the queen's champions. It was an unwritten rule of the tournament that the queen always triumphed on her day. But as Sir Henry Lee pitched ignominiously from his mount and lay on his back, flopping like an overturned turtle, it was clear that this unknown knight cared little for custom. He would have nothing short of full victory.

Then only Edward de Vere, earl of Oxford, was left to defend England's lady. Corrie held her breath as the green-clad earl took the field against the white knight. Retribution was promised in Oxford's every movement and in the way his mount danced nervously from the angry pressure of his knees.

The flag was dropped, and they lunged into motion, aiming for each other's chests or shoulders. Then, at the last minute, the white knight twisted adroitly in his saddle; Oxford dropped the point of his lance in the same instant, driving it hard into the white knight's flank in a raking motion.

Corrie choked back a scream, for it was clear that the

earl had scored a blow. The white knight curled slightly to one side, then straightened and gave his mount the knee. And they charged each other again. Oxford took a savage clout to the midsection that left him bent over his saddle. He waved his squires away as they ran toward him and valiantly straightened, turning his mount for another pass. Corrie looked up to find Elizabeth pale, her eyes glittering.

On the fifth pass, Oxford's lance splintered, and he narrowly missed being unseated. His lance was easily replaced, but not his concentration and confidence. There was an unseen tremor in his lance as he readied for the next charge. Within heartbeats, he was lying on the ground, gasping for air.

A great hue and cry was raised as the unknown knight made a triumphal circuit of the tilt floor with his lance upraised. But all quieted abruptly as he approached the dais and stopped . . . then lowered his lance toward the queen. Red-coated guardsmen came running from all directions, brandishing bladed pikes. Out of nowhere, an extraordinarily tall man in austere garb appeared beside the knight, accepting his lance and buckler. The great knight dismounted without assistance, then reached for his lance.

He strode toward the dais with the lance upraised, only to find the steps blocked by a wall of furious guardsmen. He looked up at the queen, who stood staring at him, and paused. Then, when every eye was fastened on him and every breath was bated in fearful expectation, he took his victorious lance in his hands and brought it crashing down across his upraised knee, splintering it. Tumult erupted in the galleries. What strength it must take to break a lance that was thick as an oaken beam!

Elizabeth proved her reputation for great personal courage by calling to her guardsmen, "Let him pass!" They melted back to allow him access, and he mounted the steps while the court watched with mingled horror and fascination.

Two steps from the top, he paused and laid his broken lance at Elizabeth's feet. A clamor broke out all around. He'd just given the queen back the victory he'd snatched from her champions!

"Such valor and gallantry must not go unrewarded," Elizabeth declared. "Bare your head, Sir Knight, to receive your laurels."

Corrie's heart stilled as her eyes fixed on his intriguing form. Even standing two steps down from the dais, he was equal with Elizabeth in height—and the queen was not a small woman. He worked the latches and removed his helm with a graceful economy of movement, then swept back his padded leather hauberk. Then he stepped fully onto the dais, towering over the queen and sweeping her court with a bold look more suited to a conqueror than a champion.

Corrie gasped, and that strangled sound drew his attention. His head turned slowly. His gaze fastened on her. A shocked hush settled over the galleries as the great white knight turned his massive shoulders to face her.

At that moment in the court's impressionable eye, Corrie and the unknown knight were inextricably joined by the common starkness and purity of their raiment: he, armed in glittering silver and white; she, swathed in soft, velvety white.

He was huge . . . breathtaking. Her senses were swarmed with details that went shivering harum-scarum along her nerves, some lodging just beneath her skin, some penetrating her body's sensitive crevices, and some collecting around her heart to set it beating frantically.

He was fair of coloring, with hair like ripened wheat, light skin that bore a golden patina from exposure to the sun. His features were handsomely sculptured over broad, high cheekbones and a magnificently squared, clean-shaven jaw. His eyes were vivid blue, rimmed with a thick fringe of amber-colored lashes. They began to darken as they locked with hers. Twice her eyes dipped to glance at his mouth . . . boldly chiseled lips, wide but gracefully arched on top and grandly, indolently curved below. And twice her eyes were pulled back to his sultry gaze.

His eyes were like none she'd ever seen. They were deep azure pools, cool and fathomless, as though they reached to the very center of him and beyond. She had never met a pair of male eyes so boldly, had never felt possessed by a man's gaze before now. She was suddenly lost, wandering in those seemingly endless reaches of blue. Admiration, amusement, promise, maleness, mystery . . . a hundred separate perceptions reached out to brush her awareness as she passed through those enchanted azure realms.

Her face flamed and her knees threatened to buckle beneath her. She could scarcely get her breath. Her entire body seemed to be melting helplessly into streams of raw sensation. She couldn't tear her eyes from him! But the murmuring among Elizabeth's ladies somehow penetrated his senses, and the knight pulled away, turning back to the queen with unruffled composure.

"Accept this victory, Your Gracious Majesty, as the tribute of my sovereign lord . . . your devoted admirer, King Johan of Sweden." The great knight swept the broken lance at the queen's feet with a graceful hand and bowed gallantly.

Elizabeth straightened in surprise. There was a trace of a lilting accent in his fluent English, but none hearing him would have identified him as Swedish. "Kneel, Sir Knight, and accept the victor's reward." He did as bade, going down on one knee before her, his blond head lowered. She placed a plaited wreath of laurel leaves upon his head, then presented him with a large emerald. "We know your lord, Sir Knight, and admire his generosity. We would also know your name, to welcome you among us," she declared.

Up came a wry, beguiling smile and those startling eyes that seemed to both absorb and reflect the glory of the glittering queen and her court.

"Rugar Kalisson, Count of Aelthar, Special Ambassador from the King of Sweden to Your Grace's court . . . and your servant." At the wave of her hand, he rose and stepped to the edge of the dais to receive a diplomatic pouch from a somberly clad man who was even taller than he was. "May I present Baron Sigurd, part of my mission." The lanky giant bowed, then retreated down the steps. "I offer these credentials and my sovereign's letter of greeting to you, most excellent Majesty." He lowered his head. "And I bear gifts from my lord . . ."

"Tonight, then." Elizabeth received the pouch with her own hands and studied the great, strapping Swedes before her with dancing eyes. "You and the baron must be guests at our personal table tonight, at the banquet . . . so that we may welcome you properly."

With a bow that could only have been called elegant when made in a full suit of armor, Rugar Kalisson backed away. Then he paused in the midst of turning, faced Corrie again, and removed the laurel wreath from his head. Going down on one knee before her, he laid the token of his victory at her feet. With a smiling glance at her widened eyes, he descended the steps of the dais, leaving Corrie staring after him in wordless shock.

Rugar Kalisson strode across the yard and through the knight's gate, acknowledging the clamor of adulation that poured down on him from the stands and galleries with a supremely satisfied smile. Torgne Sigurd stalked beside him, his expression customarily somber as he ignored the pandemonium Rugar had unleashed with his daring and somewhat harrowing introduction to the English queen and her court.

It was several minutes before they escaped the curious, noisy throng that invaded the knights' grounds and reached their unmarked tent, which had been erected a distance away from the others. As the commotion of tending his horse and removing his armor subsided, Rugar dismissed his grooms, saying he would finish himself. When he and Torgne were alone, he sank into a wooden campaign chair with a huge sigh. Torgne scowled and knelt to give him a hand with his greaves and spurs.

"Careful!" Rugar winced and tested his knee and lower thigh gingerly with his fingers. "It hurts like the very devil."

Torgne's eyes narrowed on the fresh bruise. "It's no more than you deserve. Whatever possessed you to break the damned lance over your knee? Those things are made of heartwood."

"I thought it added a nice touch." Rugar's grin was unrepentant. "And I could see the thing was cracked already, or I wouldn't have tried it." He prodded the large, purpling stain above his knee with a judicious finger. "Lud—I hope nothing's broken. I plan to partner the queen herself tonight, at the dancing. A broken leg might prove something of a hindrance." His handsome mouth quirked up on one side, producing a dimple in his cheek. Torgne yanked on his padded legging, causing him to both wince and laugh.

"Don't be so sour-mouthed," Rugar chided. "It worked. Elizabeth was quite taken with my little masque. Nothing like a bit of mystery and a touch of chivalry to tickle a woman's vanity. Her personal table tonight, Torgne." He punched his friend on the shoulder. "Things are going along even better than I planned." He reached for the tankard of herbed wine his groom had left on the nearby trunk and took a deep draught. When his head raised, a glint of heat had invaded his pleased expression.

"I intended to capture her eye, and I have. Now I intend to make her watch as I give her feckless court hounds and pampered champions a sound trouncing at every turn." He beamed in anticipation of victory. "Tonight I'll outdance them. Tomorrow, when the tournament continues, I'll outride and outfence them. And tomorrow night and in the nights to come, I'll take them at their gaming and out-gallant them with their own queen." His eyes narrowed, containing their vengeful glitter, and his fingers tightened around the handle of his tankard. "By the time we've finished, they won't laugh at a Swede ever again."

Torgne considered the splendid display Rugar had put on that afternoon. He had no doubt that Rugar could best the English at their trials and games. Likely he would out-shine them at their courtly accomplishments as well. He would make quite an impression on the English court, achieving King Johan's ends while settling a personal score with the haughty English. But what if Rugar's aims some-day parted company with their sovereign's, what then? He frowned uneasily as he laid Rugar's greaves and spurs in the armor trunk.

"What did she do to you, Rugar?" He turned with a frozen-fjord look about him that said he'd not be forestalled this time. He stalked closer, spread his long, hard-muscled legs, and planted his fists at his waist. "I am a party to the scheme; I have a right to know what wrong it avenges. What happened to you here that made you hate the English queen so?"

Rugar studied Torgne's angular, stem-featured face. They had been friends and companions for a dozen years; had traveled and fought together . . . lived like brothers. But there were still parts of each man that remained hidden from the other. It was the Swedish way: each man to bind his own pain and to keep his own confidence. He wrestled with Torgne's demand through a long, uncomfortable silence, then bowed to it.

"Soon after Elizabeth came to the throne, my father came to London as Special Ambassador . . . to seek her hand in marriage for Prince Erik, heir to our Swedish throne. I was permitted to come, to further my diplomatic education . . ."

Rugar's eyes darkened as he called up memories. His usually glib manner faded, and it seemed he had to drag each word from depths within him. "From the day we arrived, Elizabeth showed nothing but contempt for my father and our delegation. She refused to lodge us in the palace, kept my father waiting in corridors for audiences that were never granted, and mocked our attempts at her language. The trollop refused us her table and her society," Rugar said, staring fixedly into disturbing scenes of remembrance, "but she was quick enough to take the fine horses and chests of gold we brought as gifts."

Torgne sank onto a nearby cot, watching Rugar's expressive eyes crackle and his proud features harden with old angers. It unnerved him to glimpse the deep turbulence that lay at the core of the charming rogue he had known for so long.

"Power was like new wine to her. She was drunk with it," Rugar continued darkly. "When we were finally admitted to her banquet hall, she sat upon her high table and taunted my father into dancing . . . then ridiculed his attempts to please her. The openness of her contempt gave her wretched courtiers license to abuse him as well. I stood at the edge of the torchlight, my heart burning within me, watching as she abased and humiliated my father before her cursed English and our own delegation. My father was a warrior, a councillor, respected for his abilities and accomplishments in Sweden, but she considered him nothing because he was Swedish . . . and could not *dance*."

"It is hard for a young boy to see his father dishonored," Torgne said quietly, knowing it must have been doubly hard for Rugar, who had worshiped his proud, noble father. "But it has been a long time . . ."

"That was only the start of the trouble she caused us," Rugar ground out. "When we returned to Stockholm, Prince Erik had become king and my father had to face him with news of his failure. Word of our humiliation at English hands had already reached Erik, and he fell into a violent rage, attacking my father and banishing him from court. He swore to confiscate our lands . . . vowed he'd never see my father's face again . . ."

"Erik was going mad," Torgne interjected.

"Erik was also *king*," Rugar said bitterly. "His insane fury subsided, as it often did, but the damage was done. My father's pride had been broken by his own failure and by the king's wrath and scorn. When he was again permitted at court, he would not leave our lands . . . and soon, not even our house." His voice grew choked. "Day by day I watched him withdraw from the running of our estates . . . from me . . . finally from life itself. I was scarce fifteen when he died. My mother had died long before; I had no living brothers or sisters. England's cursed queen had taken both my father and my father's honor from me."

Moments passed before Rugar could rip his inner senses from that painful mental tableau. His heart was pounding, and his hands gripped the chair arms so hard that his knuckles were white. Exerting a control finely honed by the repeated conquering of pain, he peeled his hands from the wood and forced himself to take a deep, calming breath.

When he looked up, Torgne was staring at him with a troubled expression.

"When my godfather, Duke Johan, deposed Erik and became king, he moved to restore the honor of our house . . . made me Count of Aelthar. Now he has sent me to woo England's wretched queen. Like my father before me." He paused. His jaw flexed, and his eyes glinted. "Only, I can *dance.*"

Each submerged for a time in his own thoughts. Torgne finally met Rugar's searching gaze and nodded slowly, both in understanding and in support. But a moment later he scowled.

"Well, what was all that nonsense with that maid?" he demanded, rising to his feet. "The one you laid your laurels to?"

Rugar's engagingly wicked smile returned. "A mere whim, another touch of chivalry. A knight-errant must always have a lady fair." He laughed at the way Torgne shook his head and stalked toward the tent opening. When Torgne declared he was going to see to their application for ambassadorial apartments in the palace, Rugar only half heard that parting comment.

In his mind rose, unbidden, a pair of large green eyes with long, sooty lashes. His eyes closed to trap that image and hold it a while.

A wanton fall of hair, black as a winter night's sky. He'd never seen hair quite like that. And those eyes, green as spring wheat. Not common brown, nor watery English gray, nor even the vivid blue so common in his native land. But green. And jewel clear. Skin like the purest cream and breasts like blushed peaches. Lips in a lush, sultry bow . . . ah, God, like cherries, bursting with sweetness, just begging to be bitten. He ran his tongue over his lip in unconscious response.

He had looked around that blindingly bright assembly, and there she was. Cool and velvety, a sensual haven in the harsh, overwhelming glow of rampant gold cloth and glittering gemstones. She'd worn white, rimmed with delicate blackwork embroidery that seemed to blend with her wind-ruffled hair in a fanciful dance over her revealing gown. She was a trove of tantalizing textures: silky hair, velvety gown, satiny skin, liquid eyes, feathery lashes. His fingertips were itching now . . . wishing to touch her. And his whole body was warming to the demure, womanly silhouette he explored in his mind. No great, cumbersome farthingales or ruffs, no wired headrails or padded stomachers or unwieldy sleeves or irksome, vermin-ridden hairpieces. Just a woman. Soft. Touchable. Responsive.

And English, he reminded himself. He roused, pulling his eyes from his vision with a wry tilt to his mouth. The scant cut of her bodice and the boldness of her gaze told the rest. She was certainly of that permissive English sisterhood, but too young to be greatly jaded and appealing enough to be a sensual prize. And seated so close to the queen, she was undoubtedly one of Elizabeth's own ladies. So much the better.

He took a deep, satisfied breath as he poured water to wash. Tonight he would make it a point to learn who she was. And by week's end, he would claim her delectable textures . . . every last one of them.

At that very moment, Corrie was sitting on the edge of her bed closet, clutching a plaited wreath of drying laurel to her breast and staring off into memory. Smooth, tautly sculptured features; broad shoulders; huge blue eyes; square chin and smooth-shaven jaw. The cauldron of curiosities she'd lidded in her mind and body for the past week had finally erupted in her, brought to an explosive boil by her encounter with the dashing white knight.

Rugar. Was that really a name? He was a count of something. And Swedish. The memory of his deep, lightly accented voice sliddered along her nerves, setting her fingertips atingle. She put them to her lips, remembering his and wondering. . . .

The door flew open, and Anne darted inside, whirling to shut the door securely. "I thought I'd find you here." She stopped dead, looking at Corrie's flushed cheeks and dreamy-eyed expression. "Well, spread and spike me. Smitten." Anne huffed in disgust. "I knew it."

Corrie blushed, but turned glowing eyes on her cousin. "He's wonderful. Did you see?"

"Did I see?" Anne hooted a laugh and came to perch on the side of the bed with Corrie. "The whole damned court got an eyeful. I feared he was going to eat you up on the spot!"

"Anne!" Corrie blushed furiously, but laughed.

"Well, he is *Swedish,* after all."

"What on earth does being Swedish have to do with anything?" Corrie demanded, irritated by Anne's belittling tone.

"They're half barbarian. Natural fighters, but clumsy as bears at everything else. Ask anybody." Anne realized that here was yet another opportunity to enlighten her country cousin in the ways of the world. "I see I shall have to explain.

"You know, of course, that the Italians are the undisputed masters of the courtly graces-dancing, music, art, and fashion. Well, just below them in desirability are the Spaniards, with their dark elegance and rolling tongues . . . Lud, they have such tongues!" She shuddered wickedly, then came back to her point. "Frenchmen are next in line, and after them come our native Englishmen." She winced. "Regrettably, Englishmen are generally a paltry lot. Uninspired as poets and musicians . . . and as lovers. But at least they're better than those sorry Germans, and those Hapsburg dullards—ugh! And, lo, at the very bottom of the barrel of refinement are the Swedes. They can drink like fish and fight like devils, but they cannot dance or sing, and they garb themselves like gawky peasants gone to market. I don't know anybody who's actually bedded one, but the general impression is that they rut like boars. All grab and grunt . . ."

"He's not a grabber." Corrie's eyes narrowed fiercely. "Nor a grunter."

"Fie! How our fur does ruffle!" Anne cast a teasing eye over her. "And how would you know, my *unlicked cub?*"

Corrie sighed, sinking back into the morass of innocence again. "He is too handsome to be a grunter. And too gallant to be a grabber." Even as she defended him, she was painfully aware of how naive she must seem to her worldly cousin. Thus she was pleasantly surprised to have Anne agree with her.

"Damme, you're probably right." Anne propped her chin in her hand and her elbow on her knee, recalling him judgmentally, then declared, "But he hasn't got a proper beard."

"He doesn't need one. His face is perfect just the way it is," Corrie murmured.

Anne huffed. "Well, he's got thighs like damned tree trunks, I'll give you that."

Corrie propped her chin in her hand, copying Anne's pose. Her expression grew wistful as she recalled the shivery delight of his eyes upon her and the aura of power that flowed from his broad shoulders. "His arms are like great oak branches," she whispered huskily. "And his hands move as gracefully as swaying leaves. I think he's marvelous."

Anne tossed her a look askance and began to giggle. "Well, if I were you, I'd reserve judgment on your bloody great *oak* until I got a sample of his *root!*"

Corrie blushed and laughed in spite of herself. "I know it's sinful in the extreme, but I keep wishing Sir Christopher would hurry back to court. I'd like to see you docile as a lamb. Just once."

Chapter Five

That night, the outer corridor of the banquet hall was packed with eager courtiers when the queen and her party arrived. By custom, the doors to the hall were kept closed until the queen's revels master threw them back to unveil his handiwork to his sovereign mistress.

Corrie and Anne stood a few paces behind the queen and were among the first to witness the result of English caprice and ingenuity. The banquet hall had been transformed into a veritable Garden of Eden, replete with copses of trees, bowers of fragrant blossoms, and sylvan glades where tame deer stood tethered and turtledoves flitted and cooed. A vast silken canopy overhead was supported by massive wooden columns wrapped by garlands of ribband and fresh-cut flowers.

It was glorious, overwhelming. But Corrie scarcely heeded it as she was swept forward into Elizabeth's "faerie realm." Her thoughts were fastened on another splendor . . . a human wonder. A marvel of manhood.

She smoothed the white velvet of her revealing bodice, resettled her hair over her shoulder with a trembling hand, then checked her pearl-rimmed cap with its embroidered biliments for the hundredth time. She had borrowed a lacy ruff and a braided silver girdle from Anne, who had *tsked* and *tutted* at this surge of womanly vanity in her. Corrie had blushed, but stubbornly raised her chin. She did not intend to look like an unlicked cub tonight.

She was gravely disappointed to find the great Swedish knight missing from the gaily dressed nobles and dignitaries being seated at the queen's great, U-shaped banquet table. The entertainments began as soon as the queen's table was filled. Acrobats tumbled, minstrels strolled and sang, and servants scurried about pouring and serving.

Then above the din of merriment came the ringing of bells: small, jingling, brightly tinkling bells . . . hundreds of them, filling the hall, coming from the tapestry walls! The music warbled to a halt, and guests craned their necks to search for the source.

The bells halted, and from the main doors came a lilting tune, the song of panpipes. Four "elves" appeared in the doorway, garbed in white and wearing hats covered with silver snowflakes. Gamboling merrily, they showered white rose petals all around them as they unrolled a great silk runner of pure white, as though laying a carpet of snow all the way to the queen's table. There were more bells, and in the doorway a brace of deer appeared, then another and another. They were such odd deer, with thick antlers and wide, deeply cloven hooves, hitched together by white harnesses trimmed in silver. They pulled a small sleigh, fancifully wrought in white and hammered silver, which glided along on wheels hidden inside the runners. All turned to the revels master, who shrugged in bald shock; this was not his doing!

Then came another din of bells, and all eyes turned back to the doorway, where two figures appeared, dressed in white trimmed in silver. Murmurs and gasps rose through the hall as the tall Swedish count and his even taller companion strode along that allegorical carpet of snow toward the queen's table.

Corrie's heart gave a thump in her chest and began to race. He positively glittered. His silky blond hair, his exquisite white doublet, his slashed sleeves, and his tall white boots were dusted with flakes of silver that glinted with each nuance of assured, masculine movement. He bowed to Elizabeth, a bold gesture which displayed the extravagant grace of his manly frame.

"From the frosty reaches of my lord's realms, Your Grace," his voice rang out, "carried on the north wind . . . and kissed with snow . . . come these gifts." He gestured to the sleigh and went to stand beside the unusual animals: "These are reindeer from the frozen northlands of our country." He ran a caressing hand down one of the animal's flanks. "A gift to your deer park. And in the sleigh?"

He stepped up on one runner and picked up a great round bolt of fabric, which he held by one end and sent unrolling toward the foot of the dais. It was thick white satin, sewn with a thousand tiny snowflakes of pure, hand-worked silver. Gasps of astonishment rose from all sides as guests left their tables to crowd closer. Next he unrolled a great bolt of exquisite black velvet, adorned with those same tiny ornaments, twinkling like stars in a night sky.

The eyes of the entire court were held captive as the tall, elegant Swede unfurled an exquisite cloak of pure white ermine, secured with silver clasps set with diamonds. "Meant to warm a pair of royal shoulders," the count proclaimed silkily, "and a royal heart." There was a whole chest of gold and silver medallions made in the shape of snowflakes, no two alike. "A storehouse of precious snow to refresh England's lady in the throes of a sultry summer." There were matched gold toasting goblets, encrusted with precious stones. "Pray let these poor cups carry our affection to your lips with each sip of wine." Then came the last and greatest treasure. From the midst of the sleigh he drew a square, bejeweled box, balancing it effortlessly on one muscular hand. He turned toward the dais and stopped dead . . . as his eyes fell, then fixed, on Corrie.

All quieted in the hall, watching the great Swedish knight pause in his diplomatic wooing to stare unabashedly at Lady Corinna Huntington. His countenance warmed visibly as his eyes lingered on her.

"We Swedes live in icy, forbidding climes, 'tis true," he continued. "My lord's realm is a land of haunting forests and frozen mountains and ice-bound harbors. Our hair is light . . ." He gestured to his own pale hair, which lay in half-tamed curls about his angular face, then to his features. "Our eyes are the color of North Sea ice, and too often our tongues are as silent as the great, ever-frozen steppes themselves."

Corrie held her breath, feeling his gaze like a physical touch and responding with a warm blush. She knew he spoke to the queen and the assembly, but his eyes seemed to fashion a private meaning in each word . . . just for her.

"But we are not a cold people, we Swedes." His voice donned a velvet glove of persuasion. "We have fire in our hearts . . . and warmth in our embrace." His eyes met the lush green of hers, and his tone softened tellingly. "When we love a friend or ally . . . or a woman . . . we love consumingly, devoting ourselves to the good of our beloved." He stepped closer, almost to the edge of the table where she sat. "We are a powerful right arm, a strong shoulder . . . a tender, caressing hand."

Her heart stopped beating. Her senses filled with light and warmth and the delicious abrasion of the velvety words he massaged into her mind. He was those things . . . strong shoulders, powerful arms. Was he *tender hands* as well?

The count strode back to the queen, and the solemn baron stepped forward with him to hold the jeweled box. A ripple of amazement went through the crowd as Rugar

Kalisson mounted the dais and stood before the queen. He carried a glittering coronet, a crown made of diamond-encrusted snowflakes, so delicate, so fragile that they seemed to be made of pure ice, and in danger of melting from the warmth of a human touch.

"In token of our affection for all England and especially for England's lady, the fair Elizabeth . . . we dare offer her this Crown of Snow. And with it the kingdom of our very hearts."

Elizabeth laughed with pleasure at the irresistible charm and ingenuity of this Swedish bid for her favor. With an imperial hand, she ordered her own coronet removed, then leaned forward to allow the count to place the lacy circlet of snow upon her head.

"Great stars, Aelthar—you do know how to make an entrance!" she declared, sitting back with her cheeks flushed and eyes dancing. "It's marvelous—all of it. I shall write your lord a letter on the morrow. And as for tonight . . . I believe I have promised you a place at our table." A nod to her revels master ordered a rearrangement, and the Swedes were soon seated to the queen's right, across the open floor from where Corrie and Anne sat.

Corrie was entranced, unable to peel her eyes from him during the dining. Each time he reached for his goblet, the question boiled up in her mind and trickled down through the sensitive tips of her bubbies—those long, tapering fingers, did they tweak or squeeze? tickle or tease?

She lowered her eyes to her cup, trying to contain the shock of her brazen thoughts and these new, sliddery sensations. But when she thought herself well in hand and raised her eyes again, it was to the sight of him licking—licking!—a drip of gravy from his lip. Her gaze fastened helplessly on his boldly chiseled mouth; she ached for another glimpse of his tongue. Then it came again, a velvety softness, languorously sweeping the corners of his lips. *Slow and sinuous.* She couldn't swallow, could scarcely breathe.

She raked her tingling tongue over her sharp teeth to make it stop. But then her lips began to itch, and the twiddly feelings in her bubbies began to spread in all directions. Her whole body was coming alive, focusing on his bold and uncompromising maleness.

She was aflame with curiosity about him. How did he feel to the touch? How did he smell? How did he move, smile, and stand? Did he fold his arms, drum his fingers, or rub his chin while in thought? How did his laughter sound? How would it feel to stand beside him, dwarfed by his height and encompassed by his male presence? And how would it feel to open her lips to his slow, sinuous—

Anne was saying something to her, and she focused on her cousin's knowing look and twinkling eyes. "So you've a trace of the Huntington itch in you, after all, Cub," Anne whispered, leaning close. "Well, it's no good sniffing at the meat before you've got teeth enough for chewing."

Corrie reddened at Anne's bawdy analogy but refused to surrender to maidenly chagrin. "I'll sniff where I like, Anne Bosworth." Her green eyes narrowed. "A cub must have something to cut its teeth upon."

Anne's laughter burst around them, and Corrie turned away—straight into the Count of Aelthar's blue-eyed stare. She had a swift, hot vision of teeth, *his teeth,* nibbling her wrist, her shoulder, her— She flamed anew, dragging her eyes away. But a moment later her curiosity flared once more. *What must it feel like to be nibbled by a man?*

Through the meal, Rugar felt his raven-haired beauty's eyes full upon him. From beneath those lowered lashes she searched his movements and examined his frame with a thoroughness that confirmed his assumptions about her. Her bold physical interest produced a rogue-perfect smile on his handsome mouth and a certainty in his mind that she was the right choice as his first conquest amongst Elizabeth's ladies. She was an unexpected treat, this hot-tailed wench. It was his good fortune that Elizabeth was so vain and selective about the ladies she kept near her. *Such voluptuous little curves.* He glanced at her from beneath his own lowered lashes. *Do you like what you see, sweetness?*

He leaned toward Torgne and said, "When the dancing begins, mingle about. See what you can learn about this lady fair of mine." He chuckled at Torgne's pained look. Torgne hated mincing words and steps in courtly manners and intrigues. And he was equally adverse to courtly mores and pleasures, which was why Rugar had withheld the second part of his plan to settle old scores with Elizabeth.

He intended to make Elizabeth watch as he triumphed over England's dissolute manhood on the fighting fields. But he also intended to make Elizabeth watch while he stole her jaded ladies from her . . . one by one by one.

He canted a look at the queen he'd come to best. Elizabeth of England was no longer the young, vibrant beauty who had had the crowns of an entire continent laid at her feet. She was now a vain, strident, and unpredictable woman of well more than forty years. Since she was both an aging woman and a kingless queen, there was one commodity which of necessity grew more precious to her with each passing day. *Loyalty . . .* the devotion and affection of those closest to her. The wanton ladies of her chamber were her companions, her confidantes, her chosen family. He intended to steal their affections, to boldly woo and seduce both them and their ramping-cat loyalties from her—and to do it beneath her very nose.

Repeatedly, throughout the courses, Elizabeth drew Rugar Kalisson into conversation, calling out questions, which he answered with uncommon wit and charm. When the meal was over and the tables were removed to make room for the dancing, she made no secret of her desire for a turn about the floor; all noted the impatient tapping of her foot. And all guessed, from the way she declined Sir Christopher Hatton and the Earl of Oxford, that she was waiting for a specific invitation.

Rugar smiled as he handed Torgne his sword and ignored the line at the side of the dais to approach the queen directly, his hand outstretched to receive hers. There were glares of outrage and snarls about "another damned Viking invasion" amongst her abandoned suitors as she placed her hand in his.

All eyes were trained on them as he led her into a stately pavan. But soon the courtiers' eyes deserted their sovereign to watch the supple grace and perfect control of the tall, handsome Swede. He was like a great elm, swaying effortlessly in the wind, as he held her hand aloft, directed her in the sweeping turns, then brought her back to nestle at his side.

By the time the music ended, most of the other dancers had left the floor to watch in awe or chagrin. "This new ambassador"—Corrie heard whispers amongst the ladies around her—"he would put an Italian dancing master to shame!"

"A *Swede,*" was Anne's shocked reply. "Who would have thought it?"

When the music of a lively galliard began, it was no surprise to anyone that Elizabeth turned to the new Swedish ambassador and lifted her skirts, ready to test his skill at a brisk frolic. By the time the second dance was done, the count's reputation as one of the finest dancers at court was established.

Corrie's heart rose and fell with each rise and dip of their movements. What must it feel like to soar through the air upon his strength? To swirl softly within the arcs circumscribed by his arms? To feel his hands on hers, skin pressing bare skin? He now embodied a thousand curiosities for her and held the promise of a thousand discoveries. If only he would look at her again . . . .

A courante, called coranto in England, was next, and the Count of Aelthar partnered the queen again. Afterward, as he led her back to her chair, he slowed near Corrie's place at the table and asked if the queen might grant him a boon. "Prithee, introduce me to this lady, Your Grace. For to go on in ignorance of her name will be nothing short of painful to me."

Corrie heard his unthinkable comment and the murmur of surprise it drew from those around her, including Anne. "Lady Corinna Huntington . . . my maid of honor." She heard the queen's voice as if from leagues away. She dropped her eyes and curtseyed deeply, wondering dazedly if her legs would support her.

The count withdrew, nodding to Corrie, and escorted the queen back to her chair. But as Elizabeth reached the dais, she pulled her hand from his and bestowed it upon the handsome Earl of Oxford, who was eager to lead her out for another pavan. As they danced, the queen cast the handsome earl coquettish glances, and gave him his orders.

"Aelthar is new to our court, Oxford. He cannot know of Lady Corinna's special status with us. It would be most helpful of you to enlighten him."

A quarter of an hour later, the earl and several of his supporters caught Rugar alone, near the edge of the merriment. Their padded shoulders were puffed and bristling, and their hands rested conspicuously on their sword hilts as they surrounded him.

"You are new here, Aelthar," Oxford charged in less than friendly tones. "Allow me to offer you a bit of advice. There are many lovely ladies to provide pleasurable diversion at court. But the queen's own ladies are not among them. Ever. Lady Corinna, most especially. Set your eyes elsewhere, sirrah, or risk finding your mission forfeit and yourself trimmed shorter by the head." Oxford's dark eyes glittered. "A word to the wise, *Swede.*"

Rugar watched the dapper earl and his minions stride away. So his lady Corinna was a favorite of the queen. A slow, insolent smile crept over his mouth. He smoothed his doublet and gave the ruffs at his wrists a tug. Then he raised his chin to gaze out over the throng and laid a course straight for an irresistible swatch of white velvet.

Corrie looked up from her seat to find her Swedish count reaching for her, saying something. She looked at his hand, and her pulse skipped. He seemed to want her to place hers in it. Her naked skin against his? *Lud!* A dance, she realized; he wanted a dance. But she had danced all of twice in her entire life . . . and her father, who had valiantly attempted to instruct her, had declared that twice was more than enough!

But the need to touch him overpowered her misgivings, and she slid her hand onto his. His long, muscular fingers closed around it.

Warm, she thought dizzily as she rose to her feet. His hand was warm and hard . . . and gentle. She glanced up at him and found him smiling at her, watching her as she had sometimes watched him. His devastating blue-eyed charm loosened the knot of tension in her, and she smiled back, utterly unaware of the gawking faces turned their way.

They took up a place in the ongoing dance. The continuous turning beneath his upraised arm combined with his overpowering presence to make her light-headed. She wobbled but managed to execute one last turn, praying he wouldn't notice.

He didn't. Rugar looked down at his English jewel with undisguised pleasure and ushered her into the final steps of the dance, letting his hand float over her small waist as she turned to him for the final bow. She was absolute

perfection. Soft—Lud!—so damnably soft. He had to have
a bit more time with her.

"Dance with me anon, Lady Corinna," he entreated.

"Oh, but, sir—" The bouncy, ebullient strains of the
galliard burst around them, and he swept her up in what
should have been bold steps, quick turns, and delicate foot-
work. He skipped; she bobbled. He swayed; she lurched,
bumping into him. They jostled awkwardly through what
should have been a series of quicksilver steps, then broke
apart for a disastrous series of swags and slides and handclaps. Corrie stared at him in horror; she was utterly lost!

He read the panic in her face as they came together and
caught the lurid interest in the faces leering at them. If he
didn't do something, she was going to ruin his newly won
repute as a dancer! Another stumble, an awkward shuffle,
a nervous balk, and he simply snatched her against his side,
holding her there, while he covered her missteps with his
own movements.

With her lashes lowered, she scarcely noticed that he
had maneuvered them to the edge of the dancers. It was a
complete surprise when he seized her wrist and pulled her
through the edge of the crowd and into the corridor. When
they came to a halt in the cooler, torchlit passage, she
glanced up with her cheeks aflame.

"Pray forgive me, my lord. I would have warned you.
I—I've never danced at court before."

"Never?" He towered above her, frowning. "How can
that be, my lady?"

"I . . ." She looked up into his eyes and had to speak the
truth. "No one has asked me."

He relaxed, smiling into those clear eyes that opened so
brazenly to him. No one had asked her? She was an auda-
cious little jade, expecting him to swallow that old hook.
He watched the demure lowering of her lashes and the

tantalizing blush of her lips as she licked them nervously. *Sweet little tongue.* His own began to tingle. *Come closer, sweetness . . .*

"I am new to court," she rattled on. "I have been so busy with the queen, I have had no time to learn proper steps."

"Would you allow me to teach you, Lady Corinna?" he asked smoothly, letting his tongue linger over her name. The satin oval of her face filled with a mingling of expectation, wonder, delight . . . and possibly a little fear.

Teach her? Would she allow him to teach her? There was nothing on God's green earth she wanted more! Standing before her was the human portal through which whole new realms of knowledge and experience could open to her. Passion and joy, the pleasures of human love . . . Would he be willing to teach her such things? Or would he be put off by her ignorance?

"Please." she whispered, so quietly that he had to lower his head to catch it. "Teach me."

She knew the game, he thought. *Teach me, indeed.* His sensual features melted into a pleased smile. The muffled, reedy strains of the music inside the hall were filtering through the tapestries that separated the inner hall from the corridor. "Come, we'll begin now if you like."

He drew her down the passage and around a corner where they discovered a deserted and dimly lit area. She took her cue from his bow and curtseyed. With her gaze caught irresistibly in his, she began to move as he directed, copying his slow and exaggerated motions, point to toe point, palm to palm, turn to turn. Then he caught her against him, her back to his front, his arm about her waist, to show her the quick steps and bid her imitate them. She could scarcely mind her feet. The warmth of him, the subtle motion of him against her shoulders and back, the feeling of being cradled in his strength, were overpowering.

When he released and turned her, phantom sensations of

his warmth and hardness clung to her impressionable shoulders. Then he caught her by the waist, and she was suddenly soaring through the air on his arms. He lofted her above him again and paused, searching her rosy face and glistening eyes.

He lowered her against him, so that she slid down his length. Velvet rasping velvet slowed her shocking descent. She had time to feel each part of him against her thighs and stomach and breasts. By the time her toes reached the floor, a thousand impressions clamored in her senses. She simply stood, letting the experience of him wash through her in wave after warm, tumultuous wave.

"Pray forgive my unworthy eyes, my lady. They will not obey me," he said huskily. "I cannot seem to tear them from your loveliness."

"My eyes are equally guilty, Count," she confessed, forcing her voice past the constriction in her throat. For a long moment neither moved, neither spoke.

"In my country, no one calls me Count. There I am Rugar Kalisson," he said softly.

"Rugar . . . Kalisson." The sound of it filled her mouth and billowed in her head. "At my home in Hertford, I am Corrie."

"Coor-rrie." He gave it such a lovely, open-throated purr. Her knees went weak. He slid his hand slowly from her waist, releasing it. "In my country, you might be called Kari." With one finger he touched the moist, perfect blow of her lips and began tracing their shape with maddening leisure. "Sweet Kari. Lovely Kari."

Shock raced along her nerves in all directions. She'd never felt anything like it. The delicate friction of his fingers on her lips made them burn unbearably . . . sensations she'd never imagined! Her eyes closed as she steeled herself to withstand that exquisite torture.

Rugar swallowed hard, savoring the yielding curves

pressed against his body and achingly aware of the luxurious textures that filled his hands. He watched her still under his touch, saw the helpless flutter of her long black lashes, and felt her lips parting. He was enthralled. Such responsiveness. She seemed to drink in each sensation. He couldn't resist adding just one more.

"These wayward lips, my lady." His voice was deep, rough, and soft all at once. "Be merciful. Forgive them, too."

She felt him pressing her mouth, banishing those torturesome hot tinglings, replacing them with surges of warm pleasure, and her eyes flew open. He was kissing her! She stood, stunned, as his head tilted and his mouth slanted over hers with caressing motions. She melted under that new warmth, and her head moved instinctively to compliment the angle of his. How could lips seem so hard and so soft at the same time? So cool and so warm? How perfectly fascinating! Her beleaguered wits managed a last gasp of wonder: but . . . where was his tongue?

Rugar felt her lips parting beneath her, felt the vibration of her silent moan against his mouth, and shuddered. It was perfect. Her mouth was soft, supple, yielding beneath his. A faint hint of sweet wine clung to her lips . . . or was it honey? Or was it just her? *Gud,* she was a feast for the senses, and he wanted to taste all of her . . . to run his tongue over that delectable, satiny skin; to sworl her cool, perfect curves; to plunge into her dark, moist crevices. As his hands moved over her waist, they encountered strands of her hip-length hair, caught on her velvet gown. Soft, downy velvet—his fingers explored her—sleek, silken strands. His senses were suddenly hungry for more, and he opened his eyes . . . straight into pools of dazed wonder.

He paused, then focused on the unreadable lights flickering through her expression. This was a look he'd never seen before on a woman's face, especially the face of a woman he happened to be kissing. He had no idea what it meant. Had he surprised her? Pleased her? The heat in his senses drained abruptly.

He drew back, ending the kiss, and saw her face lower and her lashes droop. Her lovely skin was flushed—but with disappointment or pleasure? Her eyes darted beneath that sooty fringe—but with anxiety or suppressed delight? Then her brows lowered in a light frown that could only have been concentration. He blinked, staring at her in disbelief. She seemed to be analyzing his kiss—deciding whether she'd liked it or not!

Brazen little tart, he thought, judging his amorous skills before his very eyes! It had been a perfectly good kiss. Standard, perhaps, exploratory . . . Then he saw her delectable pink tongue peeping out, laving those soft, satiny lips as he had wanted to do, and a surge of raw heat filled him. Mayhap she needed a stronger sample!

His arms clamped around her, and his lips captured hers, storming her senses, demanding she acknowledge his sensual power and respond.

She was stunned by the fierceness of that sudden embrace. His lips were hard on hers, and his mouth was hot and open, searching. That searing contact turned her senses liquid and sent burning sparks of pleasure shooting along her skin in all directions. Warmth billowed inside her, filling her chest and collecting in the parts of her that were pressed tightly against him. She could not breathe. Her knees were weak, her lips were afire, and her breasts tingled and ached.

She opened helplessly to his kiss, yielding him the intimate territory he demanded. The first shock of having her mouth invaded passed as his tongue gentled to sinuous, passionate strokes that caressed her inner contours and conjured a similar motion in her. She responded tentatively, sliding her tongue over his lips as he had hers . . . touching her tongue to his.

This—she thought—*this has to be it!* This was the "kiss" the queen's worldly ladies had lauded and longed for, the strokes of a slow and sinuous tongue. It was marvelous, breathtaking. Velvet upon velvet. Wet and hot and oh, so sweet. It was shamelessly intimate and pleasurable; not at all what she'd expected. It was a new dance, an erotic oral pavan, wonderfully graceful . . . performed in the space of a mere inch, yet somehow involving her entire being.

Desire erupted in Rugar's coiled frame. The hesitant flick of her tongue, her soft whimpers of passion, the seemingly involuntary movements of her lush curves against him . . . she was slowly coming to life in his arms, responding to him with a devastatingly sweet reluctance.

Concentrating fiercely on her response, he was suddenly caught up in the heat of his own persuasion. The pleasures she yielded him, those small increments of surrender, were delicious, maddening. His every nerve was focused hungrily on the softening of her mouth beneath his, the seeking of her soft breasts against him, and the tenuous adventuring of her tongue.

When a distant sound penetrated his guardian sense, he somehow managed to lift his head. But it was a long moment before he conquered the mad heat in his blood enough to set her back a few inches. Her dreamy, desirous expression sent a quiver through him. There was no doubt of her reaction to *that* kiss. Nor of his, he realized with sudden chagrin. He was primed to a point—hot as a damned tavern poker!

"Corrie!"

The sound of her name startled both of them, and they broke apart. Anne Bosworth rounded the corner and stopped short, staring. Corrie felt Anne's eyes widening on her kiss-swollen lips, but was curiously unabashed by her brazen appearance. She felt aware of her body and her womanliness, and of Rugar Kalisson's maleness in a whole new way. Kisses, she sensed, had the power to build a connection between a man and a woman . . . a marvelous, mysterious feeling of belonging and wanting, a sense of shared intimacy. She wanted to savor these new perceptions and explore them further.

"I've looked everywhere for you." Anne came a few steps closer, casting an assessing look at Rugar. "The queen has been asking for you, Corrie."

"Oh!" At the mention of the queen, Corrie blushed deeply. She'd forgotten all about her mistress! She turned an entreating look on Anne. "His lordship was just teaching me . . . the steps of the dance."

"How perfectly *generous* of him," Anne murmured. "But really, Corrie, the queen. I think you should go to her. *Now.*"

As Corrie turned to Rugar, bootheels sounded on the nearby stone, and a deep male voice called out, "Rugar? Where on earth . . ." Torgne Sigurd loomed around the corner and came up short at the sight of them. Straightening to his full, massive height, he pulled back his prominent chin and set his fists at his waist. "I've been looking everywhere for you."

"I have been here all along, Torgne," Rugar said, annoyed by Torgne's censuring gaze on his dusky face and swollen mouth. "Come, meet my new friends at court. Lady Corinna Huntington and . . ."

"The Baroness Bosworth, my cousin," Corrie supplied.

Torgne bowed stiffly, taking Corrie's hand first. He looked boldly into her long-lashed eyes, and a rare half smile came over his lean, sinewy face. But when he turned to Anne with her tawny, catlike gaze and stunningly sensual features, his expression chilled and his body stiffened. His eyes dropped to her scandalous Italian bodice and the tempting display of flesh it afforded, and narrowed instantly. His thoughts were as clear as if he'd spoken them.

Shameless tart.

Anne stung from that visual slap of disapproval. She lifted her chin, her eyes glittering.

Juiceless cod.

"The queen asks after you, Rugar." Torgne turned with a taut, accusing look. "I think she may want another dance."

Anne and Torgne led the way back to the great doors of the banquet hall, frosting the air as they stalked along. By the time they disappeared inside, Rugar had recovered enough to delay Corrie just outside the doorway, collecting her hands in his and bending toward her.

"My wayward lips," he murmured for her ears alone, sinking his gaze into hers. "Are they forgiven?"

Her smile contained several parts wonder. *"Errare humanum est,"* she said softly, surprising him.

Latin? She answered him with *Latin?* He managed to collect her meaning.

"Human. I am that, my lady. I believe you have just proved it." He smiled ruefully, realizing he spoke to himself as much as to her. "Come and watch me ride for the rings to-morrow"—his gaze stroked her—"and I shall do my best not to *err* again."

Corrie flushed with pleasure and stepped back on unsteady legs. "I shall come."

Rugar watched the tempting sway of her skirts as she left him and felt slow heat curl downward through his long legs, weakening his knees. He recognized the feeling. Pure, undiluted desire. It was magnificent. It was also unnerving. He hadn't felt anything like this in years, and he wasn't sure he liked the fact that he was experiencing it just now.

He rolled a lingering trace of need from his wide shoulders and smoothed his doublet about his waist. His eyes glinted as he strolled back into the banquet hall, back under Elizabeth's pointed scrutiny. Her face spoke displeasure, either with his desertion of her or with his attention to one of her precious ladies. He strode toward the dais to dance attendance upon her, vowing that by week's end *her* Lady Corrie would most certainly be *his*.

Chapter Six

Late that night, Anne slipped into Corrie's room and climbed over Corrie's tiring woman, Maudie, who was already asleep on the trundle, to join Corrie on her bed. Her eyes narrowed accusingly.

"He kissed you, didn't he?"

"He did." Corrie wrapped her arms around her waist, and her face took on a sensual glow. "Want to hear about it?"

"Lud. *No!*" Anne pulled her knees up to her chest and jerked her long smock down over them. "Yes."

Corrie grinned and snuggled her toes under the heavy quilts. "One moment we were dancing, the next moment he was lifting me . . . then letting me slide down his body." She swallowed hard, staring off into memory. "His hands are so hard and warm . . . his whole body is hard. He touched me and made me feel all hot and twiddly inside. It was like being spitted and turned over a slow fire. Then his lips touched mine . . . so soft and hard . . . and his tongue—"

"Enough!" Anne groaned, squeezing her eyes shut. "Damme, I won't sleep a wink tonight for thinking about your bloody great Swede with his hard body and hot hands. I'll wager he's hung like a blessed stallion." She caught Corrie's frown of confusion and huffed in disgust. "I don't suppose you know about that either." Corrie shook her head. "Well, you can always tell the size of a man's pizzle by the size of his feet. Your Swede's got a hummer. Count on it."

Corrie's eyes glazed as she recalled the large, hard lump of his codpiece. If it *were* a codpiece. She hadn't quite gotten that far in her investigation of him. Memories mingled and whirled in her mind, and Rugar Kalisson suddenly reappeared, endowed with a two-foot sausage. . . .

"Aaghh! Stop it." She clamped her hands over her eyes, then peeled them away, finger by finger. What was he really like in his manly parts? And if it came to that someday— she glanced down at herself—would they fit?

Anne, lost in separate musings, shuddered and lowered her head to her knees. Her voice came with a trace of anguish. "Damn you, Bosworth . . . for dying on me."

Corrie focused on Anne with a scowl of puzzlement that soon melted to understanding. She reached out to stroke Anne's tawny hair. "What was he like, your baron? My father spoke of him sometimes." But always in hushed tones, Corrie recalled privately. Anne raised her head, her eyes glistening as she tossed her hair back and sighed.

"He was a rakehell and a gambler . . . a silky, incomparable beast of a man. He'd tumbled at least half the women at court before deciding to take a bride. Then he saw me and offered for me straightaway . . . I'll never know why. I went to his bed a sorry little virgin, green and trembling like a willow twig. But that very first night he took me to both his loins and his heart. Ah, God, he was magnificent. And tender. And rough. He taught me everything there is to know about loving. Turned me into a ramping wanton, he did, with his marvelous hot hands and deliciously wicked ways. And together we learned about love. You see, strange as it seemed, he'd never been in love before either." Her eyes misted. "We had three years together . . . and thought we had forever."

She drew a deep breath and stroked Corrie's cheek. "No one has *forever,* Cub. So if love comes near, you have to seize it, cherish it . . . make it bloom for you. Life is too short and too uncertain to let something as precious as love slip away."

The ache in Anne's eyes was awful to behold. Corrie rose to her knees and wrapped her worldly cousin tightly in her arms. "You'll find someone else, Anne. You have so good a heart. You'll love again and marry and have babies . . ."

Anne smiled bittersweetly, returning Corrie's tight hug, then setting her back. "No, Cub. A love like that comes once in a lifetime. I've had my *once.* I pray someday you'll have yours, too."

They were quiet for a long while, drifting separately in their thoughts.

Anne came to life suddenly, breaking the silence with a tortured groan and a roll of her eyes. "Damme—I'm bloody well on fire! You and your bigspindled Swede—" She climbed off the bed and back over snoring Maudie to stand in the candlelight with her smock hanging half off one shoulder. She glowered defiantly. "Perhaps if I wander the dark halls a while, someone will take pity on me and ravish me a few dozen times." She stomped toward the door, muttering, "Why is it you can never find a bloody regiment of horseguards when you need one?"

Corrie giggled. As she blew out the candle and climbed under the quilts, she felt a warm reprise of the discoveries she'd made that evening . . . how a touch could invade her very body . . . and linger after the hand that wrought it was gone. She'd experienced swarmy swirlings and itchy twitches and shocking hot shivers. . . .

Above all, she'd discovered just how much more there was to learn in this seemingly endless realm of loving. And she'd learned that Rugar Kalisson was willing to teach her.

* * *

Meanwhile, in the Swedish ambassador's new apartments, along a far-flung corridor of the palace, Torgne Sigurd was glaring across a tankard at Rugar Kalisson's pleasure-bronzed face. "No, I do not want to hear about your ravishing Lady Corinna in the bloody hallway."

"It was a kiss, Tor. *Gud*—she has the softest mouth and the sweetest little tongue I've ever—"

"Dammit, Rugar, do you want to hear what I learned about her or not?" Torgne slammed his tankard down on the table between them so that it sloshed and spilled, then swiped his mouth with the back of his hand. His gray eyes were sullen and disapproving.

"Let me guess," Rugar proposed with an upraised finger and a wicked grin. "She's new at court. She's one of the queen's favorites. She knows Latin better than she knows dancing, and she can't keep her eyes off me. Am I right so far?"

Torgne glowered at him. "How did you learn all that?"

"I didn't *ravish* her the entire time, Tor. I did manage a few words with her." He laughed at the sour look on his friend's face.

"And did you also learn that she's a wealthy heiress . . . will be a countess in her own right someday? Did she happen to mention the other languages she knows, or that she is the keeper of the queen's prayer book and part of the queen's library?"

"She is truly learned?" Rugar frowned as Torgne nodded. A learned tart; he turned the idea over in his mind. It would take some getting used to, if indeed it was true. Wickedly desirable and possibly learned. He drew a hard breath, feeling oddly on edge. "Anything else?"

"She's something of a musician, plays the virginal like

an angel. And she's not just one of the queen's favorites; she's Elizabeth's special pet. Her father is the Earl of Straffen, and he dotes on her."

"Troll's teeth, you are thorough." Rugar's eyes darkened. Her father doted on her. He didn't want to hear such stuff. "And her lovers?"

"She's a maid, Rugar. A maid of honor."

Rugar's expression froze to an unnerving, icy mask. "Romantic Torgne. *Maids* and *honor* . . . there are no such things at the English court."

Anger gripped Torgne at Rugar's foul assessment of English ladies while in bold pursuit of one of them. "Perhaps you've bedded and consorted with loose women for so long you can't recognize an innocent when you see one," he charged hotly.

"Oh, I know one when I see one—and when I don't," Rugar fired back through a clenched jaw. "No innocent devours a man with her eyes the way she did me this evening. Damme if she hasn't got the length of my codpiece to the tittle . . . and a fair estimate of the dimensions of what's behind it. Shall I detail for you how she rubbed her plump little ducks against me—how she wriggled and purred as I caressed her?"

Torgne rumbled a warning from deep in his throat and glared at Rugar, daring him to continue. Rugar glowered back, then finished his tankard in one gulp and rose to pace the dim chamber, feeling accused by his friend's dour stare and uncompromising moral rectitude.

"I'm no beast," he declared roughly. "If she were an innocent—which she most certainly is not—then she would have nothing to fear from me. I have no taste for innocence." His features hardened as he looked past Torgne and said, "I was an innocent myself once."

The bitterness of Rugar's words jarred Torgne. Rugar's first encounter with a woman had occurred when he was seventeen, on Torgne's father's estate. It had been the Midsummer festival, and they had all been drinking. When they began to choose partners and stagger off into the meadows, Rugar had been reluctant. Torgne had joined the others in taunting and cajoling, and had finally thrust his own first choice into Rugar's arms, threatening to stand and watch to make sure he did it. Rugar emerged from his first taste of loving a different man, jubilant but with an odd tenor of relief to his new enthusiasm for sensual pursuits. And to Torgne's slow-growing horror, Rugar spent the next two years seducing every prime wench he could lay his hands on, as if making up for his late start.

Torgne had come to feel responsible for Rugar's determined plunge into sexual indulgence, and this glimpse of bitterness in his friend stung him sharply. He fixed Rugar with a stare that could have pierced armor plate.

"What eats at you, Rugar?"

Rugar reached for Torgne's tankard, but Torgne refused to release it. Rugar looked up with hard warning in his eyes. "Leave it, Tor."

"*Nej,* I will not." For one long, turbulent moment neither spoke. Then Torgne released the tankard and said quietly, "Perhaps being drunk will help you to speak of it."

Something gripped Rugar's throat and squeezed. He pushed himself up from the table with such force that his chair tipped and went clattering over the polished boards. "Go find yourself a woman, Sigurd. Take some pleasure of your own for a change—and keep your damned righteous nose out of mine!"

The wall rattled as the door slammed behind Rugar. He stalked blindly along the dimly lit halls with his fists clenched and his eyes burning. The sights and smells of England and the dead-of-night shadows . . . He fought the memory that stirred powerfully in his senses. But those long-dormant impressions breached his defenses, setting his braced shoulders trembling, contracting his muscles into cold knots.

The echoes of his footfalls on the cold stone walls became echoes of distant laughter . . . a merciless, slapping sound. He was suddenly chilled . . . naked in a darkened, freezing-cold chamber. And the icy, relentless hands of a woman pulled at him, squeezed and prodded his gangling, still growing body. Her laughter and taunts scored his young mind like her fingernails did his broadening back, both leaving their marks.

He was again choked with fear and revulsion, unable to run, ashamed to cry out. She did things to his body, and it responded. And she laughed.

He slowly came to his senses and found himself trembling in the cold air of a moon-drenched courtyard. His fists were aching, his brow beaded with cold sweat as he faced it . . . remembered as he hadn't remembered in years.

His eyes gradually closed. It was a memory, only a distant memory. In that frigid darkness. fifteen years ago, she had destroyed his body's innocence and frozen his sexual responses, trapped him inside his own loins for a long time to come. It was five excruciating years before he recovered his sexuality in the tender and loving ministrations of a buxom young peasant girl . . . thrust upon him by his friend Torgne in the madness of a Midsummer celebration. A warm Swedish night . . . warm and willing Swedish flesh. It was a healing, a discovery, a salvation.

It had been a while before he had understood what had happened to him at the hands of that high-born English trollop. When he had realized, he had vowed never to take another's innocence. *Never.* And he had kept that vow, choosing his lovers carefully. In his varied travels, he'd learned that at a court, any court, there was never a shortage of willing and experienced ladies.

He straightened and filled his lungs with night air, smoothing his doublet. His mind drifted to Lady Corrie and her warm eyes and exquisite mouth. She was no stranger to a man's touch. And he had the jaded English court to thank for it. Perhaps there was a perverse bit of justice in this old world, after all.

The entire court turned out the next morning to watch the knights and other courtiers ride at the rings on the tilt field. It was not as formal an occasion as the tilt and bore less ceremony, even with the queen and her retinue in attendance. Most spectators watched as they strolled the field itself, choosing any of several lanes and posterns from which to view the events. Corrie dragged Anne amongst those strolling nobles, looking for Rugar Kalisson in the lists.

"He's bloody well set you afire, hasn't he?" Anne whispered as Corrie eagerly searched the contestants. Corrie's determined look melted into a wince of longing. "I have to see him again."

Anne rolled her eyes, then turned with a sigh and put her arm through Corrie's to lead her along. "See here, Cub, you've a few things to learn about men—"

"Lady Corinna!" Tall, sober-faced Torgne Sigurd appeared, striding toward them. "Rugar is riding next on this lane. Would you care to see?" He made way for her to the front of the crowd, and Anne slipped through, behind them. Rugar spotted them just behind the ropes and rode out along the barrier to greet them. Corrie's eyes shone as she unpinned the long silk veil from her cap and extended it to him as he leaned down on his great white destrier. He cast her a heart-melting smile and draped the gauzy token of her favor around his neck, then directed his horse back to the starting post.

Corrie watched him lower his visor, gather, and charge. He was fascinating . . . terrifying . . . magnificent. And to think that only last night she'd been wrapped in those powerful arms, pressed tightly against those formidable thighs.

Rugar's spear went dead on center through the spinning ring, and he reined up and turned his mount. He saluted Corrie from the saddle, then gave his mount the knee and rode back down the lane for another run.

"Two more and he will have this round," Torgne explained. "Then he will go to the main stands, for the championship."

They were prophetic words. Rugar won that round and was soon proving his skill against the winners of the other preliminary rounds. Corrie, the baron, and Anne climbed into the gallery, near the queen, to watch. With each round, each small victory, the lanky baron thawed a bit, and Corrie seized the chance to learn everything she could about Rugar Kalisson.

But for each degree that Torgne Sigurd warmed, Anne Bosworth froze a corresponding degree in response to his deepening rudeness to her. He ignored her comments and cast her disdainful looks, affronting her so that she finally excused herself to go and sit by the Countess of Main and Lord Settlesby. Corrie, absorbed in watching the trials, scarcely noticed her departure.

On the field, Rugar positioned himself for his next run and located Corrie in the stands by the white of her gown. Lowering his visor, he found he'd trapped the vision of her inside his helm. He shook his head to clear his senses, then set his heels and used his spurs to charge the spinning ring.

Just as he approached his target and began to hurl, a capricious wind blew Corrie's silken veil up against his visor, blocking his vision. He jerked his head futilely inside his helm, but there was no way to dislodge the veil. It was too late to halt the javelin. There was a gasp from the crowd, but as he reined up and turned his mount, cheers broke out. His attempt had seemed about to go astray, then had miraculously found the ring.

He pushed up his visor and grabbed the veil, glaring at it lying limp against his gleaming gauntlet. The cursed thing had damn near cost him his victory! As he took his place in line for the final round, he was tempted to grab the veil from his neck. But he looked up at that soft blur of white in the stands, scowled, and instead tucked it under the edge of his breastplate.

The next run sealed his victory at the rings. He managed to rip the final ring free of its leather thong and bear it with him to the gallery, where he offered it, on spear tip, to Corrie, who blushed as she accepted it. It was a conspicuously gallant gesture, made under the queen's narrowed eye.

Elizabeth's manner was pointedly regal as she presented him with his second set of laurels in as many days. Her countenance darkened noticeably when he strode straight from her to Corrie, to ask if she would come to watch him in the fencing that afternoon.

Midafternoon, Corrie was indeed seated in the Great Hall with the queen's entourage, watching the court's finest swordsmen crossing steel. Anne had recovered enough of her humor to join Corrie . . . until Torgne Sigurd squeezed onto the bench beside them. Anne's tawny eyes were flecked with red as she excused herself and sought companionship elsewhere. Torgne ignored her exit while explaining to Corrie some of the finer points of scoring and strategy. They watched several pairings before Rugar came up.

From the start all could see there was a marked difference in the big Swede's weapon and style, and those knowledgeable in such things identified it as a distinct Italian influence. His sword was a slim rapier, and he held his left arm up and kept his body turned to the side. Soon he was drawing both hoots and cheers from the crowd with his graceful lunges and thrusts, the renowned and controversial *stoccata* of the Italian masters. He made short work of his first opponent, and his second.

"Imagine," an outraged male voice bellowed over the spectators' benches, "a Swede fencing like an Italian!"

"Tilting, dancing, riding, fencing—is there nothing the new Swedish ambassador cannot do?" came a coy feminine appraisal.

Elizabeth watched the fencing closely, listening to the gossip and complaints of her jealous courtiers. Rugar Kalisson was giving England's manhood a drubbing, and she didn't doubt for a minute that they deserved it. Many of her would-be champions had grown soft in the ceremonial combat of court, whereas this Swede fought hard, as though he had something to win. But just what was it he expected to claim? She glanced at Corrie, who sat talking and watching the matches with the other Swede, and her queenly smile became flinty. The handsome bastard seemed to be ignoring her friendly warning about her pet. And if he persisted, he would most certainly find himself the sorrier for it. However superb he was as a warrior or courtier, he was, after all, just a *man*. And he was tweaking the nose of a *queen*.

Corrie was in thrall as she watched Rugar fence. Warming noticeably, she reached for the fan at the end of her girdle chain and found it missing. "My fan . . . it's gone." She looked all around and spotted it on the floor on the far side of Torgne's feet. Impulsively, she reached for it, leaning across Torgne's knee as he also spotted it and bent to retrieve it. He bumped into her and started back, and she lost her balance. For a moment she was caught with her body pressed full against his, half reclining on the bench. He quickly righted them and, red-faced, retrieved the fan.

"Forgive me, Baron." She blushed profusely, hoping they hadn't attracted notice. "I thought I could reach it myself." She found him smiling through his considerable chagrin. Her tension eased. "How do you say thank you in Swedish?"

He paused a moment, swallowing his embarrassment for her sake. "We say *tack* in Sweden, my lady."

"Tack . . . tack." She turned the word over in her mind and smiled meltingly at him. "Your English is wonderful, Baron. Where did you learn it?"

"The tutor who went with us on our travels was fluent in English. And, of course, Rugar was here in England for a while when he was a lad."

In the midst of his bout, Rugar flicked a glance in Corrie's direction and caught sight of her entwined bodily with Torgne. He missed a parry and narrowly avoided a dangerous rip of his opponent's blade. Appalled by his distractibility, he poured himself into the match and was soon declared the victor. Afterward, he was roundly annoyed to find her still seated beside Torgne, talking. He was even more irritated to realize that his urge to give his friend a swift kick probably originated in a proprietary impulse toward her. What difference did it make if she threw herself atop other men? Then she looked up, straight into his gaze, and smiled adorably. Inexplicable pleasure coursed through him, and he turned away to prepare for his next match with a deep scowl of irritation.

As expected, Rugar was proclaimed the victor of the fencing trials and was honored with a great silver urn, which he presented back to the queen in another chivalrous gesture. Under Elizabeth's withering stare, he smiled as he strode straight to Corrie's seat to quietly ask that she meet him later for a stroll in the Privy Garden. Corrie's mind was so filled with him, she scarcely noticed the way the queen glowered and called her to come along. When she came to her senses, she was in the queen's chambers and begged to be excused on the grounds that she wasn't feeling herself . . . which was absolutely true.

It was the longest hour of Corrie's life, waiting for her appointed meeting with Rugar. She paced her small room and had Maudie change her cap and biliments twice. She wanted to look perfect, or as perfect as she might ever look, for certainly Rugar would. He was pure manly perfection: handsome, graceful, chivalrous, physically gifted, and superbly trained. Why he would seek the company of a young, inexperienced gell like her, she couldn't guess. But she recalled and was comforted by Anne's revelation that she hadn't understood why her handsome, worldly baron had chosen her to wife. Perhaps it was something one didn't have to understand.

When she reached the Stone Gallery, she dismissed her guardsman. Rugar was leaning against the stone base of the great sundial, waiting for her. His head came up the instant she stepped into view, and it seemed the sun dawned in his face.

His blond hair was still damp from bathing, and the rich azure of his doublet lent the blue of his eyes lightning-bolt intensity. Pleasure skittered along her nerves. "Congratulations, my lord, on your victories today. You seem to have taken the entire tournament by storm."

"My only regret is that I could not give my last prize to you." He wrapped her hands in his, staring down into her face. "As ambassador, I am not always free to follow the dictates of my heart."

"In giving your victory to the queen, you honored all England," she observed.

"I would rather have honored you."

Corrie's breath stopped in her throat. He was looking at

her with a wanting that she'd never seen before in a man's face. And as his gaze lingered on her lips, she knew it had to do with what had occurred between them the night before. Was he going to kiss her again, here, now?

He placed her hand on his sleeve and led her off along one of the grassy paths. They strolled, speaking of the tournament and the splendid gardens. If there were other people around, Corrie saw none of them; her whole world was suddenly contained within the arc of one man's stride.

Suddenly there were angry shouts and violent movement in the hedges, and a panicky deer sprang from the bushes into their path. It scrambled and stumbled, turning blindly to run down the path away from them, until a human figure, a gamekeeper, jolted into its path. The animal heeled and bolted back, aimed straight for Corrie and Rugar.

Instinctively, he pulled her to the edge of the path and shielded her with his body. But she struggled to see around him, calling out, "It's one of your deer, my lord—look!"

It was indeed one of the reindeer he'd given the queen only the night before. And it was racing at them pell-mell, wild-eyed from the gamekeeper's furious attempt to corner it.

"It's frightened witless!" Corrie cried as it streaked past and darted into the bushes. Another red-faced gamekeeper came crashing through the nearby hedges, carrying a heavy club and looking determined to use it. Panic seized Corrie at the thought of that wicked truncheon bashing one of Rugar's little reindeer. She pulled away and collected her skirts, bolting into the bushes after the beast.

"Lady Corrie? Wait—" Rugar lurched after her, searching for her white gown amongst the colored leaves and half-bare branches. He finally found her on the far side of the clearing, stalking the reindeer buck and speaking to it in soothing tones. But as she came closer, it ran straight at Rugar, who managed to wave his arms and turn it back into the open.

The wily buck zigged and zagged, leading Rugar and Corrie and both gamekeepers up and down the paths, through flower beds, under arbors, and around trees. The animal finally winded itself and slowed. Corrie arrived, panting, as it stopped against one of the high brick walls that surrounded the city side of the gardens.

"Here, now," she said softly, moving slowly toward the animal. "You don't need to run anymore. We won't hurt you." Closer and closer she crept, extending her hand, letting the animal take her scent as she lulled it with soft assurances.

Rugar arrived at a run and jerked to a stop, watching her talk to the balky, suspicious reindeer until she had her hand on its leather halter. She patted and stroked its nose, then gently slipped an arm around its neck.

"I have him now," she called to Rugar and the panting gamekeepers, who had just arrived. "Come slowly." She held the animal in a hug and stroked its neck soothingly as they approached.

Her face was moist, and her eyes were alight with impulsive pleasure. The sight of her burned into Rugar's mind as she stood there, hugging a reindeer's neck, glowing with a lush, earthy radiance that seemed to come from the very core of her. He was speechless, entranced.

The shamefaced keepers confessed that the beast had chewed through its grass rope and run from where the group had been tethered as an exhibit on the far side of the gardens. Rugar came to his senses and lectured them on being more watchful, then sent them off, grumbling at their willful charge.

"You might have been injured, Lady Corrie." Sternness overlaid his upwelling concern.

"I had a fawn once as a pet, and it kept getting out." She smiled apologetically, brushing her gown. "It made my father angry, so I always tried to catch it myself, before he did. I'm sorry if I worried you, but I'm an experienced deer-catcher." Her breath was slowing, but her heart seemed to be pounding harder than ever. "I love your little reindeer. They have such bright eyes and such soft, furry noses. Will you tell me about them? And about their home?"

Caught in the captivating light of her countenance, Rugar scrambled for mental footing. His calculated seduction suddenly lay in shambles, trampled beneath a set of reindeer hooves. He finally nodded, offering his arm and leading her to the nearest path as he began to tell her what he knew of reindeer.

But her unexpected questions about his homeland did not stop with four-legged subjects. "Is there always snow at your home, or does it melt?" she asked. "Do you really see the sun at midnight? What are your houses like? And what sports and games do they play at the Swedish court? Is there much dancing? What sorts of instruments do your ladies play?"

While they walked, he sketched for her verbal scenes of life in his native land. Under her admiring gaze, his responses took on the depth and richness of his pride in his homeland. He spoke of lush valleys and rocky seashores and forbidding forests. He answered her queries about his estate and the Midsummer festival and the long, dark winter nights with stars so bright they were like diamonds. He told her of snow and mountains and of the yeomen farmers who wrested wheat and oats from the rocky soil and short season.

"And is it true that all Swedish children are blond?" she asked, her eyes dancing over the flaxen wisps around his face. Rugar nodded with rakish grace.

"All blond. And obedient. And clever." His expressive mouth twitched at the corners. "It's only natural, I suppose, since Swedish men are all strong and valiant, and Swedish women all beautiful and virtuous." When she laughed, he pretended to be shocked by her mirth. "It's true, I swear. We Swedes are paragons of virtue." His lips curled in an endearingly roguish grin. "For most of the year it's just too cold to sin."

Corrie's delighted laughter sent compelling vibrations all through Rugar. He was enchanted by the sound, and searched for ways to coax it from her again.

Sometime later, he found himself seated with her in a secluded bower, bathed in dappled light and feeling the chill of oncoming evening in her hands. He realized he'd been talking quite a while, unprompted, and that her attention had not lagged once in all his ramblings. He paused to search her upturned face, with the unnerving thought that he'd revealed a great deal about himself in those unguarded moments.

"*Tack,* Rugar Kalisson . . . for telling me about your *Sverige,* your home."

His feelings contracted, retreated inward in a heart-stopping crush that left him momentarily unable to breathe. *Tack.* On her lips the sound was stunning. Swedish settled harshly on Englishmen's ears; they thought it guttural and barbaric. *Sverige* . . . his beloved Sweden. On Corrie Huntington's lips it became a soft, soughing sound, a noble name, a desirable origin . . . or destination. He was unmanned.

"H-how do you know those words?" he said, his voice hoarse with the effort of self-control.

"Your baron. I asked him," she whispered.

"He told you of the midnight sun and Midsummer?"

"No. I have read of many places, your country among them. Will you tell me about the other lands you have visited, too?"

"Torgne told you that, too? That I've traveled?"

She nodded and looked down, fearing that she'd asked too many questions and seemed too naive. But then his voice came, pouring over her like warm honey.

"I am glad now that I spent such effort to learn your language. To talk with you so makes the hours of study worthwhile," he murmured. Corrie's eyes glistened as they came up.

"If you knew not one word of my language, you would still be fluent. Eyes have but one language, everywhere. And you have very speaking eyes, Rugar Kalisson."

"Do I?"

"You do."

"Then what are they saying to you now, Corrie Huntington?" he whispered, releasing her hands to feather his fingers over her dark hair.

What she read in his eyes brought heat to her cheeks and caused her lips to tingle with expectation. She raised and tilted her chin in wordless answer to his wordless request. And the time for speaking was past.

His arms slid around her, and his lips came down on hers, invading her senses, putting reason to flight. Caught hard against his body, she responded, opening to the lush penetrations of his kisses and melting under the sweeping caresses of his big hands. Sensation swirled through her mouth and glided down her throat to pool in her breasts . . . and spill over into her loins. Every inch of her was suddenly aching with awareness of his taut, well-muscled body and burning to learn the feel of his touch.

With a will of their own, her arms slid up to circle his neck, and her body shifted and arched, pressing closer. Rugar's hands covered her waist and hips to lift her onto his lap. His mouth dipped to hers briefly, then slid down her chin and around her jawline. He seemed to be tasting her . . . consuming and savoring her as he blazed a hot, moist trail down the side of her neck to her small ruff. When he bent to continue across the bare portion of her shoulder, the realization penetrated her reeling wits—he was *nibbling* her!

She pushed back in his embrace, breathless with wonder. So this was what it felt like! Her tongue made a tantalizing circuit of her upper lip as her gaze fastened hungrily on his mouth. "Do it again," she whispered, tilting her head. "Nibble me. . . ."

With a wry half-grin, he obliged. His lips massaged and nipped her skin. She shivered and ran a finger down her neck.

"And here."

He followed her slender hand with hot eyes, tantalized by her brazen request and consumed by the desire to know where she would lead him.

"Here . . ." She drew his sensual tongue along her collarbone, then pulled her hair aside and bent her head to give him the nape of her neck, then her ear. "Ohhh, it's marvelous . . . divine," she murmured. Small wonder the court ladies considered it a major pleasure! She straightened and pushed her sleeve from her wrist all the way to her elbow. "Here . . . please. . . ."

The sensual flow in her veins turned molten as he claimed her wrist and mousled his way up her arm. She wriggled on his lap and bit her lip to keep her whimpers of pleasure inside. More. Especially . . . She met his eyes, now dark as midnight, and drew trembling fingers down her chest to trace the swell of her breasts and the tender crevice between them.

"And here."

She arched, straining against her restrictive clothing to offer herself to him. His tongue danced like a flame over her skin, sending tremors into the hidden tips of her breasts and plunging into her tingling womanflesh.

The fierceness of his need should have shocked him. But the raw pleasure of holding her against his body eclipsed all else. She was stirring in him a compelling need for completion, for possession. Desire crowned like a raging fire in his loins, threatening to consume him. He had to find relief.

He groaned and leaned into her, pressing her back . . . sliding her bottom from his lap and levering his shoulders over hers. Then one of his knees hit the ground, and one elbow went flying into emptiness. He stiffened as his eyes flew open. It took him a moment to realize they were still perched on a garden bench . . . and that he was ranting hot as a hound . . . set to take her on the spot! Flaming, he pulled her upright with him. But his arms refused to relinquish her. He found himself staring dazedly at her lush, love-swollen lips. She was so beautiful, so unexpected and appealing. . . .

He froze. Troll's teeth! What was he doing? He was supposed to be charming her, seducing her, stealing her loyalties—not drowning himself in her sensual charms! Her eyes were great tidal pools warmed by currents of passion. Even as his worldly sensibilities demanded he recall his true reasons for courting her, her glowing smile set nerves deep inside him aquiver.

Alarm crept up his spine. She had somehow managed to invade both his vulnerable pride in his country and his volatile passions . . . worming her way into his private-most feelings without his even noticing. Even now, as he recognized and recoiled from her unthinkable impact on him, she was tugging at longings deep in the center of him.

He collected her cool hands against his lips, breathing warmly on them as he struggled for control. "I must see you inside. I'd not have you take a chill, my sweet Kari." He ran the backs of his knuckles down her cheek. "Come." He rose and pulled her to her feet, placing her hand on his sleeve and covering it with his own as he escorted her back to the gallery.

Disappointment colored Corrie's face, and small aches filled her body. But she was comforted by his concern for her and by the honor she sensed he extended in using his Swedish version of her name. He was patiently teaching her, allowing her to explore and discover her own passions as she learned about him. It was wonderful, enthralling. Perfect, as Rugar Kalisson was perfect.

Was it right to desire him thus? To want his loving and to seek his powerful sensuality as her guide?

A sage, a seeker must follow the path of knowledge wherever it led, she had always been taught. And Rugar Kalisson was the path to a whole new understanding of herself as a woman . . . and perhaps to the love that came but once in a lifetime.

Chapter Seven

"Look—another arrow straight to the center. He'll sweep the Archery Trials as well, I just know it!" Corrie declared with hushed excitement. On the third and final day of the tournament, she sat with Anne and a number of other ladies in the queen's gallery in the Tilt Yard, watching the contest under way. Old Lady Cobham leaned near to contribute:

"Astounding, really. The only one near his score is that other Swede . . . that Baron Somebody."

"Sigurd," Anne supplied with a sniff. "The baron's skill with arrows is to be expected, I suppose . . . one dry stick would have a natural affinity for others."

They watched as the targets were moved back for the final heat, then Corrie seized Anne's hand and pulled her along with a number of courtiers and ladies moving from the stands down onto the field. "Do I look all right?" she whispered, covertly tugging at her black Italian-style bodice, which was cut even more daringly than her white one. "One deep breath and I fear I may disgrace myself."

Anne cast a sidelong glance at the dozen pairs of male eyes riveted on Corrie's bosom, and muttered, "One deep breath and half the men present will most certainly disgrace *them*selves."

"There he is," Corrie said, seeming not to have heard. "Come, I want to stand at the front, to cheer him on." She dragged Anne through the spectators to the rope which marked the lanes.

The contestants each shot three arrows, and at so great a distance it was not uncommon to score a wide range. Rugar's first shaft had sunk dead on center into the painted target. Just as Corrie and Anne reached the front of the crowd, he notched and drew back his second shaft. Something caused his head to jerk. With the arrow already half released, the slight movement was devastating to his aim. The shaft landed far astray, drawing a gasp from Corrie and a great murmur from the rest of the crowd.

"He missed! Oh, Anne, how terrible—" she groaned. Then as if to comfort him, she smiled and waved adoringly. He grimaced a smile in her direction, then turned back with a great huff of disgust to prepare for his third and final shot. Corrie held her breath as his last arrow went singing straight into the heart of the target.

Rugar had forfeited first place in the archery event . . . but to Torgne Sigurd, whose consummate skill at the longbow caused a stir. The Swedish domination of the tournament was not due solely to Rugar Kalisson's individual might and skill, the courtiers grumbled; it was probably indicative of a general Swedish superiority in the martial arts.

Rugar smiled ruefully at their anger-tinged envy of the "invincible Swedes." Perhaps losing to Torgne was the best thing he could have done for Sweden. But he was still roundly annoyed.

He searched Corrie's black-clad figure and brazenly displayed bosom as she congratulated Torgne, and his skin began to heat. He'd become so accustomed to seeing her in white, it never occurred to him that she might wear something else . . . and that bodice . . . those tantalizing breasts . . . He caught the flow of his thoughts and stanched it. She had imperiled his victories twice, and caused him to forfeit his dominance of the tourney. Dread seized him. He thought of his disturbing reaction to her the evening before, in the garden, and groaned silently. She was supposed to be the instrument of his revenge, but it seemed she was becoming a recurring threat to it instead.

Elizabeth came down to the field to present Torgne with a golden arrow for his victory. He attempted to return the arrow to her, in imitation of Rugar's gallantry, but she smoothly rebuffed him, declaring he would surely find a better use for it. As the courtiers surged around them, inundating the red-faced baron with admiration, the queen withdrew a pace and sought out Rugar Kalisson. She sent him an icy smile as she called out, "Corinna!"

Corrie halted on her way to Rugar's side and turned back with a blush. Elizabeth extended a royal hand to her, ordering, "Come, accompany me back to the palace."

Rugar watched as Corrie veiled her eyes and obeyed. He stood staring after her skirts as she departed with the queen, wishing there was some way to blunt her impact on him. He took a ragged, uneasy breath. Perhaps it would be best to cry off now, to seek other, less complicated game. There was a host of willing wantons in Elizabeth's bevy of beauties.

An instant later he was mortified at the idea of letting the strength of his desire for a woman daunt his determination. He recalled Elizabeth's possessive ire and the feel of Corrie Huntington's delectable body against his, and knew no other woman could combine the pleasures of revenge and of the flesh so completely for him. He would simply have to see that pleasure, however beguiling, was kept the servant of revenge . . . then he would have them both.

* * *

The Presence Chamber was stuffy that evening, filled
with too many toadying courtiers and clashing perfumes,
and with a subtle tension that emanated from the queen
herself. She sat upon her great chair, listening to her musicians and watching predictable intrigue swirling amongst
her nobles as they postured over the chessboard and at
cards. Those well versed in her moods noted the impatient
drumming of her fingers and read a ripe distemper coming
over her.

Elizabeth's eyes drifted over the great chamber to fix upon
Corrie and Rugar Kalisson, seated together on a padded
bench along the far wall. Her jaw went taut with displeasure,
and she beckoned her august Secretary, William Cecil, to
her chair.

"Get me Morris Lombard," she ordered in an angry hiss
as he bent near. "Have him come to my private closet after
the others have gone for the night."

The Secretary stilled at the sound of the name, then
nodded. His scowl hinted at discomfort as he followed the
queen's intense gaze to Lady Corinna Huntington and
the new Swedish ambassador.

Corrie flushed as she felt Rugar's fingers claiming hers
under the edge of her skirts. The secret pleasure of his hand
on hers as they talked started warmth trickling through her.
Each time she was with him thus, she experienced something new in him: strength, tenderness, wit, patience . . .
consideration. But she had little time to talk with him or to
relish his attentions, for Anne arrived with news that the
queen desired Corrie's presence. Corrie's heart sank, but
she excused herself and came to the queen's side with her
lashes lowered.

"I've a mind for some soothing music," Elizabeth declared. "I would that you play for me, Corinna. Something

Italian, I think." There was a terseness that bordered on annoyance in her tone, and Corrie knew she was being subtly chided for inattention to her mistress.

"Here, Your Grace? In such public—"

"But of course—you play beautifully," Elizabeth said loudly. "Edgerton," she ordered the nearest earl, "evict that clout from the virginal so that Corinna may play for us."

Attention collected on Corrie as she seated herself at the instrument and warmed her fingers on the keys. The strains she produced floated over the chamber, drawing numerous courtiers from their games. Some came to stand nearby, but were careful to leave a clear path for the queen to view her.

Elizabeth's icy hauteur melted as Corrie's slender fingers bent to her will. The way her gaze flicked in Rugar's direction said that this command performance was more for his benefit than for Corrie's. It was a demonstration of her sovereign sway over her pet. It was a challenge which Rugar Kalisson could not allow to go unanswered.

He defiantly set a course through the crowd, straight for Corrie's side. He stopped short as her notes struck him, assured and clear, lively in expression and personal in tone. She sat erect, her fingers flying nimbly, her lower lip caught in a bite of concentration. When his shock passed, he came to stand on the other side of the boxy instrument, a mere arm's length from her, letting the dulcet tones of what he recognized as a difficult Italian piece wash over him.

Corrie looked up to find Rugar staring at her. The notes began to slow and soften. Under his admiring gaze, she became one with the music she made . . . and sent each note as proxy for her fingers, stroking him the way her hands dared not.

Her earnest desire to please him with her playing coaxed him to respond in kind. He put words to her music with a full, sonorous baritone, crafting each deep, jeweled tone to fit perfectly within the setting of her accompaniment. And he sent each wooing word straight to her vulnerable heart.

Above the astonished murmurs of the court, Corrie played and Rugar sang, paired in virtuosity, each complementing the other's skill. And it was clear to all, the queen most especially, that the music each made was meant for an audience of *one*.

Standing nearby, Torgne Sigurd listened and watched. His stern features softened with surprise, then pleasure. His gray eyes began to glow with warmth.

Across the chamber, Anne Bosworth also watched. The way Corrie and Rugar looked at each other produced a dull ache in her, a hunger for the love that had once been hers. Her burning eyes swept the room and caught on Torgne Sigurd's lean, aristocratic features. The softening of his customarily hard-set jaw and rigid shoulders lent him a sensual and manly aspect that held her eyes for one moment too long.

His head turned, as if responding to the heat of her stare, and his gaze slid straight into hers. Anne was a woman much practiced at reading men's eyes. And what she read in Torgne Sigurd's said he was a hungry man indeed. Desire prowled the flickering lights in his eyes like a panther trapped inside him, coiled and sinewy, eager to spring free. The insight caught her by surprise and turned her mouth up at the corners.

Torgne's eyes fastened on Anne of Bosworth's sultry smile, a cool, knowing curve that mocked restraint and beckoned him to lose himself in her. Alarm and temptation struggled mightily in his heating blood and aching sinews. She was beautiful; those lush, pouty lips, that skin so delicately shaded with passion's blush, those succulent breasts. But she was also a court woman, a voice inside him sneered, a fancy-dressed strumpet with the morals of a cat. His fists clenched.

Anne's face burned fiercely as he ripped his eyes from her and strode from the Presence Chamber. She felt positively scorched by his look of disdain. Yet her pride surged. The righteous prig! She'd seen his kind before. He might want her, but he wouldn't stoop to taking her. And no doubt he thought his abstinence made him a saint of some sort.

Her fury hardened into determination as she lifted her skirts and sailed for the doors. The torchlit hallway seemed deserted. She turned one way, then the other, and in a window nook several yards away, she spotted boots . . . large, pompous boots. Her tawny eyes narrowed. She swayed down the corridor toward that selfrighteous footgear with her skirts twitching.

Torgne, a shoulder propped against the window frame, was staring out over the moonlit courtyard. He turned at the sound of her footfalls and straightened with a snap, glowering at the sight of her. She paused, smoothing her skirts with dainty pats, and regarded him with a ferocious smile.

"You don't care much for me, do you?" she demanded.

"I have no use for court women." His mouth curled, as though the very term sullied his lips.

"Not even a single use?"

"No."

"Liar." She advanced on him. He retreated a step, and his back smacked against the stone wall. With a dangerous glint in her eyes she inched closer, tilting her sultry, defiant gaze up to watch him. He stiffened tellingly, his face bronzed, his eyes glowing darkly. She smiled. He was so tall . . . such a convenient height.

She leaned into him and rubbed her body slowly across his contracted belly . . . and loins . . . and codpiece. She felt his convulsive jolt as she raked his roused manly parts, and her eyes glittered with sensual challenge as she lifted a brazen, triumphant face to him.

"Hypocrite."

And she turned and left him standing there, stewing in his own righteousness.

Late that night, by the light of a pair of candles, the queen herself admitted a thin, ferret-faced fellow in blue servant's livery into her private closet. She went to sit in her chair by the glowing candlestand, but her visitor stayed outside that circle of light. His dark, piercing eyes raked the small chamber, probing every nook and crevice until he was satisfied they were alone.

"Yea, Mistress?"

"You are like the walls themselves, Lombard. Ever-present. Inconspicuous." The queen's determined eyes settled on his wiry form. Though he was currently garbed as an ordinary servant of the royal household, his service to her had nothing to do with sweeping hearths or carrying trays. "You have as many eyes as Argus, and ears that reach to the edge of London and beyond."

"My eyes and ears are at your service, Mistress . . . as always," he said in a raspy voice, bowing his head without lowering his watchful eyes from her.

"Then I would have you direct them upon this new Swedish ambassador, this Rugar Kalisson."

"The 'invincible' one?"

"The very one." Elizabeth's laugh was mirthless. He probably knew a great deal about the Swede already, she thought; there was very little in the palace that the devious but useful Morris Lombard did not know. He had a knack for collecting information of an unsavory or clandestine nature and had proved useful to her several times in recent years. "I wish to know who he sees and where he goes and where he sleeps—if he sleeps. And I want to know each time he meets with a lady . . . particularly, Corinna Huntington."

The name struck a spark in his feral eyes. "Corinna Huntington?"

"The Earl of Straffen's daughter. You knew she was here, of course," Elizabeth prodded, lifting her chin. She noted the tightening of his thin lips as he nodded. "She is dear to me, Lombard." It was a declaration intended to warn as well as instruct. "I will allow no one, not even that invincible Swede, to trifle with her . . . if you take my meaning."

Lombard hesitated, weighing her words, then nodded curtly. Her rigid posture eased. "I thought you would understand. You have been most helpful in the past, Lombard. Be diligent in this task, and you will be rewarded. There will always be a place in government for men of certain . . . talents."

A place in government. It was as if she had cracked a whip at his ear; he started visibly, and his sallow face flushed.

Elizabeth waved a dismissing hand toward the rear door, and he backed into the shadows and disappeared. She stared thoughtfully after him. Morris Lombard had long lusted for a place at court, a position of some influence where he might use his legal education and reclaim the respectability he had lost. Ambition was a powerful motive for diligence. But there was yet another reason for Lombard to be especially watchful of Corinna; he had crossed paths with her father, Jack Huntington, years ago and, as a result, had no love for the house of the Earl of Straffen. He would be quick to report anything untoward concerning a Huntington.

Elizabeth rose with a fierce little smile and made her way to her empty bed. If that smug Swede was intriguing against her, she would soon catch him up in it. And he would regret ever tangling with Elizabeth Tudor. They did not call her "Old Harry's Cub" for nothing.

The next afternoon found Corrie mired in the library, dawdling miserably over a translation of a passage from Cicero that had already been translated and retranslated at least fifty times. What need could the queen possibly have for yet another version? It seemed more the punitive assignment of a displeased tutor than a regal command meant to enhance a queen's collection of wisdom. She sighed, feeling guilty for her inattention toward the queen of late, and tried again to concentrate. But her mind kept drifting to the rousing memory of Rugar Kalisson's bold lips and sultry eyes.

As if conjured by her longings, Rugar appeared in the doorway, crossing his arms and leaning a shoulder against the doorframe. He stood surveying the chamber. Every available inch of wall was lined with stacking shelves that reached the ceiling, and much of the floor space was taken up by book stands and cabinets stuffed with velvet and leather-bound books, leather packets, and cloth-wrapped rolls of parchment. Sunlight streamed in the long, narrow windows at the far end, casting a golden glow over everything, including Corrie Huntington's lustrous raven hair. A glint appeared in his eye. It was quiet here and secluded. Perfect. His gaze drifted over her stark, high-necked gown, modest ruff, and demure cap . . . .

Responding to the heat of his scrutiny, she looked up from her writing desk and started up—"Oh!"—sending her chair thumping back over the wooden floor and awakening Sir Ethan Blackwell, the chief librarian, who was enjoying his usual afternoon nap at his desk.

"Eh? W—who's there?" His wizened head bobbed up from behind several stacks of books nearby.

"It's all right, Sir Ethan. It's just me—Lady Corrie." She blushed and hurried to the old fellow's side, taking his arm to usher him toward the door. "I'll be here to see to your books. Why not go to your chambers and finish your 'reading' there?"

As the door closed behind Sir Ethan, she was achingly aware of Rugar's eyes on her, searching her movements, her body—and most especially her high-necked bodice. She groaned mentally. She was wearing one of her father's protective styles, intending to save her "Italians" for the evenings. She could only hope she didn't look too nunlike.

"I hope you do not mind. I asked Baroness Bosworth where I might find you," Rugar said, breaking the tension. "She was good enough to direct me here." He glanced around the crowded chamber. "I cannot imagine what the queen must be thinking, keeping you closeted away with these moldy old tomes."

"Oh, but I love these moldy old tomes!" She came forward, her face alight at the knowledge that he'd sought her out. "It is a rare privilege to use the queen's library. It was on this account that the queen brought me to court, to companion her and to translate and help in her library." When he frowned, she grew determined to convince him. "Come, let me show you."

She took his hand and led him around the library, showing him numerous old books, detailing what she knew of the history of each. Some were ancient illuminated texts copied by monks and some were early printings in German and English. Pulling one volume after another from the shelves, she opened them with reverent fingers and read to him in Italian and in courtly French. Then, beaming scholarly pride, she brought him to a great oaken cabinet filled with charts and showed him a recent rendering of a map that included both England and Sweden, asking him to locate his home for her.

"I am sure," he remarked drolly, "that Sweden is much larger than this on the maps we have at home."

She laughed and set her fingers next to his on the map, measuring the distance between Stockholm and London. Holding up her splayed hand to show him the result, she smiled irresistibly. "You see, England and Sweden are not so far apart."

"No," he found himself saying, "not so far apart." As their eyes met, he wished it were true . . . and refused to think any further than that.

Next, she led him to her desk and showed him her work on Cicero. His eyes widened as she read a passage, first in fluent Latin, then from her own English translation. As he listened to her commentary on the merits of one interpretation over another, the full impact of what he was hearing finally broke upon him. She truly *was* learned!

"You really do know Latin." He fairly strangled on his surprise.

She lowered the parchment to the table, realizing belatedly that her learning might offend him. "My mother taught me. Then after my twin sisters were born, I had tutors—rusty old fellows with thinning pates who drank too much wine at dinner, so that they nodded off during my recitations." His wondering smile sent reassuring warmth through her middle, and she had an urge to tell him more. "My father used to bring me books each time he came home from London. In them, I read of other lands and customs and about philosophy and nature . . ."

Rugar noted her pride and affection as she continued to speak of her family and her life at home. It unmanned him to think of her as someone's daughter . . . someone who bought her books and provided her with tutors, and got angry when her pet fawn escaped but let her keep it anyway. The sight of her with her arms around the neck of a reindeer recurred with poignant clarity in his mind. That tender, impetuous gesture suddenly spoke volumes about her. Some of the warmth in his loins migrated to his chest.

"It was my learning that prompted the queen to bring me to court, and my love of learning that made me want to come. There is so much to discover here!" Eyes glowing, cheeks flushed, she reached for his hands and pulled him to a wide padded bench which was reserved for the queen's use whenever she visited the chamber.

"The whole world comes to England's court." Her hands squeezed his. "Here I may study other people and languages and cultures, and the ways of governance and power, and all the intrigues and marvels of human nature."

"And have you learned?"

"Oh, yes. A very great deal, indeed . . . and some of the most interesting things."

"Such as?" he prompted, fascinated by his expanding view of her.

She rolled her eyes and caught her lower lip between her teeth, trying to decide where to begin. "Well, I've learned that Spaniards do not keep well in antechambers. After three hours they become overripe and raise a powerful stink." She grinned impishly when he threw back his head and laughed.

"And I've learned that the wise sayings of the sages are meant to have many applications; the more applications, the wiser they are. For example, it is said: 'A clean glove oft hides a dirty hand.' That is usually taken to mean that there may be secret sins or unworthiness in a man who seems upright. But does it not also teach that outward impressions may mislead in a number of ways? And might it not also imply that men find ways to cloak or excuse their sin, to make it seem less reprehensible?" She saw Rugar's smile fade at her thoughtful observations and sought to coax it back to its former brightness.

"And I've learned to beware old Dunberry." At his puzzled look, she explained. "Gilbert Estreen, earl of Dunberry. A crotchety, wasty-faced fellow who is positively haunted by his own bowels. Pray to God that you are never cornered by him, or you'll be made to endure a thorough interrogation of your bodily habits . . . and a detailed recitation of his favorite purgatives!"

Rugar choked on his astonishment, then erupted in peals of laughter. He fell back on the cushions, holding his sides, and she laughed, too, with delight at having pleased him. "And never depend on Lady Blanche Parry to escort or direct you about the palace. She's an old dear, but she herself wanders about lost half the time." Her voice lowered to a conspiratorial whisper. "And never play primero with Lord Settlesby. He picks his nose to make bum-cards of the spades, and none dare accuse him of it openly, for he wields a wicked tongue—and a wickeder blade."

It took Rugar full minutes to recover. He wiped moisture from the corners of his eyes and regarded her incredulously.

"*Gud*—anything else you've learned?"

The mirth-mellowed glow of his face made her stomach go limp and slide, leaving an aching hollow behind.

"I've learned about reindeer," she said very softly, watching him as the sense of her words struck. "And about Midsummer celebrations and how blond and clever the children are in Sweden . . . and I've learned to say *tack*."

He snapped upright, roused massively by those unexpected words and the soft caress she gave each one as it tumbled from her lips. It was a gentle offering of admiration, an overture of acceptance that poured through him like liquid lightning. He touched her cheek and saw her shiver in response. Did she feel that same nerve-burning jolt, that same deep, compelling need?

In that long, scintillant moment, he recalled and savored every aspect of her he'd uncovered. She kissed like a delicious little wanton and analyzed it afterward like the veriest of scholars. She translated classics, made music like an angel, caught wayward reindeer with hugs, thought in philosophic conundrums, and captured the essence of court eccentrics with irreverent wit. She made him burn. She made him melt. She made him wonder. And now she'd made him laugh. . . .

"Sweet Kari." His fingertips drifted over her face. "Is there anything you cannot do?"

"I do not know." Her eyes darkened as he drew tantalizing spirals on her skin. Her gaze met his, testing the mysterious, intangible bond she sensed growing between them. "I only know there are things I have never done."

Both felt the sudden lash of desire as it uncoiled like a whip between them. He pulled her into his arms, stopping her breathy gasp with a kiss, binding her to him with the liquid heat of his mouth. He laved her lips, tasted the honeyed silk of her depths, and claimed the succulent length of her tongue with bold strokes as she opened helplessly to his possession.

Their kisses deepened as he lowered her onto the cushions, pressing her beneath his chest, molding her as he shifted his body fully against hers. Her arms lapped around his wide shoulders and her hands flowed over him, exploring his broad, muscular back. There was a ferocity to his tenderness, a reined strength to his touch, that were mesmerizing. With her last rational thought, she managed to realize he was using his elbows.

"Kari . . . Kari . . ." He breathed his name for her into the corners of her mouth, along the line of her jaw, across her closed eyelids. When she responded with his name, it was like an incantation that set his body in motion against her, rippling, undulating as she tightened and arched beneath him, seeking him in an unfocused way.

She felt his hands gliding down her hips, cupping her buttocks, and stiffened . . . before conquering that virgin impulse and surrendering to the new delight of his touch in such private places. He explored both her shape and the limits of her garments, seeking an inward passage and finding none. His groan of frustration echoed in every aching sinew of her body.

Her clothes, she moaned silently, her bloody wretched clothes—her father's intentional impediments to passion!

But even through her thick velvets, his searching touch aroused her response. His hand drifted below her waist to splay across her belly. Her breath stopped in her throat as his fingers slid onto her woman's mound and closed gently but possessively over her, sending molten excitement toward one burning point at the center of her woman's cleft. Her whole body tensed with fearful and wondrous expectation as her skirts began to rise and she felt his hand on her bared knee, then riding up her naked thigh. When he lifted his head to look at her, she wet her dry lips and whispered the deepest longings of her heart.

"Teach me. Please . . ."

Her plea struck sparks as it dragged across the steeled sinews of his body. Need flared like a hot blue flame in his loins, even as alarm sounded in his mind. He felt the dread realization coming, onrushing, inescapable . . . a flood of recognition that could no longer be misinterpreted or ignored.

Oh, God. He shut his eyes and plunged hotly into her mouth, trying not to think, desperate to keep reason at bay just long enough. . . . But the crush of evidence and the weight of his own conscience forced it into his mind. There were things she hadn't done, she said. He lifted his head to look at her, searching for something to allay his fears, to prove him wrong. She was staring at him with a look of awakening. And desire, new desire, freshly stirred. And trust. *Teach me.*

"You . . . you've never done it before?" he whispered hoarsely. She shook her head, her eyes glowing with expectation.

God's Merciful Knees. She *was* an innocent!

A storm of conflict broke in him with a vengeance. The sheer magnitude of his desire horrified him. He was poised on the brink of disaster, felt it prickling up and down his spine.

It was his worst nightmare come true. Fouled in his own net . . . caught in a quagmire of his own conflicting desires and motives. And if he didn't peel his hands from her now—this instant—she'd be caught in them as well.

Corrie searched his face as he paused above her. She was breathless to know what came next. She touched his face, and he nuzzled her palm. When he turned back to her, he seemed to be struggling with something inside him. Then he shuddered, the dark wells of his eyes became oddly luminous, and his mouth formed a pained smile.

"The library is a place for learning," she coaxed softly. She felt him quiver as her words struck.

"Lovely Kari . . . but not for learning this."

To her aching disbelief, he rolled aside and pulled her up with him. Her face flamed, and her lashes lowered to hide her confusion and embarrassment. Why had he stopped? Had she done something wrong? He lifted her chin on his finger and stroked her face gently with his other hand.

"There will be another time and a better place, sweeting," he said. *And another man,* he thought grimly. When she raised her eyes to him, he struggled to produce a dazzling smile for her.

The heat of her disappointment was transformed into a glow of expectation. It was undoubtedly consideration for her and his own noble character that demanded he remember honor and withdraw. He was coming to care for her, she somehow knew, and she marveled at the new womanly sense which told her so. She relaxed and stroked his hard cheekbones, letting her feelings for him flow through her adoring fingers.

After another lingering kiss and a last impulsive caress, Rugar sent her back to her work and escaped the library.

His stride had lengthened and his pace had quickened to a near run by the time he reached the Stone Gallery. He scarcely saw the courtiers who greeted him or the ladies who cast him come-hither glances. His mind, body, and emotions . . . his whole being was a tumult.

Innocent, he thought furiously. It had been there in every demure touch, every tremulous shiver, every artless flick of her tongue. And he'd let his craving for her delectable flesh and his burning need for revenge blind him to it. *Teach me.*

Corrie Huntington was a rare treat, a bright little jewel—who had imperiled his plan for revenge several times already! She was an intriguing, impetuous, curious little minx—and a bloody menace to both her sanctity and his peace of mind! She was indescribably lovely, instinctively sensual—and she'd damned near caused him to violate his long-standing prohibition against seducing innocents!

She ought to be locked up. Instead, they let her traipse around at court with her delectable ducks on display! Well, if *he* were her father—

But he wasn't her damned father, his long-ignored conscience sneered. He was the slavering letch who had charmed and cozened his way into her delicious curiosities . . . and named her heart a prize in his game of revenge. He'd used her, for no more reason than that she was English . . . and Elizabeth's. He countered that crush of guilt with a desperate vow: *from this moment on, he would have naught to do with Corinna Huntington. Nothing at all.* No kisses, no touches, no talks—not even looks. Thor's Aching Hammer— even thinking about her was dangerous!

He found himself near the great wooden doors that led into the Privy Garden and barreled through them, hoping the cold outside would dispel the heat still smoldering in his loins and rid him of her troublesome aura. It did . . . and it didn't. The crisp air curled reassuringly through his lungs and seeped into his blood as he stalked along the drying paths and scuffled through fallen leaves. But every breeze taunted him with the memory of his encounter with her and a reindeer in this same garden.

He stormed through the doors to the Privy Gallery on his way to his chambers and stumbled awkwardly into Lady Beatrice Smallwood, who was strolling the great passage with a few of her intimates. He righted her and framed a suitably charming apology. But when he would have released her, her hand lingered on his sleeve, and he found himself staring down into a pair of flirtatious eyes and treated to a thorough glimpse of the bounty perched inside a brazenly cut bodice.

From long-standing habit, he sent her a purposefully dazzling smile. She dragged a sultry, coquettish look down his body, then flicked him a quick glance of invitation before turning to continue with her companions.

Rugar watched the swing of her wide-hung skirts as she departed and realized he'd just stumbled, quite literally, into the solution to his problem. He took a harsh breath and smoothed his fashionable doublet, assembling his shattered control. The court was full of accommodating ladies . . . loose, luscious creatures who required a minimum of coaxing. It shouldn't take him long to lose the memory and feel of Corrie Huntington in their plentiful charms. It was high time he got on with his plan, he thought grimly. He had a number of hearts yet to steal.

Setting his mouth at an insolent cant, he fastened his gaze on Lady Beatrice's seductive sway, and set a course straight for it.

Chapter Eight

Corrie glowed with anticipation as she scanned the forms and faces entering the Presence Chamber that evening. All afternoon, and through supper with the queen and vespers afterward, she had relived the thrill of Rugar's kisses and the loving light in his eyes. And with each reprise of those warm, powerful experiences, her longing for him broadened into complex new realms of feeling she was breathless to explore.

Her eyes took on a distracted and desirous look that betrayed the drift of her thoughts. Anne, seated beside her, gave her a covert elbow in the ribs.

"If you have to go glassy-eyed with lust," Anne whispered, leaning close, "can you at least wait until the queen's not watching?"

Corrie looked up to find Elizabeth regarding her with a cool expression. She managed a contrite smile and focused polite interest on the antics of the queen's fool.

Minutes later, Corrie became aware of a growing interest turned her way. Rolling eyes and furtive whispers . . . knowing nods and purposeful nudges; some gossip was spreading amongst the courtiers on the far side of the chamber. Her puzzlement grew as the murmurs increased. A rustle of disquiet went through her shoulders.

Then she spotted a flash of blond above the crowd near the main doors, and her countenance lit with expectation. The knot of courtiers surrounding Rugar dispersed, giving her a clear view of him . . . and of the lady standing beside him. It took Corrie a moment to recognize Lady Beatrice Smallwood and to notice that her hand rested possessively on his sleeve as she leaned close to him with her brazen bosom and coquettish smile.

At first Corrie didn't understand. Then dread quickened her pulse as she watched Rugar squire Lady Beatrice around the chamber, pausing here and there to chat. Not once did he glance Corrie's way or give the slightest notice of her presence. The color in her face slowly drained. She was unable to tear her eyes from the bold, chrming smiles he fashioned for Lady Beatrice—smiles so very much like the ones he'd given *her* a short while ago.

The curious stares and knowing smirks directed at Corrie intensified as she struggled to deal with the sight of Rugar's attentions to another woman. Each admiring sweep of his eyes over Lady Beatrice's beautiful face and bountiful charms tightened a band of anxiety around Corrie's heart. Her eyes began to sting, her throat burned dryly, and a deep, aching hollow opened in the pit of her stomach. Just as every part of her had responded to the wonder of his presence, every part of her now reacted to the shock of his abandonment.

The air grew charged as speculation escalated. Anne watched the darkening of Corrie's eyes and reached for her hand beneath their skirts, offering what small comfort she could in so public an arena.

Corrie blinked and looked at her. The sympathy in Anne's eyes released an overwhelming wave of hurt in her, and moisture sprang into her eyes. Panicking, she looked up—to find the queen staring at her with the same taut, pained recognition. Anne knew her distress. The queen knew. Corrie raised her trembling chin to confront the lurid interest in the other faces turned her way. They all knew.

Elizabeth rose abruptly, declaring she was fatigued, and waved to select a few of her ladies to accompany her as she retired to her Privy Chamber. It was a thinly veiled conceit which allowed Corrie to retreat gracefully from the chamber. Once in the corridor, the queen dismissed all but Lady Blanche and Corrie, whom she led straight to her private closet.

Elizabeth seated herself with an air of gravity and waved old Blanche into the other chair. "I am of a mood for Seneca, Corinna. I would have you recite for me." It took a moment for her command to take root in Corrie's mind.

"P-please, Your Grace . . . I-I . . ." she protested weakly. Her throat was so constricted she could scarcely speak, but the look on Elizabeth's face was strangely compelling. Through the haze of her misery, she braced and began to recite. "'Life is neither good nor evil,' as Master Seneca once wrote to Lucilius, 'but a field for doing good and evil. . . .'"

Words begat more words, and the stream of her remembrance broadened, salving her painful feelings with the cool, clear balm of wisdom. She continued for some minutes, each word leading her deeper into truths that had weathered the ages. "'Fire is the true test of gold,'" she ended softly, "'and adversity is the true test of men.'"

"And of women," Elizabeth added solemnly. "And God knows, the greatest adversities women must endure are always the work of *men*."

Corrie understood now why Elizabeth had demanded she recite at so difficult a time. There was comfort in those wise, familiar words. Tears sprang to her eyes, and Elizabeth rose and took her hands.

"Few men know how to give loyalty to a woman, Corinna . . . fewer still to a queen. It is to women that the

Almighty entrusted the virtue of loyalty. It is our crown of thorns . . . our greatest virtue and our greatest bane." Her voice softened as she wiped a tear from Corrie's cheek. "It is a bitter lesson that all women must learn, little heart. It grieves me that you must learn it in my service."

Corrie nodded mutely; she could not produce a single word from the great emptiness inside her.

Late that night, Corrie lay in her bed, going over and over it in her mind. As the storm in her emotions abated, her thoughts began to clear. Could a man kiss and touch a woman the way Rugar had her, then forget she existed in the space of a few hours? He'd called her lovely; had he lied? He'd told her of his beloved home and called her by a Swedish name. They'd talked and laughed and made music together; did those things mean nothing to him?

A quiet rapping at her chamber door interrupted her thoughts. As soon as the bolt was thrown back, Anne burst inside and engulfed Corrie in a great protective hug. She dragged Corrie back to the bed, stuffed her between the quilts, then climbed over Maudie, on the trundle, to perch on the edge of the mattress.

"He did it to you this afternoon, didn't he?" she declared, burning with indignation. "And on the damned floor of the library!" She could think of no other reason for the wretch's callous desertion of Corrie. "He's gotten what he wanted, the handsome bastard, and he's on to fresh game."

"No. He didn't take me." Corrie blinked away tears as they formed. She confessed miserably, "He . . . wouldn't."

"He didn't—?" Anne's anger was stunned by a blow of incredulity. "*Wouldn't* take you?"

Corrie shook her head. "He wanted to. At least I thought he did." Her shoulders knotted and her voice grew hoarse as she sprang up in bed and leaned closer to Anne. "He kissed me over and over . . . long, deep kisses, with his tongue slow and sinuous against mine. And he lay atop me and touched me. And he rubbed his manly parts against me and moaned from low in his throat, like a growl." Her hands clamped frantically on Anne's wrists. "Would he do such things if he didn't want me?"

"Lud—" Anne choked, eyes widening at the artless eroticism of Corrie's revelations. "I believe it would be safe to say . . . *not*."

"Then . . ." Corrie swallowed hard and continued. "He raised my skirts and touched my naked thigh and ran his hand ever so slowly up . . ." Her eyes were huge, shimmering. "A man doesn't put his hands beneath a woman's skirts unless he really wants her, does he?"

"Lud." Anne was purely bewildered. "You mean to say he did all that to you and then just . . . *withdrew?*" At Corrie's nod, she wilted with confusion. "Why?"

Corrie shrugged, unable to speak, her hands grasping the bedcovers in fists of frustration. "Everything was wonderful until . . ." She thought of those last moments in the library . . . of the odd look on Rugar's face as he set her away from him, and of the revelation that preceded it. Her eyes filled with tears of dismay. ". . . until he learned I'd never had a man before. Oh, Anne, is that why he chose Beatrice over me? Because I'm so green and inexperienced?"

"Lud, Cub, I've never known a little thing like a bit of innocence to stand in a man's way—not once he's stoked hot and looming proud as a poker." Anne scowled. She had a brief, steamy vision of a well-primed Rugar Kalisson wedged against Corrie's voluptuous body in urgent passion. She couldn't imagine any man pulling away from the opportunity to initiate desirable little Corrie into the realm of sensual pleasure—much less a virile beast of a man who had spent the past four days in fevered pursuit of her. Rugar Kalisson was of too carnal a bent and had carried his sensual game too far to have withdrawn for the sake of nobility. That left only Corrie's explanation, that he'd found her innocence unappealing.

"'Pon my arse, these Swedes are a perverted lot," Anne muttered. "They have no taste for either tarts *or* virgins. Who the hell do they diddle?"

Corrie scarcely heard her. She was immersed once more in the splendor of Rugar's touch and the deep, speaking looks they had shared like a phantom whispering, *Another time, a better place.* The liquid ache draining through her was set ablaze by fresh sparks of determination.

"I want him, Anne," she said with quiet finality. "And I know he wanted me . . . at least until he learned I was untried."

Anne recognized the look on Corrie's face as one that came straight from the depths of an awakening heart. It all but took Anne's breath.

"Ohhh, Cub . . ." She looked perfectly horrified. "Don't tell me you're falling in love with him."

"Love?" The word seared Corrie's mind. Was this unquenchable hunger for him the same divine madness that the poets and sages had named "love"? The prospect fired both her curiosity and her longings. "I cannot say. I only know I cannot let Beatrice have him until I have a chance to find out." She pushed onto her knees and seized Anne's shoulders. "And you have to help me!"

"Ohhh, Cub . . ." Anne pulled back, appalled.

"Anne," Corrie insisted, shaking her cousin by her voluminous sleeves, "this could be my 'once in a lifetime.'"

Anne winced, realizing that she had put that romantic notion in Corrie's head. "See here, Cub, certain men . . . I'm not certain Rugar Kalisson is the sort to be anybody's 'once in a lifetime.' Men like him don't fall in love . . . not for more than an hour at a time, anyway, nor in any position other than on their knees and elbows."

Corrie sobered with determination. "Then I'll just have to get him *on his knees and elbows*—and keep him that way until it's too late for him to stop loving me!"

Anne stared at her extraordinary cousin with a sinking feeling, realizing that there was no dissuading her. Corrie Huntington, she had learned, could be a very stubborn little thing indeed. She thought of the warm, golden glow of Rugar Kalisson's face as he had watched Corrie play the virginal, and she prayed that his worldly heart would be as susceptible to Corrie's loving nature as everyone else at court. And that the queen didn't find them out.

The queen. Anne stilled as the wider ramifications of Corrie's determination arrayed in her mind. The thought of defying Elizabeth's suffocating possessiveness sealed her decision. When she nodded, Corrie let out a whoop and hugged her.

She lost no time in plotting a course of action. "Now, we'll have to snoop about to discover when he is alone with Beatrice—Anne, you're good at that. Then I'll have to find ways to interrupt them."

Even as Anne was entering Corrie's chamber, the all-seeing Morris Lombard was making his first report to the queen: Rugar Kalisson had been closeted with Lady Corinna that afternoon in the library and had emerged looking wrought up and irritable. He had stalked through the gardens before taking up with Lady Beatrice. The twosome spent time together, parted for a while, and met again outside the Presence Chamber that evening. They had stayed in company for some time after the queen withdrew, then strolled along the dimly lit Stone Gallery. Later, they were seen kissing and fondling in a darkened window nook before they parted to their own chambers.

Elizabeth listened, regarding her chief informer furiously

over her templed fingers, then exploded. "He attempted her in my library? Damme—but the bastard has ballocks of brass!" But her outrage quickly melted into a vengeful smirk as the implication of such events unfolded in her mind. *Wrought up and irritable.*

"Well, well. It appears our Swede is not so invincible after all. He undoubtedly failed in his seduction of Lady Corinna today, and was forced to cast about for more willing game." Her expression warmed to a smile of genuine pleasure. "The gell clearly has her wits about her . . . and she's not likely to forget the sting of being discarded so publicly. I believe she is safely through." She focused on Lombard's gaunt features. "Still, watch this Rugar Kalisson closely. I'll not have him trifling with any of my ladies—that whore Beatrice included."

She dismissed him with a sweep of her hand and turned back to the papers littering her desk. Lombard bowed and melted back through the shadows, into the palace walls once again.

As it happened, Lady Beatrice was not Corrie's only rival for Rugar's attentions. During the next day, Anne spied him with no less than three of Elizabeth's other ladies, strolling, playing at cards and tables, and composing lyrics of courtly love to their feminine graces. The rest of England's jaded courtiers also watched, scandalized by his bewildering taste in potential paramours; The Countess of Main nudged sixty years and scarcely had a tooth in her head. Lady Clarice was an acknowledged, but notoriously frigid, beauty. And Lady Mary Guestmark was as plain and pitted a woman as the smallpox could possibly make her. Yet when his formidable charm focused intently on them, they blossomed like roses, growing dewy-eyed and shedding years and imperfections as they basked in his compelling attentions.

Torgne Sigurd was equally mystified by Rugar's wide-ranging dalliances. He had watched in raw consternation the previous night as Rugar spurned Lady Corrie to traipse about with loose-hipped Lady Beatrice. It had always been his policy to look the other way regarding Rugar's amorous adventurings. But the sight of Lady Corrie's sweet face, so confused and bereft, had generated an un-characteristic fury in him toward Rugar's casual sexuality. Then the next day, watching Rugar charming and cozening ladies almost twice his age and ugly as bull beef to boot, he grew incensed.

"What in hell's gotten into you, Rugar?" he demanded as they strolled toward the palace tennis courts that after-noon, at the edge of a group of spirited young nobles and ladies. "Abandoning Lady Corrie before the entire court—"

"She proved . . . unsuitable," Rugar hissed from behind a perfectly amicable smile which was aimed at Lady Devon-rie, who was just then casting him inviting glances. "Not to my taste at all."

"Not to your—*för guds skull,* Rugar," Torgne said with hushed ferocity, then in English: "For God's sake. She's not to your bloody taste? And I suppose those dried-up crones and draggletailed trollops are?"

Rugar's keen Nordic features bronzed with suppressed anger as he turned on Torgne. His eyes crackled and his nostrils flared, forbidding another word on the subject, then he strode off—straight for flirtatious Lady Devonrie.

Torgne was left glaring after him in confusion, until insight struck: only one thing marked a woman as untouch-able in Rugar's casually hedonist ethic. *Innocence.*

He watched as Rugar's carefully crafted charm worked its will on yet another of Elizabeth's bold lovelies, and his

mouth quirked up in a wry grin. So Lady Corrie had proved
to be a maid after all. And from the cold fury in Rugar's
face, the discovery had made quite an impact on him. He
wasn't used to misjudging women or to having his desire
thwarted. Torgne tugged down his doublet with a broad,
vengeful smile and struck off after the party.

Elizabeth sat in her darkened closet that night, hearing
the list of Rugar Kalisson's flirtations with a scowl of
puzzlement. "God's Blessed Knees. One certainly cannot
accuse him of being too choosy in his conquests. Does he
think to swive toothless old Main and have her gift him
with her estates out of gratitude?" She squinted at Morris
Lombard, who neither blinked nor smiled at her gibe. "Yet
you say he sleeps alone?"

"Yea, Your Grace. Alone."

"Well, he shan't much longer. He'll soon settle his desires
on another . . . and have her heels in the air before you can
say Jack Sauce." She fixed Lombard with an imperative
stare. "And when he does, *I* must be the first to know."

A few darkened corridors away, Corrie was receiving a
report from Anne, who had spent the better part of her day
at her infamous pastime: spying. The subject of her efforts
had been the same as Morris Lombard's, and her information
was equally juiceless. But when beautiful Lady Devonrie was
mentioned, Corrie paled.

"I have it on good report that he had no more than a bit
of tip and tickle from either Beatrice or Devonrie," Anne
reassured her. "And he spent this entire evening stripping
the pockets from Essex, Oxford, and the other earls in the
Guardsmen's Chamber. He won nearly every hand at cards,

and they're red-eyed with rage at him." She reached over to pat Corrie's folded hands. "He's kissed a few fingers, Cub, but I doubt he's dipped his stick into anyone else's honey."

Corrie was in no mood for cold comfort. "Tomorrow, Anne. I must find some way to get him alone."

Chapter Nine

The next afternoon, Anne hurried into Corrie's chamber. "I've just learned your Swede's got an 'appointment' with Devonrie shortly. Tennis, I believe"—she rolled her eyes—"or some other bit of ball sport." Corrie was out the door in a trice.

As they hurried down the corridor outside the Presence Chamber, they came across Sir Christopher Leighton, who had only just returned to court. He greeted them stiffly, then inquired whether they had seen Lady Devonrie of late. When he learned they had not and departed, Anne turned to Corrie, whispering: "Here's your chance, Cub. Devonrie's madly in love with Chris."

Rugar and the dark-eyed Lady Devonrie were crossing the gravel yard outside the tennis courts when Corrie finally spotted them. They were carrying gut-strung wooden rackets for playing tennis but were headed for the secluded nooks created by the groomed hedges and brick walls outside the tennis courts. From their direction and the way they pressed close as they walked, it was clear that tennis was not the only game they had in mind. The sight caused Corrie's throat to tighten, but she squared her shoulders, tugged her bodice lower, and hurried after them. They had just strolled around a corner and into a secluded nook amongst the hedges when she caught them.

"Lady Devonrie!" Corrie said airily, halting squarely in the middle of the opening to the small hedge-bound niche. They started apart, their faces crimsoning with surprised irritation. Ignoring Rugar's furious expression, Corrie fastened her attention on the sloe-eyed lady. "I almost despaired of finding you, my lady." She smiled directly into Devonrie's crackling hot look. "I've only just left Sir Christopher Leighton. He's newly arrived back at court . . . and searching everywhere for you."

The ire in Devonrie's expression melted at the sound of Sir Christopher's name. Her hand withdrew from Rugar's sleeve, and her skirts seemed to shrink from all contact with him. The bold, seductive hauteur of her usual manner softened into a stricken look.

"B-but I was only just about to—to p-play . . ." Both conflict and color mounted in Devonrie's expression as she glanced guiltily at Rugar and handled the tennis racket as though it burned her fingers.

"I shall be happy to take up your game with the ambassador," Corrie offered with the sweetest duplicity, extending open hands toward the racket. Devonrie thrust it at her, lifted her overskirts, and fairly flew down the graveled path toward the Privy Gallery. In the charged silence, Corrie peered up at Rugar's angry countenance from the safety of her lashes.

"I've never played at tennis before," she said, clasping the wooden handle to her breast. Her voice had a rushed, breathless quality. "Perhaps you could . . . instruct me."

It was an invitation to pleasure, a guileless seduction, an achingly sweet temptation. It made his fingertips vibrate alarmingly. "I fear that will not be possible."

"But"—she stepped closer—"you would have played with Devonrie."

"Lady Devonrie"—he backed away a pace—"has played before."

"Well"—she advanced again—"how difficult a game can it be?"

"Vastly more complicated than you realize," he declared, backing up yet another step, which brought him crashing into a giant privet hedge. He was excrutiatingly aware of the twin currents of meaning in their exchange . . . and of the dangerous eddies of warmth those submerged messages were stirring in his blood.

"If Lady Devonrie can do it, surely so can I." She nudged closer, tilting her face up to him. "Women are not so very different from one another. What is it the French say? *La nuit taus les chats sont gris.*"

He twitched as the translation bloomed in his mind. *All cats are gray at night!* He knew the saying and its crass English counterpart: "Jane is as good as milady in the dark." He'd tossed off such sayings himself on occasion, but to hear that jaded sentiment on her innocent lips was something of a shock.

He reached for her, intending to escort her from the hedges and straight back to the safety of the queen's possessive thrall. But the instant his hands closed on her upper arms, he was struck motionless by a tidal wave of need. His eyes defied his frantic control to slide into the warm, forbidden pools of hers. He could only stand . . . holding her, immersed in her presence. Then without conscious will he drew her closer to his hardening frame. In that pause, her pose softened, her lips parted, and her eyes grew luminous with longing.

From that moment on, he realized, women would never be "cats in the dark" to him again. Now there would always be her . . . a separate enchantment, utterly unique . . . proving that callous sentiment false. Every nerve and sinew in his body was alive with the pleasure of her warm, sweet curves pressed against him. His lips hovered, almost touching hers, craving her luxurious softness.

"Teach me, Rugar," she whispered against his mouth.

The seductive urgency of her prompting sent a quiver through his loins which brought him hurtling back to his senses. Conflict spiraled through his chest as he beheld the guileless desire in her face. Teach her? The only things she seemed not to know were lovemaking and deceit, he realized grimly. And he didn't want to be the one to teach her either. He wouldn't be the one to take her inno—

För guds skull! She was doing it to him again . . . turning his blood to steam and his mind to mush!

She had watched his thick blond lashes lower and felt the deep shiver that racked his body. Her heart soared. She closed her eyes and melted against him, raising her chin to meet his lips fully.

Instead, she found herself being spun about and propelled along the path by one big, sinewy hand on her arm and another at her back. She blinked in disbelief. Her knees were wobbly, and her head spun. It took a moment for her to collect herself and dig in her heels to resist him.

"W-what are you doing?" She struggled in his grip and managed to halt them both. Embarrassed anger bloomed crimson in her cheeks and bosom.

"I'm taking you back to the queen, where you belong," he gritted out, looming above her. "But if I were your father, I'd be taking you to a bloody convent!"

"Well, you're not my father," she declared hotly. "I already have a father, thank you—a perfectly wonderful father." The heat of his hand on her wrist radiated up her arm and curled its treacherous tendrils through her body, making it impossible to maintain her anger. There was more than righteous ire in his eyes; there was a vibrato of undamped desire that found answering resonance in the deep sinews of her body. He was so close, and the wanting in his eyes was so real. He was the portal, the guide, and the journey . . . and she understood for the first time that he was probably the goal of her heart's quest as well.

"Rugar . . ." Her voice was filled with promise and plea, and it ignited a raging fire in Rugar's susceptible loins. His arms were suddenly trembling; his breath came in short, hot blasts.

"No!" he snarled, lurching into motion and dragging her behind him. She scrambled and tugged, stopping them again.

"Why?" she demanded in a choked voice.

Why? Rugar's guts were tying themselves in knots. Because she'd somehow gotten into his blood . . . because of all of Elizabeth's ladies, she was the one he didn't want to seduce or ruin . . . because she was innocent in a way he'd never had the luxury to be . . . There were at least a hundred reasons that he shouldn't teach delectable little Kari Huntington the volatile pleasures of sensual love. But in the end they all came down to one: he wanted to protect her.

And by God's Blessed Knees, he was going to protect her whether she wanted it or not! He pulled her gruffly into motion again.

In a scant few moments, Corrie found herself standing alone in the deserted Privy Gallery, caught between the dying echoes of Rugar's footsteps and the growing clamor of the queen's entourage as it approached. Her cheeks were afire, her eyes were stinging, and her heart felt small and bruised. She placed her hand on the center of her breast and rubbed, trying to soothe the ache there. He would love other ladies—*any* other lady, *every* other lady—but he wouldn't love her. There just had to be a way. . . .

* * *

That evening in the Presence Chamber, Rugar added several more feminine hearts to his undisputed possession, including crass-spoken Lady Alyce Edmondson, snappish Lady Gwendolyn Partridge, and deaf-as-a-post Dame Agatha Cutterly, who jostled and elbowed each other openly, vying for the honor of having his sleeve for a promenade.

"I have to be on the right side!" old Dame Agatha declared loudly, her wrinkled countenance drawn up like a prune. "That's my good ear."

"You don't have a good ear," Lady Gwendolyn sneered, refusing to relinquish Rugar's right arm.

"Oh, but she does." Rugar intervened, speaking exaggeratedly to the old woman so that she might understand him. "In truth, you have lovely ears . . . pink as shells . . . exquisite. Men write sonnets to such ears." He lowered his head as if to brazenly drop a kiss on one sagging earlobe, then slyly veered away to press his lips upon her knobby fingers instead. Dame Agatha flushed and giggled toothily and Rugar sent Lady Gwendolyn a warm, lascivious wink, coaxing from her a sigh of acquiescence—and a shiver of anticipation.

Lady Alyce Edmondson managed to insert herself between Rugar and Dame Agatha. "My dear count, however can I persuade you to speak with my stable master about the services of that marvelous white stallion of yours?" she said suggestively.

"I wish I might oblige you, my lady," he murmured, gazing into her coarse, heavily painted face. "But I made him a gift to the queen only yesterday." He made to kiss her fingers and, as if overcome by impulse, pressed his lips boldly against her inner wrist instead. "Perhaps if you applied to her . . ."

"Apply to the queen for a stallion?" Lady Alyce laughed, then rubbed covertly against his arm as she crooned, "I am a renowned horsewoman, my lord. I choose my own stallions." The slow, tactile sweep of his smile raised gooseflesh on her skin.

Bess of Hardwick sailed up with her daughter in tow, and managed to separate Lady Gwendolyn from Rugar's other sleeve by an ill-disguised bandying of rank. But Bess was soon expelled by Lady Lennox, who was in turn displaced by Lady Clarice LaSalle. . . .

With all his attention seemingly trained upon whichever lady occupied his sleeve, Rugar still managed to make every lady who had ever possessed that coveted position feel that he longed to have her, and only her, occupy it once again. Everywhere he strode, he collected dewy-eyed looks from ladies whose fingers still tingled from his adoring kisses and whose ears still hummed from his seductive whispers. A tangible wave of feminine heat followed him wherever he went, borne on currents of cloying perfumes and hot, desirous looks.

His plan to woo Elizabeth's ladies was succeeding beyond his dreams. Yet there was something increasingly oppressive about their excessive finery and exaggerated femininity; about their overpainted faces, yellowed smiles, and hungry adoration. He clenched his jaw and reached deeper into his resolve, finding it alarmingly empty. The pleasure he'd imagined taking from such conquests was somehow missing. Even the most alluring ladies around him seemed stale and drab, their eyes not as jewel-clear or intriguing, their laughter not as bright or genuine, their lips not as expressive or desirable . . .

He suddenly realized what comparison he was making and glanced irritably across the great chamber to where the object of his desires sat, cloaked in forbidden virginity, seemingly oblivious to his presence.

But Corrie wasn't indifferent to his presence. It took every bit of her nerve to steel herself against a public display of her feelings toward him, even as the male courtiers smothered their raging jealousy with shows of disinterest. Pride demanded it. But all in the chamber were fiercely conscious of his location and occupation.

Elizabeth observed the growing competition for Rugar Kalisson's attentions with a cold disdain that was slowly condensing into icy fury. She cast dark glances at several empty chairs around her, and at her ladies, who now buzzed about Rugar like witless bees, eager to be robbed of their honey. Ponderous cows . . . giddy, distractible tits . . . the devil take the lot of them! she thought venomously as she watched them preen. She jerked about angrily in her chair, and her gaze fell on Corrie, nearby, who was engrossed in a game of tables with another honor maid. At least her precious Corinna had escaped unscathed.

When she looked up, her eyes slid straight into Rugar Kalisson's. Her heavily ringed fingers tightened on the exotic feathers of the fan in her hands, crumpling them. He was staring at her with a trace of mockery in his sensual features, a smug male presumption that filled her with outrage. *Watch me,* those devil-blue eyes taunted; *watch me with your ladies . . . and wonder.*

Through a sulfurous haze of new wrath Elizabeth suddenly understood that the wooing of her ladies was aimed at *her*—an insolent boast of male prowess and potency, an exhibition of the one power that Elizabeth, however mighty or imperial, would never wield. His hot, personal stare taunted her to think of the naked, breathtaking splendor of that unique male sovereignty to which she, as reigning queen, could never yield.

With fierce, queenly grace, Elizabeth raised her chin and endured the sight of her ladies paying homage to a man's treacherous charm. And with fierce Tudor vengeance, Elizabeth vowed that Johan's Swedish studhorse would sorely regret his cursed male challenge of her.

The next afternoon, Rugar invited the cool, elegant Lady Olivia Barreton, Countess of Windedeigh, for an intimate stroll in the Privy Garden. His determination to make her his first conquest in the flesh before the afternoon was out, bordered on the grim. After his encounter with Corrie Huntington the previous day, he was frantic to purge the accumulated heat in his blood and convinced that the only way to kill his ill-begotten craving for her was to drown it in another's charms. He squired Lady Olivia along the paths near the centrally located sundial, then gradually led her farther afield.

"How lovely you are today, sweet Olivia . . . a rare lily, awaiting a warm, caressing breeze to open your sleek, silken petals . . ."

"You turn my head, sir," Olivia murmured seductively.

"I would turn back time and tide themselves, to win your favor. For only your pure affections can soothe the ache in this hollow breast . . ."

He cultivated the glow his words generated in her with feather-light touches and increasingly heated looks. When they paused in a secluded bower, he drew her closer and read with some relief the sultry permission in her knowing eyes and parting lips.

"Lady Olivia!" A familiar voice burst upon them, jolting him with frustration as he started back a step. A heartbeat later, Corrie Huntington rounded the corner of the green hedges and jerked to a halt, staring wide-eyed. *Her again?* He groaned, as dread crept up his neck.

"Countess—" Corrie panted, ignoring him as she addressed the cutty-eyed lady. "The queen is calling for you, and—oh, my lady—she's in a foul mood!"

Olivia paled. "The queen is angry? But what could I have—"

"Prithee hurry, my lady"—Corrie gave Olivia's mounting fears a judicious prod—"do not anger her further." The lady lifted her skirts and turned to go with a doleful look at Rugar. Corrie made as if to accompany Lady Olivia, then suddenly discovered that her gilt-trimmed cedar ball had somehow fallen from the end of her girdle chain. "Oh, my pomander!"

She searched the ground, locating it mere inches from Rugar's left foot. "There it is!" She hurried back to retrieve it, brushing against Rugar as she swooped to pick it up. Regrettably, one of the two great strings of pearls she wore managed to catch on the hilt of his short sword. When he stiffened and lurched backward, she recoiled in kind, and the long strand snapped, sending luminous spheres flying all around.

"Nooo!" Corrie wailed, fumbling at the remnants of the strand which was still unstringing itself around her neck.

"Merciful—" Rugar reacted belatedly, grabbing at the last few pearls that fell and seeing them plummet past his fingertips into the dried grass at his feet.

"I have to find them! You'll have to go on without me," Corrie told Olivia with a groan. "Make haste, my lady. The queen is in the Stone Gallery." As Lady Olivia gathered her skirts and whirled away, Corrie sank to her knees and began sorting through the thick, dried grass, groaning, "Oh, if I've lost them . . ."

Rugar stood watching her, his eyes narrowed with

suspicion. He should stalk off, give her the broad of his
back and be done with it—if he had a jot of sense, that was
exactly what he'd do. But he couldn't make his feet move.
He looked around at the tangles of drying shrubs, vines, and
trees. In the isolated reaches of the chilled gardens, alone,
on her hands and knees, she'd be vulnerable . . . unpro-
tected. Deep inside, he felt his finely honed instinct for
self-preservation going soft around the edges, and that
mushy, sinking sensation sent him fleeing back to the safe
haven of male authority.

"Just what in hell do you think you are doing?" he demanded. "Come up from there." He bent to drag her to her
feet but stopped halfway down, recalling vividly the last
time he'd attempted to take her in hand bodily. He straightened abruptly, curling his itchy, unreliable hands into fists
and planting them on his hips.

"The pearls are not mine, they're Cousin Anne's—a gift
from her late husband. They are very precious to her. I must
retrieve them"—she lifted a rueful look to him—"if it takes
me all evening."

He couldn't just walk away and leave her there, yet he
knew if he stayed, there was the appalling possibility that
he'd end up entwined with her again. The conflict that
prospect generated in him sent a quiver through his shoulders which was amplified by anticipation until it shook the
very foundations of his resolve. He knew he would probably regret succumbing to her stubbornness, but succumb
he did. With a muffled groan, he lowered himself to his
hands and knees beside her, telling himself it was only to
help her search.

"I seldom wear jewelry," she explained, her voice breathy.
"But Anne insisted, saying the pearls would complement
my new bodice. You see, I've never worn red before. . . ."

Red. Rugar knew it was pure folly, sheer lust-spawned

idiocy, but he had to look at her just then. He found her half facing him, looking up at him from beneath black, feathery lashes. Her lustrous dark hair was uncapped, swirling over her shoulders, and her bodice—what he could see of it— was not the customary white or black, but a sultry maiden's blush red. He hadn't noticed the color until now . . . and suddenly his entire vision filled with the pale, creamy bounty spilling from a shocking red Italian neckline. Heat scored his body from his eyes all the way to his loins, where it struck a key nerve, dead on center.

His head snapped up, but his gaze refused to accompany it. Those plump, delectable ducks; how many ways he could adore them . . . mold and caress, nuzzle and lick— *Gud*. His sight broadened to include her sleek, half-naked shoulders. He was in absolute tumult inside. Then she added one final persuasion: one word, infused with all the longing of her awakening sensuality.

"*Rugar . . .*"

The virgin hunger in her eyes was irresistible.

Pleasure engulfed Corrie as he dragged his knuckles down her cheek, and across her bare shoulder. She melted to a sitting position, and he surged over her, pressing her back onto her elbows, claiming the space above and around her. The sight and feel of his powerful body surrounding hers filled her with sweet triumph. She had him on his *knees* at last—and well on his way toward his *elbows*! Her lips felt hot and naked, and every inch of her skin came alive, craving him.

All at once he lowered her onto the grass and his mouth poured over hers, sinking into the deep opulence of her lips and the honeyed surfaces beyond. She opened eagerly to him, meeting the bold seductive spirals of his tongue with her own. His mouth drifted across her face and down her throat to stop at her small ruff. She shifted in his arms, offering herself up to him, seeking the lush decadence of his mouth on her body once again.

His kisses brought her quickly to the limits of her experience, then plunged beyond. She felt his fingers slide to her front lacings, and held her breath, anticipating what came next. He peeled back her bodice and worked the ties of her corset. Her breath caught in her throat as he pried back her boning and brushed her shift aside to bare her breasts in the chilled air. A low moan sounded from deep in his throat as his fingers slid over the hardened, tingling tips of her breasts, melting her every maidenly qualm. She was swirling . . . plummeting . . . soaring!

His palm swept over her nipples in wide, maddening circles that sent pleasure through her belly and down the backs of her legs. He brushed her lips with his, then bent to excite each taut rosy peak with long, liquid swirls of his tongue. It was as though he had stripped her senses bare, to expose each to the maximum intensity of his touch. When be took one nipple into his mouth and suckled it, she moaned and arched against his mouth, vibrating with each expert flick of his tongue.

Each sensation was new and brilliant; each hot draft of pleasure carried her further onto uncharted seas of desire. She whimpered softly as her body contracted about a taut emptiness in her loins that she hadn't realized existed within her. With a will of their own her hips moved restlessly, seeking relief for the turgid heat collecting in her womanflesh and finding the promise of it against his hardness. For the first time she truly understood how their bodies could merge . . . and the inexpressible pleasure such a joining would bring.

"Love me, Rugar," she whispered from the depths of her woman's heart. "Touch me . . . and love me."

He rose shakily on one elbow, feeling out of breath and out of control. Beneath him, she lay bared and love-rumpled

amongst the autumn grasses, her breasts swollen and lush
nipples contracted amidst an erotic sworl of blush-red
velvet. Her lips and eyes glistened seductively above the
prim border of her narrow ruff. Her black overskirt and
pristine petticoats were tangled about her shapely legs like
a half-opened blossom, sheltering pleasure's secrets. Heart-
stopping tenderness rushed through him. He wanted nothing
more than to—

Love? The word bit sharply into his passion-sodden
nerves, and he found his whole body recoiling before he
managed to understand why. He focused on her clear eyes,
and what he read through those revealing windows on her
heart set his chest tightening around his lungs. She spoke
of love . . . and meant far more than acts of passion. She
meant the wild yearning of hearts and mawkish upwellings
of emotion that overflowed into courtly avowals of unending devotion. He trembled as that revelation clamped a
harsh check on his desires. Inside that curious, ramping-hot
little body beat the heart of a dewy-eyed virgin. A hopeful.
An *innocent.*

His muscles bunched and he shot up onto his arms with
a savage growl.

Corrie was stunned by his withdrawal, unable to react at
first. It was happening again, that cold, intractable retreat
that always followed a flare of hot passion in him. And
just when her heart had begun to take flight! Frustration
welled as he began to drag the edges of her bodice over her
exposed flesh. She held his hands against her breasts to
still them.

"Did I . . . do something wrong?"

"No—yes!" he said with strangled vehemence, ripping
his hands from her as if she'd scalded him. "Nothing—
everything!"

She blinked against the sudden stinging in her eyes and
the burn of humiliation in her skin. How could he say such

things to her after the way he'd touched and loved her? She wavered between hurt and anger.

"Well, if I did things wrong, you're partly to blame," she charged. "You taught me everything I know!"

He stiffened, looking as if he'd just been doused with hot pitch. *You taught me.* He'd taught her, all right; the heat of a man's kiss, the feel of a man's hands on her delectable little body, the tantalizing preludes to passion. The knowledge positively gored him.

"Dammit—"

"Then tell me what I've done amiss, and I'll try to do better."

She'd try to do better. He groaned silently. It wasn't possible for Kari Huntington to do any better; she was already sensual perfection! He shut his eyes but found he'd trapped the sight of creamy mounds tipped with crinkled rose velvet in his head, and frantically opened them again.

"For God's sake . . . lace yourself up!"

His command scorched the air while he tried to stare fiercely at her without actually seeing her love-tousled look and alluringly disheveled bodice. Then with defiant deliberation, she leaned back on her arms and lifted her chin, refusing to obey, refusing to let him deny his eagerness for her yet again.

"I said—"

"*You* undid me," she said, her voice deep with smoky challenge. "*You'll* have to do me up again."

He recoiled as if struck. *You undid me.* Not yet he hadn't! She was suddenly back in focus, her gaze aglow with feline awareness as she arched her back slightly and thrust both her shambled laces and her lush breasts with their erect nipples toward him. She was daring him to touch her without wanting her again.

It was a challenge he couldn't ignore and would be daft

to accept. Raw male pride was his last bastion; he had to show her who was in control, had to assert some proper male authority. With an outraged growl, he reached for her laces, tugging at them, fumbling, his ineptitude a measure of the power of her ploy.

"Do not ever—*ever*—let a man do this to you again— do you hear?" he ordered. "Don't ever let a man kiss you with his tongue, or lie atop you, or put his hands inside your clothes. Never." His throat constricted around his next words. "At least, not until you're safely married ." He swallowed hard and made himself add, "Someday you'll marry and . . . and men expect their brides to be . . . innocent."

Married. You'll marry. The words struck Corrie like a great suffocating sea wave, toppling her from her determined stand into a churning white water of confusion. As she floundered, she began to understand: Rugar wanted her, and he might even have a bit of tenderness for her tucked away in some remote corner of his heart. But he had just declared that he would not ever marry her. And in such a situation, his noble, knightly code demanded that he defend her, against both his ignoble desires and her own.

She was suddenly lost, adrift. She had never seriously thought of marriage as a possibility until this very moment. Now she knew with dreadful certainty that she would never consider it again, for she could never allow any other man to do to her what Rugar had just done. She would never want to be with another man the way she wanted to be with Rugar, watching him, talking and laughing with him, learning from him. Terrible loss engulfed her—desperation for the pleasure of being held in his arms, for the sight of his eyes glowing with intimate delight, for the heady joy of giving up her breath to his kisses, for the tenderness with which he'd taught her.

Rugar Kalisson, she realized with new and crushing awe, was most certainly her *once in a lifetime*.

"Rugar," she whispered, clasping his hands to still them as she sought his stormy gaze. Her eyes were wet and luminous, filled with equal measures of fear and hope. She had to say it. She had to try.

"You . . . you wouldn't have to marry me."

No other words in all of Christendom could have had such a devastating effect on him. He felt as if he'd been hammered in the ribs; he could scarcely breathe. Kari Huntington, his learned, sensual, curious little virgin, was offering herself to him. Without promise or qualification. Just for the sake of loving him. *Loving him.*

He exploded to his feet with such force that he staggered, his head reeling. He quelled a flash of panic and grabbed her by the wrists, pulling her to her feet before him. He completed her laces with a few fiercely determined jerks, gave her small, crumpled ruff a cursory fluff, and curtly dragged a few stray grass straws from her hair.

He tried not to look at her . . . didn't want to see that her lashes were wet, that her cheeks were crimson with shame, or that she was biting her lip to keep back tears. He only wanted to get as far away from her as he could before he took her back into his arms and loved her past the brink of reason . . . all the way to *ruin*.

There were three witnesses to their harried entrance into the Stone Gallery.

Anne had waited there to divert Lady Olivia from the summons they had concocted and had lingered, hoping to learn the outcome of Corrie's latest gambit. One look at her cousin's love-rumpled appearance and downcast eyes, and Anne was spurred to action. She collected Corrie against her side and led her quickly into the private, stone-walled passage leading toward the ladies' apartments. Once reasonably shielded from prying eyes, Anne gave Corrie a fierce hug and cupped her chin with a tender hand, demanding to know if she was all right. Corrie's chin trembled as she made her anguished report.

"Oh, Anne, I'm afraid your lovely pearls went for naught."

Torgne Sigurd also saw Rugar deposit Corrie in the empty gallery, then stride off. The image of her sweet, miserable face and disheveled gown branded itself into Torgne's outraged moral sense. He caught up with Rugar in the courtyard just outside the Cock Pit. His ire was scorching as he wrestled Rugar back by the arm and demanded in furious Swedish: "She looks like you wallowed her to Stockholm and back—just what the hell did you do to her?"

"More than I should have . . . but a damn sight less than she wanted!" Rugar answered with equal heat. Feeling beset on all sides, especially from *in*side, he added pugnaciously: "It's not my fault her arse is always getting tangled up with mine! I don't want any part of her. I've never had a taste for virgins, remember?" But as he wrenched his arm from Torgne's punishing grip and headed for the comparative sanity of a cockfight, a beleaguered voice inside him taunted, *Never . . . until now.*

The third pair of eyes to witness Rugar and Corrie's dismal parting belonged to the canny and opportunistic Morris Lombard. He stepped quickly back into the shadow of a stone buttress as Anne Bosworth and Corrie Huntington passed by and thus kept them from seeing him.

As he took in Corrie's shame-stained cheeks and littered skirts, he surmised what sort of activity had brought her to such a state, and his restless, all-seeing eyes glowed hotter. Jack Huntington's daughter, he thought with a nasty smirk, had deliciously disastrous taste in lovers. What an unholy opportunity for a bit of revenge . . . delivered straight into his crooked fingers! It had been eighteen years since the Earl of Straffen had wrecked a perfect Lombard scheme, costing him a brace of years in Newgate Prison and a profitable career at the law. But the long wait had been worth it. At last he had a Huntington's fate in his hands once again.

Chapter Ten

A program of plays was staged that evening in the Great Hall, but Corrie was not present. Earlier, she had sent word to the queen that she was not feeling well and begged to be excused from the evening's festivities. Anne Bosworth, who had carried the message, was given leave to sit with her for the evening. But Corrie and Anne seemed to be the only ones missing; the other courtiers turned out fully, prodigiously powdered, perfumed, and pomandered.

Speculation that evening centered on which of the costumed players were actually highly placed nobles of the court in roguish disguise. But a major scandal came after the performances had ended and the court musicians provided music for dancing; there was suddenly a dire shortage of ladies for the gentlemen to partner. A number of the court ladies had withdrawn to the Presence Chamber, where they were being entertained, the queen was reliably informed.

Dread crawled up Elizabeth's spine as she looked around the empty dance floor. Her artificially whitened face paled even further, and her icy fingers dug into the pearl-crusted smocking of her overskirt. It was *him* again, she was sure of it.

For the past two days her immediate world had been

turned on its ear on his account. Her maids and ladies now jostled and hissed and clawed at one another like she-cats in heat. The merest slight or verbal misstep would bring them out biting and scratching. And yet, let Rugar Kalisson appear, and they all grew bright-eyed and docile, openly coveting his gaze and competing for his touch. Bile rose up the back of her throat. They'd deserted her, the faithless trollops, and for no more than the promise of a bit of petting from one man's hand.

She quitted the Great Hall in high dudgeon, heading straight for her Presence Chamber. It was as she had feared and worse. Rugar Kalisson was seated amidst a throng of court ladies, some standing, some in chairs, and some seated on pillows by his feet, their colorful skirts spread around him like a bouquet of bright blossoms. The spectacle was magnified by the long mirrors on the wall behind him; he appeared to be engulfed on all sides by a veritable sea of elegant femininity.

Elizabeth stood watching with her male court at her back. She did not miss the message intended in his bold choice of location: he was clearly holding court in *her* Presence Chamber, and with her very own ladies. He was *usurping* . . . stealing the love and loyalty which rightfully belonged to her.

Rugar felt her stare and looked up to find her surveying the scene with controlled fury. He lurched to his feet, produced his most dazzling smile, and bowed extravagantly.

"Your Grace. I was but sharing a few poor Swedish folk tales with these lovely ladies. And they insisted upon learning a few words of my native tongue."

Elizabeth's face remained chillingly calm, and several ladies got to their feet and stood with fidgeting hands and uneasy looks. A trill of warning slithered across his broad shoulders, and he wondered fleetingly if he'd pushed too far. Would she move openly against him?

But Elizabeth had survived both her long and perilous route to the throne and her first seventeen years as an unmarried queen by dissembling, not by confronting. As the unparalleled mistress of the use of calculated inaction, she was always at her most dangerous when appearing to hesitate or to retreat. And she chose that treacherous course once again.

"You entertain my ladies well, Aelthar." There was ominous indignation in her tone. "But they have duties, sirrah, as do we all. Devonrie, Beatrice, Bess, Clarice, I shall have you accompany me. And my honor maids . . . come." He bade her good night with a deep obeisance. Her only response was the glitter in her eyes as she motioned curtly to a number of others and decamped.

After Elizabeth and her women had gone, Torgne made his way through the palpable tension in the grand chamber to Rugar's side, looking thoroughly shaken. "*Gud,* Rugar, that was close. Perhaps it is time to give thought to returning to Stockholm." But Torgne's shock deepened when Rugar grasped his shoulder with a look of fierce pleasure.

"We cannot leave yet, Tor," he said in a rasp. "I'm just beginning to like it here."

The stale air in the queen's gilt-crusted closet was as turbulent as her mood when Morris Lombard came that night to make his report. Elizabeth had earlier vented her rage on her women, denouncing them as faithless, jaded tarts to whom decency and loyalty and the honor of her crown meant nothing. They had cowered gratifyingly, and at least one honor maid would likely bear the outline of a regal hand upon her fair cheek the next morning. But that portion of Elizabeth's anger which burned toward the insolent Swede was not yet banked, and Lombard's report only stoked it higher.

The ambassador's adventures had increased. That same day, he had carried on flirtations with several ladies of the queen's own chamber; had enjoyed long, private interviews with De la Varga, of the Spanish mission, and Pasquier, the French Ambassador; then had wagered and won on cocks in the Cock Pit.

"And between the ambassadors and the cocks"— Lombard's mouth twitched—"he managed to keep a tryst in the gardens with . . . Lady Olivia Barreton."

Elizabeth's rigid shoulders sagged briefly beneath her gold-stiffened robes. "Olivia? In my own gardens?" Her wiry body coiled as if preparing to strike. "God's Blood— does the bastard mean to plow them all? The hideous guile, the monstrous conceit!" she raged, springing to her feet and pacing with swishing flourishes of her robes. When her anger was spent enough to master, she lifted her head slowly.

"Put your ears closer to the walls, Lombard." Vengeful determination pinched her thin features. "When he plans another assignation with one of my ladies, bring me word, so that I may join them."

Lombard gave an inscrutable nod and withdrew. When the small, arched door, which led into a narrow stone passage, had closed behind him, a thin-lipped smile creased his face. He had purposefully made no mention of Corinna Huntington's renewed involvement with the Swede and would make none . . . until the chit's indiscretions were too deep and ruinous to be denied by the queen . . . or forgiven. Then, loyal servant that he was, he would inform the queen of the Swede's latest perfidy and let her glimpse for herself.

"A buffled head, trembly knees . . . alternating chills and fevers, bone-deep aches and gnawing hungers. If this is love, then it is a most peculiar strain. It's naught like the sonnet writers' descriptions," Corrie mused as she watched the single flame of the oil lamp burning lower in the gloom of her chamber. "It seems more like the recorded accounts of the Great Plague . . . only without the hideous red spots."

"Sonnet writers . . . notoriously unreliable," a sleepy Anne mumbled, curling around a bolster at the foot of Corrie's bed and propping her cheek wearily on her palm.

"A plague without spots." Corrie sighed. An apt description. She was indeed learning about love from Rugar Kalisson, and today's lesson had clearly been that the stuff of "love" was far more complicated than she'd expected and not always filled with joys and raptures. Some of it was perfectly awful!

In the evening hours just past, she had relived her afternoon's encounter with him over and over. He had gone to heroic lengths to protect her wretched maidenhood. How ironic that the prime obstacle to the fulfillment of her love seemed to be her own virtue, Corrie thought. And how perfectly monstrous of fate to make her once-in-a-lifetime love too blessed noble to actually love her.

"It isn't fair . . . none of it," she said, groaning. "If I ran the world, rich, handsome noblemen would never be too gallant to make love to green young gells—or to marry them." She thought on that, and her spirits began to plummet. "He isn't married, but it's clear he wants no part of marrying me." She looked down at the pale shoulder bared by her drooping smock and winced. "It's because I'm not beautiful enough, isn't it?"

"Don't be a ninny. You're as comely a piece as any at court," Anne declared, forcing her eyes open yet again.

"Then perhaps I'm not rich enough."

"'Pon my liver, Cub," Anne swore halfheartedly, "you're a full heiress. Three estates, ships, boodles of . . ."

But Corrie's mind had raced ahead, and her eyes widened in horror as she glimpsed a more devastating possibility.

"Or not *Swedish* enough." Anne had no rebuttal for that, and Corrie's heart hit bottom. "I hadn't thought of that. He has position and responsibilities and a home—a whole life—in a faraway land. And he loves his native country deeply. Perhaps he can't think of marrying anyone who isn't Swedish . . . and blonde."

"Imagine wanting to m-marry a Swede," Anne mumbled, half coherently, teetering on the brink of consciousness. "Some s-sins are their own punishment."

Oblivious to Anne, Corrie stared balefully at a lock of her hair. She couldn't help that she'd been born English, with hair black as midnight.

For the first time she understood that she and Rugar were separated by more than just the boundaries of innocence and worldliness. They came from very different countries, lands set apart by far more than merely miles of sea. There were great differences of language and heritage, custom and belief; differences that she, in her wretched ignorance, hadn't recognized because of Rugar's accomplished use of her language and his smooth, seemingly effortless entry into the English court. But Rugar, being wiser than she in the ways of the world, had undoubtedly seen it.

How could she battle his noble principles, his deep love for his homeland, and his hard-won experience in life, when all she had was hope enough to fill one small heart?

Corrie rose from her bed the next morning, hollow-eyed and listless. Surrendering to Anne's good-natured bullying, she groomed and gowned herself smartly and accompanied Anne to join the queen in the Privy Gallery that afternoon. They found Elizabeth in a rare mood, wielding her rapier-sharp wit mercilessly as she held forth amongst her nobles and ambassadors. Her increasingly pointed barbs produced a volatile atmosphere in the crowded gallery; a stark tension ran beneath the courtiers' display of forced gaiety. It was as if, with her stabs and pricks, she prepared them for the spectacle she had ordered for the afternoon—the baiting of a bull, a bear, and an ape in the Tilt Yard.

Anne insisted Corrie go, hoping it would take her mind off her troubles. Corrie had certainly heard of baiting; indeed it was a popular attraction at fairs and celebrations of most any kind. But her overprotective father had sternly prohibited her and her sisters from witnessing such sport.

"Baiting and beheading always bring them out in hordes." Anne wrinkled her nose and gathered her skirts protectively as a surge of London's unwashed citizenry rumbled past them on their way to the Tilt Yard. "Never been particularly keen on baiting myself." She leaned close to Corrie and quipped, "A bull, a bear, *and* an ape . . . I wonder what's given Bess such a taste for blood."

A taste for blood. Disquiet settled on Corrie's shoulders, but she was soon caught up in the unbridled excitement of the crowd. A dais had been hastily prepared for the queen's chair, but it was too small to accommodate her retinue, so her courtiers filled the few permanent stands and spilled over onto the grounds to mill with the Londoners around the wooden ring where the baiting would occur. Corrie and Anne squeezed onto the end of a bench in the stands, where they had a close view of the proceedings.

The crowd roared to its feet when the beasts were brought in. The bull was huge and fierce; it took half a dozen men to secure the chains from the ring about his huge neck to the iron stakes in the ground. The bear bellowed and lashed at his captors, egged on by men with pointed sticks who prodded him to excite him for combat. And the ape was next, smaller than Corrie had expected, and not so very different from the pet monkeys that were popular with the ladies of court. When the three were securely chained to the stakes, a hush fell over the crowd, and the keepers withdrew. Then the dogs were unleashed, more than a dozen large, frenzied hounds whose hunger was evident from the racks of ribs visible on their sides, and a great cry of excitement went up.

The lathered hounds snarled and lunged, working in instinctive packs, harrying and snapping at the chained beasts, which bellowed, reared, and swung at them.

One dog darted in and ripped the ape's leg, and the smell of blood mingled with the rising dust to excite both the animals and spectators to a fevered pitch.

Corrie winced, unable to tear her eyes away as the dogs attacked again and again, each time ripping further into the ape's flesh as it screamed with pain and strained against its chains to fight back. Soon the bear's side lay open and the bull's flanks glistened with blood. All around Corrie the courtiers' faces were crimson and their eyes glittered as they demanded more blood and laid wagers on which beast would be the first to die. Corrie's spine went rigid and her hands balled into fists at her sides. She could scarcely draw breath.

On and on it went, the staged "battle" between beast and dog . . . bloody mayhem that called to the beast in man himself. When she could take no more, Corrie lurched from her seat and pushed blindly through the jostling crowd. She was buffeted on all sides by the explosive shouts and gyrations of the frenzied throng. Just as she approached full panic, she found herself caught in a pair of strong hands and looked up into the glowing eyes and ruddy grin of the Earl of Oxford.

"Lady Corinna! You're missing the fun, my lady." He

thrust her gallantly ahead of him toward an opening at the edge of the ring. "Here, take my place and I'll stand behind!"

She was suddenly trapped at the edge of the wooden barrier, viewing at blunt range the spectacle of rending flesh and spurting blood. Her vision filled with gore-spattered ground, with maddened animals clawing and fighting over possession of a mangled carcass, with human faces contorted by bloodlust into fiendish masks. Savage snarls and the humanlike screams of beasts in pain mingled with dreadful laughter in her head. Her stomach heaved, and she wheeled and shoved frantically through the gentle-men crowded in behind her.

She wrestled through the crowd, gasping, ears ringing, vision constricting into a long, dark tunnel. As she reached the edge of the spectators, she staggered to a halt and fought the urge to sink into that comforting darkness. Sweat trickled like icy fingers down her neck and shoulders. She looked up, forcing her eyes to focus, and there, a few paces away, was a familiar face . . . a haven, a refuge. . . .

Rugar had stood along the baiting ring with the other spectators, but his mind was occupied by the timing and logistics of a very different sport. He was fiercely intent on claiming the promises of pleasure he'd been receiving all afternoon from the voluptuous red-haired woman who occupied his sleeve. He looked down at Lady Sophie Gran-tham, appraising the heaving of her plump, pillowy breasts and the way her cheeks were flushed and her eyes glistened as she watched the bloody spectacle. He was probably in for a hot time of it, he realized with less than proper appre-ciation. He attempted to smile at her when she snuggled insinuatingly against his arm, then he turned his head to glance around the ring with strained forbearance. In that chance movement, his gaze fell on a small feminine figure pressed against the railing some distance away.

His belly did a slow contraction. Corrie Huntington. He couldn't see much of her, but he'd know that raven-framed face anywhere. *No!* Not when he was finally about to purge her from his sensual memory with another woman's charms. His attention snapped back to Lady Sophie, and with renewed determination he leaned close to whisper into her ear. Her lashes fluttered coy agreement, and he drew her in his wake through the half-intoxicated crowd.

It was the perfect opportunity for a rendezvous; with the whole court up to its gullet in gore, no one would notice them slipping off. His apartments were conveniently close by, and they wouldn't be missed for another hour or two. When they reached the edge of the crowd, Rugar put his arm around Lady Sophie with a conspiratorial wink and started for the gates of the Tilt Yard.

But they hadn't gone half a dozen steps when a small, dark-clad figure burst from the heaving crowd and staggered to a halt just ahead of them . . . a demure little figure . . . *a disaster in the making!* Not this time, Rugar thought desperately. He tried to draw Lady Sophie around the obstacle in their path, but she didn't understand and balked in confusion. "This way, quickly!" he whispered, but not in time.

Corrie stumbled straight into their path. Rocking unsteadily, she looked up—straight into his face. In one heart-stopping minute he went from burning with frustration to freezing with anxiety. She was as pale as ashes, and her eyes were unnaturally dark and unfocused.

"Lady Corinna?" She looked ready to collapse. What the devil was wrong with her? His protective instincts rose against his will. He groaned silently, hesitated, then dragged the reluctant Sophie forward, since she would not relinquish his sleeve.

"R-Rugar . . . ?"

"What's happened?" he demanded, watching Corrie stagger toward him and feeling those first awful pricklings of dread that now heralded one of his unholy encounters with her. She lurched against him, and he just managed to catch her around the middle as she fell. Gritting his teeth in frustration, he grappled for a better hold on her and managed to circle her waist—which left her bent, headfirst, over his arms. She whimpered, clamped a frantic hand over her mouth, and tried to straighten. But instead she stiffened, and her shoulders convulsed once, twice . . .

"God—no!" Rugar growled. "Don't be—"

But she *was* sick—all down his elegant half-gartered hose and all over his costly kidskin shoes with the fancy Italian filigree buckles.

"Not my shoes," he groaned.

"Ugghhh!" Lady Sophie recoiled with a shudder, pressed her pomander beneath her nose, and quickly abandoned them to their vile condition.

Rugar scarcely noticed her departure; he was too busy trying to keep Corrie's limp body from hitting the ground. There was no help to be had around them, only a few ragged Londoners who covered their noses and scurried away at the sight of sickness. Growling through clenched teeth, he gathered her ungainly form as best he could and lifted her against him.

A moment later he was striding from the Tilt Yard with Corrie Huntington, instead of a paramour, in his arms yet again.

He kicked open the door to the apartments he shared with Torgne and carried her through the outer room straight to the draped bed in his private chamber. Her eyes were closed and her breathing was shallow as he laid her down and removed her dangling cap. Alarmed by her unresponsiveness and the clamminess of her skin, he sank onto the edge of the bed beside her and called her name urgently, shaking her shoulders. When she roused slowly, he took her chin in his hand and searched for signs of recovery in her eyes.

"För gud skull," he said with gruff relief. "You are the most troublesome female I've seen in my entire life. You lurch from one damned catastrophe to another. Don't move."

He returned moments later with a wet cloth and a goblet of brandy, and with his legs bare from the knees down. He had stripped his hose and shoes and washed hurriedly. As he wiped her face and brushed back her tangled hair, a few raven tendrils curled about his fingers. There was a strange tightness in his gut as he freed his hand and reached for the goblet.

"Come, up with you and drink some." He shifted on the side of the bed to cradle her shoulders against his hard chest. She twitched and gasped as the fiery liquid burned a path to her abused stomach, and he snorted amusement. "Brandy. It will settle your heaves and put some heat back in your blood." She obeyed, shuddering after each sip until she felt a blessed warmth spread through her.

"I'm s-sorry." Her cheeks went from pale to blushing pink. "I must have been sick."

"Indeed you were." He scowled and lifted a bare calf and foot in evidence. "All over my best hose and shoes." His words blamed, but his tone absolved her of guilt.

"Forgive me. I—I'd never seen a baiting before. My father never let us . . ." The sickening sights, smells, and sounds still clung powerfully to her senses, so that the mere mention of it caused those horrors to billow again in her mind: the stench, the gore, the frightening bloodlust in human faces.

She sat upright and seized his sleeves with panicky hands. "There was so much blood—and the beasts' screams sounded like human cries. I thought a baiting was supposed to be a battle between wild beast and dog, but the beasts were so weighted down with chains that they couldn't possibly fight. It was no more than foul slaughter . . . starved dogs ripping at their flesh, killing them bit by bit." She choked, unable to continue as her eyes and throat filled with tears.

The distress in her delicate face took hold of him. Suddenly there was no distance between them, no rational, dispassionate separation of self from other. Her feelings permeated him in a way he'd never experienced before with another human being. With a new and devastating awareness he not only perceived her misery but participated in it.

Impulsively, he wrapped her securely in his arms. As her tears turned to earnest sobs and her shoulders quaked against him, he wished with all his heart he could wipe those vile impressions from her mind.

"W-why did they do it?" Leaning face-first into his chest, she managed a gulping breath or two. "The animals didn't want to fight . . . they had to be starved and goaded to it." She raised tortured eyes to him. "Then it must be . . . those who make them fight and those who watch . . . are more savage than the dumb beasts themselves."

Rugar saw her face pale as the awful realization of just how cruel a beast man could be replaced a precious bit of innocence in her soul. It was terrible for him, watching the world grow tarnished in her eyes.

"Plautus wrote of it, but I didn't understand really until today. *Lupus est homo homini.* 'Man is a wolf to man.' He spoke of how cruel men are to one another, preying viciously out of hatred, vengeance, and greed." She paused, then her voice came softly. "I suppose it would be futile to expect men to be less cruel to dumb beasts than they are to one another."

That raw, painful new wisdom found resonance in his deepening feelings. He had an overwhelming urge to draw her inside him, to safeguard her against the disillusionment that inevitably came as one learned more about the world.

He slid back against the bolsters at the head of the bed and pulled her onto his lap, sheltering her with his strength as he offered her what comfort he could.

"Sweet Kari." He lifted her chin. "Yes, sometimes men are wicked, unprincipled, and unmerciful, but that is not the final sum of mankind, else we should all have perished from the earth long ago. Men can also be noble, honorable, and compassionate. To know the truth about mankind, you must weigh both in the balance." He gave an odd, bitter-sweet smile and rubbed her reddened lip with one finger. "I believe you have just discovered the dirty hand that sometimes inhabits the 'clean glove.' But, Kari, you must not let it lead you to expect dirt on *every* hand."

The warmth and wisdom in his azure gaze was like a balm to Corrie's heart. Relief washed over her. Before her very eyes was the proof; Rugar Kalisson was the embodiment of all that was good and decent and noble in mankind, the living example of the perfection of human will and intention. There might be flawed men whose appetites led them to be cruel and indecent, but there were also men like her father and like Rugar whose higher nature and moral standards led them to set their personal interests aside for the good of others.

Her arms slid around his ribs, and his answering embrace tightened around her waist and shoulders. They sat for some time, Corrie cradled in Rugar's arms, both savoring an intimacy that had nothing to do with the proximity of their bodies. She nuzzled his doublet front with her cheek and felt him do the same to the top of her head. She could hear the muffled beating of his heart, could smell the muted blend of spicy herbs that was used to scent his clothing in storage, and could feel the hardened contours of his body giving way beneath hers. Gradually the fluid warmth swirling between them focused into more familiar streams of sensation.

She raised her eyes to his and found them darkening. Her pulse jumped, and her gaze fled his to travel over the large, velvet-draped bed with its soft mattresses and plump feather pillows, and the comfortable, stonewalled chamber beyond.

"Where are we?"

"My apartments, not far from the Tilt Yard." His voice was deeper, softer. "It seemed the quickest place to find you a bed . . ."

Bed. Both of them froze. They were indeed abed, entwined bodily, and already intimate in a way neither had anticipated or was prepared to resist. All that was needed was a word, a look; a spark to ignite the volatile potential for passion that had been seeping through their encounter like a subtle but compelling perfume.

"I am in your debt once again, my lord. *Tack.*"

Rugar's eyes went black, and his body hardened instantly against hers.

"Say it again," he demanded hoarsely, staring at her lips.

"Tack." She felt his shiver all along her body. His voice was deep and enthralling as his head bent toward hers by torturous increments.

"Ingenting att tacka för."

"What does that mean?" she whispered, running her tongue over her upper lip as she watched his mouth descending.

"It means . . . it's nothing to thank me for."

Then his lips crushed hers softly, and suddenly the gates of perception were thrown wide open. A great churning flood of perception came rushing through their hungry senses. There was no hesitation now. He slid her bottom from his lap onto the bed beside him, and in one smooth movement he was above her, bearing her down into the soft covers. His kisses were both fierce and tender; silky, restrained strokes and voluptuous wet bites, demanding a breathtaking range of response. She gave herself to him with a moan of eagerness and a helpless undulation up the length of his body.

"Rugar . . . Rugar, where are you?" Torgne entered their connecting apartments, scowling, intending to have it out with his friend and insist that they withdraw from the English court and set sail as quickly as possible for Sweden. Hearing a muffled noise in the bedchamber, he strode through the antechamber and threw back the half-opened door. His gray eyes narrowed as they located Rugar on the bed, and he stalked forward, demanding, "Dammit, Rugar, I must talk to you. And for once, you shall listen!"

At the sound of Torgne's voice, Rugar was up and around in an instant, coiled and braced, looking shocked and red-faced. Beyond him, in the bed shadows, Torgne glimpsed movement, then a womanly shape struggling up from the bed. In the space of a breath he recognized Lady Corrie, her raven hair atangle, her lips love-bruised, and her face aflame. He stopped, sputtered, and stumbled back, unable to tear his eyes from the sight of her. Rugar had Lady Corrie in his bed!

Rugar was on his feet in a flash and quickly dragged Corrie after him. Both frantically smoothed their rumpled clothing and rattled disjointed bits of explanation as to how they came to be there. The baiting came into it somehow, and the Earl of Oxford; Corrie was sick, and Rugar had the misfortune to be in the way when she emptied her stomach, which explained his notable lack of footgear; then she fainted, and he had to carry her . . .

Their excuses dwindled and halted under Torgne's righteous glare, and Rugar cleared his throat and quickly escorted Corrie from the bedchamber. Burning with humiliation, she insisted she could find her way to her own chambers without further assistance, and he bade her farewell at the door with an awkward kiss of her trembling fingers. Then he found himself facing the combined fury of his own self-recrimination and Torgne Sigurd's towering wrath.

"How dare you bring Lady Corrie here—into your own bed! If I had been anyone—*anyone*—else, servant or noble, she would have been utterly ruined! And you could damn well be on your way to the Tower!" Torgne paced away, quaking with the unaccustomed release of emotion.

"Dammit, Rugar, we were sent here to woo the queen and her damnable court, to make a good impression and smooth the way for Swedish interests. We've worked hard to prove that Swedes are to be respected and reckoned with. Then you go and endanger it all with this nonsense with the women. . . . What do you think Elizabeth would do to you if she learned you'd seduced her pet?"

Every word could have come from the ravings of Rugar's own embattled conscience. It was no good making excuses or blaming circumstance or even protesting his own good intentions; the bald truth of it was that he'd had Corrie in his bed and Torgne had found them there.

"Your treatment of Lady Corrie is beneath contempt." Torgne seized the chance to air a simmering resentment, storming over to thrust his face into Rugar's. "She's nobly born, Rugar, a maid who's gone from her father's house to the queen's protected circle. She knows naught of the world or of the sort of men who would ruin her and cast her aside." His glare made it clear he considered Rugar one of that contemptible class. "She deserves better . . . an honorable marriage, someone to protect her and see to her interests."

The raw emotion in Torgne's hulking frame stunned Rugar at first. With each poignant word he spoke, the source of that unaccustomed passion had become clearer, and by the time Torgne mentioned marriage, Rugar felt as if he'd been dealt a clout to the gut. The shock of recognition cloaked itself in a harsh laugh.

"Damme if you're not half in love with the gell yourself," Rugar charged.

Torgne flinched as Rugar's taunt struck, but he would not retreat. Instead, with the steeled nerve of a true Viking warrior, he said, "She is a jewel, Rugar. She has a rare sweetness about her, a genuineness of heart to equal her rare beauty." His throat constricted and his eyes darkened. "A man would be a fool *not* to be in love with her."

Rugar twitched as Torgne's burning countercharge bit deep. He strode for the door, oblivious to everything but the turmoil inside him. When he reached the cold stone passage outside, he was rudely reminded of his bare legs and feet, and blew back inside to snatch up a pair of boots and storm out again.

He stalked the cold corridors with his fists clenched, his lungs aching, and his shoulder muscles bunched into knots. Torgne's impassioned words haunted him. *A man would be a fool not to be in love with Corrie Huntington.*

Chapter Eleven

Sometime later, his confused heat mostly spent, Rugar found himself in an upper corridor, beside a small leaded window that overlooked the Privy Garden. He was now a study in bewilderment; his jaw and shoulders had gone slack, and his arms dangled awkwardly at his sides.

He was in love with Corrie Huntington. There was no other explanation for his wretched behavior and the turmoil he was experiencing just now. He was absurdly, distractedly in love with an eighteen-year-old *English* gell—and a *virgin* at that.

The fates must have a perverse love of irony, he groaned silently, for they couldn't have chosen a less suitable female for him to want beyond all reason. One of the cursed English, the race of people for whom he'd nursed a long-standing vengeance. And a virgin . . . after long years of avoiding them as if they carried the plague. The plague. A fair description of Corrie's effects on him: fevers and night sweats, and mad, marrow-deep longings.

She, who was to have been a conquest of his charm, had now made him a captive of hers. And how thoroughly he was ensnared was evident in the unholy concern he'd felt for her that afternoon and the delight he'd taken from just holding her in his arms to comfort her . . . without a single thought of carnal pleasure.

He stumbled down the stairs and made straight for the Privy Garden. Sinking onto an isolated bench, he put his head in his hands and expelled a harsh breath. Things had gotten appallingly out of hand. If it had been anyone besides Torgne who came upon them, Corrie's future, their mission, and his neck might have all been forfeit.

He was engaged in a dangerous game of cat and mouse with England's reigning queen, and last night's tacit challenge of her had been a reckless stroke. Sooner or later, when he'd dared too much, prodded Elizabeth once too often, she would lash out at him, and at anyone she felt had betrayed her because of him. He couldn't allow Corrie to be caught up in the conflict between him and the queen, or in the vengeance Elizabeth might exact upon him. As much as he wanted Corrie, he wanted her safety even more. He would have to find a way to put distance between them, a way to put her beyond his reach.

The opportunity Rugar sought came more quickly than he could have imagined, literally with his next turn of a corner. As he approached the sundial in the midst of the garden, he spied Anne Bosworth parting from a group of courtiers and coming toward him.

"Perchance, have you seen my cousin, my lord?" she inquired anxiously.

"I believe I did see her, going toward the ladies' apartments," Rugar answered with a stiff nod.

"Thank you, my lord." As she turned to go, her eyes lingered one instant too long on his strapping frame.

With senses long trained to detect the subtlest of sensual signals, Rugar caught that brief betrayal of womanly interest, and it stopped him in his tracks. He assessed Anne of Bosworth's comely form as she walked away and found her a stunning combination of delicate features and voluptuous curves. She was a woman who'd known pleasure, but in whom passion was banked and smoldering. As he watched her enter the Privy Gallery, he knew he'd found the answer to his dilemma.

Not long after that evening's vespers, the queen decided to retire to her inner Privy Chamber with a select few of her ladies. The other courtiers, nerves dulled and passions sated from the afternoon's excitement, drifted from the Presence Chamber to their own amusements.

Rugar stationed himself in an alcove down the corridor and waited for Anne Bosworth to exit. When she emerged and turned toward her chambers, Rugar strolled into her path.

"Why, Baroness, what fortune to find you here." His eyes glowed with unmistakable admiration. "I was just having a quiet moment gazing at the stars." He visually caressed her liberally exposed skin. "They are magnificent tonight. Would you care to see?"

Anne was stunned by his unabashed visual stroke, and in the moment she took to respond, he extended his hand to her with the clear expectation that she would take it. Quelling a small shiver, she did just that. "I would be pleased, my lord count."

He drew her into the darkened alcove and, once there, put his hand boldly on her waist to guide her near the windows. He pressed against her skirts and pointed up at the clouded night sky, in which not a single pinpoint of starlight was visible. "Look there." His chest nudged her shoulder. "Is it not glorious . . . the smooth, velvety blackness of the sky, the brilliant twinkle of ten thousand stars."

"Yes . . . glorious." It was glorious, the way his deep voice slid over her bare shoulder like a physical stroke.

How many ways, she wondered dazedly, could he caress a woman without touching her? It was breathtaking, being the object of his intense and compelling charm.

Slowly, he drew one finger down the nape of her neck, across her ruff, and along one fashionably bared shoulder. It was a brazen touch for all its lightness; it boldly inquired and more boldly promised. When she turned to face him, trembling, he did not move away. Her senses were engulfed in unexpected male heat and the answering warmth rising in her own body.

"You are a beautiful woman, Anne of Bosworth. And lonely." His eyes glistened in the dim light. "Let me ease your loneliness." His hand claimed her cheek softly, and when she made no protest, it quested further, massaging its way down her neck. Then his fingers molded over her liberally exposed breast, claiming access to the passion within it.

"How dare you touch me so?" Anne whispered hoarsely, drawing back just beyond his fingertips. How dared he make her feel these torturous stirrings of passions long dormant in her? It had been nearly a year since her furtive trysts with Christopher Leighton. And despite her bawdy tongue and penchant for an illicit bit of tip and tickle, Chris was the only lover she'd had since her husband.

"I dare to offer . . . what your eyes say that you desire."

She averted her face and shut her traitorous eyes. Her heart was pounding. He knew, damn him. He knew exactly how she was responding to him.

"Come to me . . . tonight, after midnight." He both entreated and commanded, adding the superfluous persuasion of his fingertips stroking the lower curve of her lip. "My apartments are discreetly placed. You will be safe in my bed, Anne of Bosworth. Safe in my arms."

She swallowed hard, drowning in sensation, floundering

for direction. His coaxing smile provided it. She nodded, helpless against the combined force of his sensual persuasion and the hot taste of desire rising in the back of her throat.

Rugar watched the sultry movement of her body as she left him and thought of the bittersweet pleasure in store for them both. Once he had made love to Anne, there would be no going back to Corrie. Together they would have betrayed her unforgivably. And when she learned of it, as she would when he and Anne were seen in public together afterward, Corrie would be safely beyond his reach.

As Rugar strolled off toward the Privy Gallery and the Cock Pit beyond, Morris Lombard stepped out of the shadows near the alcove with his ferretlike eyes darting and his mind racing. So the randy Swede meant to have another Huntington as well, did he? His thin mouth drew up into a smirk. This would bear watching. He stole on silent feet down the corridor after Anne Bosworth, keeping to the sides of the passage and scurrying to avoid being caught in the glaring light thrown by the torches.

In the corridor outside Corrie's chambers, Anne stood staring at her cousin's door. Her desires, her pride, and her deep affection for her young cousin were all aflame. She thought of Corrie's clear, innocent eyes shimmering with new love as she spoke of Rugar. Then she thought of them as they had been at his abandonment: rimmed with tears, eloquent with pain. She recalled the way Rugar had looked at Corrie as the two made music together and the way his countenance had lighted whenever she appeared. There had been no tender glow in his handsome features for *her* just now, only the dark urgency of blood heat.

The clamor of conflict reached deafening proportions in

Anne, then stilled abruptly as her higher nature took control.
It was Corrie he truly wanted; it was Corrie he'd gone to
such pains to protect by his unthinkable male abstinence.
And it was Corrie's tender heart that had blossomed with
womanly feeling at his first glance.

Loyalty rose to bolster the embattled nobility of Anne's
heart. For all her own attraction to Rugar and the mad urgings of her long-starved desires, she could not betray Corrie's
trust in her. In these past weeks Corrie's companionship
had come to mean a great deal to Anne; it had restored some
balance, some humanity, to her life. No pleasure, she realized with dawning wisdom, was worth sacrificing loyalty
and love to obtain. Two long years at Elizabeth's rapacious court had taught her well that true love and loyalty,
whether between lovers or friends, was a rare and precious
commodity.

She took a deep breath and knew exactly what she had
to do. Rushing into Corrie's chamber, she swept her cousin
up in a wildly exuberant hug, then set her back at arm's
length.

"Oh, Cub—" she squeaked, jiggling as if something were
boiling about inside her, eager to get out. "Your Rugar, he
pulled me aside. He wants to see you tonight—at midnight,
in his chambers!"

From a nearby corner, Morris Lombard watched
Baroness Bosworth pause in the passageway, then square
her shoulders and enter Corrie Huntington's chamber. His
brow furrowed as he tried to search out what it meant. Anne
Bosworth had an assignation with Rugar Kalisson . . . he'd
seen the Swede brazenly fondling her, had heard the invitation with his own two ears. Yet she'd come straight to the
Huntington chit's chambers. What sort of game was afoot

here? He settled down in the concealing darkness to watch the door.

Well more than an hour after that portal had closed behind the baroness, it opened once again. Two cloaked figures emerged with hoods pulled low to conceal their features. Lombard didn't need to see their faces to know it was Anne Bosworth and Corrie Huntington. They hurried down the hallway toward the Privy Gallery, keeping to the shadows, walking on tiptoe. He scurried along behind, moving when they moved, stopping when they stopped.

The two of them together, Lombard thought with some confusion. They both appeared to be bound for the Cock Pit and the Swede's apartments. Perhaps they thought to make it a *threesome*. His mouth quirked up nastily at the idea of Elizabeth discovering her virginal little pet in such a depraved indulgence. But when they reached the apartments, the women paused and embraced; then one of them turned back.

Lombard ground his teeth in frustration and glanced at the retreating figure, then back at the doorway to the apartments. Which of them had stayed to meet the Swede? He hurried after the one who'd left, hoping to discover her identity from her destination. He couldn't unleash the queen's fury upon the Swede until he was certain it was Jack Huntington's daughter who would be caught up in it.

A quarter of an hour later, he leaned against a stone wall in a corridor in the queen's women's apartments. Sweat trickled down his neck, and his breath came in wheezes and rattles, but there was a wickedly satisfied smile on his face. He'd followed his quarry to Anne Bosworth's chambers, and in the last moments she'd allowed her hood to slip, revealing a glorious blond head. That meant Corrie Huntington was with the Swede!

* * *

Not precisely *with* the Swede, as it happened, but awaiting him in his bedchamber. Corrie stood in the light of a single candle, holding the cloak she had shed, feeling breathless with expectation and a little fear. It was not yet midnight, but she'd been so eager, so delirious with joy, that she couldn't have waited another instant to traverse the dark halls and cross the silent yards to reach his side. He'd sent for her. And she'd read beneath that invitation a deeper purpose, more urgent and thrilling.

Corrie had closeted herself in her chamber that evening on a pretext of illness. She was humiliated to the core at having staggered, fainting, from a court "amusement," emptied her stomach on Rugar's feet, and been caught wriggling wantonly beneath him on his bed. By all logical accounts it was an unredeemable disaster. But her stubborn heart kept recalling Rugar's tender care of her and the feeling of closeness between them that had naught to do with physical pleasures.

Something important had happened that afternoon while they sat on his bed, holding each other, taking comfort in being together in a different way. And tonight Anne had proved it, bringing her a secret message from Rugar. The afternoon's unthinkable encounter had apparently accomplished what her schemes could not. Rugar was ready to love her!

She closed her eyes and imagined slipping into his arms . . . his eyes glowing softly as he called her "Kari" and pressed her to his heart . . . Returning to her senses, she laid her cloak across a chair and straightened her smock and kirtle. She smoothed her hair and tugged at the bosom of her sleeveless bodice. She had purposefully omitted her corset, overskirt, and sleeves. "No use putting it all on," Anne had teased wickedly, "when it's only going to come off soon anyway." Hearing Anne's insinuating laugh in her mind again, Corrie shivered nervously.

Evidence of Rugar was all around her. She lighted another candle in the stand and carried it about the chamber, running her fingers over his belongings: his handsome bed hung with claret-red velvets and covered with down-filled comforters, his great trunks made of fine burled oak fitted with polished brass. On the wall across from the bed hung a heavy silk banner: a field of azure blue divided by a cross the color of golden buttercups. Recognition slowly dawned; it was his Swedish flag. Warmth welled in her, pride in his devotion to his king and his land, as she touched those regal colors.

Her explorations completed, she returned to the bed, biting her lip uncertainly. She removed her shoes and climbed onto the soft mattress, testing it, then leaning back on the thick bolsters. Looking up into the canopy, she let herself imagine . . . and closed her eyes. It was so soft and warm. The covers carried a hint of the same spicy herbs used in his clothing.

Lulled by the late hour and comforted by her imaginings, she drifted slowly to sleep.

Rugar's steps lagged as he returned to his quarters. He'd been drinking, but was still wretchedly sober, and dreading who and what awaited him in his chambers. He'd purposefully delayed returning from the rout in the Cock Pit by more than an hour, on the chance that Anne Bosworth might be so piqued by the delay that she would leave before he arrived. But when he opened the door to his bedchamber, his eyes fell first on a woman's cloak draped neatly across the chair, and he knew he'd hoped in vain.

A quick glance around the silent chamber sent his eyes to the shadowed interior of the bed, where he glimpsed a dim figure. He squared his shoulders, drew on his seductive mien like a well-worn glove, and strode forward. Halfway to the bed he stopped, then froze, staring at the form which occupied it. Hair as black as ravens' wings?

He lurched forward, his stomach contracting. He halted two steps later, staring in mute horror at the unmistakable shape of the one woman in the whole world who shouldn't be in his bed.

Corrie. His eyes flew over her curled, kittenish form and her long hair, which was carelessly rumpled around her shoulders and over his pillows. She wore a gathered smock and sleeveless bodice, and her bare feet peeked from beneath a simple kirtle. His gaze lingered on those feet, slender and delicately arched, so artlessly provocative, so trusting.

Dammit, how could she have learned of his tryst with Anne? But then—if she knew the truth of it, she would hardly be here in his bed waiting for him, he realized. His ears caught fire as the linkages were made in his mind. Anne Bosworth was apparently a far better friend than he'd guessed, and a vastly more honorable woman. She knew of Corrie's desire for him and had sent Corrie to take her place in his bed. Fierce longing filled his loins, just as her eyes fluttered open and she turned to him with a sleepy smile and a voice still weighted with dreams.

"Rugar."

The way she said his name sent a curl of heat through him, and he straightened and stepped back, stiff with panic. She sat up and stretched, holding his eyes captive with the way she dragged her fingers through her hair and pulled her bare feet under her skirts.

"I didn't mean to fall asleep. But you were so late . . ."

"I was . . . detained."

An awkward moment followed, and she glanced around them.

"I didn't see much of your chambers earlier today. They're very comfortable." She looked at him, then away again, suddenly embarrassed at having claimed a place so boldly in his bed, and her eyes fell on the silk banner hanging on the opposite wall. "That must be the flag you spoke of," she said, pointing to it. He nodded, occupied with desperate thoughts of how to get her out of his bed without touching her. She met his frown of concentration with a shyly adoring smile. "How fitting that the flag of your *Sverige* . . . is just the color of your eyes."

He was totally disarmed. She had the most uncanny ability to bring together his volatile need for her and his pride in his country, and to touch them both with a single irresistible stroke. He watched her eyes growing luminous and her shoulders softening as she rose onto her knees and tucked her feet beneath her. His voice thickened as he spoke.

"This—this was a mistake. You should not be here. I had no right to—" He cleared the huskiness from his throat and tried to be more authoritative. "Come, put on your shoes and cloak, and I'll take you back." The disbelief in her face pained him, and he bent to pick up her cloak.

"I won't go," she said quietly.

"Gud förbjude." He straightened and backed up a step. "You cannot stay. If anyone were to learn of it . . ." Desperate resolve filled his voice as he fought the pull of her eyes. "It was a mistake."

"Why?" She slid toward him on her knees.

"You know why." He backed up yet another step.

"You're afraid of taking my innocence." Her heart was pounding, her mouth was dry, and her stomach was quivering. It was now, she sensed, or never.

"But you already have my innocence, Rugar. Bit by bit, you've already claimed it. You've quickened my senses and my body to the pleasures of physical love . . . and with it awakened in me the desire for such delights. You've invaded the tenderest, most private realms of my heart . . . and stirred in me a need for loving communion with a man."

He was dumbstruck, both awed and horrified by the prospect. He searched her face with burning eyes and deepening shock. Could it possibly be true? There was a womanliness about her, an air of knowing, a heart-deep glow that owed nothing to innocence. All his life, in his convenient male view of things, he'd equated a woman's innocence with virginity, never imagining the subtle differences that set them apart in a young gell's heart and allowed them to be conquered—and surrendered—separately.

"The feelings you have brought me to—affection, desire, jealousy, loneliness, joy, and even sadness—can they be so different from the feelings of women who have lain in a man's arms? Could they change so much upon the rending of a maidenhead? What more would I know, what less would I be, for the joining of our flesh in sweetest pleasure?"

Her gentle words sank to the very core of him, accusing him yet somehow absolving him. Her wisdom, her knowledge had nothing to do with flesh at all, he saw now, but with the understandings of the human heart. In that awful moment, he felt totally exposed, a moral fraud. He had greedily taken her innocence while piously denying her the loving pleasures that were meant to replace it in a maiden's heart . . . leaving her empty, without even memories for solace.

"You have made me a woman in all but the flesh. Teach me the rest, Rugar." Her eyes glistened with promise and expectation. Her voice grew hushed, intimate, and compelling. "Touch me. Let me learn the feel of your body on mine . . . the rasp of your skin, the weight of you on my breasts. Teach me the wonders of your man's body . . . and of my own woman's form." Then she whispered, a vow as much as a statement:

"For I'll have no other teacher. Ever."

The desire in her eyes shimmered like potent wine. Rugar was trembling, hot, and intoxicated by the sight of it. There was no resistance left in him, no empty chivalry, no self-serving restraint meant to protect self as much as other. There was only a deep, shattering need for this woman-child who had discovered a longlost part of him, a purity of feeling, an innocence of heart, and now was returning it to him.

"Kari, my sweet Kari . . ." He took one shambling step. Then another. The third was easier yet, and it brought him to the edge of the bed. His hands cradled her face, and his thumbs stroked her cheeks with fervent tenderness.

"I'll teach you."

Joy erupted in her countenance. She sprang up to embrace him at the same instant his arms clamped fiercely around her. Their mouths joined eagerly . . . then again voluptuously, tasting and tantalizing each other with sleek, sinuous tonguings and a feast of gently rapacious nibbles.

Slowly they moved back onto the bed, facing each other on their knees, their hands hot and feverish to caress, their bodies pressed tightly, seeking fuller sensation. He groaned, running his hands down the curve of her back to cup and clasp her bottom, and his arms and back flexed powerfully as he lifted her against his swollen male need and thrust seductively against her.

She gasped and clung to his broad shoulders while his movements coaxed and tutored hers. Dimly, she understood what he wanted and parted her thighs for him. He made a throaty noise of approval and pressed her bottom tighter against him, arching again and again in graceful, hypnotic rounds. Each rasping stroke both incited and assuaged a burning ache in her sensitive woman's mound and sent a quiver through her pliant body. With each thrust, her thighs parted a bit more, and her hips tilted instinctively, seeking more intimate contact with that tantalizing hardness.

Slowly, the sense of their motions came clear in her mind. These were *those* motions! Then this was . . . He meant to take her like this? On their knees in the midst of the bed . . . without even loosening her clothes? She slid her mouth from his and leaned back to look up at him through her lashes.

"Don't you have to peel me first?" she whispered hoarsely.

"What?"

"Peel me. Shouldn't you peel my clothes away before we . . . do this part?"

He huffed a soft, distracted laugh as he continued to hotly nuzzle the base of her neck. "Peeling, I believe, is an option, not a requirement."

"Oh." She stilled in his arms. "It's just that I expected . . . I wondered . . ."

She flushed and buried her face in his shoulder. But his own curiosity was piqued, and he let her slide down his front until her knees touched the bed again. He tilted her chin up to stare into her darkened eyes.

"What was it you wondered?"

"What it would be like to be . . . to be . . ." She couldn't say it.

"Naked," he answered for her. The word stirred a ripple of excitement in her eyes, and he cocked a rakish grin as he savored the sight of her helpless arousal. "So you wanted to be naked, did you? And with me? Wicked, wicked gell." His expression curled into an irresistible leer.

"You know what happens to wicked gells, don't you?" He paused as she shook her head, and his voice coarsened to a sexual rasp. "They usually get exactly what they want."

With a lustful grin he slid his hands down her chest and over her breasts. He both saw and felt the pulse of desire that stopped her breath. A deep, charming laugh rumbled up as he began loosening her laces, then pulling them out altogether. When the tie of her smock lay asunder as well, he drew her gaze to his hands as they pushed back the sides of her bodice and dragged her soft linen smock slowly down over the tight velvet sworls at the tips of her breasts.

Deliberately, he kissed and caressed each inch of her shoulders and breasts as they were revealed and proceeded down her waist to dispatch the ties of her kirtle and petticoat. He pushed her skirts down over her hips and flung them aside, leaving her covered only by her smock, which lay open to the waist and swirled about her. She sat before him on her knees, her soft skin aglow, her hair flowing over her pale shoulders and rosetipped breasts like a dark, erotic river. Her eyes shone, her lips were kiss-ripened—red and swollen from his attentions—and her nipples were contracted into long, luscious spouts that fairly begged to be tasted.

"My wicked little innocent," he murmured huskily. "What do you want now?" His eyes fastened on the way her tongue seductively probed the corners of her mouth.

"I want . . . to peel *you*."

Heat roared through his lungs, leaving him scorched, panting. Without a heartbeat's pause, he led her hands to the buttons of his doublet and the ties of his shirt.

"Oh, Rugar." she breathed, pulling his shirt down over his wide shoulders. "Ohhh, Rugar." Her eyes widened on the smooth, mounded muscles of his breast and glimpsed his taut male nipples. Awed, she reached out to touch them, then pulled back to brush her own. "They're so much like mine . . ."

When she looked up, his eyes were fixed on her curious little fingers. "Hurry, love," he rasped.

Tossing his shirt aside, she feathered her fingers over the muscles of his upper arms. "What wonderfully strong arms you have."

"To hold you with . . ."

"And what marvelous, big hands you have." She picked

one up and ran her tongue over the toughened creases of his palm.

"To touch you with . . ." Then he led her hands to the band of his bloused breeches and helped her drag them down his heavily muscled thighs. When they were shed, he returned to his knees before her, watching her eyeing the columnar ridge in his hose. And he held his breath as she reached for the ties and pulled them. Her eyes widened hugely as she shyly parted that conforming silk to reveal his swollen, upright member.

"Ohhh, Rugar. . ." She strained to produce even a whisper. "Such a big . . . you're so . . ."

"To *fit* you with . . ."

She glanced down at her own half-bared body with sudden apprehension. "Ohhh . . . I'm not sure we'll *fit* at all."

The laugh he choked back showed in his eyes. "We'll fit, love. Men are not made so differently from one another, nor are women. And they usually manage to . . . fit. Touch me . . . don't be afraid."

Her cool fingers stroked him tentatively, gliding up and down his shaft and around its velvety tip. He groaned and closed his eyes, and she felt him lurch against her fingers. Then his hand closed over hers, wrapping it around his hardness, and he rocked, thrusting gently in the soft sheath they made together. She watched, realizing he was showing her what would happen, teaching her there was nothing to fear. By the time he released her hand, her body was flushed with anticipation.

"Please," she entreated, wetting her lips, "touch me, too."

They toppled backward; she landed gently on the bed with her knees bent and parted and he landed softly on her, wedged snugly between her thighs. His kisses melted the tension their unaccustomed position created in her, and as she relaxed, his body molded to her intimate contours.

Then his hands began to move. Wherever they ventured, his mouth followed to lavish kisses and lush nibbles over her skin.

"Ohhh, Rugar . . ." Desire billowed in her like a hot cloud as he shifted his body aside and slid his fingers beneath the garment tangled about her waist to caress the sleek curve of her hip and the dent of her belly. That cloud condensed into a hot, stormy shower of sensation as his fingers quested lower, grazing wispy curls before they continued down the side of her thigh.

He kissed her deeply as he raised her smock and stroked her thigh and hip. Then his fingers drifted purposefully to the silky thatch covering her woman's mound and began to toy shockingly with that downy softness. With gentle motions he gradually spiraled inward, seeking the sleek coral flesh at the heart of her. Sensations came in overlapping waves when he found that burning point around which all her woman's heat revolved. Vivid flashes of rapturous white heat streaked along her nerves as he stirred her flesh, over and over in slow, heart-stopping circles. Each round deliberately brushed that fleshy pearl of response, and her senses swelled, filling with a limitless, expanding delight.

She arched and writhed beneath him, biting her lip, clutching his shoulders, caught in the deepest throes of ecstasy while soaring toward the summits of passion. Then with a sudden surging updraft, she was flung through a dense wall of sensation and shattered. Her muscles spasmed, her senses exploded, and she felt herself splintering into a thousand pieces that showered like sparkling crystal prisms through endless realms of light . . . casting joyous rainbows everywhere around her.

As she floated back to self, she was aware of Rugar all around her. He was on his side, holding her close against his chest, stroking her hair, and massaging her back as he murmured soft reassurances in her ear. After a while she drew a deep, shuddering breath and lifted her rosy face to him.

"That was it, wasn't it?" she said, awed. When he nodded she closed her eyes, concentrating on the echoes of release lingering in her blood. "But I don't understand how it could have happened when you only touched me."

"Pleasure can be made in many ways, little love. With touches as well as . . . other things." His smile was intimate; his eyes were soft and wise. "And soon I'll prove to you just how well we'll 'fit.'"

One of the chamberers who slept at the royal bedposts roused the sleeping queen in the dead of night with news that Morris Lombard waited in her private closet.

"A thousand pardons, Majesty." Lombard greeted her with a grave countenance and the cryptic apology: "But treachery never sleeps."

"What have you, Lombard, that is worth either my sleep or your own pitiful neck?" Elizabeth demanded, batting away her chamberer from the frogs of her furlined dressing gown and ordering, "Leave us." When the door closed behind the servant, Lombard answered.

"The Swede. This very moment, Your Grace, he lies in the arms of one of your women."

Elizabeth's heavily swathed frame jerked taut, now fully alert. Her nerves began to vibrate in anticipation of the coming confrontation. She spoke one word.

"Who?"

Lombard braced. His ferretlike eyes scoured her bilious countenance as he spoke his prized half-truth. "Tonight I followed Baroness Bosworth to the Swede's quarters."

"Anne? My Anne of Bosworth?" Rage erupted into ruddy splotches over her face. "Damn his eyes! He leaves me no one! Anne . . . and after I took her to my bosom, made a place for her at my court." Her eyes closed for a long, perilous moment, then reopened with a vengeful glitter.

"Go for the Captain of the Gate, Lombard," she ordered harshly. "There is treason afoot."

Chapter Twelve

Corrie's hands slid over Rugar's bare shoulders and up his neck to tangle gloriously in his flaxen hair. Her eyes danced with flames he'd sparked and fanned in her, and she wriggled wantonly beneath him, hungry for the feast of new delights promised in his gaze.

"Love me, Rugar," she panted softly, with passions not yet subsided, now resurging and rising faster than before. Her body was afire; the hollow between her legs ached and burned as he lay wedged against her sensitive cleft. "*Fit me . . .* now."

"My greedy kitten." He gave a wicked laugh and sank his arms beneath her, arching his body so that his hardened shaft rode the satiny groove of her woman's flesh. He flexed and thrust gently, over and over, coaxing instinctive movements from her hips that merged with his own in perfect rhythm. It was maddening, breathtaking. She writhed in a delicious agony of arousal and anticipation. Fluid tremors that she now knew as heralds of the powerful release to come began to shudder up her spine and vibrate along her nerves. The vast, mystifying scope of his male power filled her senses, a huge engulfing presence that invoked and commanded her responses, that roused and satisfied needs she hadn't known she possessed.

"More . . . oh, Rugar . . . please . . ."

Something—a noise, an echo perhaps—sent a ripple of warning through his passion-fogged senses. An old wariness roused groggily in him, and he lifted his head. Was that a creak of hinge or a voice? A footfall? The *clank* of steel on stone was a distinctive sound . . . .

Suddenly violent voices, scuffling, and banging broke out in the antechamber, and above the din came what sounded like Torgne's shout. Rugar was immediately up on his elbows, frozen, staring into Corrie's widened eyes. In that awful moment, their hearts spoke without the encumbrance of words: the same fears, the same desperate tenderness.

"Rugar—"

"Kari—" He cupped her face in his hand and kissed her with aching gentleness.

The door burst open with a splintering crash, and a red tide of fury erupted into the bedchamber, a heaving mass of coiled muscle and honed steel: the tyrannical forces of righteousness come to do battle against the treasonous power of love. Rugar turned to meet the threat, pushing Corrie behind him to protect her. "There he is—seize him!" There was a mad rush at the bed, and Corrie screamed as the queen's guardsmen dragged Rugar from her side, wrestling and grappling fiercely to contain his formidable strength.

When he'd been subdued, a second force surged into the chamber, led by Elizabeth herself. Her face was crimson with rage as she blazed at Rugar. "So this is how you repay my hospitality, by foully seducing—" As she spoke, she turned toward the bed and stopped dead. In those treacherous confines, where she expected to find a traitorous blonde, there was instead a jumble of dark hair which blended with the bed shadows.

Her eyes drifted in growing horror over a pair of huge jewel-green eyes, love-reddened lips, and naked shoulders which hovered behind bedclothes. She gasped, clutching her breast and paling as she stared at Corrie's tousled beauty and shame-stained cheeks. She lurched back, stunned breathless, pierced to the heart by this unexpected turn. It was her precious companion, her beloved Corinna, in his bed, not Anne Bosworth! She turned on Morris Lombard in disbelief, and he sputtered and stammered as if stunned himself. Then she wheeled on Rugar.

"The others weren't enough," she choked out. "You had to take my Corinna, too? You corrupting filth!" She flew at him and smashed the heel of her palm so viciously into his cheek that his head snapped to the side. "You vile, defiling devil! You'll pay for this treachery!"

"Please, no—" Corrie cried out. But when Elizabeth turned, the tumult of outrage and pain in her face silenced Corrie's protest.

"Take the whoreson away—throw him in the deepest hole in my dungeons!" she ordered the guardsmen holding Rugar. Then she turned on her captain. "You—escort the gell back to her chambers and lock her inside. She's to see no one, do you hear, no one! I hold you personally responsible!"

The queen fled the chamber in high dudgeon, and as the guardsmen half dragged, half carried Rugar out, Corrie cried out his name. But he could only delay them long enough to meet her eyes with one last, agonized look.

The captain barked an order to the rest of the guardsmen, and they withdrew, slamming the door after them. Corrie sat huddled in a miserable ball in the midst of the bed with tears streaming down her face and shame searing through her heart.

She was allowed to dress and was taken straight back to her chambers and locked inside. She was forbidden all human commerce, even the company and comfort of her own tiring woman, Maudie, who wailed so in the hallway outside that the guardsmen threatened her with a good cuffing if she didn't "clammer off." Corrie pounded on the door, first demanding, then begging that she be allowed to see the queen, and finally pleading for permission to at least write a letter to her mistress, to explain and to intercede for Rugar.

All was in vain. A deep, fearsome silence loomed from the far side of her locked door, and Corrie realized for the first time the vast scope and dread importance of that mercurial commodity: the royal favor. With it, everything was possible; without it, nothing was. One could approach the queen in person or even in writing only if she permitted it . . . and by shamelessly giving herself to Rugar Kalisson, Corrie had forfeited access to her mistress as well as the queen's love and favor. The memory of the hurt and betrayal in Elizabeth's face as she had stared at Corrie's half-naked form tore at Corrie's heart.

But it was the anguish in Rugar's expression as they had dragged him away that was the most difficult to bear. She relived that awful moment over and over. He had known the risks, had tried to warn her, to protect them both, from her impetuous desire for him. But, ignorant fool that she was, she had charmed and brazened and, yes, seduced her way past his better sense. And in so doing, she'd brought catastrophe down on both their heads. She had never meant to disgrace and imperil Rugar or to betray the queen's trust. Yet she'd done both, wounding the man she loved and her beloved queen. Was there no justice in life at all?

Rugar fared far worse. He was taken to the dungeon beneath the palace gates, clapped in irons, and thrown into a hewn stone cell without even a blanket to cover his half-naked frame. He knew without being told that he would have no hearing, no access to appeal, and no recourse in whatever fate Elizabeth's anger conjured for him. He'd seen firsthand the fate of nobles who transgressed a monarch's will, and to that would be added the special vengeance of a vain and aging woman, betrayed. Stockholm was too far away and too little feared to be of help to him.

He had no illusions. He stood in clear peril of his life. Yet for all his troubles, the thing that afflicted his heart was the sight of Corrie, wrapped in bedcovers and deepest shame, calling to him with tears running down her face as they dragged him away.

For all his noble intentions, for all his desperate attempts to keep her and her delectable passions at bay, he'd led her into disgrace. His worst fear had been realized, and he had no remedy, no excuse.

He had pursued Corrie at first to spite Elizabeth, and his love for her had been sown squarely in the midst of his loathings, where it had grown side by side with the grim crop of his revenge. Now the time for the harvest had come, and the yield was bitter indeed.

He felt his way through the frigid darkness to the pallet and drew some of the moldy straw about him for warmth.

What would happen to her now? A cottage, a convent, or a cell—he shuddered—like his own? What punishment would she receive for the sweet treason of loving him and trying, with such meager success, to give him her virtue? He ached inside to recall the tender crime he had not yet committed, but for which he would most certainly be punished.

Early the next morning William Cecil, Elizabeth's sage and loyal Secretary, answered a curt summons to the queen's Privy Chambers and found her already gowned and groomed and worked into a full, lathering fury.

"That bastard Swede!" she hissed. "He's seduced my Corinna—I caught him at it! Had her in his damned bed, in the chambers *I* granted him, rummaging her as if she were some filthy little kitchen scull! He'd stripped her mother-naked. . . and God knows what other perversions he practiced upon her." She choked on the vile memory and had to halt to collect herself. "I sent to Straffen for the earl at first light, but by God's Death, I'd rather have my liver plucked out by crows than face him."

The grave look, the fatherly fears in Jack Huntington's face as he surrendered his daughter to his queen's care now returned to Elizabeth with a vengeance . . . as did her own arrogant assurances of her power to ensure the gell's safety. His greatest fear for his daughter, that which Elizabeth had emphatically, even scornfully dismissed, had come to pass . . . foully seduced under her very nose, and by a foreigner. Worse! a damned *Swede!* It was bad enough to have lost her precious pet, her lovely, sweet, sage Corinna. But to have to face Jack Huntington's paternal outrage and what would undoubtedly be his male contempt . . .

"What will you do with the Swede?" Cecil asked.

"I shall alter him like a tailor," she answered without a heartbeat's hesitation. Her nostrils flared, and her dark eyes flecked with red. "Trim him shorter by the head!"

Cecil sighed quietly. "Your Grace," he intoned, "with all respect, the count is not your subject. He is a credentialed foreigner, an *ambassador*. It is neither prudent nor queenly to lop off the head of a foreign emissary."

"I want him dead!" she cried. "In seducing my honor maid he has trespassed my sovereignty, disparaged my authority, and affronted both my moral code and my dignity. Worse yet, he has abdicated his duty to his king and gravely wounded English relations with Sweden. He deserves to *die,* and I want his insufferable blond head on my gatepost by nightfall!"

The august Cecil had learned much during the two decades he had implemented Elizabeth's will, assisted her rule, counseled her decisions, and weathered her scorching blasts. He chose his course carefully.

"And what of Lady Corinna? What's to become of her if you kill the Swede?"

The high color in Elizabeth's cheeks drained. She clasped and unclasped her hands, and Cecil detected a telling quiver in her chin. She was truly wounded, he realized. But his sympathy was tempered by dread, for there was no more dangerous creature in the world than a wounded Tudor.

"I shall send the gell from court . . . to her home or, if they won't have her, to one of my country houses until she's had time to recover. And after a time I shall restore her to my side, where none shall dare berate or accuse her."

"And if there is a babe?"

"There will not be—cannot be!" she railed bitterly, on the verge of tears.

"With all respect, Your Grace," he said softly, "not even queens may dictate to nature. If I may suggest . . . there is an alternative to execution and bastardy and the strife and infamy which such entail." He saw her shoulders sag and judged her as ready to hear it as she would ever be. "Give him the choice of marrying the gell or forfeiting his neck."

"Give her to him? Damn your wretched bones, Cecil— he'll not have her! By my own death—he'll not have my pet!"

Cecil diplomatically ignored both her vanity and her blasphemy to continue. "Then, after the nuptials and after the scandal subsides, in a month or two, you may quietly order the wretch from the country, and things will be as they were . . ."

Elizabeth argued and swore, turned over a stool, and smashed a silver goblet against the wall as she rampaged up and down her apartments. But she eventually tired, and in the end, Cecil's counsel held sway. She relented to his diplomatic solution; she would not behead the Swede without first offering him a chance to redeem his neck by marrying her beloved Corinna.

When Cecil departed, Elizabeth sat sprawled on a foot-stool looking forlornly at the door. Her face was bloated, her eyes were dark-ringed, and her thin body was slack with exhaustion. Losing her Corinna was heartbreaking enough, but the thought of handing her into the clutches of that smug, rutting Swede was intolerable. Slowly her Tudor spirit rose to assert itself anew, and a fierce glint crept into her eyes. She straightened, then stiffened, then struggled to her feet beneath a weight of gilt-crusted velvets.

She might be forced to marry her pet to Rugar Kalisson, to satisfy both church and society, but she could certainly see to it that the cursed Swede would never live with her . . . *nor even have a wedding night upon her!*

Calling for one of her pages, she gave him succinct orders: "Fetch my chief steward to my chambers. I wish to plan a wedding feast. Then"—her voice lowered and her gaze darkened—"find Morris Lombard and tell him to come to my closet *immediately.*"

Jack Huntington arrived within the glooming, fog-shrouded confines of Whitehall Palace late the following night and, despite the untimely hour, was shown straight to the queen's Privy Chambers. Such speedy access to her presence was a sure sign of disaster. He managed to make a leg to Elizabeth before blurting out, "Where is she? What's happened to my daughter?"

"Corinna is . . . well." Elizabeth dismissed her attendants and musicians, then bade Jack "sit" in a tone that brooked no resistance. He obeyed, but barely; he balanced on the edge of the chair, ready to bound up at the slightest provocation. She studied him, reading in his eyes that he already guessed what she was about to tell him, and she came straight to the point.

"Corinna, I fear, has fallen prey to the clever manipulations of a charming and duplicitous rogue."

"Dammit! I knew it!" Jack was on his feet in a trice.

"Sit!" Elizabeth bellowed, flinging an imperial finger at the chair and meeting his burning glare full on. After a long, dangerous moment, Jack subdued his rash impulses enough to obey. "Make no mistake, Straffen, I am wounded, devastated by such treachery. Corinna has owned a coveted place in my heart and at my side."

She related what incidents she could while judiciously omitting the sordid details of Rugar Kalisson's other dalliances at court. When Jack demanded what sort of name "Rew-garr Kalli-son" was and was informed it was Swedish, he grabbed his belly and groaned as if gored by the news.

"A *Swede?* Good God—they're raging barbarians! They treat their women like cattle—beat them publicly!" The thought of his precious daughter in a Swede's crude, bearish paws sickened him. "How could it have happened . . . my Corrie overpowered and abused by such a beast?"

"At least as to manners, no beast," Elizabeth declared. "He's smooth as any Italian . . . handsome as Lucifer and twice as subtle. The ladies find him entertaining in the extreme." She turned Jack's accusing stare back upon himself. "Not so unlike yourself in earlier days, sirrah."

It was true—Jack flinched visibly—handsome, smooth with the ladies, entertaining . . . such words had often been used to describe him in his youth. Elizabeth's purposeful glare linked his past and this present calamity, implying that this current distress was a sort of penance for his old sins. That very thought had plagued Jack all the way from Hertford to London. It was too cruel, too base an irony to be borne; his precious daughter seduced and foully used by a rake such as he had once been.

"However, the knave has two redeeming features, Straffen," the queen continued in a stern, deliberate tone. "He is wealthy. And unmarried."

Jack's eyes bulged as the intent of her revelation came clear, and he nearly strangled on his own juices. He turned on the queen with his face crimson and his neck veins at full swell.

"*Marriage?* I won't allow my daughter, my heir, to be carted off to some barbaric, frozen wasteland! I'll send her to a French nunnery first—I swear it!" Jack ranted and railed, treading perilously close to open rebellion as he wrangled with his sovereign. But Elizabeth was set upon marriage as the only solution, and no manly bluster or fatherly appeal could move her queenly determination.

"The church and the moral requirements of society are quite clear on the matter of the seduction of a maid," she declared imperially. "Whatever my personal feelings, I may make no exception in Corinna's case. There is precedent to think of, a standard to uphold. Corinna must marry the Swede on the morrow, and no one can do anything about it." She released a genuinely pained sigh. "Not even myself."

The two days she had spent locked in her chambers were the longest of Corrie's life. She had raged until she had no anger left in her, cried until she had simply run out of salt to make tears, and prayed until she couldn't utter another single syllable of supplication. She had begged repeatedly for some word of Rugar, but all she got from her keepers were a tray of food, a basin of water, and a sullen stare. She felt spent and bereft.

The days and nights themselves had lost meaning for her. She slept in fitful naps and, while awake, paced or lay on her bed staring up at the top of her bed closet. Thus when scraping and voices came at her door in the dead of night, she was quickly on her feet, watching the door and mustering a frantic prayer that it would be the queen. But when the door swung wide, she was horrified to find her father standing on the other side.

"Corinna," he said in a deep voice that seemed to boil out of the mists of her childhood memories . . . a haunting voice that carried disappointment and reproof, but always mingled with the possibility of redemption. "Are you . . . all right?" She could only nod.

They faced each other in silence, each hurting and yet more concerned for the hurt in the other, each uncertain how to say what must be said.

"Can you ever forgive me?" she whispered, her eyes rimmed with tears, her chin quivering.

What was to forgive? Jack thought miserably. Her innocence and vulnerability? Her stunningly sweet sensuality? Cut to the quick, Jack held out his arms, and she stumbled into them, grateful for the grace they offered. He held her close and stroked her hair as she rested her cheek against his shoulder. At length, he set her back and lifted her chin.

"You have my forgiveness, Corrie, and your mother's. She would have been here as well, but she is with child, and at her age . . . It seems you are to be a sister yet again." His chest tightened around his lungs as tears spilled down her cheeks. "But the queen is not so easily appeased. I am sent to declare your punishment to you." His face was so grave, so tortured, that Corrie's heart seemed to beat in her throat.

"You are sentenced to marry this great boar of a Swede before another day is past."

"Marry . . . Rugar Kalisson?" She was stunned. That

was to be her punishment? Her eyes flew wide, and she staggered back a step.

"'Tis monstrous, unthinkable—I pleaded with her and argued, but she will not be moved," he declared.

"But . . . I don't think he wants to marry me." Corrie sniffed.

"He will, damn his eyes. He will."

Rugar sat in his dank stone cell, listening to the scurry of god-knew-what in the unrelenting blackness around him. He was weak with hunger, parched with thirst . . . and his mind seemed to be conjuring moonflaws and fancies, flashes of light and rumbles of sound, to fill his deprived senses. It took him a few minutes to realize that the noises and dim bursts of light weren't coming from inside his head, but from the grating in the cell door. When an oil lamp shone directly through the opening, he scrambled awkwardly to his feet.

The guardsmen dragged him from the cell, and as he shielded his eyes from the glaring light and demanded to know where they were taking him, he spotted Torgne down the passageway, standing in shackles like his own, but wearing a blanket about his shoulders and a bewildered grin.

"Ye must live 'neath a charmed star, Swede," the captain of the guards grumbled, tossing a blanket over him and shoving him forward. "Another fellow in yer scrape would be on 'is way to the block, but ye be on yer way to the altar."

"A charmed star?" Torgne muttered as they were trundled up the dingy stone stairs. "More like a whole damned constellation. A female one, no doubt. Probably Virgo . . . the *virgin*."

* * *

The impending marriage of Lady Corinna Huntington and the Swedish Count of Aelthar was announced amongst other decrees and affairs of state at the queen's regular public audience that afternoon. The pronouncement included a pointedly offhand reference to Elizabeth's personal sponsorship of the nuptials and wedding dinner, which, to the dismay and titillation of court gossips, was to be held behind closed doors in her private apartments.

The witnesses and principals to the marriage assembled that evening in the vaulted and oak-paneled Privy Chambers. The archbishop himself presided, and the official witnesses included the only duke of the realm, two earls, and an assortment of Elizabeth's countesses and ladies.

From the outset, the proceedings were overset by tensions and rife with resentments that threatened to erupt into open conflict.

The noble guests watched with lurid fascination as the Earl of Straffen faced his daughter's devilishly handsome bridegroom for the first time. Everything about Jack Huntington's future son-in-law appeared to rub salt in some private wound: height which topped his own; a bold and intriguing face; a powerful, well-muscled frame; and an arrogantly sensual carriage. But what galled him the most was the way the Swede seemed unruffled, even slightly pleased, by these forced nuptials.

All watched raptly as the marriage contracts were read and the count was informed that his wife's considerable dowry was to remain in her own hands and that he was precluded from ever inheriting any of her numerous English holdings. Rugar swallowed the insult, understanding that this was part of his penance and refusing to be goaded . . . until the earl leaned across the writing table on his fists and declared his son-inlaw would not profit by his illgotten marriage, nor would he in future from the untimely or unexplained *death* of his wife. Rugar lunged forward, hot-eyed at the slander of his intentions toward Corrie, and was caught instantly in Torgne Sigurd's vigilant grasp.

By the time Corrie entered the main Privy Chamber, accompanied by Anne and crusty old Lady Cobham, scarcely a breath was being taken or let around the room.

She stood just inside the doorway, looking demure and delectable in a high-necked bodice and overskirt of soft white velvet. Her hair was tamed beneath a white cap and silver biliments that Anne had given her as a gift, and she wore a dainty lace ruff, a silver filigreed brooch, and a worked-silver girdle hung with a fan of white feathers. She lowered her lashes and colored becomingly at the attention fastened on her. Like a dutiful subject and daughter, she went first to the queen, curtseying and kissing the proffered hand, then to her father, to whom she also curtseyed.

"Is it too selfish of me to wish Mother were here?" She blinked back tears, and her father took her cold hands in his, raised and boldly kissed them, defying all who might look askance at such a display of affection.

"No, little heart," he said quietly. "Had she known such as this was afoot, she would have been here, babe or none."

Corrie nodded, her eyes glistening, and laid a kiss on her father's cheek. Then, duty discharged, she was at last free to turn to Rugar. From the moment she entered the room, she had felt his eyes on her, and her hands had grown icy and her throat tight with anxiety. She was desperate to look at him, yet afraid to face him after all that had happened. Surely he must blame her for these forced vows—in a foreign land, with a foreign bride—which would rob him of the chance to wed one of his beloved Swedes.

He was indeed staring at her, his blue eyes startlingly intense and the lines of his face sharper somehow. He seemed whole and hale, standing there in his white velvet doublet, silver-trimmed sleeves, and white boots, the same clothes he'd worn the first night she'd seen him. Warm remembrance swept her, and suddenly everything about him was reassuringly familiar: his silky blond hair, the set of his shoulders, the bold curve of his lower lip, the hard planes of his shaven cheeks.

To Rugar's aching eyes she was indescribably lovely, appealing, bright, and generous of heart . . . deserving of a far better fate than to be forced to wed in disgrace and carried from her home and her people into a foreign land. When she turned to him, he could see the smudges under her eyes and the uncertainty in her chin. *Gud,* how he wished he could pull her into his arms.

As their gazes met, the tension in his face slowly yielded to a guarded warmth that gave her the courage to speak.

"In Sweden, when the priest asks a man if he takes a woman freely in marriage, what does he reply?" she asked quietly.

"He simply says *Ja.*"

"And will you say *Ja* here today, my lord?" Her heart paused as she searched his expression for some clue to the state of his heart.

"I will say it, Lady Kari," he answered softly.

All witnessed the first tentative curve of her mouth and the answering upturn of his. A small, wistful smile grew on her face, matching the breadth and tenuousness of his, then growing bolder as his broadened. Audible relief passed through the guests even as it surged through both Corrie and Rugar.

During the ceremony, the bridal pair glanced often at each other as they repeated the vows. Rugar agreed to take Corrie to wife first in English, then, as promised, in Swedish. There was an unmistakable tenderness in his expression as she gazed up at him and repeated his words as her own.

As they stood a pace apart before the archbishop, the picture they made touched every heart present, comforting some, searing others. Torgne and Anne heaved separate but similar sighs of relief to see an honorable end to a dangerous situation in which both bore some complicity. Jack Huntington looked on with a mien like hewn granite, and Elizabeth watched with both a vengeful, queenly pleasure that her will was being done and a deep, ineffable sense of loss.

Then it was over and the nuptial kiss was given. Congratulations were quick and compulsory-sounding under the queen's tight-eyed scrutiny, and the party soon repaired to the cloth-draped tables in the adjoining chamber. The air was scented by fine beeswax candles, evergreen boughs, and the spicy aroma of mulled wine. Court minstrels provided music as the drink was poured and course after course of food was served. But beneath the pleasantries and stilted toasts to wedded bliss grew a deepening tension that flowed from the queen's darkening mood.

Elizabeth watched Rugar leaning ever closer to Corrie, subtly asserting his new claim to her with small, declarative touches and warm, proprietary looks. Let the smug bastard enjoy his moment, she thought furiously. He would soon rue his wretched insolence toward her. She looked to the main doors and located Morris Lombard standing, half hidden, amongst the footmen bringing their food. His dark eyes, which had been fixed on Jack Huntington, met her inquiring look, and he gave a discreet nod that indicated all was in readiness. She straightened in her massive chair and put on her most regal and enigmatic smile.

Had Rugar been watching, he might have found Elizabeth's expression unnerving. But he had eyes only for Corrie this night. She was his now, before the eyes of God and men, and not even the desires of a queen could change that. The thought set his mood soaring.

He had won his covert clash of wills with Elizabeth of England. He'd defeated her knightly champions and wooed her ladies and stolen her beloved pet—and still kept his head. But now, when he looked at Corrie, his vengeance seemed oddly unimportant, a thing completed, too costly by far in the coinage of honor and spirit and feeling, and already fading into his past along with the pain that had required it.

He cradled Corrie's hand in his and vowed, starting that very moment, to separate the bitter satisfaction of revenge from the sweet possibilities of the marriage he had just made. It was the mistake of ten lifetimes that he had ever sought to make loving pleasure the servant of vengeance, and he was grateful beyond measure that he had a chance to make it right. Revenge, he realized with humbling insight, could never be as sweet as the promise he glimpsed in Corrie Kalisson's eyes.

Chapter Thirteen

The evening drew on, and tension rose as the time for the bedding approached. At Elizabeth's nod, Anne and old Lady Cobham claimed Corrie from Rugar's side and escorted her out to prepare her for the bridal bed. Things became steadily more strained as wine cups were drained again and again, and Rugar glanced ever more frequently toward the door where Corrie had disappeared. It seemed an eternity before the archbishop took note of the late hour and proposed one last toast to send the bridegroom on his way.

Freed at last, Rugar bowed handsomely to the queen and to the company, then beckoned Torgne to follow and strode out into the wide, arched hallway.

"It's damned well about time!" He grinned, his heart racing at the thought of Corrie waiting at the end of that hallway. He grabbed Torgne's arm and drew him to a halt. "You'll keep watch outside the door?"

Torgne gave him a sour look. "Only if you swear you'll keep it quiet. I do not intend to pass the night on a cold stone floor, listening to you . . . pleasure your bride."

Rugar grinned. "I'll do the same for you someday."

"You'll never have to. Your experience has cured me of

women altogether. Court women are too loose, and virgins are far too treacherous," Torgne grumbled. Rugar laughed.

"And my package?"

Torgne looked startled and glanced back over his shoulder. "I must have left it . . ."

"I can't have a proper wedding night without a gift for my bride," Rugar declared. Torgne huffed in disgust and turned back to retrieve it while Rugar strode on alone. His blood was humming, his mind fixed on Corrie and on the unexpected delight of knowing that she belonged to him.

As he passed a cross-hall, he heard a scuffling noise off to the right and turned to look, coiling from defensive habit. But the hallway to his right was empty and dark.

It was out of the left hallway, behind him, that three burly figures suddenly sprang at him and bashed him over the head. His knees buckled, and he crumpled into a heap on the stone floor. His grizzled, rough-clad attackers paused, listening and peering up and down the hallways, seeming confused. After a cursory search of the passage, they dragged his limp body down the side hall to a little-used set of servants' stairs.

Within the space of a few heartbeats, all trace of Rugar Kalisson was gone.

Torgne retrieved the small, cloth-wrapped package which he'd left on the banquet table, nodded again to the queen, and hurried out to catch up with Rugar. But the corridor was empty, and though he followed it all the way to the end, there was still no sign of his friend. He retraced his steps, recalling uneasily the queen's dark looks, when a rasping male voice burst upon his ears from a side hallway.

"The baron, pisshead," the voice scraped harshly, "where the hell is he?" Torgne darted to the wall and flattened against it. Then, inching slowly forward, he peered around the corner. "You were to take them both!" a slight, pinch-faced fellow in blue livery snarled at three roughs carrying clubs. "Damn and double damn your flea-bit hides! Well, don't just stand there with your maws gaping—search! When you find him, dump him in the cart with the other one and get them down to the ship. Move your lazy arses— find that Swede!"

They were searching for *him,* Torgne realized, and *the other one,* the one they'd already taken, had to be Rugar. So the wedding that was too good to be true was too good to be true! They intended to abduct Rugar and him, and carry them from the palace to a ship. He had to find Rugar and free him. And his one chance of rescuing Rugar was to follow the men who were searching for himself.

Thus the hunted became a hunter. With grim determination, Torgne stalked them from the shadows, following first one and then another, hoping they would lead him to Rugar. They scoured the halls and corridors, from the Privy Gallery to the stables to the apartments near the Cock Pit, with no inkling that the man they sought was often mere feet away. Eventually they crept back across the palace grounds to a small court and dingy servants' entrance which, judging from the powerful stench, must have been near the kitchens.

In the ill-lit courtyard, Torgne sank wearily among stacked barrels, crates, and piles of kitchen wood, and watched the queen's henchmen arguing and shoving one another. His eyes fell on a small wooden horsecart filled with straw and covered with heavy felt. As if responding to Torgne's interest in it, one of the roughs separated from the others and tossed back the covering to check the cart's contents. Torgne caught a dull glint of white, a boot on the straw, and broke into a relieved smile. They had led him to Rugar. Now all he had to do was wait.

Corrie sat in her smock in the middle of a brocade-draped bed in the middle of a huge, elegant but drafty bedchamber which had once been the repose of King Philip of Spain. The queen had insisted they have new quarters in which to start their wedded life, and had assigned them apartments near her own. There were heavy tapestries on the walls, a thick rug on the wooden floor, an ornate brazier filled with hot coals, and a rich array of beeswax candles burning, but the chamber still felt chilled and unwelcoming to Corrie. Anne, who was putting the finishing strokes to her hair, watched the way she licked her lips repeatedly and heard the anxiety in her constricted sighs.

"You'll be fine, Cub." Anne climbed onto the massive bed beside Corrie and picked up her icy hands to warm them. Too well she recalled the jittery nerves of her own wedding night. And this bedding was fraught with more than the usual tensions and emotions which attended a maid's first time, primarily because it wasn't supposed to *be* Corrie's first time. "Would you like me to stay until he comes?"

Corrie's tension eased, and she smiled. "No, Maudie will be here. You've done enough already."

Anne winced. "That I have. Cub, I'm completely to blame. I'm no puling innocent. I should have seen what was happening and been more responsible with you. I guess I've been at court too long."

"Anne, you're the best friend in the world." Corrie gave her a tight hug. "And it's all worked out for the best. I love Rugar and I believe he cares something for me. If you're to blame for us being married, then I should be thanking you."

Anne sighed and gave Corrie's cheek a brief caress. Her mood changed as she slid off the bed. She tilted her head to eye Corrie from different angles. "'Pon my rosy arse . . . if you aren't the most adorable thing." She seized the chance to divert Corrie's anxiety with one last bit of advice.

"Oh, and don't be afraid to make noises . . . men rather take it as a compliment." When Corrie looked at her blankly, she explained: "You know—rapturous groans and moans, hisses of pleasure, shuddering sighs. Panting is always good, although some men prefer that you talk your way through." Corrie's eyes were as big as hens' eggs. "'You're so big, milord,'" Anne mimicked in a wicked falsetto, "'we'll never fit!' and 'I never dreamed it could feel like this,' and 'Do it again, milord.'" She laughed. "There's not a man born who can't use a little direction from time to time, but you have to be clever about it: 'A little to the left, milord . . . ahhh, yes. Very nice indeed. You do have wonderful hands, milord.'"

"Anne! You're impossible!" Corrie blushed hotly; she'd already said some of those very things to Rugar.

"Not true," Anne declared impudently. "All this talk of 'ramping and tamping' has made me appallingly *possible*. Only I've no one to exploit my"—she wriggled her body suggestively—"possibilities. Perhaps I'll just hang around outside your door and enjoy the sounds of your wedding night along with you."

"Anne!"

"Greedy little cub, aren't you—keeping it all to yourself. All right, I'll go. Feel free to howl like a bloody cat if you get the urge." Her voice and lashes lowered. "Your Swede looks the sort to wring a good howl out of a woman."

"Out—out!" But Corrie couldn't help laughing.

Soon she was alone, except for old Maudie, who huddled with a blanket on the trundle, nodding off. Corrie stared at the flickering bank of candles, then at the door, and waited.

And waited.

From barrel rack to crate to woodpile . . . Torgne crept through the gloom toward the cart and the muscled oaf who was assigned to guard it. He paused, taking stock of his chances against the beefy lout, and cast about for something to use as a weapon. He took a practice swing or two with a stout piece of firewood, then rose to a crouch, moving into the open behind Rugar's guard.

His approach went unnoticed; the guard stood by the cart, stolid and unsuspecting. At the last second the man began to turn, but Torgne brought the firewood crashing down on his head and sent him sprawling onto the cobblestones. Just as Torgne managed to pull the groggy Rugar up onto his shoulders, there was a noise from the nearby doorway, and he staggered hurriedly back into the shadows with his burden.

From their hiding place behind the wood rack, Torgne watched another member of the gang discover his unconscious comrade and make a furious but cursory search of the yard. Assuming his captive had gotten well away, the fellow went barreling back into the kitchens. Torgne managed to carry Rugar to the comparative safety of the stables and, with the help of some frigid water, revived him. But when he related all he'd seen and heard, Rugar, true to form, ignored his advice and charted a course straight for the royal apartments.

"How is your head?" Torgne asked breathlessly, joining Rugar against the brick wall outside the Privy Gallery.

"Terrible." Rugar winced as he rubbed the back of his neck. "Damn Elizabeth's hide—I should have smelled a moldy rat. But give me an hour alone with my wife, and I'll be in fine fettle."

Torgne sent him a deadly look. "You don't mean to say, after what just happened—"

"Do you honestly expect I'd leave Corrie alone in our marriage bed?" Rugar's grin contained equal measures of pain and lust. "That's clearly what Elizabeth wanted, and I'll be damned if I let her have it."

He scowled and tested his reasoning aloud: "She wants rid of me, but in secret. She's taken pains to give public sanction to this marriage, for Corrie's sake, and sent her henchmen to abduct me privately. That means she is reluctant to move against me in the open," he concluded with a wry grin. "And I intend to take advantage of it." Rugar shoved off from the wall and started for the garden sundial.

"Where are you going? The royal apartments are this way!" Torgne pointed back over his shoulder.

"Have you noticed any myrtle growing here?" Rugar murmured when Tor caught up with him.

"*Myrtle?* Have you gone mad?"

"A bridal crown, she has to have a bridal crown," Rugar declared, veering down another path.

"This is daft!" Torgne followed, copying his crouch and stalking gait. "The queen has you abducted, I risk my neck to rescue you, and all you can think about is finding some wretched sprig of greenery?" He pulled Rugar back by the arm and found himself facing the most determined expression he'd ever witnessed.

"She's a bride, Tor. *My* bride. And she needs a crown. You lost the one I made for her this afternoon. It was in that package . . ."

Torgne began tearing at the buttons of his doublet and pulled out a flattened cloth-wrapped object. "You mean this?"

Rugar snatched it from him and turned it over inspecting it. It wasn't much the worse for wear. His expression softened in the dim moonlight, and Torgne shook his head.

"You really do care for Lady Corrie."

"I do." Rugar looked irresistibly sheepish.

"Ye gods," Torgne swore lamely, creeping off with him toward the royal apartments. "I hope this wedding night of yours is worth both our necks!"

* * *

The candles had burned low in the bridal chamber, faithfully keeping their vigil and filling the air with their sweet scent. Rugar slipped inside, dropping the doorlatch after him, and crept toward the bed. A less-than-genteel noise halted him, and he swung around the end of the bed to find Corrie's old tiring woman on the trundle, snoring. He awakened her and caught her startled cry with his hand, whispering she wouldn't be needed for the balance of the night. She glowered at him, hitched herself out of her warm bed, and stumped stiffly for the door. Rugar nodded to Torgne in the hall outside and slid the bolt on the latch home.

Corrie was asleep, curled around a bolster. Her eyes seemed a bit puffy, and his stomach slid. She'd probably been crying, perhaps had cried herself to sleep. He squared his chin and clamped a firm hand on his rising desires. He was determined to replace the hurt she must have felt at his absence with more pleasurable emotion . . . and determined to make her first experience of sexual love as warm and sweet as humanly possible.

"Kari, love, wake up." He sat on the edge of the bed, stroking her arm, then the bow of her back.

Corrie opened her eyes to a waking dream: Rugar bending close, calling her name, his eyes alight with pleasure. His hand was making small, thrilling circles over her shoulder and back, and she could feel the warmth radiating from his body. It was that delicious sensation that suddenly brought her wide awake.

"Rugar?" She rolled onto her back and touched his face, testing his reality with one hand, then with two. "It is you!" She threw her arms around his neck, but then pushed him back before completing her hug. "Where have you been? I waited and waited."

"I was . . . delayed." He made to nuzzle her ear, but she

pushed back out of reach, frowning. "I'm sorry, sweeting, I didn't mean to keep you waiting." He tried to pull her closer, but her arms braced against his shoulders, preventing it.

"Delayed by what?"

Perhaps if he told the truth. "I was abducted."

"What?" Her eyes grew wide with alarm.

No, clearly not the truth. "B-by Torgne and some others," he added with a spurt of dubious creativity. "It's . . . an old Swedish custom, abducting the bridegroom on the wedding night and taking him to a special . . . drinking rout . . . called a . . . *supkalas*. Not one of our better traditions, I daresay. I didn't think of him doing such a thing after all that's happened. I wouldn't have worried you for the world." That last part, at least, was true. The gentle reproach in her eyes was difficult to bear. "Sit up, sweeting. I've brought you something." He leaned against the bolsters at the head of the bed and lifted her onto his lap.

She shivered as he stroked her bare shoulder above her drooping smock and smiled his charming best. She watched warily, rubbing her hands up her arms as he produced and unwrapped a flattened bundle of cloth tied with string. From it he lifted a cloth-covered coronet, wrapped with a rainbow of ribbands and tied with streamers. He shook out the ribbands and held it up for her inspection.

"In Sweden, brides wear a sort of bridal crown, a *huvudla*, something like this. The old women usually make them. But without an old Swedish woman around, I had to do it myself. I had to bribe a few guards to get the ribbands . . ." He watched her eyes begin to glisten, and her chin and shoulders soften, as she gingerly stroked the colorful silk streamers.

"You made it?" she whispered. In that admission, and in the ill-concealed knots and rumpled ribbands of a makeshift crown, she read the answer to the question that had weighted her heart in the long, miserable hours he was gone. He didn't hate her for her part in these forced vows. This was proof! He cared enough to want to make her a bride according to his customs.

"I could hardly have given it to you in front of the queen, but . . ." He took it from her trembling hands and placed it on her head, smoothing the bright ribbands over her soft, dark hair, savoring the sensuous way they blended. She looked so perfect, so artlessly tantalizing, sitting there with her smock slipping off one shoulder and a rainbow of silken strands swirling around her. He brushed a kiss on her ripe cherry lips.

"I'm a Swedish bride, then?" she asked, her eyes sparkling. He nodded. "Then make me a Swedish wife"— she grabbed fistfuls of his doublet and pulled him close, demanding against his mouth—"and quickly . . . before something else happens to prevent it!" When surprise caused him to hesitate, her voice dropped to a throaty whisper. "*Now,* Rugar." And she startled him by taking his lower lip between her teeth and raking it with a light, sensual bite. "Do it now."

He erupted around her, banding her fiercely with his arms and matching the rapacious hunger of her kiss. He dueled with her tongue and nibbled and caressed her lips, then plunged deeper to probe and claim her sleek recesses. She pushed back in his arms, holding his mouth hostage on hers as her fingers flew to his buttons and frantically unfastened them. She groaned in frustration at her slow pace, and he chuckled, ending their kiss and setting her off his lap so he could slide from the bed and remove his doublet and boots.

"There's no hurry, love." He smiled, both tantalized and amused by her eagerness.

"Oh, yes, there is. We've suffered distractions, interruptions, intrusions, and abductions. Who knows what more the night has in store for us? I do not intend to end my wedding night a virgin bride!"

His eyes widened. She was closer to the point than she knew! "You won't, sweetness." He laughed, entranced by her determination. "I promise you."

While he ripped open his breeches and pulled off his shirt, she scooted back on the bed and lifted her smock over her head, taking care not to disturb her crown. Flinging the garment aside, she nestled naked on her knees in the midst of the lush covers and shook her midnight hair with its rainbow of streamers around her pale shoulders.

Rugar let his eyes feast on her curvy body: those voluptuous breasts with their long, impudent nipples; that tiny waist; those generously curved hips and elegantly rounded buttocks. She was a living, breathing paradox; a lascivious innocent, his virgin temptress.

"Lady Cobham vows it's best to get 'rogered' the first time on a chair," she informed him in a constricted voice.

"She does?" His mouth quirked up at one corner.

"But Lady Beatrice insists a gell should always be deflowered on her back."

"Lord. How very opinionated of her."

"H-how do you usually . . ." She closed her eyes, flushing scarlet from head to toe. When she opened them, he was standing by the bed, clad only in his conforming silk hose. She couldn't meet his gaze.

"I don't have a *usual* for deflowering virgins," he said with an odd thickness to his voice. When she looked up, his eyes were dark and tender. "I've never had a maid before. You're my first, sweet Kari. And my last."

Mist bloomed briefly in her eyes. *Once in a lifetime.* She would be his . . . as he would be hers. The joy of sensual triumph erupted in her, and she grabbed his hands and dragged him onto the bed with her.

"Then I don't care how you do it." She fell back onto the

bolsters and pulled him atop her, wrapping her arms around his neck. "Just pluck my blossom, Swede," she demanded seductively, "before I wither on the vine!"

With a deep, throaty laugh, he seized her head between his hands and kissed her breathless. Long, liquid strokes of his tongue alternated with voracious nibbles over her mouth and down her throat and then onto the burning tips of her breasts. He sworled her nipples, suckled and kneaded and caressed until she was gasping, arching into him, filling her hands with his taut muscles, demanding more.

Obeying the impulse of sensation, she shifted, aligning their bodies and inviting him into the warm, silky cradle between her thighs. She sighed raggedly as his hard weight settled on her softer frame. His answering groan vibrated in her mouth as he molded intimately to the receptive curve of her woman's mound. She tilted her hips against him, seeking him with virgin certainty, knowing what she sought while never having known it.

The urgency of her desire ignited in him a driving need for completion, for a union that could not be altered by mere mortal powers. He filled his greedy senses with her, dragging his fingers over her intimate crests and hollows, tasting the honey of her mouth, inhaling her musky-rose scent, watching her pale shoulders arch and writhe in an erotic tangle of dark mane and soft ribbands. His hands skimmed her sides to sink beneath her and cup her buttocks, holding her tightly as he flexed and thrust his swollen shaft against the delectable cleft of her womanflesh, parting, penetrating its soft underside . . . sliding along that responsive channel, thrusting over and over against that liquid, alluring heat.

She was turgid with sensation, scarcely able to breathe. Each unerring stroke of his shaft against her set her shuddering, rising; soaring. Her body contracted around voluptuous bursts of pleasure, and her senses constricted around a golden point of light that grew to engulf her with its radiance.

"Oh, Rugar . . . ohhh . . . it's—"

He felt the quivering, upward spiral of her arousal as if it were his own and sensed in her sudden stillness that she was prepared . . . launched. He fitted himself in the hot, tight opening of her body, and as her senses erupted, he thrust forward, taking her maidenhead.

That dazzling light suddenly pierced her to the core and exploded, flinging her to the very edge of existence. She felt the burning rend of Rugar's stroke, and suddenly all the wild, swirling pleasure in her focused on that breathtaking heat and fullness. More, she wanted more. And as her arms tightened around him and her body shifted, seeking his, he withdrew partway and thrust again, a bit deeper, then deeper still, again and again. His silky, restrained motions rose higher against the resistance of her untried flesh, and soon each additional measure of fullness was welcomed, assisted by the creamy response of her body.

She yielded, savoring the sharp, stinging tingles that were assuaged only by the gentle lapping motions of his body against hers. Her senses slowly cleared, and she realized that he'd paused, lying full inside her. He'd taken her in her moment of climax, submerging whatever discomfort she might have felt in that lush, drenching pleasure. Now she felt so deliciously stretched and full and hot . . . so very hot. Lud! it was wonderful!

Opening her eyes, she found his features almost fierce as he held himself still within her.

"Is it done?" she whispered.

"Consider yourself *plucked*," he rasped, with a devilish grin. "But sweetness, we are most certainly not *done*."

He plunged into her kiss and began to move inside her . . . small, exploratory motions at first, then stronger, more powerful thrusts. Instinctively, she moved with him, absorbing, exploring these new feelings. Through a haze of warmth, she felt the force gathering in his body, focusing on release, and him struggling to control it. His muscles bulged, his body quivered as he groaned her name over and over. Suddenly he contracted fiercely around her, his body racked by spasms, his face a mask of exquisite strain as he writhed in the throes of white-hot splendor.

"Now, my wicked little blossom . . ." He sighed tenderly when he could breath again. "*Now* we're done."

Later, Corrie lay in his arms, suffused with warmth, unwilling to surrender to exhaustion. His damp head rested on the bolsters, and he lay on his side, holding her against him. His big body spent heat recklessly, providing so much warmth that they needed no cover.

She was a woman now, she thought, turning the idea over and over in her mind. A *wife.* The mystery of physical loving had been both dispelled and intensified by her first joining with Rugar; it had been both soothing and shattering, a deeply satisfying agony of body and soul. The vows they had made were now sealed in their very flesh, promised and now given. Each belonged to the other in a way that they did not belong even to themselves. That profound sense of holding some part of him inside her while yielding up a part of herself to him brought a shimmer of wonder to her eyes.

Imagine a lifetime of such loving, the deepening closeness it would bring. Imagine exploring him freely by night—his body, thoughts, and feelings—then going about the dignified "ordinaries and propers" of living by his side during the day. Would she be able to walk with him, to meet his eyes, to be in the same room with him, without feeling her body growing warm and liquid? She felt his slow, even breaths brushing her hair and smiled dreamily, closing her eyes to luxuriate in his presence. Soon her jumbled thoughts were claimed by sleep.

The candles had guttered out long before Rugar wakened in the gray light of early dawn. It took him a moment to orient himself in the unfamiliar surroundings and to discover that the bed beside him was cool and empty. He started up, looking for her, and found her sitting behind him, her body delectably bare and her knees drawn up under her chin. She had a rosy, fresh-scrubbed look about her.

"Good morning, wife," he said huskily, leaning back on an elbow. "What are you doing?"

"Looking at you." She colored slightly. "Watching you sleep. Is that all right?" She held her breath, wondering if the heated intimacy they'd shared would withstand the cool of dawn. When he smiled and nodded, reassuring warmth curled through her. It was still there, she marveled, that intangible connection.

"Do you know, I could see your heart beating at the base of your throat as you slept."

"Where?" he asked, reaching for her hand and carrying it toward his chest. "Show me where." His husky tone said he was feeling that same warmth.

She felt the thud of his pulse beneath the smooth skin of his neck. "Here," she whispered, watching his eyelids lower as he held her hand against him. There was an unmistakable increase in his heart rate.

"Ummm." He pulled her closer, and she rolled onto her side, facing him. He reached up to sink his fingers into her hair and pull her head toward him as he arched to offer her access to his throat. "There's yet another way to feel it."

She bent close and let him press her lips against that vital, throbbing point. His blood surged to meet that contact, and she was suddenly caressing him with her lips, kissing that succulent spot, then tracing it with her tongue.

"There are other places you can feel my pulse," he offered, glancing down his casually sprawled nakedness. "Shall I show you?"

She bit her lip and nodded. He led her eyes and fingers to his wrist and inner elbows, and her lips soon followed. Then he directed her touches and kisses to the backs of his knees. He watched with bated breath as she feathered fingers and kisses up his powerful thighs and sinewy hips and muscular ribs.

"Your body is marvelous . . . beautiful. So different from mine and yet so similar. Do you feel the same things as me? When I do this"—she dragged her nails lightly up the inside of his thigh and felt him quiver—"do you feel shivery and cool, like water is trickling beneath your skin?"

"Something like that," he said, swallowing hard.

"And when I touch you here"—she ran her palm in slow circles over his flat nipple and saw him stiffen—"does it feel like something is twiddling and stirring your insides . . . spiraling round and round, from your breast all the way to your . . . male parts?"

"I believe that describes it . . . adequately," he said thickly, catching her wrists and kissing her busy fingers.

But she wasn't finished. She caressed his big hand, measuring his span against hers, then placed it over the hardening swell of her breast, where it made a very nice fit indeed. She covered his chest and back with curious hands, measuring him, memorizing him . . . tantalizing him with licks and nuzzles up the trickle of blond hair from his belly to his chest. Suddenly she raised her face to him, her expression filled with wonder.

"What is it like to be a man?"

He laughed, surprised by her question and utterly at a loss on how to answer her. "Do you mean, how do I feel? Or what do I think . . . or what things do I have to do?"

"All of it. Everything." She studied him intently, her curiosity aflame.

"Well, I'm not sure how to tell you . . . if it can be explained," he said, roused and somewhat disturbed by her question. Who but Corrie Huntington would think to ask such a thing?

She looked down with a thoughtful scowl, and her eyes lighted as they landed on his doublet, lying on the rug. She slid from the bed and picked it up, whirling it onto her naked shoulders and shoving her arms through the ornate silver-trimmed sleeves. She struck a bold and shocking pose—feet spread, fists settled on her hips. Then she lifted her chin in a wicked parody of courtly male arrogance and appraised him from insolently lidded eyes.

"Well, I know a few things about men," she declared. "Men get to look at whomever they please, however they please. Nobody chides them for too bold an eye." He chuckled his surprise, and she turned aside and began to swagger up and down in outrageous mimicry of a courtly swain's exaggerated gait. "And men get to wear breeches instead of a cumbersome farthingale . . . so they may strut and stride about on their long legs . . . as if measuring the earth itself for a suit of clothes that only they could possibly make."

Her own strutting drew his eyes to her shapely legs and his mind to the fact that she wasn't wearing a farthingale either at the moment . . . or anything else on her saucy bottom. He heated a few degrees.

"A man need make no apology for his fascination with a rosy breast or a pouty lip . . ." She paused before him and slowly pushed back the sides of his doublet, as if to demonstrate. He watched, desire like a flame licking up his belly, as his quilted white velvet dragged across her succulent nipples and slid aside to bare her generous breasts.

"While a woman must deny she owns such interests."

She lowered her lashes and lapped coy, splayed fingers over her breasts in a most insincere attempt to cloak them.

He was mesmerized, roused and primed by her playful seduction. He slid from the bed, but she danced away with a mischievous grin, and he lurched across the room and snatched her back with a wicked laugh. She came to rest against him, engulfed in his huge doublet and encircled by his arms. Her expression softened with wonder as she ran a finger down the smooth bulge of muscle at the top of one of the arms that held her captive.

"It must be wonderful, having arms like oak branches, strong enough to lift whatever you wish. I wish I could have them . . . just for a little while."

This glimpse of the curious and quixotic workings of her mind was as irresistible as it was unexpected. Everything in the middle of him seemed to be going soft again, and he had the most overwhelming and irrational wish to reorder all of creation so that *he* might give her exactly what she wanted. But since that wasn't within his power, he did the next best thing.

"You do have them." He carried her hand back to his arm and laid it over his flexed muscle, covering it with his own. "These are yours."

As she stared at him with huge, bright eyes, he carried her other hand to his chest and slid its coolness up his shoulder. "And these shoulders . . . are yours. And these eyes." He stroked the precious contour of her cheek with his knuckle. "And these hands."

She could scarcely breathe. He was offering himself to her . . . offering her the chance to experience maleness through him. The insight struck her with gale force: that was what marriage did! It joined a man and a woman such that each could touch and learn from and participate in that separate experience of humanness . . . that other sex. Through him she could understand manhood. And through her he could explore all the wonders and contradictions, the unique strengths and joys, of womanhood!

She was suddenly dizzy, giddy with the delight of discovery. Laughing, she seized his hands, led them to her breasts, and molded them to her. "Then it's only fair that these are yours." The dark centers of his eyes registered an understanding of what she offered him.

"And hair . . . I've a yen for long, silky hair."

"It's yours," she vowed, pulling him toward the bed. "Now come and claim the rest of your new possessions!"

He swept her up onto the bed with him, sliding quite naturally onto the soft pillow of her breasts and into the warm, receptive cradle of her thighs. He sent trembling hands inside his doublet to claim her . . . savoring the contrast of stiff garment and soft skin, and the forbidden, erotic sight of her feminine curves occupying his male clothing.

They kissed and caressed, exploring and tasting each other until desire welled liquid between them and overflowed, first trickling, then flowing as sensation was collected and channeled into a deep, coursing river of arousal.

Dalliance gave way to more intentional pleasures. He stroked her slowly, knowledgeably, and watched her curl under his hands, beguiling him with the luxuriant responses of her body. Stretching, purring, she reveled in the beautiful new feelings he was stirring within her. Then she sought to return them.

Her eager caresses were unlike any he'd known, sweet and adoring, experimental yet unerringly aimed. Through his passion-steeped senses he managed to realize that she was copying his movements, knowing now that what pleased her also pleased him. In touching her he had unwittingly directed her hands on him.

Now it became a deliberate and tantalizing new game. Eye to eye, breast to breast, they played. He kissed, then she kissed; he palmed, then she massaged. He rubbed;

she stroked. He tickled; she teased. It was enthralling. And it soon led them both to the brink of climax.

He pulled back, panting. Then she rubbed her wet, silky heat against him in one long, languid round of her hips and whispered, "Now."

He sank slowly into her warm, honeyed sheath, struggling for control and barely maintaining it. She arched and sighed beneath him, stunned by that rapturous, prolonged invasion. Then, when he lay imbedded fully in her, she slid her legs up his and wrapped them around him, an instinctive claiming, a primal feminine urge for possession.

He moved, gently at first, his short strokes lengthening as he worked to release his reined power in judicious increments. She sensed his struggle and began to wriggle kittenishly, fondling and teasing him, tempting him to abandon control, to plunge heart-first into warm, foaming seas of pleasure.

The sweet ecstasy of climax took them both by surprise, engulfing them like rolling surf, sending them gasping and tumbling. Pleasure drenched them like playful ocean spray, filling their senses with crystalline sea hues of cyan and sapphire, lapis and silver. It was clear, shimmering delight, capricious and fanciful, like vibrations of laughter along their nerves. This was the light heart of sensuality . . . hidden in the shadow of roaring, volatile desire, awaiting the calm when need was satisfied and there was luxury enough for indulgence that had as its only driving impulse, love.

It left them shivering and laughing into each other's eyes. It left them wondering, touching, and snuggling close. And it left them a bit deeper in love as they drifted toward sleep.

Later, she turned on the hard pillow of his arm and found his eyes closed and his mouth curled into a male smile that she was surprised to understand completely. It said he was pleased and satisfied, proud of his potent performance and of her uninhibited response. She stroked his jaw, and he turned to her with love-weighted eyes.

"What would Lady Cobham say to learn I ignored her advice?" When he looked confused, she jogged his memory. "The chair, remember?"

"Ahhh. But you weren't rogered, sweetness," he said with a wicked waggle of his brows. "You were Rugar-ed."

And she laughed.

Chapter Fourteen

The queen emerged from her royal apartments at noon the next day, sweeping through the public chambers of Whitehall in a rare, ebullient mood that drew her courtiers to her like bedazzled moths. One moment she flirted outlandishly and played the coquette, the next she traded spirited banter and merciless witticisms with her favorite court wags and gossips. The courtiers caught her mood and imitated her gay and strident manner as they followed her about the palace and grounds, from galleries to gardens to work yards.

All watched in lurid surprise as she called for Lady Corinna, paused, and made a show of suddenly recalling last evening's nuptials. "Perhaps she is not yet permitted out of bed," she crooned cattily. There was coarse, knowing laughter, and she straightened, donning her most imperial mien and tone. "Dare we allow such sloth in our royal service? Methinks not! We must roust these newly-weddeds . . . make them an example to all slugabeds in the kingdom!" With a lilting, ironic laugh, she lifted her voluminous skirts and waved her companions along with her.

She led them, jesting and jostling, along the Privy Gallery and up the main stairs toward the royal apartments. She knew exactly what they would find in the bridal chamber: a missing bridegroom and a distraught bride. It was regrettable, of course, but necessary, this intrusion into Corinna's privacy and grief. The shame and pain of being abandoned on her wedding night would be imprinted indelibly on the gell by their firsthand discovery of it. Elizabeth's smile became almost grim.

In her mind's eye, she envisioned driving the gawking courtiers from the chamber and then offering the gell a shoulder to cry on and a continuing place at court—at her queenly side, in her queenly service. After a restorative visit to her home, Corinna would return to court a solitary young matron, wise to the treachery of men and unlikely to let her heart be lured away from worthier pursuits again.

The nobles drew up around the door, pressing close, their faces ruddy with lurid glee at the prospect of perusing the outcome of the virile Swede's night upon delectable little Corrie Huntington. They watched, transfixed, as the queen tugged at the doorlatch and found it locked. An oily, collective "Oooh" went up. "Ye gods, he's locked her in!" she quipped. "Or has he locked us out?"

Her followers laughed, and she set the heel of her palm to the door in several sharp raps. When there was no response, she gave the Earl of Oxford the nod and he took it up, smacking the great oak planks with his gloved fist and calling out in a deep, commanding voice, "Aelthar . . . Countess! You cannot lie abed all day—open up!"

All held their breath and "shushed" as the scrape of the bolt was heard . . . then the creak of hinges . . . and the door was swung open. The queen's eyes flew wide, and her face drained, then mottled with furious color. She was speechless.

Rugar Kalisson stood inside the doorway, clad only in silk hose and a half-opened shirt which revealed a large, tantalizing slice of chest. His legs were spread and his arms were crossed over his chest as he faced her and her unruly delegation. Behind him, peering at them from the midst of the great sunlit bed, was a sheetclad Corrie, looking charmingly tousled and thoroughly tumbled.

The courtiers boldly ogled Corrie's bare shoulders and made sly, admiring whistles and groans. Rugar waited just one moment too long to be truly respectful, then greeted Elizabeth with a deep, flourishing bow.

"How good of you to come to waken us, Your Grace," he said, his deep voice velvety with satisfaction. "But as you can see"—he flicked a pointed glance over his shoulder at Corrie—"I have been up for some time."

The scarcely muffled titters, groans, and giggles his double-edged declaration drew from her followers poured over the queen like boiling oil. She was incensed to find him there, seething at the way he'd despoiled her little treasure, and purely outraged to have to suffer his brutish insolence on top of it all!

"Then we shall expect to see you this afternoon at the tennis courts, Aelthar," she declared shrilly, not caring that her ire tainted her tone. "In three hours' time." Her eyes were flecked with red as she whirled and exited with a flourish, dragging her reluctant courtiers from the tantalizing sights of the nuptial chamber.

Rugar closed and bolted the door, and stood staring at it before turning back to the bed and Corrie's worried frown.

"She's very hurt and angry with us . . . with me," she said as Rugar came to sit beside her. Her sense of responsibility and her loyalty to Elizabeth caused a tightness in his chest.

"No," he said truthfully, "she is angry with me. I've compromised you and now I've married you." He brushed the tip of her nose affectionately as a huge grin spread over his handsome face. She sighed as he pulled a helpless smile from her.

"Then for her sake—and ours, my lord—couldn't you try to seem a bit more miserable and repentant?"

The princely chamber filled with his laughter. "I'll try, Kari. But I warn you, it won't be easy."

Elizabeth paced her closet a short while later, feeling caged and burned, raw to the core. When Morris Lombard scratched at the back door and she bellowed permission to enter, he cowered like a hound before his angry mistress.

"I have had two disagreeable shocks of late, Lombard," she ground out, her voice hoarse as she advanced on him, "and *you* have been associated with both!"

"Let me explain, Majesty—" He bowed and sniveled his way forward with his shoulders rounded and his hands clasped in supplication. "We had them—"

"I won't hear it! You vowed he was out of the way, and yet there he was—smug as the devil himself—fresh from his carnal plundering! I swear, Lombard, if that cursed Swede spends one more night defiling either my pet or good English soil, your wretched blood will be let to purify the taint! You're to carry him and his cursed accomplice off tonight. I shall arrange a great, noisy dinner and have him called away . . . led straight into your hands."

"B-but he's been warned now. H-he'll be alert to an—"

"Curse it—there are but two of them! How difficult can it be to subdue a paltry two men? Tonight, Lombard! Take some of my guardsmen if you must. Carry the bastards to the ship as planned, or kill them outright—I care not which. But if I see Rugar Kalisson's face on the morrow, I swear to you, no one will ever see yours again!"

* * *

Rugar and Corrie emerged from their bridal chamber that afternoon into a veritable storm of curiosity and congratulations. *Sly devil;* the men clapped him enthusiastically—if somewhat enviously—on the back while ogling Corrie's rosy glow. *Clever chit*; the ladies squeezed Corrie's hands—some wishing they were her throat instead—while eyeing Rugar with wistful memories of his potent male charm. Rugar grinned and pulled Corrie closer to his side, and she smiled shyly, stroking his sleeve in an unconscious but distinctively feminine display of possession.

But from that promising start, things went steadily downhill. When they joined the queen at the tennis courts, she made an effusive show of welcoming Corrie while ignoring Rugar altogether. Through the tennis matches, a visual battle raged between her and Rugar over Corrie . . . quite literally over Corrie's head. Afterward, the queen stridently declared that all present should sup with her that night and enjoy an evening of dancing . . . most especially the newly wedded couple. No sooner had the queen sailed off on a sea of cloying adoration than Corrie's father planted himself before Rugar, demanding to know when he intended to leave for Sweden.

Corrie looked up at Rugar, surprised. Until that moment, she hadn't given thought to the fact that as a wife she would be expected to reside in her husband's house—and that her husband's house was in Sweden! Her sudden excitement was quickly tempered by the misery in her father's face.

"I cannot yet say. I have made no arrangements," Rugar replied in a controlled tone.

"Then you will stay in England for a time," Jack declared, some of the angry rigidity of his shoulders melting. He looked at Corrie. "I would have my daughter visit her mother for a while . . . before you carry her off."

Rugar noted the poignant longing in his father-in-law's face and made himself nod, even as he realized he could never accede to the demand. Elizabeth's every glance this afternoon had carried the threat of renewed treachery.

"It seems a reasonable enough request," Rugar said. "I would have you know, my lord earl, you will be welcome to visit us in Sweden. My wife's family will always be welcome in my house." The way the earl bristled at his invitation rubbed Rugar the wrong way entirely, and he retaliated. "And I understand you have two younger daughters, my countess's sisters. I would be pleased to help you find them desirable Swedish matches as well."

Jack Huntington sputtered and stepped back, his eyes hot with indignation. "Until later, daughter." He snapped a nod at her, then strode off.

Rugar looked down to find Corrie staring at him reproachfully, and had the grace to redden. "Well, you would like having one of your young sisters settled near you, wouldn't you?"

Her eyes narrowed. "I think we should let my father get used to having one foreigner in the family before asking him to consider *two*."

Rugar escorted Corrie back to their new quarters and reluctantly deposited her there, excusing himself to keep an appointment with Torgne. She spent the balance of the afternoon ordering and arranging Rugar's and her things, and enduring Anne's curiosity about her wedding night.

"Then . . . at least say he was out of his head with delight," Anne insisted, frustrated to the core by Corrie's reticence.

Corrie paused, folding a smock, and her eyes flitted over a remembered picture of Rugar's face in the most critical moments. A secretive smile curled her mouth. "I believe he was . . . well pleased."

Anne huffed in disgust. "Fine. Be pinch-beaked and

ungrateful. I was only asking to learn whether you heated him up enough to melt the locks on his coffers." When Corrie frowned at her, she announced: "You'll have to have a raft of new gowns, Cub. Now that you're a married woman, a full *countess,* you simply cannot go about looking like a nun anymore . . . all that virginal black and white."

"Anne!" Corrie was genuinely appalled.

"Sorry, Cub, but it's true. And it's best to train him properly right from the start: if he wants you to be generous with him in bed, he'll have to be generous with you outside of it." She smiled smugly. "You'd need new gowns soon anyway; I hear from Beatrice, who has relations in France and Italy, that bodices are on the rise again."

"B-but . . . I've just had most of my bodices lowered!" Corrie stared in disbelief as Anne gave an impish laugh.

"Well, that's the price you pay, Cub, for being so dead set on following fashion."

As it happened, Rugar spent the rest of the afternoon arranging things as well: foremost, transportation to Sweden. Spurred by Rugar's abductors' mention of a ship, Torgne had learned there was indeed a merchantman in London harbor which would soon put to sea for Stockholm. Together, they paid the grizzled Swedish captain a secretive visit and crossed his callused palm with silver to learn that he'd sold passage for two to Sweden to some knotty, ferret-faced fellow claiming to represent someone very high up in the palace. The gold had been plentiful, so he'd not bothered with questions. But the promised passengers hadn't been delivered. And though he was eager to lift anchor, he dared not until he heard from the little wretch, for fear of offending someone in the palace and losing his right to unload his cargoes of Swedish timber in London harbor.

"Troth, I think we may be able to help you, sir." Rugar

smoothed his doublet, looking pleased. "We"—he gestured between Torgne and himself —"are the two passengers you were to have carried." He smiled beatifically at the captain's dark, mistrustful look. "And we intend to leave within a few days. Would you be willing to wait a week . . . for a hundred gold dalers?" When the captain pushed back his hat and scratched his woolly head, making a dour face, Rugar upped his bid.

"And another hundred upon arrival."

They finally agreed on four hundred, but only after a lengthy recitation of Rugar's holdings and credit, and a desperate review of Torgne's acquaintances in Stockholm's merchant families. Aelthar . . . the captain seemed to have heard the name. And Sigurd . . . his wife's brother's wife was a Sigurd by birth. He was finally persuaded that he would lose nothing by the bargain and agreed to make ready for *three* passengers, instead of two, and to say nothing to the weasel-beaked fellow from the palace if he showed his face again.

Rugar and Torgne furtively made their way back to the alley where their horses were being held. By the time they reached Whitehall Palace, it was well past dark, and they exchanged grim nods as they parted. Torgne went off to his chambers to pack his trunks for Sweden, and Rugar went to his new apartments to prepare for the queen's banquet . . . with a clear memory of what had happened after her last show of hospitality toward him.

The dinner was a spirited affair, held in the drafty, unadorned banquet hall. The broader court was abuzz with the news of Lady Corinna's marriage, and they vied hotly for a seat at the cloth-draped tables in order to glimpse the new countess and her husband. The gentlemen eagerly awaited the start of the dancing, hoping it might prove easier to pluck Lady Corinna from her husband's clutches than it had been to pry her from the queen's. And the ladies' hearts fluttered, anticipating that the handsome Swedish count would give up his bride to other hands, leaving him obliged to partner them once again.

Corrie and Rugar were seated not far from the head table, alongside Corrie's father and Anne. Torgne Sigurd was conspicuous by his absence, and Rugar mentioned offhandedly that he'd had affairs to tend and would likely join them later. He was keenly aware of the queen's notice, and Corrie was miserably aware of her father's scrutiny. Both Corrie and Rugar wished for all the world that they were back in the privacy of their own apartments.

When the tables were dismantled and the dancing began, Corrie was besieged by invitations, which she declined as gracefully as she could. She read in Rugar's twinkling eyes that he, too, was recalling her last disastrous attempt at dancing. She smiled back, feeling reassured and somehow lighter inside.

Well along into the third dance, a footman approached Rugar with a message that Baron Sigurd wished to see him immediately and would meet him in the court at the end of the Privy Gallery. Rugar's mind worked furiously. It honestly might be Torgne, having learned something important and needing to consult or to warn him. But it might also be a lure, he realized, meant to draw him into an ambush: the very thing he and Torgne had hoped to forestall by not attending the dinner together tonight. Was he truly summoned by Torgne or by the queen's vengeful trap?

He spied the queen, caught up in a lively volta, leaping gracefully, then whirling coquettishly under Sir Christopher Hatton's upraised arm. There were no clues to his fate in her buoyant mien, nor had she betrayed any secretive delight or special malice during the dining. He sent a hand down to the short sword at his side and knew he could have the answer only by risking walking into a potential disaster.

He murmured to Corrie that he'd been called away for a few minutes by a message from Torgne, pressing a covertly ardent kiss on her palm. She nodded and squeezed his hand as he left. Then she turned back to whatever Anne was trying to say above the din of music, loud voices, and laughter.

Rugar strode through the door with his senses keenly pitched and his muscles coiling. His left hand gripped the scabbard of his blade, and his right clenched and unclenched in anticipation of action. The corridor was much cooler than the banquet hall and more dimly lit. As he walked along the passage, each wooden column and stone pillar in the broad hallway loomed as a potential threat, a hiding place for abductors or assassins. But each proved empty as he passed, and he let out the breath he was holding; the Privy Gallery was empty as far as he could see. He turned toward his old apartments, from which he expected Torgne would come. He moved quickly, staying close to the wall, keeping his sword hand ready. But by the time he reached the end and the doors leading to the Cock Pit and the ambassadorial apartments, there was still no sign of Torgne. Coiling with expectation, he slipped between the doors, then felt his way along the darkened stone archway that rimmed the court. Clouds were drifting over the moon, veiling its light, but Rugar managed to glimpse a motion, a figure across the courtyard, and darted to a nearby pillar to watch with his heart pounding against his ribs.

Torgne! Rugar sagged with relief. He relaxed his grip on his scabbard and stepped out into the court to wave a hand. But as Torgne approached, Rugar could make out a puzzled scowl.

"I got your message," Torgne called in a loud whisper. "What's happened?"

Torgne had gotten a message, too? Rugar's whole body contracted at the realization of what was happening . . . just one heartbeat before the courtyard filled with furious red-coated guardsmen. The queen's trap was sprung!

Rugar's sword swooshed from its scabbard, cutting a broad arc around him as they charged, and the guardsmen fell back. He saw Torgne draw his blade and then saw no more as he met their second charge, full on. The guardsmen carried six-foot bladed pikes, and as they came, protected by the range of their weapons against his short blade, he feinted and struck their blades aside with the flat of his. He scarcely had time to recover before others were upon him, two, then three at a time. He parried and slashed and lunged, driving his blade between muscle and marrow more than once. But as some groaned and fell back, others surged in to take their place.

A hooked pike smashed against his blade from the side, knocking it from his grip, and he was left to defend himself bare-handed. Through the roar of his blood, he heard someone shouting orders to take them alive. Spear points were stayed mere inches from his chest, only to be replaced by coarse, sinewy fists and the blunt ends of the wooden shafts. They were everywhere, surrounding him, jabbing, gouging as he wrestled with one brawny guard after another. Then a dull thud shook his head, and everything seemed to explode—a blinding flare that consumed his consciousness and left him sinking into charred blackness. Within moments, Torgne joined him, unconscious, on the cold paving stones.

A slender form in plain brown woolens pushed through the wall of royal red coats. A cold glint of satisfaction appeared in Morris Lombard's eyes as he surveyed the results of the queen's vengeance and his own skill at connivance. As he had anticipated, each of his quarries had loyally answered the other's call. An absurdly noble sentiment, *loyalty*. See where it had gotten them.

"Well, don't just stand there, you clouts," he snarled. "Get them out of here before anyone sees them."

Not far away, in the banquet hall, Corrie watched the queen, alone on her regal chair. In Rugar's absence she had decided to approach Elizabeth, to try to mend the rift between them caused by her own wretched breach of faith and honor. Only the fact that the queen had both sponsored and attended her vows with Rugar held out hope of reconciliation and emboldened Corrie enough to approach her mistress. She moved closer to the dais, then closer still, and paused a respectful distance away. She held her breath, gaze downcast, waiting to see whether Elizabeth would receive or reject her.

The queen turned to her, and Corrie gradually lifted her head, asking with her luminous eyes the question in her heart. Could she ever be forgiven? The queen's expression softened slowly; her guarded air of responsibility and privilege lowered . . . enough for Corrie to glimpse that the wounded affection between them had begun to heal. In that meeting of gazes, much was said that could never be spoken aloud. A small, tenuous smile crept over her features, and Elizabeth responded in kind. A wave beckoned Corrie forward, and soon she stood a pace from the royal knee. Elizabeth extended her hand, and Corrie knelt and pressed it to her forehead with a misty-eyed smile.

Still on her knees, Corrie found her mistress regarding her warmly. "Thank you, Your Grace."

"Welcome back to our side, my dear Corinna." Elizabeth sighed with deep satisfaction and squeezed Corrie's slender hand as she added in her thoughts: *This time, to stay.*

Corrie sat on a stool by the queen's feet for a long while, talking, laughing, exchanging news. It felt like former days . . . almost. Her attention wandered with increasing frequency to the far reaches of the hall, searching the jostling, milling throng for some sign of Rugar. She hadn't seen him since the dancing had begun, and that had been nearly two hours ago. She excused herself from the queen and sought out Anne to ask if she had seen Rugar.

"Nary a glimpse," Anne vowed. Then, noticing the concern in Corrie's face, she added. "Don't fret, Cub, he'll be along in time for bed." Corrie's frown only deepened, and Anne pulled her aside. "What is it? Has something happened?"

"Pray, help me look for him, Anne. Please," Corrie said in a tight voice. Anne rolled her eyes, but nodded.

Separately they made a circuit of the banquet hall, then together they questioned the boistrous courtiers gathered about the hall. Then they checked the dimly lit corridors outside and stopped some gentlemen returning from the Cock Pit. Rugar hadn't been seen there, either.

"Perhaps his old apartments. The baron sent for him—" Before Anne could protest, Corrie pulled her into the chilled Privy Gallery and toward the far doors. Panting from the run across the courtyard, they drew up before Torgne's door and knocked, then pounded. Silence answered, and they slipped the latch and crept inside. A palace page looked up sleepily from his vigil near the warming brazier and informed them the baron had left hours ago.

Outside again, Corrie grabbed Anne's hands and set her in motion. "I have to find him. Come on!" She dragged Anne through the Great Hall and the Presence Chamber, into the dim Stone Gallery, through the royal apartments and lesser courtyards, then past the odoriferous kitchens, and even through the chapel and vestry. No Rugar Kalisson. No Torgne Sigurd. Not a trace.

* * *

Rugar awakened for the second time in as many days to a blast of icy water. He battled back the pain in his head and the fog in his senses to sit up, and discovered he was lying on something moderately soft . . . and that a face was looming indistinctly above him. He rubbed his eyes and shook his head, feeling as if his wits were sloshing back and forth inside him, and finally focused on the face of the crusty old Swedish sea dog he'd struck a bargain with earlier that day.

"Didn't expect to see ye back so soon," the captain growled, bending over him. "Nor in such foul fettle."

Rugar discovered he was lying on wool bales in the cavernous cargo hold of a ship. Torgne lay sprawled beside him, still unconscious. Rugar's first coherent words carried a measure of disbelief.

"T-they brought us here?" he rasped, holding his pounding head in his hands.

"Dumped ye off and said to set sail straightaway." The captain squinted at him. "But I figured I'd hear what ye had to say first, since yer payin'. Anyhow, I tho't there was supposed to be *three* of ye."

Three. The word cut through Rugar's head like a knife. He struggled to his knees, and the captain lent him belated assistance. "Throw some water on him." Rugar gestured toward Torgne. "We have to go rescue my bride."

"Bride?" The captain scowled at Rugar, who shot him a pain-riddled glare.

"She's number three."

"You don't understand, Anne." Corrie sniffed as she drooped on the edge of the empty bed in her new chambers. They had spent the hour before midnight combing the palace for some sign of Rugar and Torgne, and finding none. Now, well past midnight bells, Corrie confessed: "This isn't the first time he's . . . disappeared. He didn't come to our chambers last night until the wee hours of the morning."

Anne's expression froze with surprise. "You mean he didn't come to you when he left the wedding dinner?"

Corrie shook her head. "He said it was an old Swedish custom . . . abducting the bridegroom on the wedding night. Torgne and some other gentlemen spirited him off to a drinking rout." Even as she said it, she realized how suspicious it sounded and recalled how shamefully eager she'd been to embrace his excuses. Her tears began in earnest, and Anne collected her into a tight, protective hug.

"Torgne Sigurd." Anne spat the name as if it fouled her mouth. "Trust that dry codpiece to ruin a gell's wedding night . . . getting your husband drunk as a brewer's pizzle."

"But he wasn't drunk. He'd scarcely been—" She lifted a horrified look to Anne. "If he wasn't drinking, where was he? And where is he now?"

Anne comforted her as best she could, but as the hours slipped by—one, two, then three—the awful feelings of abandonment she'd felt once before swamped her, and guilt over their forced marriage settled cruelly upon her heart. The delights of the second half of their wedding night seemed like a dream, far less real than the distress she'd felt at his initial absence and the anguish of having it repeated on the very next night!

She wrung her hands and swiped away tears, conjuring one dismal possibility after another. He'd been set upon and injured by some of the bullies and thieves who crept into the palace and stalked the maze of corridors; Anne snorted that "invincible" Swedes would certainly hold their own against a few padders and pitchfingers. Corrie's spirits plummeted as the lesser troubles were dispelled. Another woman? she choked out. Anne hooted that one down. Then he could be angry at their forced marriage and avoiding her. Anne declared hotly that no one had *forced* him to make love to her the previous night, nor had he been forced to smile at her and caress her when he thought no one watched them, that afternoon. Round and round Corrie went, her guilt at their forced marriage outpacing Anne's rebuttals.

"You're not making sense anymore, Cub! And if you keep this up, you'll make yourself sick." Anne took charge, bullying Corrie into bed and insisting she take a dose of sleeping powders. "I'll be here, Cub, all night"—she stroked Corrie's hair back from her face—"in case you should need me." Corrie was too exhausted and dispirited to protest. The strain of the past two days had finally taken its toll. As Corrie fell asleep, Anne felt her own fatigue and rousted Maudie to help loosen and remove her bodice and over-skirts. Then she dismissed the tiring woman and wrapped herself in a comforter on the trundle.

In the early hours of the morning, the candles guttered and went out, sinking the chamber into a gloom as deep as that in the heart of its mistress.

Chapter Fifteen

In the deepest hour of the night, well before the sullen sky would brighten with the first hint of dawn, the royal apartments were dark and still . . . but for the two figures slinking past the dozing guardsmen at the rear stairs. Rugar Kalisson and Torgne Sigurd climbed the winding stairs to the uppermost floor and felt their way along the narrow, inky servants' passage that ran like a labyrinth through the heart of those princely lodgings. Rugar, in front, stumbled over a human form sprawled across the passage, and they both froze. But a soft wine-soused snore was the only response, and they each made an audible sound of relief.

Farther along, they half saw, half felt a doorframe and paused, pressing their ears to the panels, listening. A full, blustering snore could be heard on the other side, and Rugar chuckled grimly, then pulled Torgne farther down the passage. They stopped before a thick door, and Rugar fingered the latch.

"I'll get her . . . you get her things."

Torgne grunted agreement, and Rugar quietly jiggered the latch until the door creaked open. The great chamber was as dark as the passage, but they were able to make out looming gray shapes. Rugar headed for the bed. He stopped short, realizing the trundle had been rolled out, and crept around to the other side.

Torgne turned toward a tall shape by the wall, knowing it to be a wardrobe of sorts, but didn't see the low metal brazier in the way. His big foot caught in its legs and sent it crashing across the wooden floor. "Dammit!"

A bundled human shape pushed up from the trundle, weaving groggily, and Rugar and Torgne froze. Corrie's tiring woman! They'd forgotten about her.

"Troll's Teeth!" Rugar growled. "Don't let her—"

But Torgne was already in motion. He pounced on the old woman, knocking her back down onto the trundle and smothering her startled cries with the comforter. He managed to feel for her face through the bedcover and clamped his hand over her mouth just as she started to wail.

"Dammit—hold still!" he panted, subduing her struggling form with his own weight. "It's your lady's husband—come to get her—"

But the old woman continued to thrash and moan, apparently unconvinced of either their identity or her own safety. When she got her mouth free and started to scream, Rugar croaked out, "Shut her up!"

Grappling wildly, Torgne found her thrashing head again, then her face, and finally succeeded in muffling her cries. Gradually her protests ceased, and she went limp beneath him. He rolled off the trundle with a soft thud, and he and Rugar both held their breath, listening furiously for sounds of detection.

When the quiet remained uninterrupted, Rugar expelled a ragged breath and lurched onto the bed beside Corrie, trying to awaken her. "Come, sweetness, open your eyes—" But patting her cheek, shaking her shoulders, rubbing her hands . . . nothing availed. She was fast asleep. "What's happened to her? I can't arouse her."

A distant noise penetrated the gloom, coming from the

main hallway, and Rugar had no more time to ponder. He had to take her now and find out what was the matter with her later. He wrapped her in the heavy comforter, pulled her up into his arms. There was a distinct *clank* from the main hallway, and he strode around the bed, picking his way through the gloom. Torgne was frantically plowing through the wardrobe, dragging out handfuls of linen and velvet until Rugar growled, "Forget the clothes; get her tiring woman instead. I can buy her new clothes, but she may need the old woman for comfort."

Torgne began to protest, but another, even closer sound from the main hallway made him empty his hands. He rushed back to the bed, misjudging and banging his foot on the trundle. "Mmmda mmmmr—" He bit his lip to keep it in. The old woman was limp as a rag as he hoisted her comforter-wrapped form onto his broad shoulder, rump up. "What if she's dead?" he hissed, groping through the darkness toward Rugar and the door. "What if I've strangled her?"

"It takes more force than a bit of bedcovers in the face to strangle a body," Rugar whispered, shifting his own burden gingerly in his arms.

"Wonderful—then I've merely smothered her," Torgne snapped. They slipped into the opaque blackness of the narrow servants' passage and felt their way along. "I've never hurt a woman before in my life. If I burn in Hell for this, Rugar Kalisson, I intend to tell the devil it was all your idea!"

The winding, unlit stairs provided a slow, torturous descent. Inch by inch, they crept along, wincing at each creak of a wooden stair tread, fastening their minds on the waiting cart, on the ship, and on home. The prickliest moment came when they pushed open the outside door and slipped past the sleeping guards, holding their breath and giving each footfall the deliberation due a military maneuver. But

all remained blessedly peaceful, and soon they were across
the courtyard and unloading their burdens onto a bed of
straw in the back of a two-wheeled cart, then covering the
cart with felt.

When they pulled the cart through the alleys and arch-
ways toward the main gates of Whitehall, borrowed hats
shielded their faces and woolen doublets, inches too small,
strained across their shoulders. They might have been farmers
or the servants of a merchant who had made a delivery to the
palace kitchens. Once outside the gates, they were indistin-
guishable from the growing predawn trickle of feet and
wheels trundling up and down London's dank and smelly
streets.

The ship was already spreading sail to catch a steering
breeze when they arrived at the quay. They slunk across the
gangway and carried Corrie and her servant quickly belowdecks to a modest but comfortable cabin. The bunk was
wide enough to accommodate two, and Rugar lowered
Corrie onto it, then peeled back her cover. She was flushed
and tousled, but seemed, nonetheless, to be merely sleeping.

"Faith! this old one's heavy," Torgne grumbled, eager to
unload his burden. When Rugar stepped back, Torgne bent
over the bed and let the body slide from his shoulder onto
the straw-stuffed mattress. He pulled back the comforter,
praying the old woman wasn't injured or—*gud förbjude*—
dead. He froze.

Blond hair, not gray. Smooth, youthful skin, not a prune-
like countenance. Exquisite, classical features, long amber
lashes, and a bold, velvet-rimmed mouth that was provocative even in repose.

"*Gud,* Rugar. What have we done?"

Torgne stood staring at beautiful Anne Bosworth in abject
horror. With her head turned to the side, her slender throat
was visible . . . temptingly bare, with a faint pulse fluttering.

Torgne's eyes fixed on that dainty but disturbing throb,

then closed, and he shuddered. He hadn't killed her; he wasn't going to burn in Hell. But he was going to be punished all the same. He was absolutely sure of it.

Everything in Corrie's world was gray and swirling, like a wind-borne mist that seeped both through and around her, brushing, then escaping all her senses before she could examine it. As her awareness grew, that soft shroud gradually thinned, then vanished, and her senses were once again solid, able to collect and hold perceptions. Her first sense was of swaying, both her and the things around her; then came the smells of dampness and wood, a tang of salt and oil, and a hint of acrid pitch. It was a strange array of smells, new in combination, yet individually familiar. There were sounds, disjointed at first: creaking, the caw of gulls, human shouts that seemed far off.

She opened her eyes and beheld wooden planking above her. She was lying on a bed of sorts, beside a planking wall, beneath a planking ceiling from which an oil lamp was suspended, swaying back and forth. She raised her head, squinted, blinked, and made out a small chamber, a chair, a paneled door, a small carved table, an ironbound chest. Cool yellow sunlight came through a long, narrow window at the end of the bed, and as she watched, the entire chamber seemed to pitch slowly to the side, and the lamp swung oddly with regard to the tilting walls. She grabbed instinctively for something to brace herself, and the movement pushed her cover back.

Cool air flooded over her half-bare chest and thin linen smock. She shivered and looked down, realizing she was all but naked. Where in heaven was she? The swaying, the salty dampness . . . a *ship?*

She sprang up as quickly as her sodden reflexes allowed

and was startled when a voice burst forth from almost beside her.

"Corrie? Thank God! Are you all right?"

Anne bounded up from a chair near the head of the bunk. Corrie scowled and blinked, staring at her disheveled hair and the thick down comforter she was clutching around her with whitened fingers. For a moment she thought she glimpsed Anne's bare feet!

"Anne?"

"Oh, Cub, say you're all right," Anne begged, squeezing onto the side of the bunk by Corrie, frantically snatching up her hands. "I've been so worried—you slept for so long—"

"Fine, I think. A bit addled." Corrie rubbed her temples and sat up farther, then pulled her cover tighter about her. "Wh-where are we? What is this place?"

"A ship. We're on a damned ship!" Anne declared, flinging a hand around her.

"Wh-what are we doing on a ship?" Corrie sat bolt upright, her eyes suddenly wide with alarm.

"We've been abducted," Anne said furiously, "by your ranting hound of a husband and that brute of a—" The cabin door swung open, and Rugar ducked inside, followed closely by Torgne.

"We heard voices—Kari!" Rugar rushed toward the bunk, but Anne lurched square into his path. "Are you all right?" He tried to slip around Anne, but she planted herself in front of him and jammed her fists on her hips, ignoring the ignominious slide of her cover.

"She's in fine fettle, no thanks to you!" She stuck her chin up at him with her cheeks flushed and her golden-brown eyes flecked with crimson fire. "I demand you take us back this very instant. Turn this vile, wallowing tub about and set us on solid English soil by nightfall or—I swear to you—I'll see you hunted down and dressed out like the ruthless beast you are!" Rugar's face bronzed as he tried to sidestep her challenge to reach Corrie, and she jolted to prevent it, facing him with blazing defiance. Corrie watched, dumbstruck, disbelieving her eyes and ears.

"Will you move, woman?" he bellowed at Anne, looming big and powerful above her. "Or must I take you in hand and move you myself?"

"You daren't touch me again, you rogue," Anne spat, her ire and volume rising steadily. "I've been attacked and smothered—banged about until I'm sore and bruised all over—abducted from my cousin's bed in the dead of night—kept half naked in a cold cabin with no food—" She was beset past all bearing and ready to use her claws on any who crossed her. "Worse yet," she raved, "I'm being carried to *Sweden,* the same godforsaken barrens that spawned both you and that juiceless"—she flung a finger at Torgne—"sanctimonious cod!" She flinched as Torgne jerked forward, then smirked nastily when he bashed his head into the hanging lamp.

"I'll see the queen has your ears on a string for this," she vowed, punching a finger at Rugar's chest. Her voice dropped to a gritty scrape as she turned that finger on Torgne. "And I shall personally have *his* guts for garters!"

Rugar's face reddened as he saw Corrie's eyes growing owlish and confused. He grabbed Anne's shoulders, dragged her bodily out of his way, and thrust her into Torgne's arms, bellowing, "Get the witch out of here—*now!*"

Scarlet-faced Torgne clamped furious arms around her rebellious form and hauled her to the door as she kicked, screeched, and wrenched violently in his grasp. She swore in shocking terms that they'd rue this barbaric treatment of her and any harm that befell Corrie while in their vile clutches. Rugar opened the door. As Torgne wrestled her out into the passage, she began to scream bloody murder.

Rugar slammed the door. He was across the cabin and down on his knees in three strides. "Tell me you're well." His hands flew lightly over Corrie's shoulders, her face, her hair.

She stared at him, still hearing Anne's muffled screams and a door slam, and she managed to nod her head. "Rugar, what Anne said—that you abducted us from the palace— did you do that?" She watched him shift knees on the floor and gather her hands into his. The contact felt strange; warm and pleasant, yet somehow foreign.

"We did. Torgne and I. I came to get you and couldn't awaken you. We couldn't wait. . . . We didn't mean to take the baroness; we have a problem there. We thought she was your tiring woman and that you'd want her with you on the voyage and once we reach home."

Home. The word caused sudden confusion in Corrie. Her father's face rose unbidden in her mind, along with images and impressions of Straffen and her mother and sisters . . . the queen's library and her cozy chamber in the palace. She felt a sudden chill, and he pushed himself up to sit by her on the bunk and drew the comforter around her.

"You couldn't wait? But you told my father we would stay . . ." As she searched his face, she suddenly saw the cut and swelling at one corner of his mouth, the gash above his left brow, and the dark ring that ran from his cheekbone upward, encircling his eye.

"Rugar, what happened to you?" she whispered, stroking his battered face. Anxiety stopped her breath. As he caught her fingers and kissed them, she stilled, remembering more.

"Where did you go? I searched everywhere. It was the second time you'd disappeared." She looked down at his hands covering hers. "I thought you'd left me."

"Kari, I would never leave you." He traced her cheek with

his thumb, looking as if he were struggling with something inside him. His hand withdrew. "I—we—were abducted."

"Abducted?" It was as if he'd delivered a huge, ugly, indecipherable lump into the middle of her mind, and she hadn't the faintest idea what to do with it. "Why? By whom? Who would try to abduct you?" She stared at the bruising and at the cuts on his face with the alarming feeling there had been a great deal happening around her, just outside the limits of her awareness. "Why would anyone want to hurt you like this?"

"It was the queen," he said bitterly. "Your queen had Torgne and me abducted. Twice." She watched his shoulders stiffen as he steeled himself, and realized there was more to come, much more. Her expression darkened with dread. "The first time was on our wedding night."

"But you said . . ."

"I know what I said. I didn't want to worry you. But it wasn't Torgne who abducted me that night, it was Elizabeth. She intended to deport us secretly from England, so that it would seem I had abandoned you. And she might have succeeded, except that her henchmen failed to take Torgne at the same time, and he was able to find and free me." As he spoke, his face grew perceptibly harder. "That was why I was so late to our marriage bed, Kari. I damn near didn't arrive at all." His voice lowered to a menacing snarl. "Which was Elizabeth's intent all along . . . to keep me from having you."

Corrie pulled back one inch. One very telling inch. "Oh, Rugar, you're wrong." Her throat constricted around each word she uttered, so that her voice sounded forced. "The queen would never do such a thing. She endorsed our marriage, sponsored our vows in her own apartments, and even gave our wedding feast. She's a noble woman—wise beyond knowing, and moral and upright—compassionate beyond our deserving. Think, Rugar—she might have imprisoned me or banished me from court for my dishonor, and she might have done far worse to you. But she chose to forgive and to have us marry instead. Why would she have you abducted and sent from the country after insisting that we marry?"

Her disbelief was physically painful to him. Her loving, loyal heart, her innocent spirit, could not believe ill of anyone she loved, not even when they used and manipulated her, as the queen had. As he himself once had. And as much as it hurt him to disillusion her, he had to make her see what Elizabeth had done, how ruthlessly she had dealt with them and why he'd had to take such drastic measures with her future.

"Why?" she demanded stubbornly, her chin aquiver. "Why would she do such things?"

"Because she's declared you hers, body and soul. Her favorite. Her pet." Then he added on a indrawn breath, "And because she hates my very liver."

She recoiled from his harsh tone, staring at him with pained confusion. "Rugar, you don't understand how it was between us." She pushed onto her knees, letting the cover slide. "I was her friend, the companion of her thoughts, the confidante of her feelings. She allowed me to see the trials of her queenhood and to hear the secrets of her heart; things she could share with no other. She was deeply hurt that I'd disappointed her and betrayed her standards—"

"No, it's you who doesn't understand," he declared hotly. "Elizabeth is a cold, grasping, devious shrew, who knows how to use flattery and a young gell's innocence to hold her captive. It was well known—she made it well known—that you were out of bounds to all the men of court and a goodly number of the women as well. She intended to keep you to herself, her own possession, for her exclusive amusement." He got up from the bunk, unable to bear the denial in her expression, and paced away. Then he turned back. He had to say it, had to make her see.

"Did you never wonder why no man ever asked you to dance at court?" When that seemed to register with her, he pushed on. "I can tell you why. When I showed interest in you that first night, she sent the Earl of Oxford and his men to warn me to keep away from you. And I cannot have been the first she'd banned from seeking you."

Each word burned deep into Corrie's vulnerable heart in a way Anne's bitter charges against the queen had been unable to do. Her care for him and her belief in him made it impossible not to listen. She had been a possession, a thing to be used, a trifle? The queen's diversion? She'd been avoided by the courtiers because the queen had declared they were to keep away? She thought of Sir Christopher, of Anne's charge that he'd been sent from court on her account, and of the queen's denial. Was it possible Elizabeth had lied to her? Even the questions, earnestly admitted, sent a breath-stealing stab of pain through her heart. She shook her head, resisting it with all her heart. "No . . . no . . ."

"She wanted you, claimed you. And as much as she loved you, she *hated* me," he insisted, frustrated by her disbelief. "We were both demonstrations of her power—you the scope of it, and I the limits of it." He stalked back to the bunk and stood over her, his eyes aflame, his hands clenching and unclenching at his sides. His voice dropped to an ominous growl. "She hated me because I challenged her and I *won.*"

"What do you mean, you won?" But the moment she asked, she dreaded the answer. She had never imagined him like this. Beneath his rumpled doublet, his chest and shoulders swelled frighteningly, and she could see the slow-coiling fury in his posture.

"A battle of wills raged between us from the day I arrived at her court. And I bested her on every front." He hurled each word like a javelin, and each struck her reeling heart, dead on center. "I defeated her soft English champions and

taught both her and her jaded, dissipated courtiers respect
for Swedish might at arms. I outdanced, outgambled, and
outgallanted her pathetic English swains, putting their pro-
vincial English ways to shame. And then the final stroke . . .
I stole her precious pet from her."

Corrie was dumbfounded by the loathing in his voice
and face when he spoke of the English, and by the vengeance in his voice when he spoke of besting Elizabeth.
But her deepest shock came from the raw, pulsing triumph
in his tone when he spoke of stealing her from the queen.

Stealing her. Her heart sank like a stone in her breast as
her mind fastened on those words. He spoke of her as if she
were a prize, a lifeless trophy, the spoils of his conquest of
a queen's pride, rather than a flesh-and-blood woman, a
loving, giving being who had shared the deepest, most intimate parts of herself with him.

"You stole me?" She forced the words past the painful
lump in her throat. Tears welled in her eyes, mercifully
blurring the sight of his beloved features now hardened by
vengeful anger. Was that truly what he thought of her? She
was a "thing" to be won and possessed? She blinked, dis-
lodging tears to roll down her cheeks.

"I was her plaything?" she whispered, anguished. "And
you stole me?"

Their gazes met, blazing blue to pain-singed green. She
searched him desperately, seeking some trace of tenderness
and warmth, finding only gall and bitter marrow. That acrid
mixture began a terrible alchemy within her, turning all the
precious faith and trust she'd borne him into base metal.
She lowered her eyes and turned her face from him.

The sight of her sitting in her bare smock, her eyes filled
with sorrow, slowly penetrated his fog of anger, and it
began to lift. He'd hurt her, he realized. Her loyalty and
innocence, the qualities that made her unable to see Elizabeth's darker side, were part of the same loving nature

which had blinded her to his own carnal schemes and made her see only goodness and worthiness in him. In his determination to expose Elizabeth's ruthless possessiveness of her, he'd inescapably bared his own base and wretched motives toward her . . . and put at risk all that had been good and right between them.

His stomach did a slow, burning grind.

She had been a prize at first. But only before he'd seen her hug a reindeer, listened to the joy in her music, been beguiled by her questions, and reveled in her lush, irresistible sensuality. Only before he'd fallen deeply and irrevocably in love with her. And how could she believe him if he told her that now? He had to try.

"Kari—" He sank down on the edge of the bunk and reached for her hands, but she shrank from him, feeling as if she were looking at a stranger. They were the same handsome features, the same silky blond hair, the same long, graceful frame. But the man behind that face, inside that beautiful, noble form, was altogether different from the tender lover who had come to their marriage bed with a crown of ribbands in his hands. This man despised her queen, spoke harshly of her home and her people, and reduced her womanly heart to an object, something to be coveted, acquired, and perhaps discarded at will.

She didn't know this hard, angry man at all. And yet he held the deepest and most precious parts of her, her love and her dreams, in his hands. She'd given them to him.

"No, Rugar, you didn't steal me," she whispered, her voice ragged with hurt. "I'm not a prize granted the victor in some contest of wills. I'm a woman. I have a heart and a mind and a God-given will of my own. You didn't steal me." She couldn't hold back the tears anymore. "I gave myself to you."

Her words landed like a punch, square in the middle of

him, and he blanched. "Kari—" He reached for her shoulders, but she pushed back, resisting him for the first time.

"My name is *Corrie,*" she said with tears streaming down her cheeks. "I am English, remember?"

Trembling, he rose to his feet and stood looking at her with aching eyes, then stumbled from the cabin. And Corrie put her face in her hands and sobbed.

Torgne had carried Anne kicking and screeching from the cabin. When the door slammed behind them, he found himself in the cold, drafty passage, holding a half-naked Fury by the waist and feeling doom settle over his straining shoulders like a cloak. He spotted the door of the small cabin he'd been assigned and dragged her toward it while she flailed and roared unladylike threats. By the time he had wrestled her through the doorway, her feet were back on the floor, and she'd begun to turn in his arms. She wrenched one arm free of his grasp and wriggled about—coming suddenly belly to belly with him.

"You'll pay for this—"

Her arms snapped up and her hands arched—nails pressed into the tops of his cheekbones, set to rake him stem to stern. But something—the tightness of his arms around her or the controlled intensity of his hard frame pressed against her half-naked body—stayed her vengeance for one exquisitely agonizing moment.

Molten passion soared inside her. With her shift raised and twisted about her, she could feel every part of him along the length of her body. His steel-thewed arms all but crushed her against his hard chest and ribs, and his long muscular thighs, and the thick bulge of his manhood seemed to burn against her body. She absorbed the strength that bound her in a parody of a lover's fierce embrace; drank in the feel of his smooth, taut skin beneath her fingers;

searched the full, insolent curve of his lower lip; and breathed the salty, musky male smell of him.

Heat sworled in her tawny eyes, a parched desert heat, craving a drenching shower of passion, burning for the sweet flow of love in her drought-stricken depths. Her heart pounded wildly as she dragged her fingertips down his cheeks, leaving a trail of tingling flesh instead of red marks. And as those passion-gentled fingers slid to his lips and traced them, she felt herself going molten inside. Such full, velvety lips . . .

His body was beginning to tremble against hers. She caught the scent of the oncoming storm, felt the rumble of approaching thunder in the flesh and marrow of him.

The need between them erupted . . . massive, searing . . . too explosive to continue. She shoved against his chest and won unexpected release. Staggering back, she caught herself and stood balanced precariously between raging and bursting into sobs. She feared letting him speak; a single word of disdain from him, and she would shatter. So she tossed her blond head and lifted her chin with desperate sensual bravado.

"The next time you set hands to me, Swede," she challenged in a throaty rumble, "it had better not be to restrain me."

He fell back a step, then another, then ducked out the door, slamming it behind him. Anne's knees buckled, and she sank onto the nearby bunk. Her entire body was trembling uncontrollably, aroused to a fever pitch. Desperately she wrapped her arms across her aching breasts and about her waist, as if afraid she might fly apart.

Never. She had never felt anything like this before. It was a pure sensual rage, a primitive, elemental hunger that consumed both sense and sinew. And this roaring, voracious need had been aroused in her by stern, moralistic Torgne Sigurd. Not Chris Leighton, or even handsome Rugar

Kalisson, but by that great, surly Swede with his hard body
and big hands, his stormy gray eyes and bold, disdainful
mouth. By the man she'd battled and despised for his self-
righteousness.

Her golden eyes flew wide. How perfectly hideous of
fate to do this to her!

Torgne stumbled up the steps onto the deck with his
knees trembling and his chest heaving. He lurched to the
railing and turned his face into the wind, letting it draw
heat from his burning face. He closed his eyes to quench
the telling flame in them and was engulfed again in the feel
of a wriggling body . . . so soft against him, so curvy and
voluptuous and hungry. His lean, hard cheeks tingled anew
from the feel of her fingertips, and his lips itched so that he
dragged his teeth harshly over them. He was speechless
with horror. Anne of Bosworth. Wanton Anne. Witty Anne.
Wayward and waspish and wily Anne.

The turmoil in his body and senses sent him into full
panic. He was trapped in close confines with that beautiful,
seductive, half-naked *temptation* . . . for the next fortnight!

He groaned. Was that any way for the good Lord to treat
an upstanding Lutheran?

The halls of Whitehall's royal apartments trembled like
a web when the spider stalks across it. The black-clad
queen surged along the main corridor with her guardsmen
at her back and her servants and courtiers scurrying from
her path. She stormed into the apartments she'd granted to
the Count and Countess of Aelthar to see for herself what
had been described to her minutes earlier.

As reported, the princely bed was stripped of comforters,
and the bolsters lay strewn about. The cold brazier had been

overturned, and the wardrobe stood ajar, with garments tumbling from it onto the floor. There was not a trace of Lady Corrie.

"Gone," she croaked, her throat half paralyzed with rage. "The bastard's taken her."

She flew through the halls and chambers to her private closet, sending pages scurrying and shouting orders to the captain of her guardsmen to search the palace from top to bottom. She sent immediately for Jack Huntington, who was preparing to leave for Straffen, and for Morris Lombard, who was being fitted for a new suit of clothes in anticipation of his advancement in the royal service. Both paled at the summons and hurried into the queen's inner sanctum.

"You!" Jack Huntington roared as he faced Morris Lombard. Something foul must be afoot with his old enemy, Morris Lombard, present. When the queen related that Lady Corrie was missing, Jack pointed furiously at Lombard and declared him the culprit.

"Don't be a horse's arse, Straffen," the queen snapped. "He's the one who abducted your son-in-law and put him on a ship bound for Stockholm." She turned to Lombard with dangerously narrowed eyes. "He was put on board the ship, wasn't he?"

"Yea, Your Grace. By my own two hands!" Lombard protested.

"Then explain to me how the bastard managed to abduct my Corinna."

Lombard paled and shuffled and stammered.

Elizabeth's face flushed hot with fury. "You little wretch, how much did he pay you?"

"N-nothing, Your Grace, I swear it! I delivered him, and the ship left this morn with the tide!"

"The cur lies—" Jack snarled, lurching at Lombard.

"Enough!" Elizabeth caught him by the sleeve, then cast a furious eye over her erstwhile spy. "I'm of the same opinion as the earl, Lombard. Something smells rotten about your failures of late. But what matters now is getting my Corinna back. And you will most certainly succeed when I hold your family in the Tower as surety against further failure." She smiled vengefully as he went chalk white. "She has left the country without my permission, a *treasonable* offense." Her eyes darted as her mind worked. "One which justifies sending a ship and her father and my agent to arrest her and bring her back."

"Arrest her?" Jack was appalled.

Elizabeth's smile was the essence of cunning. "Quite. I doubt I should get my privy councillors to stand the expense of the venture if I told them I was 'rescuing' the gell from her lawfully wedded husband."

Chapter Sixteen

That evening, as the cold daylight faded, Corrie sat on the bunk in the chilled cabin with her knees drawn up, sniffling. She'd cried until she'd run out of stamina for it and now leaned her head against the wall at the head of the bunk and wished her racing mind would simply stop. Yesterday she was a bride of one glorious night with eyes only for her handsome, charming husband; now she was a bride of two days with eyes red and swollen from crying over her catastrophic marriage. Yesterday she'd been restored to the queen's favor and was sleeping in chambers once reserved for visiting royalty; now she was stuck on a ship bound for an icy foreign land, with no clothes, no shoes, and a husband she didn't seem to know at all!

She hugged the comforter she'd pulled from the bunk tighter about her, fearing in her depths that she'd never feel warm again. A bitter wind had blown through her heart, chilling it, and as long as it was cold, the rest of her could never truly be warm again.

Her last words to Rugar drummed relentlessly in her head: she had given herself to him. Now with the harsh clarity of hindsight, she revised them: she had thrown herself at him. She had schemed and connived and flaunted herself and chased after him like an innocent—ignorant!—

little fool. She'd been so eager to experience life, so hungry to learn the joys of love, that she'd ignored all else. She'd rushed headlong into things she knew nothing about, taking events and people at face value, trusting that they were what they seemed.

She should have known better; she'd certainly been well warned. The memory of her father's face and voice came to her above the clamor of both sense and recall: *"At court . . . men and women . . . using deceits to satisfy their foul urges for lust and power."* Then came Elizabeth's sage observation: *"At court . . . appearance and impression become all-powerful. Then who can say when impression becomes illusion?"* And the sage little scholar in her head stepped forward: *"A clean glove oft hides a dirty hand."* But she'd ignored all such advice and caution, pursuing her own disastrous course with Rugar until they were caught and it was too late.

Had it all been illusion, then? Had her wretched ignorance made Rugar and her love for him into something too wonderful to be real? He'd been so considerate, so gallant, so noble . . . and all the while he was tallying the damage every kiss, every caress inflicted upon a queen's pride. His golden, manly perfection had cloaked dark motives . . . the dirty hand inside a beautiful, pristine glove.

There was a noise by the door, and she looked up to find Anne scurrying back into the cabin, wearing a threadbare blanket, which she quickly traded for the thicker, warmer comforter she'd dropped earlier.

"Anne, are you all right?" Corrie stared at her tousled form, suddenly remembering her screams.

"I'm half bloody frozen," Anne declared shivering as she climbed next to Corrie on the bunk, rubbing her chilled legs and feet together to warm them. "And I'd give what's left of my virtue for five minutes with a brush." She paused in the middle of pushing her tangled hair back over her shoulder and stared in alarm at Corrie's red eyes and swollen nose. "You look terrible, Cub. What did that cur do to you?"

"I . . . Rugar . . ." The wretched tears started to fall again. "Anne, I've made a terrible mistake, marrying him. I should have begged for a cell or a nunnery instead."

Compassion filled Anne's expression. She sat back against the wall and opened her blanket enough to slip an arm around her cousin. "It can't be that bad, Cub. Tell me."

Corrie drew a deep, shuddering breath and blurted out: "Rugar hates both England and the queen, and he bragged that he *stole* me from her—like some peddler's trinket! And worst of all . . . he's nothing like I thought he was."

To which Anne replied: "Faith! Hordes of people hate moldy old England, and legions more hate our viciously virginal Bess. He undoubtedly *did* snatch you from Bess's suffocating clutches, Corrie, and he deserves nothing short of undying gratitude for it. You'd have been a cloistered virgin until you were too old to remember what made you one!" She paused as she considered Corrie's last lament, and her tone softened.

"As for the rest . . . shockingly few women marry the man they think they're marrying, Cub. But it's probably a mercy on us all." She sighed. "Do you think I had any idea when I married my Bosworth that he'd bedded half the noblewomen in England and a quarter of the peasantry?"

"Lud, Anne." Corrie's eyes widened as she began to understand what the baron's prodigious philandering meant in real human terms. She looked at Anne with fresh insight and a new bond of womanly compassion.

"It was a disillusionment, I'll say," Anne admitted wanly. "But we got past it, Cub. Later, he would waggle his brows at me and say he'd just been practicing . . . to get it right for me. And oh, Cub, he did get it right for me, both in bed and out." Her eyes misted for the second time in Corrie's memory. "He wasn't a perfect man, Bosworth. But he was perfect for me, and that was all that mattered." Her smile was bittersweet. "Whatever your Swede has done, Corrie, you must find a way to get past it."

They sat in silence for a long while, each sunk in separate musings, each contemplating an unknowable future.

"They didn't mean to take you, you know," Corrie finally said. "They thought you were Maudie."

Anne's eyes narrowed to slits as her head turned. "Thanks ever so much. Being mistaken for a frump of a tiring woman just caps my day."

The only human they saw that night was a young cabin boy who brought them a tray of food, two extra blankets, a pail of cold water, and a brazier of sizzling hot coals. When they asked questions, the lad stared blankly at them, then scowled, and they realized he spoke no English. Corrie ventured one of· the few Swedish words she knew, *"Tack,"* and was rewarded with a smile and a deep bow.

They devoured the hot stew, bread, and strong ale, washing what body parts they dared bare to the cold water, then huddled together around the brazier to warm themselves. Corrie regarded Anne with a forlorn expression.

"I suppose we'd best get used to the cold. This is probably what Sweden will be like. Rugar said it gets too cold even to sin."

Anne looked at her, horrified. "'Pon my arse—then let me off this bucket! I'm not going!"

The next morning, it was ale and cheese and bread and another box of coals. Corrie tried to make the cabin boy understand that she wanted to see the tall blond nobleman, but to no avail. Then she and Anne took turns walking up and down the cabin.

"I've worn this blanket for so long, I'm beginning to feel like a horse," Anne said tartly, then scowled. "A horse without a rider." She wriggled suggestively, and Corrie stifled a shocked laugh.

Anne picked the strangest times to get "itchy."

But they weren't to wear blankets much longer. Rugar and Torgne appeared in their cabin, midmorning, with grim faces and unpleasant news. The captain had confined them to the cabin for the duration of the voyage, due to their lack of clothes. Anne groaned in outrage, but Rugar hastened to offer an alternative. Torgne had managed to smuggle one of his trunks aboard the ship before they were abducted, and they had rounded up a few spare garments amongst the ship's officers. If Corrie and Anne would agree to try to alter and wear them, they would be granted permission to go on deck while the seamen were belowdecks.

There really was no decision to make. The clothes were brought, and after some awkward explanations of what went where on the body, Corrie and Anne were left to fit themselves into male garments. Their own smocks made do as shirts and were tucked into trunk hose, while leggings were trimmed, rolled, and gartered. Doublets and sleeves were tucked, stitched, and donned. Then the only pieces missing were hats, ruffs, and shoes.

That evening, Rugar swung through the opening when they called for him to enter. He paused, staring at them, trying not to let his eyes slide down their revealingly clad legs. "You look like young gentlemen," he remarked, his eyes fastening on the front of Corrie's oversized green doublet. He was suddenly remembering how she looked in his own doublet a few nights ago, and how she'd felt. Sharp longing shot through him from heart to groin, followed by abrasive guilt.

The night and day just past had been the longest of his life. He'd paced Torgne's cabin and deck above, his fists and jaws clenched until his hands and head ached. He'd gone over every angry, arrogant word he'd said to her, again and again, and each time he shriveled a little more inside. His only excuse was that he'd been hurting physically, still furious at the queen's treachery, and frustrated by Corrie's stubborn faith in her jaded sovereign. A whole continent lay between them now, placed there by his vengeful pride and her loyalty to a queen who wasn't fit to touch her skirts. He had to talk with her, to try to set things right between them. Their future, their life together hung in the balance.

He came to his senses to find himself standing in silence, staring at her in her boyish garb. "Well, it seems you get your wish, wife," he said huskily. When her eyes slid into his, his voice and gaze softened. "I recall distinctly: you expressed a desire to try wearing breeches instead of hoops and farthingales."

Corrie, engulfed by the azure of his eyes, was unable to move or speak. He had just conjured in her memory the most important night of her life.

"I'm still missing shoes," Anne declared, eyeing the promising exchange between them. "But I cannot wait another minute to get out of this stifling cabin!"

They scarcely heard the door close behind her. They stood looking at each other, testing the turbulent waters between them. Finally Rugar took a step closer and spoke.

"Corrie, I never meant to hurt you." He paused and swallowed hard.

She searched the earnestness in his eyes and felt her heart stirring around the hard lump of pain and disillusionment. Did he mean to be honest with her now? And if he was honest, if she truly learned what sort of man he was and all that he had done, would her love for him survive?

It wasn't wise to hope for much, the wounded part of her heart cautioned. But in spite of that pained little skeptic inside her, she nodded, accepting his words as the apology they were. His shoulders relaxed noticeably, and she realized that his anxiousness matched her own.

"I believe it is best that you know the truth of why I came to England. Then if you judge me harshly, at least it will be on what I have done, not on what you fear I've done." He offered her his hand and led her to a seat on the bunk. He backed away and stuck his thumbs in his belt, fastening his gaze first on the toes of his boots, then on the wooden sideboards of the bunk, then on the hands that she clasped fiercely in her lap.

"My father came as ambassador to England years ago, on a mission to win Elizabeth's hand for our Crown Prince Erik. I was young, only twelve years, but I came with him to learn of England and of the diplomatic trade. From the start, Elizabeth abased my father and ridiculed his attempts at wooing. She denied him a proper ambassador's lodging and place at court, even while greedily accepting the gifts he brought from our prince. For months I watched the English whisper and snigger at us, and mock our use of their language and our 'clumsiness.'"

Anne's derisive description of the status and character of Swedes suddenly returned to Corrie: they drank like fish and fought like devils, but could not dance or sing, and "they garb themselves like gawky peasants gone to market." Corrie had dismissed her words as simply another bit of Anne's insolence or, at worst, sour grapes. Rugar was the only Swede she'd ever met, and he was handsome and accomplished, the very essence of courtly elegance and grace. But Anne's crass summary now lent veracity to Rugar's story, and Corrie blushed, chagrined, as more of her wretched ignorance fell away.

"Elizabeth was the worst of all, sitting high upon her dais, laughing in her sleeve at our attempts to please her." His eyes darkened with old pain and loathing. "My father was no skilled courtier. He could wield a sword and buckler the day long, and he could negotiate peace terms with a man-eating ogre. But he could not dance, or play the lute, or compose pretty verse. Elizabeth bullied and humiliated him to make him take the dance floor; then, when he obliged, she hurled insults at him. 'Prithee, someone give that Swede a hand; he cannot get his knees up past his girdle!'" he mimicked bitterly. "'Better yet, get a hoist and tackle for the ambassador. God's Teeth, but they grow these Swedes large . . . a pity they cannot grow them with feathered heels as well!'"

Rugar's every word carried smoldering heat. "It was bad enough that he was humiliated before the English court, but our own delegation witnessed it as well, including Duke Johan. Upon our return to Sweden, Erik, now king, attacked and banished my father from court for the scorn Elizabeth had heaped on him and upon Sweden. A lifetime of service and loyalty crushed beneath Elizabeth's vain and reckless heel. Eventually he was pardoned, but his pride . . ." Rugar drew a shuddering breath. "The time for statesmen was past, he believed; the world would be run henceforth by peacocks and toadeaters, pretty fellows whose skills ran to fawning, dancing, and deceit. Two years later he died . . . of a heart that no longer wished to beat."

As dark emotions swirled in Rugar's face, Corrie was assailed by memories of her first impressions of him. Elegant, powerful, handsome, courtly, noble . . . perfect. The perfect courtier. He had both challenged and charmed the English court; he'd been unstoppable with weapons and arms, and irresistible without them. *He had become all that his father had been and*—the insight staggered her—*all he had not been. Perfect.*

"I learned to dance as well as to fight," Rugar continued, watching her with a tight, defensive expression. "I studied both arms and the courtly graces all over the Continent preparing myself . . ."

"To return to England," Corrie whispered, her heart sinking under the recognition of the source of that darkness in his countenance. She could scarcely say it. "For revenge."

Rugar met her eyes briefly, then turned away, pacing to the window and bracing an arm against the wall as he looked out over the cold, wind-whipped waves.

"I swore when my father died, I'd teach that whore Elizabeth a lesson in things Swedish. And when the king ordered me to London as his ambassador, I knew the time had come. I was prepared. I intended to take her wretched tournament by storm, to embarrass her paltry champions as she had embarrassed us." He took one ragged breath, then another, as if gathering the strength to say it. "And I intended to woo and win the hearts of her ladies from her . . . to steal the loyalty due her as she had stolen the loyalty due my father."

It was like a blow to Corrie's stomach. She could scarcely breathe. She struggled up from the bunk, fighting back a surge of tears. "You needn't say any more," she choked out, starting for the door.

"Corrie—" In a flash he was blocking her way. She tried to dart around him, but he grabbed her shoulders and held her fast as she squirmed in his grip.

"Please, just let me go—" She strained her face away from him, hoping to escape before a wall of tears came crashing down on her.

"Corrie, listen to me! I have to say it and you have to hear it, because we both know it's true." He groaned, grappling with her wriggling form. "I courted you at first to spite the queen. You were her pet, her prize." Corrie lost her struggle against tears and against his superior strength; she stilled in his hands, tears burning down her cheeks. "But make no mistake, Corrie"—he paused and his voice softened—"I wanted you, from the first moment I set eyes on you. Look at me, Corrie."

She shook her head and kept her eyes shut against the sight of him. It hurt too much to look at him, to love him so and to know that he'd sought and used her love only as a means of revenge. His hands fell away and her eyes flew open—just as he grabbed her about the waist and hoisted her, carrying her to the bunk and dropping her on it.

"Ohh! Stop—*no!*" She gasped, arching and straining as he levered his body down over hers, trapping her with uncanny precision. "Please—don't do this—"

"Corrie," he rasped, sliding his arms beneath her shoulders and propping himself up on his elbows, cradling her as he braced above her. He took her head between his hands and turned it, making her face him. "Look at me."

Her heart was convulsing in her chest. Why was he doing this to her? Was he so determined to punish her for her disastrous pursuit of him and their forced marriage?

The silence between them was deafening. After a long moment, she finally opened her eyes. Rugar was staring at her, his face filled with pain.

"You turned all my plans upside down. You were everything I wanted and nothing I expected. You honestly couldn't dance, but you kissed like the sweetest little wanton. You chased reindeer and surprised me with all manner of questions about my home. You translated Latin for me and made brazen, public love to me with your music." As his words recalled their encounters and the feelings that had passed between them, Corrie began to remember more.

"Each time I saw you I grew more enchanted. Somewhere along the way you ceased to be just a prize and became a woman to me, a bright, enchanting, desirable young woman. And everything got confused—my desire for you, my desire for revenge. Lord help me, I tried to give you up. I didn't want to take your innocence or to have you caught between the queen and me. I wanted to protect you. I honestly tried."

He *had* tried. Oh, how he'd tried! She bit her lip, letting his warm words penetrate her chilled inner recesses. They soaked into her heart, thawing it, bathing it in new warmth that freed the hope frozen inside. He had wanted to protect her; he must have cared something for her!

"But I didn't want to be protected, I wanted to be—" She bit back the word "loved." "I wanted to learn, to experience the feelings between a man and a woman. I knew you wanted me, and I thought you were being noble, rejecting me because . . . you didn't want to marry me." The pain in his laughter was so close to a sob that her heart contracted.

"Lud, how much more do I have to confess?" he asked. "I didn't honestly think about marriage one way or another. I only knew I wanted you, and I was deathly afraid of ruining you. I'd never felt that way about a woman before, never put a woman's needs ahead of mine. But when I watched you . . .

"You sparkled, Corrie, from deep inside you, like sunlight dancing on waves." His eyes became bluer still, matching the velvet persuasion that crept into his voice. "Everything seemed so good and wonderful and fascinating to you. You were so eager for life, so untouched by the darkness of the world. So innocent."

"Ignorant, you mean—" she choked.

"No." He touched her cheeks until she looked at him. "Innocent. It's nothing to be ashamed of, Corrie. Rather, it's something to be treasured, a precious part of you that goes beyond virtue, a rare quality of looking for the good in things and in people, and always managing to find it. Too many of us have our innocence wrenched from us before we realize that we have it." Pain glinted in the depths of his eyes as he drew a ragged breath and told her what he'd only revealed to one other living soul.

"I lost mine at the age of twelve, in England. The innocence of both my body and my heart. I was cozened and petted by Elizabeth's court women, then foully seduced . . . and then I had to watch as my father was whittled to insignificance before my eyes." Her breath caught in her throat as she watched his eyes fill with mist. "I swore then I'd never take another's innocence. And then . . . you gave me yours."

That old hurt now reached across the years to them, and she felt the ache that must have been in his boyish heart. If only she could have been there for him.

"Your innocence is dear to me, Corrie. In you I can enjoy the wonder and faith I was never allowed. Perhaps that was what drew me to you on that first day, at the tournament. You looked so fresh and unspoiled and lovely, so unlike the other court women."

"But I'm not so unlike them," she confessed ruefully. "I schemed and chased and tempted and seduced—" He put his finger against her lips to stop her.

"No more than I had. And, heaven help me, I don't regret any of it . . . except the tears you've shed." He brushed away her last teardrops with his fingertips.

"None of it? You're not sorry you had to marry me?" She held her breath.

"Not one bit."

"Even though I'm English?"

"You'll always be more 'Corrie' to me than 'English.'" It was the perfect answer, his way of telling her he had separated her from his distrust and dislike for England, from his revenge, at last. "You'll always be the heart of me, Corrie. The finest and best part of me. You've given me back so much that I'd lost. I want to live with you, to make my home around you. And yet I think that can only be in Sweden now. Do you mind so much, me taking you to my home?"

"No, Rugar, I don't mind," she said, beaming. "I've always yearned to see other lands, to experience the wider world.

Now, with you, I have the chance to do it!" She threw her arms around his neck and pulled his head down to hers, sharing her joy with him in the most direct way possible.

Passion rose with their spirits, and soon their hands and kisses roamed, claiming the sweet pleasures of their love and renewing their vows to seek their future and whatever it would hold, together.

When Anne left the cabin, she looked around the narrow whitewashed passage, which contained several doors, then mounted the short rise of steps toward the daylight visible through the hatch door at the top of them. A damp, chill breeze swirled around her as she stepped out into the cold sun and onto the dry wooden deck. She was struck by the activity all around her: men scrubbing, climbing ropes, mending sails, hauling and checking lines. And as she approached the railing, staring up into the maze of rigging and canvas above her, she became aware of slowing activity and of male eyes turned her way.

She had no chance to see more, for Torgne Sigurd suddenly loomed before her, demanding that she go below. He dragged her through the hatch and down into the relative privacy of the cabin passageway. "We've an agreement with the captain that you won't go on deck unless his men are below. He and most of his crew believe it's an abomination, next to blasphemy, that you're garbed in men's clothes."

"Well, I cannot stay in there!" Anne jerked a thumb over her shoulder toward Corrie's cabin door. "Corrie and that beast of hers are . . . talking . . . and I have no place else to go."

His jaw flexed noticeably, and after an awkward moment, he shoved her toward his own cabin door. He tried hard not to look at her shapely legs or to think about the fact that her lush breasts were rubbing against the inside of his doublet and her rounded bottom was wriggling about in a pair of his breeches. It was a sure route to sin and madness, thinking about Anne Bosworth's tantalizing body inhabiting his clothes. But he couldn't keep his eyes from sweeping her, and he couldn't stop the heat and pressure from collecting in his loins. And when she turned in the cabin to face him, he couldn't help staring at the flash of white that appeared through a slit at the front of the breeches she wore.

"Good Lord, woman, what have you done? Where are the rest of my breeches?" His long, angular face flamed as his eyes widened on the sight.

Anne looked down at the small slit in the front of her belly, where a suggestively padded rectangle of cloth was missing; then she raised her chin, narrowly overcoming a burst of chagrin. "You mean my codpiece? Forgive me— *your* codpiece. I refuse to pretend to parts I shall never have."

"It's more than—they're supposed to cover the front!" he declared hotly. "They hold the bloody breeches together!"

"I'm smaller around. I simply tied the sides themselves together," she declared, sticking her thumbs in the tied band to demonstrate. "It's bad enough I'm stuck in your clothes— I refuse to wear one of those male contraptions of yours! They're vulgarly huge . . . monstrous, in fact." Her tawny eyes burned a trail down his front to his codpiece, and she added wickedly. "Not very modest of you. Do they represent the truth . . . or are they just wishful thinking on your part?"

Torgne's jaw dropped. She was utterly shameless—the most brazen woman he'd ever met! Excitement raced up his body like rasping tongues of flame, and he was seized by an urge to possess her, to tame that naughty mouth and claim the forbidden pleasures she exuded like perfume. He was suddenly fully aroused, trembling, afraid to move lest he betray his state. His voice came deep and fierce.

"You've a foul mouth for a woman, Anne of Bosworth."

She was achingly aware of his arousal and of the way he

struggled with it. That great sinewy cat of need again prowled the backs of his darkening eyes, clawing at him, roaring, eager to get free. She took a shivery breath and threw down her sensual gauntlet.

"There's only one way to sweeten it, Torgne Sigurd."

It took half an instant for her ultimatum to sink in. His face darkened visibly. He lunged at her, and before she could even gasp, she was banded by his steely arms, clasped fiercely against his hardened body, and being kissed to within an inch of her life. His mouth was hot and rapacious, demanding total surrender, pulling from her every bit of passion she possessed and wrapping her in it, engulfing her with it. She caught flame against him, clasping him, pressing closer as she opened helplessly to the masterful penetration of his kisses.

Suddenly she was being lifted by the waist and carried onto the narrow bunk with him. She moaned as his body covered hers, reveling in the way her soft woman's frame accepted his weight, giving, molding to him. With her trapped securely beneath him, he gentled, his mouth tasting, teasing, dancing over hers. Then his hands flew to the buttons and ties he knew so well, and in moments his hands were sliding beneath his former garments onto the soft, velvet-tipped mounds of her breasts and around the silken flare of her hips.

He invaded her smock and pulled her breeches from her in a sweet frenzy of desire. He knew just how to touch her, knew just how to make her squirm and sigh and press against him, wanting more. Then she felt his touch at the center of her femininity, and warm surges of pleasure flooded upward and outward, sweeping through her whole body. She held onto his shoulders as he caressed her, stronger, faster. She was so ready, so hungry . . . she

shattered into a thousand white-hot embers and cried out
his name.

She lay in his arms, quivering, stunned by her own
volatile response. He was still against her, his eyes were
stormy with the deep emotions churning visibly in his core.
He raised his hand to her cheek and caressed it tenderly,
then rolled from the bed and strode for the door.

Two great bounds brought him up onto the deck in the
chilled December wind. His whole body was screaming
protest; his senses were in turmoil. Stumbling to the railing,
he faced into the wind and closed his eyes. She rose in his
mind's eye as she had risen from the bunk when he left in
a tangle of half-shed garments, her blond hair tumbled
about her shoulders, her eyes luminous with release, and
her lips bruised from his kisses.

He was shocked to his marrow. He wanted Anne of
Bosworth past all morality, past all reason. In her kiss he'd
felt things he never imagined existed. His lovemaking had
always had a dour, furtive sense about it, which became
shame-tainted in the light of day. But with tart-tongued
Anne—daring, delectable, defiant Anne—he wanted to
plunge into his desires, wanted to wallow shamelessly in
them, revel in them, glory in them! And he somehow knew
he'd feel no gnawing regret afterward. Just passion, free,
pure. Just *Anne*.

He fingered his bruised and throbbing lips. What was
he doing just standing here—he had to talk to her! Hell—he
had to love her!

He blew through the hatch, ignoring the steps to land
directly on the passage floor, and raced for the door. He
stepped inside the cabin and stopped dead. It was empty.

He bolted out into the passage, trying every unlocked
cabin door. He found her seated in the captain's cabin,
being poured a civilized cup of wine. He stiffened with a

dour expression that scarcely covered his chagrin, declined to join them, and backed out the door—but not before he caught the burning accusation in her tawny eyes.

Hypocrite.

As he closed the door behind him, he knew she was right. He pulled himself up the steps into the comparative comfort of the frigid sea wind, thinking that he probably should have strangled her when he had the chance.

That night, as Corrie and Anne supped in their cabin, Rugar and Torgne appeared to offer Anne the use of Torgne's cabin for the remainder of the voyage. Anne regarded Rugar through narrowed eyes. "Eager to get on with married life, are we? As much as you've inconvenienced *me,* I should sleep with your wife for the next ten years!" Then she turned haughtily to Torgne. "And where, pray, will you sleep, Baron?"

"B-belowdecks, or with the crew, I suppose." Torgne scowled and reddened.

"Won't that be terribly discomfitting for you?" Anne purred.

"Very likely."

"Good." Anne turned to Rugar and Corrie with a fierce smile. "Then I accept."

That night Torgne watched Rugar slip into Corrie's cabin with a knowing smile and felt roundly irritated. He started for the crew's quarters in the forecastle of the ship, but the door to Anne's cabin swung open, and he froze. When no one stepped out, he made his feet move toward the dim, seductive glow coming from the opening, dreading what he'd find.

Anne stood inside the doorway, wearing her smock, her feet bare and her fair hair twisted into a rope that hung over one shoulder. He braced his arms against the frame as if afraid of being pulled inside and felt his blood start to pound in his veins. In the lamplight, he could see the outline of her body beneath the thin garment and small, erotic bumps where the tips of her breasts nudged the fabric.

"My bed is soft and warm, Torgne Sigurd." Her voice was filled with exotic promise. "And you're welcome in it. But you must say what I need to hear, first."

"And what is that, Anne Bosworth?" Torgne managed a dry whisper.

"You know," she said quietly. After a moment, she closed the door and left him standing in the passage, his face, his blood, his whole body aflame with the want of her.

No, dammit, he didn't know. He didn't even have a clue!

Chapter Seventeen

The next afternoon, Corrie came up on deck for the first time. She was amazed and a little frightened by the unending expanse of sea around their vessel. She knew of the sea from her studies, had pondered and charted its great distances in her head. But until now she'd had no way of understanding how truly immense it was, or how small it would make her feel. She stood by the quarterdeck railing, looking out over the dazzling, sunlit water, realizing that her world had just expanded a thousandfold. She began to understand how such vast distances could separate people, cause their ways to diverge, and allow them to mistrust each other for their differences.

She caught sight of Rugar, amidships, and watched him striding back and forth, exercising his long legs. She saw him with wiser eyes now. He wasn't perfect; she was mildly chagrined that she'd ever thought he was. But, as Anne had said of her Bosworth, Rugar was perfect for *her,* the mate to her body, her mind, and her spirit. And having seen the whole of him, his loves and hates, his beliefs and feelings, having experienced both his bitterness and his joy, she felt closer to him. They had weathered a fierce storm, a test of their love, and they had survived.

In Sweden, they would start anew, just the two of them.

Just Corrie and Rugar. A new land, and a new life. They were from two different countries, two different cultures. There would always be some part of that between them. But knowing that, she determined to work all the harder to make their life together a good one. She would come to love Sweden, she knew she would. There must be a thousand things to love about a country that Rugar loved as much as he did his home. And she was determined to find and love every one of them, too!

When Rugar joined her by the railing, he found her eyes sparkling and her face flushed with excitement. "Starting right now," she declared, grasping his sleeve and pulling him against her, "I want you to talk to me in Swedish. Slowly, so I can hear it all, and repeat it."

He laughed, surprised. "Well, what shall I say?"

Her eyes caught on the fiery crimson streaks in the sky and the great orange ball of the sun as it set. "The sky, the sunset, the weather . . . And tell me how to say 'My name is Corrie Kalisson.'"

He smiled handsomely, took her into his arms, sensing why she was so eager to learn, and gladly obliged her.

The rest of the fortnight's voyage passed with surprising speed. Corrie worked hard at learning the Swedish words for commonplace items and actions and simple phrases. She enlisted Torgne to help with her lessons, too, and tried to get Anne to join her. But Anne snorted in contempt.

"I have no need of Swedish, beyond a few foul names for stubborn servants and balky horses, and"—she glanced pointedly at Torgne—"*difficult men.*" He reddened tellingly. "Besides," she continued, "I shan't be staying in Sweden long. Your husband has agreed to buy me a new wardrobe and to provide me with funds for servants and passage back to England as recompense for the hardships I've suffered.

I shall stay in that frozen, barbaric wasteland only long enough to collect my due; then I shall gladly be on my way!"

While Corrie and Rugar reveled openly in each other's company and positively glowed with newly wedded love, they watched with increasing distress as relations between Anne and Torgne plummeted steadily. Anne's changeable, irascible moods and Torgne's increasing stoniness made it difficult for Corrie and Rugar to have both friends in the cabin with them at the same time.

They had no way of knowing that Anne was purposefully, even gleefully, making Torgne's life pure torture. They didn't see the way she brushed against carefully chosen targets on his body whenever she passed him in the passage or availed herself of a door he'd opened. They didn't notice the way she drank her ration of wine with exaggerated pleasure, toying with the rim of her cup, letting the wine wet her lips, then licking it off—knowing he was hungrily watching every dart of her tongue. They did observe her new obsession with keeping her male attire in perfect order, but didn't mark the suggestiveness in the way her slender hands fidgeted with the empty front placket of her breeches and continually ran up her legs to straighten her leggings. Nor did they see the way she sometimes paused by his chair or rubbed, catlike, beside him against the railing when they were allowed on deck, whispering seductively, *"Say it."*

But they did hear her vaguely insulting references to the size of his feet and his dour, mirthless countenance. And they winced on his account. When Corrie made to speak to Anne about it in private, Anne scoffed and declared, "The wretched baron should be flattered to have attention of any kind, even abuse." Corrie was left sputtering and scowling.

* * *

On what the captain assured them would be the last night of the voyage, they had an especially good meal of hot stew, dried-apple pudding, raisin cakes, and wine instead of ale. Corrie was unusually quiet and not particularly hungry. Rugar astutely guessed that her stomach was already filled—with excitement and anxiety. That afternoon, he had made it a point to be near her as some of the first landmarks were sighted, pointing out bits of shoreline, telling her what he knew of them and what to expect in Stockholm. He'd glimpsed the nervousness behind her brave smile. Now, when Anne left their cabin and Torgne finally bade them a long-faced good night, Corrie turned to her husband with tears in her eyes.

"I feel as if something is ending . . . and I don't know what will take its place. And I can't bear the thought of Anne leaving us. I know you think she's difficult, but she's really very dear at heart, and I treasure her friendship."

Rugar wrapped her in his arms and drew her head against his chest. "I know she has been a good and loyal friend to you, sweet. For that reason, I shall be sorry to send her back to England. But in truth, I won't miss the scrape of her tongue one bit."

Topside, Torgne stalked the deck to and fro, staring at the moonlight dancing on the water and seeing in it the glisten of wine on Anne's lips and the shimmer of desire in her eyes. He knew that the moment they landed he'd lose her, first to Rugar's house in Stockholm, then to England again. He groaned at his own moonflaws and fancies—as if she were ever his to lose! He'd spent the better part of the past ten days trying to resist her, then trying to come to terms with his unholy fascination with her, then trying to figure out what it was she wanted from him, besides the obvious. He had the inescapable feeling that with a woman like Anne there would always be lots of things that weren't obvious . . . and he was a pathetically "obvious" sort of fellow. All she had to do was glance at him and he was hot as a tavern poker. All she had to do was smile at him, which she had done all of twice in those miserable ten days, and his spirits soared.

What was it she wanted of him, what was it she needed to hear as much as he needed to touch her? It was his last night, his last chance. . . .

Anne sat on the bunk in her cabin, staring at the door, dying a little more inside with each minute that passed. She'd been so sure it would work. She'd been convinced her taunts and seductions were bearing fruit. Bosworth would have succumbed long ago and had her flat on her back . . . and probably six other ways as well. But Torgne Sigurd wasn't Bosworth, wasn't anything like him at all. Torgne was upright and stern and hard and uncompromising . . . and he had hands like a magician and a kiss like a tiger. Time and again she had found herself staring at him, watching him move, absorbing the way he used his hands, and examining the tilt of his head when he was in thought. Now she thought of how tall and strong and proud he stood, and imagined what sort of children he would make.

Children. She bounded up from the bunk to pace, hoping the chilled air would distract her. Thoughts of children always made her feel vulnerable and a bit wounded. She had wanted them so badly, and Bosworth always said there would be plenty of time, that he wanted her to himself yet a while. He'd taken steps to see that she didn't conceive . . . then he'd died and left her childless. It was the one thing she could not bring herself to forgive him for. And now she wanted Torgne Sigurd's powerful loving and wanted children and wanted to wake up next to him of a morning and wanted to complain about his big boots being left in the middle of the floor . . .

No more than a heartbeat later, those big boots thudded to a halt outside her cabin door and those big hands hovered, then seized the latch.

She skittered back as the door flew open. Torgne ducked inside, and when he straightened, her mouth drooped. His eyes were like molten silver coins, and his tall frame was coiled as if to attack. He trapped her gaze in his, and all the raw need in his body focused in his throat as he said it.

"I want you, Anne. Dammit—I need you."

She blinked, then gasped as her heart gave a wild lurch in her chest and burst open, freeing all the love and passion trapped inside. Explosive with joy, she snatched up the tail of her smock and launched herself into his arms, wrapping her arms and legs around him, calling out, "Torgne—yes, you big, stubborn Swede—yes!"

Somehow, between kissing her madly and holding her, he managed to kick the door shut behind him. Then he carried her straight to the bunk and sank onto it with her. His kisses were breathtaking, hot, and voracious; everything she'd remembered and more. She opened to his deep, plundering strokes and whimpered as his hands sank beneath her to knead and caress her back and shoulders, then her neck. She shifted beneath him, seeking his touch on her meagerly clad breasts and moaning when he found them with his hands, then his mouth. He was hungry, so hungry—and she could scarcely wait. Her fingers flew to his buttons and his ruff and then his shirt—he wore so many cursed clothes! He slid from the bunk and quickly shed his clothes, even his hose, with no thought of modesty.

Her eyes glistened as she watched his lean, hard body

emerging, and when he was naked and straightened, she gasped, staring at him. Her eyes grew round as goose eggs as she watched him slide onto the bunk with her and pull the comforter over them. As he took her into his arms and began to cover her throat with kisses, she managed a heated whisper.

"We'll never fit."

"Yes, we will," he murmured against her breast as he bared it. "Trust me."

She curled her fingers into his sober brown hair and used it to lift his head so that she could see his eyes. They were shimmering, smiling, matching the wry cant of his broadly curved mouth. "I do trust you," she said softly. "I don't know anyone I trust more."

He laughed, the most wonderfully lusty and triumphant sound she'd ever heard—a deep, rolling, thrilling vibration that seeped through her entire body. Then he gradually fitted himself into her creamy softness and proved just how trustworthy he truly was.

There was no time for quiet passions, for deep gazes and sweet caresses. The tensions between them demanded a full storm, a raging fury of release. He clasped her fiercely, possessing her with the white heat of his mouth and the burning rod of his passion. Her senses blanked to all but the powerful awareness of that gorgeous impalement and the searing-hot motion of him within her, around her. He plunged over and over, and she met his every thrust, driving harder, faster, taking him deeper . . .

Her senses peaked, then exploded, and her body convulsed as wave after wave of fiery release roared through her. She clawed at his back and moaned his name over and over, in a crescendo of ever wilder response. Then he flexed and spasmed as his own release cut him free from mortal bounds, flinging him after her into those vivid crimson realms of pleasure where sense and sensation faded and being—being together—was all that mattered.

They lay together for some time, unable to move, content to savor the sweet, steamy feelings lingering in their passion-charred bodies. When at last he stirred and moved to lie beside her, she turned to face him, feeling all manner of confusing emotions: awe, elation, fascination, and even fear. He lay facing her, his head propped on his hand, his eyes smoky, his aquiline features softened, burnished and beautiful in the glow of spent passion. As she felt the tenderness of his hand on her face, the final padlocked door of her heart swung open, a door she'd thought would never open again.

She sat up quickly and drew her legs up, wrapping her arms about them. Her expression was pained, bewildered, and she dropped her head to hide her face against her knees.

"Anne?" Torgne sat up beside her, concerned by her sudden withdrawal. He ran a hand down her bare shoulder and felt her respond . . . with a shiver or a shudder? "What is wrong?" His throat constricted. "Did I hurt you?"

She shook her head, but her lashes and cheeks were wet, and she swiped at the tears as if trying to hide them.

"I . . . I . . ." She straightened her legs and slid toward the edge of the bunk, fumbling in the covers for her smock. "I . . . I . . ." She eluded his hands by scrambling off the bunk and backing toward the far side of the cabin, clutching the garment to her.

For the first time since Torgne had met her, Anne Bosworth was at a loss for words. A wave of tenderness crashed over him, then subsided, leaving a sweet ache in his chest. He'd never imagined her crying, or embarrassed by her own tears. Vulnerable Anne. The ache in his middle grew to grand and splendid porportions. Lovable Anne.

She watched him come toward her with that superior male prowl of his and drew back, wishing she could hate him for being so self-possessed when he'd just shattered every defense she had and reduced her to tears. She hadn't really cried since Bosworth's death. When he reached for her, she struggled. When he dragged her onto the bunk with him, she braced against him. When he pulled her onto his lap, she wrested in his grip and resisted him. But he managed to put his arms around her all the same and held her close.

"Let me go! I really—I cannot—"

"Tysta!" he hissed, pulling her head against his chest and holding it there, above his heart. She struggled for a minute longer, then slowly went still.

"What does that mean, 'tisssta'?" she demanded.

"It means 'hush.' Hush . . . and let me hold you." She sat stiffly, struggling with her chaotic emotions as she listened to his steady heartbeat. Then he added, "And let me love you."

She wilted completely against him, turned her face into his bare chest, and sobbed. Minutes later, she slipped her arms around him and said into his tear-dampened chest:

"I guess it is possible . . . *twice in a lifetime.*"

Torgne frowned, puzzled, then grinned and gave her words his own interpretation. "It's possible more than that, my little cat. More like . . . twice in a night." His devilish grin coaxed a teary smile from her. "Trust me."

She did trust him.

And *twice in a night* it was.

Stockholm lay beneath a thin blanket of new snow that made the steepled spires and housetops glisten in the cool winter sun. Corrie and Anne were hurried from the ship and bundled into an ornate covered cart and given thick fur lap robes to cover their boyish garb, while Rugar and Torgne mounted and rode just ahead of them on horses that

Rugar always kept at a hire stable near his city house. They wound their way slowly through the docks, to the din of creaking wheels, clopping hooves, thudding and trundling barrels, the cries of gulls, and the flurry of human voices chattering, talking, and shouting—in Swedish. Those voices, rattling on quickly, were the first significant indication that they were in a foreign land.

Until that moment, Corrie had watched with equal measures of disappointment and relief the familiar sights and sounds of Stockholm's harbor. It was surprisingly like London harbor, and it struck her that it was possibly like every busy harbor on the Continent, since these ships necessarily sailed between countries. Stockholm itself, seen from the mouth of the harbor, seemed very much like London, too. The buildings were of stone, brick, and timber, stacked close together along narrow streets, punctuated by occasional spires and towers. It was a city built atop islands, thus filled with waterways and connected by bridges.

Corrie's heart was thudding wildly as she peered around the cart's canvas covering. She strained to make out distinct, recognizable words in the clamor of noise and voices around her. The people in the streets wore mostly woolens, though a few showed costlier velvets. The women wore caps and shawls and skirts tucked up out of the dampness, and the men were garbed in doublets and simple breeches, hats and boots—not so very different from what might be glimpsed on a London street. Tousle-headed children—ruddy fair—darted into the street and were warned off by the cart driver with a snarl that needed no interpretation.

"Isn't it wonderful?" She turned to Anne with a beaming smile and was too preoccupied to be surprised that Anne glowed with good humor and agreed. "He says his house here is modest, but that it's both close enough to the palace and far enough away from it to be ideal. And he keeps horses in town. Did you see that gray he is on? Oh, I wish we could have ridden instead of being stuck in this cart."

"But we can't possibly be seen in public until we've some decent women's clothes," Anne reminded her primly. "Who knows but what they still stone women here for such an offense."

Anne seemed so serious that Corrie laughed. But she knew Anne was right to be concerned. They had agreed on the strategy of slipping quietly into the city and into Rugar's house in order to have some time to acquire proper clothing for Corrie and Anne, and to give Rugar and Torgne time to prepare some reasonable explanation of their ill-fated mission to Elizabeth's court. Rugar and Torgne had reason to be nervous about the king's reaction; they were fiercely aware of the trouble they'd stirred by abducting the female heir to an English earldom and an English baroness from the English court and then carrying their contraband females straight to Stockholm. And they knew that news of their disastrous flight from England might not be far behind them—possibly on the very next ship that docked from England.

The ride to Rugar's house took them over two bridges and past copses of trees and occasional open squares, where pushcarts and wagons displayed merchants' wares and farmers' stock. They drew up before a warm red brick house, nestled snugly among several others on a well-tended thoroughfare. At street level there was a large double door with an iron ring knocker and one very small window, but above, where the house rose to five stories above the street, there were larger windows of leaded French glass.

Rugar ushered them past a bowing footman he called Jens and up a set of steps to the second floor. Servants came running from upstairs and down, their faces flushed with surprise that their master was home unexpectedly from his great journey abroad and had brought guests. A dignified woman in black, wearing a pristine white cap and a girdle draped with keys of office, came hurrying from upstairs, shouting what appeared to be orders to the gawking servants. She was introduced as Fru Ola Nilsson, the housekeeper, and the hoary-headed fellow in somber velvets who came puffing up from the storehouse in the lower levels was introduced as Steward Ars Berg. They curtseyed and bowed, respectfully. Then Rugar announced that Corrie was *Grevinnan* Corinna Kalisson, their new mistress, and the other guest was *Friherrinnan* Bosworth, their new countess's kinswoman from England.

The pair blanched with shock, then flushed as their eyes widened with stifled horror at their new mistress's shocking appearance. Their reaction, Corrie noted uneasily, was exactly what she'd feared, and she hastened to practice her best servant-greeting in Swedish, to which they nodded in bewilderment and bobbled awkwardly again.

Rugar hastily explained that the women's garments had met with a misfortune during the voyage and that they required immediate assistance. He delegated Herr Berg to quietly send for the best seamstresses and cloth merchants in the city, and ordered Fru Nilsson to freshen the beds and make the chambers and kitchen ready for them. As the servants hurried off to do their master's bidding, Rugar led Corrie, Anne, and Torgne upstairs to the family quarters.

The family apartments contained large, airy chambers with tall ceilings that were trimmed liberally with carvings. The walls were plastered and painted white, and the floors and wooden trim were made of dark, mellowed oak. Each chamber contained a bottle-shaped earthenware stove decorated with colorful glazed tiles. The furnishings were an odd but pleasing assortment of stately carved pieces, imported from the capitals of Europe, and brightly painted and intricately decorated pieces that displayed the skill of

Swedish craftsmen. In each of the upper chambers there were large, well-curtained beds, richly colored Swedish weavings, which hung side by side with elegant tapestries collected in Rugar's travels, and assorted trunks, chests, tables, and chairs. And in the master's chamber there was a princely bed, hung with sendal green brocades, and two thick Persian rugs that made Corrie feel as if she were walking on pillows.

"It's beautiful, Rugar, all of it." Corrie beamed up at him, then insisted he say it back to her in Swedish so she could tell him in his language as well. He laughed and obeyed, then took her into his arms and gave her a kiss before Torgne's throat clearing made him recall where he was.

"I've been thinking, Rugar, perhaps I should stay here with you for a while," Torgne intoned gravely. "Opening my house as well will only make our presence in the city twice as evident."

Rugar agreed, but assigned him to a chamber on the next floor up instead of the one beside Rugar's, where he had usually stayed when passing the night under Rugar's roof. That chamber, Rugar declared, would be Anne's. He escorted them into the next room and waited tensely as the haughty baroness surveyed the handsome bed and turned to him.

"It's quite enough for my needs, your lordship," she said demurely. "Quite charming, actually."

They stared at her in complete surprise.

That evening, after a fine supper of fresh and smoked fishes, capon, and roasted veal, which was served in the hall on the second level, the foursome retired to an upstairs withdrawing room, where servants had stoked the stove. The chamber was surprisingly warm, and they settled close around the stove. Anne and Corrie removed their shoes and baked their feet for the first time in weeks.

Rugar glanced at Torgne, then raised the delicate subject

of Anne's unfortunate status as the "victim" of their abduction. "Corrie is married to me, and a strong case can be made in common law for a man having the right to carry his legal wife with him, whether or not a monarch approves. But our unintentional abduction of you, Baroness, an English noblewoman unrelated to me or Torgne, has taken the situation from a 'domestic matter' into the realm of an international affront. In English eyes, you are being held hostage by a foreign nobleman who, as an ambassador, can be seen as acting in his sovereign's stead. A rather sticky problem, you will concede, for two men who were sent to England with the mission of *improving* relations between our two courts."

Anne listened intently to Rugar's dilemma and, afterward, sat quietly. "Then my abduction puts you in grave difficulty?" she questioned, as if clarifying things in her mind. "You could be punished, disgraced, or at least chastised for your hideous treatment of me?"

Rugar nodded grimly, recalling Anne's earlier threats.

"Well, that won't do a'tall," she declared in a shockingly sweet tone. "There is no earthly reason that anyone should object to my accompanying my newly married cousin to her new home for a visit. For surely that is what I've done, accompanied my dear cousin . . . of my own free will."

Rugar went slack with surprise, and Corrie jumped up to give Anne a sound hug. But it was the glow of promise in Torgne Sigurd's eyes that brought a smile to Anne's lips.

Later, in their stove-warmed chamber, as Rugar peeled Corrie's boyish garb from her, perhaps for the last time, he remarked on Anne's apparent change of heart. "I could scarcely believe my ears: 'of my own free will.' You don't suppose she'll change her mind, do you?"

"No. Anne is a very honorable woman, Rugar," Corrie answered, dancing away from his hands toward the great bed and climbing into it. She slithered under the pan-warmed covers and held out her arms to him, her eyes full of deviltry.

"Now quit worrying so much and . . . come and 'Rugar' me."

Torgne Sigurd, tiptoeing past Rugar and Corrie's door a moment later, heard her triumphant squeal. His face reddened, but his eyes glowed that much hotter. Anne's door was unlatched, and he slipped inside to find her brushing her hair by the stove, clad only in her smock. He crept up behind her and slid an arm around her waist to pull her back against him, where she melted. His other hand traveled down her flat belly to rest with gentle possession on her woman's mound.

"This has been the longest day of my entire life." He groaned into her neck as he nibbled her. "Seeing you, wanting you . . ."

"Ummm." She smiled dreamily as her eyes closed. "Tor, when you love me tonight, tell me everything you're doing to me . . . in Swedish. Slowly, so I can learn the words."

"Hmmm?" He lifted his head and breathed into her ear. "That sort of Swedish has few applications. Wouldn't you rather have a tutor, like Rugar has promised Corrie?"

"Let her learn her way," Anne said, laughing, "and I'll learn mine."

The next three days were a quiet flurry of activity in the Count of Aelthar's household. Merchants, tradesmen, and seamstresses were trundled secretively in and out, behind closed doors, receiving lucrative orders from the handsome count for his beautiful new wife and her kinswoman. Corrie and Anne were stunned to be able to choose from a rich, colorful array of French velvets, taffetas, and brocades; Flanders silks, Venetian and Alençon laces, and the greatest surprise of all, *knitted* stockings. In England, the queen herself had only recently begun to wear hand-knitted silk stockings!

The clothing worn by Sweden's wealthier nobility, they quickly learned, was the equal of courtiers' anywhere on the Continent. "Who would have thought it?" Anne mused. "Fashionable Swedes." Apparently King Johan and his predecessor, King Erik, had taken pains to bring the court and the nobility into current Continental fashion by appropriating and importing the best of Italian, Spanish, and French arts, manners, architecture, and clothing styles . . . just as the English had so eagerly done.

With a judicious use of coin, Corrie and Anne were able to obtain a complete gown or two that had been intended for other patrons, and were able to again dress as ladies, which smoothed some of the dour lines from the housekeeper's forehead and made Corrie breathe easier.

When the fabrics for the rest of their new clothes had been chosen and the merchants and seamstresses withdrew to their workshops to begin cutting and stitching, Corrie turned her attention to her pursuit of Rugar's native language and the workings of his comfortable household. She drifted from chamber to hall to chamber, naming aloud the objects she saw, practicing phrases, and speaking directly with servants, who frowned or stammered as they answered her imperfect queries.

Table, chair, window . . . *"bord, stol, fönster."* Rain, snow . . . *"regna, snöa."* Isn't it cold today? . . . *"Är det inte kallt idag?" "oktober, november, december . . ."*

She stopped dead, standing in the midst of the master chamber, where she practiced aloud. *December*. It was well along in December—a fortnight, no, three weeks into the month. Then it must be . . .

"Christ Mass in three days," she murmured aloud. A peculiar, empty feeling opened in her, and images of her last Christ Mass flooded in to fill it. Her mother and father . . . her twin sisters . . . the lavish and boisterous feasts that marked the celebration of Yuletide at Straffen Manor.

She swayed on unsteady legs. How long would it be before she saw her family again? Would her mischievous, red-haired twins be grown and married and settled, with passels of children of their own? Shaking off such gloomy thoughts, she submerged that homeward longing in her determination to make a life with Rugar in Sweden. There was no better time to start than with a joyful occasion like Christ Mass. Perhaps she could surprise Rugar by arranging for a few traditional Swedish observances.

Corrie located Fru Nilsson directing servants who were cleaning the great hearth in the dining hall on the second floor. With a resolute smile, she settled before the dour housekeeper and inquired in her most careful Swedish, "I wish to learn your customs for Christ Mass . . . Yuletide. Tell me, please?"

Fru Nilsson regarded her blankly, lifted her nose a bit higher, and tightened her already taut mouth a bit more. Nearby, the lesser servants paused in their work to stare at Corrie and exchange speaking looks.

"Yuletide . . . Christ Mass . . ." Corrie prompted, resorting to English, wondering if the words could be so different in Swedish. "Customs . . . like Yule logs, feasting, hanging the greens . . . ?" Oh, how did she say such things? A flush of frustration trickled into her cheeks as the silence around her deepened. The housekeeper shook her head as if she didn't understand, but the look she wore contained an unmistakable taint of satisfaction. Did she truly not understand, or did she simply refuse to speak with Corrie?

"Fru Nilsson, please," Corrie said quietly, her throat constricting as the other servants rose to their feet and stood appraising her in a critical manner. "Yuletide? Christ Mass?" The silence elongated and grew pointed, aimed at her like an arrow. She recoiled a step, feeling utterly isolated and alone. "Is there no one who can answer me?"

"Yuletide?" came Rugar's voice from the arched door-

way behind her, and Corrie whirled to find him leaning a
shoulder against the frame. His eyes glinted as he spoke in
clipped English. "Surely you remember Christ Mass, Fru
Nilsson. The word is *Jultid*. It sounds the same in both languages. You *do* remember?"

The housekeeper blanched and nodded, fidgeting with
the ring of keys dangling from her waist. She had understood
her lord's English words well enough, and the displeasure
they both concealed and conveyed.

"Then by all means, answer your lady. And make yourself understood."

"Ve make *julstock* . . . Yule log, *grevinnan*. Ve make
much feasting. And Santa Lucia comes in a *krona*—a
crown—of lights," the housekeeper said with a guarded
expression and a notable waver in her voice.

"Much like England, except for our little Lucia," Rugar
commented, strolling forward to take Corrie's hands in his
and kiss them with telling reverence. "I shall have to explain about her. Lud, Christ Mass is upon us—I hadn't
given it a thought."

"I hoped to surprise you . . . only . . ." Corrie said quietly,
embarrassed at being caught in such a strained encounter
with the head of Rugar's household.

"And I *was* surprised." His smile wrapped her in reassuring warmth. "But now I shall have the pleasure of teaching
you our customs myself." The tension in her shoulders melted
under his masterful charm.

Rugar sent her up the stairs ahead of him and paused
long enough to impale Fru Nilsson with a furious glare. His
voice came deep and ragged. "I will not permit such insolence toward my wife. She is *mistress* here, in this house.
And you will give her every assistance, answer her every
question—or you will find yourself in the streets! Do I
make myself clear?" When the ashen housekeeper swallowed hard and wobbled a deep curtsey, he turned to the

other servants, extracting chastened nods and bows from them as well.

Minutes later, he found himself in the hallway at the top of the stairs, his fists clenched, his gut tight. He had returned to the house just in time to witness his servants' disrespect to Corrie. It had never occurred to him that the household staff who had served him for so long would behave sullenly or resentfully toward his bride. How dared they!

But as he paused before his chamber door with his hand on the latch, he forced himself to calm and thought more reasonably about the incident. They were servants, after all, with little experience beyond the narrow confines of their duties and their small area of Stockholm. And they were accustomed to an uncommon amount of independence during his frequent absences. They would have to adjust to Corrie's role and authority, just as she had to adjust to her new life among them. He vowed to be more watchful in future, to see that Corrie's experiences in his household were worthy of her eagerness to embrace his home and his people's ways.

"Now, about Christ Mass," he declared as he swung through the doorway.

Corrie turned to him with a bone-melting smile and a renewed determination to learn Swedish ways and thaw the suspicion in Rugar's household. She spent the rest of the afternoon in Rugar's loving tutelage.

Christ Mass was indeed celebrated, with the traditional greens and log and a small but lavish feast. Rugar relented to Corrie's desire to attend church service on the eve of Christ Mass; he and Torgne escorted her and Anne to a late service in the great Riddarholm Church. The next morning, one of the servants' daughters played the part of Santa Lucia, bringing the master and mistress of the house honeyed buns and ale in their bed. The foursome spent the rest of the day in quiet pursuits, playing cards and tables, talking, listening to Corrie play the virginal, which Rugar had managed to purchase and smuggle into the house for her. After a number of songs, which Rugar sang to her accompaniment, Corrie looked up to find the doorways to the main hall filled with Rugar's servants. A number of them were even smiling.

Despite the precaution of long, concealing cloaks and the lateness of the hour as they attended church, Rugar and Torgne had been noticed and recognized. Thus on the very day after Christ Mass, a courtly older gentleman dismounted at the street door, asking if the count had indeed returned, and, after some consternation amongst the staff, was shown upstairs and into Rugar's presence. A short interview later, the fellow hurried off to the palace with news that Rugar Kalisson had come home . . . and with an English bride!

The next morning, the king sent messengers for Rugar and Torgne, and they bade Corrie and Anne farewell as if trudging off to the executioner's block. At the last minute, Corrie recalled something she and Anne had seen in Torgne's trunk when they were aboard ship. She ran up the stairs, returning minutes later with a long object wrapped in dark velvet. When she drew back the cloth, there in a velvet-lined box lay the solid gold arrow Torgne had won as an archer.

"Tell him that the queen sends it to him . . . as a token of how his offers of friendship have found their target in her heart," Corrie proposed breathlessly.

"You are a devious little thing," Rugar quipped, grazing her lips with his as he took the arrow from her. "I keep forgetting that. Pray your gambit succeeds, sweetness, or your career as a *grevinnan* may be short indeed."

* * *

It did work. Red-bearded King Johan listened to Rugar's colorful recounting of tournaments and banquets and interviews and appointments with numerous councillors and ambassadors. Then he informed them that Elizabeth had already sent him a letter, which had arrived less than a fortnight ago, thanking him for the magnificent gifts and for sending the Count of Aelthar as a gallant addition to her stellar court.

"So yes, yes, you were a splendid success"—he waved an impatient hand—"but what of this bride I hear you've brought us? And what in heaven are you doing back so soon? I expected you to stay the winter at least."

"My bride." Rugar reddened and looked a little pained. He searched the eager glint in his godfather's eye and the way he scooted forward in his chair. "I beg you to be forgiving with me, Majesty, for I'm afraid it is a bit of a tale." The king had apparently sensed something was afoot and now grinned, settling back in his chair and calling for wine.

"I'm of a mood for a good tale."

Rugar spun a precariously candid story of his courtship of Corrie, starting with the tournament day, when he'd first seen her, and taking roguish male credit for all of the seduction that had led to their marriage. Then he admitted that he'd cut short his stay in England because his wife's family was vehemently opposed to the marriage, even though the queen herself had sponsored the vows and given the marriage feast. He ended by saying, quite truthfully, that he prayed his abrupt departure from England would not injure relations between the two courts.

Johan was greatly entertained and obviously satisfied with, perhaps even a bit envious of, Rugar's performance on all counts. He jovially insisted on giving a dinner to introduce Rugar's bride to the court. And Rugar and Torgne left the palace feeling buoyant . . . as if they'd been given a second life.

But when they arrived home, Corrie was less enthusiastic about the honor the king was about to do her.

"Four days hence? But, Rugar, I haven't a thing to wear!"

Chapter Eighteen

Corrie did find something to wear: a lovely gold brocade bodice and overskirt which were trimmed with fanciful gold wire embroidery on green velvet bands at the neckline and skirt hem. Her voluminous sleeves were of the same exquisite green velvet, smocked and lavishly embroidered with gold wire, and her French-style cap and silk hood were adorned with pure gold biliments. For the first time in her life, she wore a proper Spanish farthingale beneath her skirts and felt and moved like a true court lady.

Rugar had tutored her in Swedish court ranks and greetings and had helped her create a proper Swedish speech to use in greeting the king. She practiced it over and over in her head, then aloud. She was still practicing when the covered cart drew up to the street door. Rugar gave her a hasty kiss, then tucked her into the conveyance beside Anne for the trip to the palace.

The palace was ablaze with light. Torches hung in the main courtyard and lined the halls of the long stone corridor leading to the hall where the banquet was held. They were scrutinized closely as they passed elegantly clad nobles who dotted the corridors, and Rugar nodded to acknowledge friends and acquaintances. Corrie tightened her grip on his sleeve and reminded herself that the banquet was being given to celebrate Rugar's marriage; it was only natural that they would be the object of attention.

In the banquet hall, King Johan and Queen Katarina stood on a stepped dais, before a massive head table draped with white and hung with great embroidered estate cloths and fragrant evergreen boughs. Rugar bowed and Corrie curtseyed. At a wave of the king's hand, Rugar lifted Corrie by the hand to present her to his sovereign as Lady Corinna Huntington Kalisson, the new Countess of Aelthar.

"Välkommen, grevinnan . . . och gratulerar!" The king extended his hand, his smile growing as she curtseyed deeply again and pressed his ring to her forehead. Finally, she spoke her Swedish piece.

"May God bless you for this generous welcome, Gracious Majesty. And may I prove a worthy addition to your realm."

"By the north wind, Aelthar . . . she's a treasure," the king declared, clearly delighted with her. When Anne was introduced as a baroness and Corrie's kinswoman, the king's admiration for English femininity overflowed, and Corrie was pleased to understand: *"Vakar, skön . . . den engelska!"* Beautiful, lovely . . . these Englishwomen.

The moment the king released them, they were swarmed by curious guests. Corrie smiled determinedly as she strained to decipher one word in five of what was spoken to her. It was a pure mercy when a footman approached and guided them to a seat at the foot of the main table, in plain sight of the assembly, and the music and serving began. Torgne was seated some distance away, according to his rank, and Corrie found herself separated from Anne and seated between Rugar and a number of older, austere-looking ladies wearing dark velvet and pinched expressions. Rugar introduced them to Corrie, and she greeted them properly and tried to converse with them.

"How lovely the king's hall is . . . such a wonderful carved ceiling," she said in her accented Swedish.

They regarded her in silence. Had she used the wrong word? she wondered. *Innertak,* "ceiling" . . . *snideri,* "carvings"? She drew a deep breath and tried again.

"The food and drink are delicious."

Their eyes narrowed ever so slightly, and they glanced at one another, then smiled condescendingly at Corrie. She blushed and looked down, going over it frantically in her head: *Mat och dryck . . . . delikat.*

Through the balance of the serving, whenever she ventured a comment or question, one of the ladies chose a word she had spoken and repeated it behind a concealing hand, giving it that peculiar emphasis which implied some deficiency in either the choice of word or its pronunciation. Their icy responses set Corrie's heart thudding and her hands chilling.

Whenever Rugar turned to her, she smiled as sweetly as she could and hoped he hadn't seen her poor efforts or the ladies' reactions to her.

But he *had* seen, and his handsome smile had frosted noticeably. The influential old cats were taking exception to Corrie's Swedish. It was subtle, of course, but not so subtle that Corrie would miss it. He found himself coiling with irritation at having Corrie's impressions of his fellow nobles tainted by such vile company. They were acting worse than his wretched servants! Soon the old cats began to whisper amongst themselves, eyeing Corrie and her gown disapprovingly. Their behavior, in so prominent a place in the banquet hall, was observed by a large number of the guests. As soon as the servants were called to move back the tables for the dancing, Rugar whisked Corrie away to seek more congenial company.

All watched the handsome count squire his countess

about the hall, and while some remarked on the striking pair they made, an equal number whispered that he would have done better with a *Swedish* bride. Among those present were several mothers and maids who had been disappointed in their campaigns to bring wealthy Rugar Kalisson to the altar. They were inclined to see his foreign wife through jaundiced eyes, and their disapproval spoke loudly to husbands and fathers who could not afford to seem too eager to welcome another man's wife.

The king himself strolled out to speak with them, and when he asked Corrie a few simple questions in his language, she endeavored to answer him in kind. Her pronunciation was good for her having studied the language for so short a time; there were only a few dropped sounds and misplaced words. Rugar studied her pale face and determined smile, and glanced around them at the critical expressions evident on some faces.

Then she mentioned that Rugar had followed Swedish custom and made her a *huvudla* . . . only she confused it with *huvudlös* and said he made her "featherbrained" instead. The king chuckled indulgently, but a number of others laughed raucously, their mirth a thin cloak for derision.

Corrie's face flushed hotly, and Rugar's began to glow red. He felt her embarrassment as if it were his own, and it roused a jumble of painful feelings and memories in him. In these familiar faces he saw scorn and condescension that he'd never witnessed in them before, a disdain that darkened his countenance and stiffened his spine.

When the king insisted Corrie grant him a *dansa,* she cast Rugar a panicky look. But there was no gainsaying the King of Sweden, no matter how graciously she protested, and Corrie was soon escorted to the center of the floor.

It was her worst nightmare: being forced to dance before Rugar's people, with his king. It was a lively courante, and she was lost from the start. Her face flamed as she tried valiantly to follow his slides and handclaps and quirksome hops and turns. The king seemed surprised by her lack of skill and slowed his movements to direct hers, which put them all out of time with the music and only deepened Corrie's humiliation. She glanced up at Rugar, and the raw anger evident in his face caused her to stumble as tears sprang to her eyes. All around her she heard laughter that ranged from muffled sniggers to malicious hoots. She wished with all her heart that the floor would just open and swallow her whole.

Rugar watched helplessly as his own kinsmen inflicted such pain on her. He stared at the people around him, some of whom he'd known for most of his life. They were smirking, smiling, some laughing outright. Then he heard it, a harsh feminine rasp ending with "a fine sample of English grace," followed by more vile laughter.

He was suddenly murderous with rage. Trembling, he turned a scorching glare full upon the catty source of that remark. God, how he wanted to wring the old crone's scrawny neck! Then, one by one, he impaled the other smirking faces near him with his savage stare, and the laughter close around him slowly died. Not long after, the music died as well.

The king escorted Corrie back to Rugar and nodded to the dark question in Rugar's gaze, dismissing them. Then he brusquely ordered the musicians to play again, and the noise rose precipitously as he selected another partner. Rugar seized Corrie's hand and pulled her into the hall.

Corrie looked up at him through a haze of tears as he thrust her ahead of him, toward the entry court. He was crimson-faced, and a vein throbbed visibly in his temple. She opened her mouth to apologize, to beg his forgiveness, but the angry heat radiating from him caused her mouth to dry, so that the words stuck in her throat. Then he stuffed her into the cart and climbed aboard to drive them home himself.

"I'm s-sorry, Rugar," she managed to say in a small, constricted voice once they were under way. But his back was to her, and she had to scoot forward in the cart before she could touch his broad shoulders. He turned to her with his face set like granite and his eyes smoldering. His face blurred as tears surged in her eyes.

"I didn't mean to embarrass you. I tried to dance, I truly did. And I know now I shouldn't have tried to speak your language, but I wanted your people to like me and I thought . . . Please don't be angry with me." Her breath came in gasps as her heart twisted, anguished, in her breast. He was so silent, so stony, so deeply wounded that she grew frantic to build a bridge between them, even if it had to be made of the timber of her pride.

"I . . . I shall try to do better in future, I promise. I'll study Swedish every day—all day, if I have to—and I'll learn your customs and ways, and I'll even find someone to teach me to dance." Tears flooded her throat even as they burned down her cheeks.

"I'll try, Rugar, I truly will." Her voice dropped to a desperate whisper. "Only please . . . please don't be angry with me."

His face froze as his eyes fixed on her misery. He was a-tumult inside, and incapable of speech. Old memories and new ones mingled powerfully in him, evoking devastating feelings. Remembered shame and sorrow blew through his core like a typhoon, sweeping sense and reason in their path. He couldn't say anything to her—not with his whole world turning itself inside out. In pure chaos, he turned away and slapped the reins to race toward home.

Her heart shriveled in her breast, and she slumped onto the cold seat.

The cart lurched to a stop outside Rugar's house, and he blew past old Jens at the street door to carry her up the stairs to their dimly lit chamber. He laid her on the bed and stood watching her cry . . . wishing he could cry for her; wishing he could call out the whole damned Swedish court, one by one, to uphold her honor; wishing he could bash some sense and decency into the whole wretched, merciless world.

But he couldn't. He was just one man. And as wealthy and physically powerful as he was, he hadn't even been able to protect one loving, innocent heart which had been entrusted to his care.

He had to leave, had to move, had to somehow let this fury out of him. He rushed down the stairs and into the night with the sight of Corrie's tears digging into his heart like spurs.

Torgne and Anne arrived some minutes later and hurried upstairs to find Corrie weeping and Rugar gone. Anne sent Torgne to look for Rugar, closed the door against prying servants, and took Corrie in her arms.

"I made a fool of myself, Anne, and I embarrassed Rugar. Now he won't even speak to me," she sobbed. "I begged him to give me another chance. But he wouldn't talk to me or even look at me. Oh, Anne, what am I going to do?"

Anne choked back tears as she searched for some hope to hold out to Corrie. "He loves you, Cub, you know that. He's proved it these past weeks. This will pass, you'll see, and you'll talk and find a way to get beyond it." She rubbed Corrie's shoulder, feeling a burst of loathing so strong that it startled her. "Lud—those vicious old crones—I could have gleefully strangled them with my own two hands!

I don't think I've ever truly hated anyone in my life until tonight."

"He didn't want to marry a foreigner in the first place," Corrie whispered brokenly. "Now if he has to choose between me and his Sweden . . ."

"Hush, Cub!" Anne hissed, swiping at her own tears, then setting Corrie back to scowl at her. "You're working yourself into a state again. I'm going to get you some brandy from that bilious old trot of a housekeeper. Don't you move."

Torgne came through the street doors with his fists clenched and his lean face grim. He paused in the street, deciding which way to go, then turned in the most likely direction and strode off to search for Rugar. He didn't see the figures huddled at the edge of a small alleyway two doors from Rugar's house. But they saw him.

"It's one of them." The fatigue-ringed eyes of the Earl of Straffen cut through the gloom to study the retreating figure. "It's that brown-haired one, that baron. Now all we have to do—"

"I know what we have to do!" Morris Lombard snapped. He turned to one of the two rough-clad men with them and jerked a nod toward the door of Rugar's house. The fellow slipped around them and crept down the street to knock on Rugar's door. The footman answered and they spoke; then the fellow shrugged and left, strolling casually back toward the alley. He shook his head and uttered one Swedish word. *"Nej."*

No. A yellowed smile crept over Lombard's face. "The count isn't home either. This is our chance."

* * *

Rugar blew along the cold, wet streets of Stockholm like a dried leaf driven by the wind. The frigid night air provided meager relief, drawing some of the heat from his body and condensing the steam in his blood to an icy sweat along his brow.

For the first time in his life, he was ashamed of being Swedish. He'd always been fiercely proud of his home, of the basic goodness and decency of his people. He'd defended them time and again, lent his strong arm to uphold their honor at tournaments and on battlefields. He'd touted their virtues and sung their praises from one end of the Continent to the other. Whenever he'd been called or sent from his home into other lands, he'd carried his native land with him in his heart, enshrined there, noble and inviolate.

Now he'd brought his bride, his sweet Corrie, home to his countrymen, eager for them to love her as he did, eager for her to love them as well. But instead of accepting her, they'd rebuffed and ridiculed her. How could they do that to her, to someone he dearly loved? How could they do that to *him?*

His Corrie, who knew Latin and French and Italian, who played the virginal like an angel, who was lovely and learned and good and forgiving; they had treated her as if she were a common, ignorant little trull. She had worked so hard to learn their language and customs, and for love of him, was willing to make his home and people hers. And they had looked at her beauty and grace and seen the sweetness that shone in her countenance and declared that it wasn't enough. She was nothing short of extraordinary, yet none of the wonderful things she was mattered to them, all because she hadn't been born of their blood, on their soil.

Again and again, as he strode those icy streets, he saw their faces, heard their sneers and muffled laughter. Memories of another court, another humiliation, rose in his mind, and he saw the two wrongs side by side, past and present. His father and his wife.

For fifteen years he'd blamed Elizabeth and her cursed English court for the way they'd shamed and humiliated his father. It was a dread flaw in the English race, he'd convinced himself; they were by nature cruel, immoral, and self-serving. And now he had seen his own people display the same little-mindedness and prejudice toward his sweet Corrie. It was the past repeating itself, and it called forth double anguish in him.

He sank down on a low stone wall at the edge of a dimly lit square and put his head in his hands. Everything inside him seemed to be in turmoil: his beliefs, his standards, even his hatreds. He'd spent half a lifetime preparing to avenge a wrong, only to learn that the basis of that wrong lay not in the character of a country but in the character of mankind itself. And now as he looked deep into his own heart, he found traces of it even within himself.

If it hadn't been for Corrie, he realized, he would have gone along his destructive, vengeful course, never seeing the truth, never understanding that the goodness and decency of the human heart, like the deceit and malice of it, knew no national boundaries.

He got to his feet and stumbled along, knowing he had to purge both old loathings and new angers from his soul before he could face Corrie . . . and do what he could to make it up to her.

The rear alley door of the count's house was unlocked, and the hallway leading past the kitchen and the servants' hall was ill-lit and concealing. Four sets of feet slipped past the storerooms on the ground level and crept steadily up the main stairs. On the second level they froze and scrambled against the walls as a footman bearing an armload of wood came trudging up the steps behind them. In the dim light, the footman caught sight of one of the intruders and started to call out, but a stout truncheon came down against the back of his head. They waited to see if the noise would bring others. But quiet settled over the house, and they dragged the fellow aside and resumed their climb toward the bedchambers.

Anne heard the latch, but ignored it as a servant's noise. Suddenly remembering Rugar, she straightened and turned toward the door. A great burly figure lunged at her from close range and she jolted up, only to be caught and engulfed in a crushing hold. She struggled and opened her mouth to scream, but a cloth was stuffed into it, and her panicked cries sounded only inside her head as other men appeared and bound her hands and feet. She had just managed to realize that muffled cries were coming from Corrie on the bed before a heavy blanket was thrown over her head and she was hoisted and carried squirming in impotent fury from the chamber.

Corrie also fought her attackers, but her responses were dulled by the brandy Anne had insisted she drink, and soon they had stuffed a cloth in her mouth and bound her hands and feet. They hastily threw something over her head and hoisted her onto their shoulders. Through the haze in her senses and the darkness inside that heavy shroud, she could still make out that they were carrying her down the stairs, down and down. Was there no one in the house to see them? Surely the servants— She struggled against her bonds, but her captors continued on, and soon she heard the scrape of hinges and felt a cool blast of air about her feet. She was outside—they'd managed to carry her from the house!

No amount of thrashing hindered them, and she was lowered onto something soft and felt something heavy pressing over her. She squirmed and rolled partway onto her side, to get her face free. The smell of musty straw filled her head, and everything around her lurched into motion. She was in a cart. She'd been abducted from her home, from Rugar, and was being carried off in a cart!

Jack Huntington slouched in the front of the cart and glanced back at the precious cargo it carried: his daughter and his niece. He took a deep breath, but relaxed none of his guard as they wound their way through the darkened city, over bridges and through cobbled squares. Their long journey was now half over, but they would not be out of peril until he got them onto the ship and set sail with the tide. He found Morris Lombard staring triumphantly at him.

"I told you it would succeed, Straffen," he declared nastily. "No one manages an abduction quite like a Lombard."

That taunting reminder of the time Jack himself had been abducted by treacherous "Lombards" set Jack quivering with suppressed rage. "Curse you, Lombard! By the queen's command we're forced to work together on this mission. But bear in mind . . . the queen's orders don't require that we both return to England in one piece!"

Torgne returned to Rugar's house after nearly two hours of fruitless searching and found the place in an uproar. One of the footmen had been bashed senseless in the upper hallway, and when he was found and they hurried to tell the mistress, it was discovered that she and her cousin were missing! Torgne rushed upstairs and burst through every door, calling for them. On the empty chair beside the empty bed in the master chamber, he found a packet of parchment in their stead, bearing the name of Rugar Kalisson, Count of Aelthar. He stared at the elegant hand and at the impression in the wax seal which bore a chillingly familiar monogram. "ER." Elizabetha Regina. And he knew, without even reading its contents, that disaster had struck once again.

When the blankets were finally lifted, Corrie and Anne found themselves again aboard a ship, lying helpless on a cabin bunk. The ship was swaying and creaking around them, sure signs that they were under way. A short, scrawny fellow with a sallow face and dark, piercing eyes was working the ropes that bound their feet and hands. As soon as she was free, Anne dragged the wretched cloth from her mouth.

"Who are you?" she demanded, her chest heaving, her eyes flashing.

"My identity is unimportant," the man said smugly as he dispatched Corrie's bonds. "What is important is that you are safe and on your way back to London . . . and to the queen."

"London?" Anne screeched.

"The queen?" Corrie croaked as she dragged the cloth from her mouth. "You're carrying us back to London and the queen?" Horror and anger warred in her expression, and the victor was declared when she launched herself from the bunk, straight at their captor, knocking him back with a furious shove. "Ohhh, you—"

The shock of Corrie's action ignited Anne's fury and she flew at him, too, bashing him in the shoulder with a fist. He staggered back, stunned, and they attacked together, slapping, punching, kicking. He scuttled back with his neck drawn in and his arms upraised to shield his head. Then his bootheel caught on a board and he tripped, sprawling onto his back. Together, they pounced on him, pinning him to the floor, Corrie on his chest and Anne trapping his feet.

"How dare you abduct me from my lawful husband!" Corrie raged, grasping the front of his doublet and shaking him so that his head banged against the floor. "You'll turn this bucket about and set us back on land or—"

The cabin door swung open, and Jack Huntington burst inside, his body coiled for danger. He stopped dead, his eyes widening in disbelief at the sight of the two women sitting on Morris Lombard.

Corrie and Anne looked up and froze.

"Father?"

"Uncle Jack?"

"It's *you?*" Corrie slid from her victim onto the floor and stared at her father in complete confusion. "You've carried us off? But what—why?"

"I came to rescue you!" Jack declared, hurrying forward to help Corrie and Anne to their feet. As he engulfed his daughter in a tight hug of parental relief, the furious and humiliated Lombard scrambled up and fled the cabin.

"But I don't need rescuing," Corrie said, pushing back in his arms, remembering more. "I was perfectly all right— Father, you have to take us back!" Her heart began to pound. "I have to talk to Rugar, to—"

"I shall do no such thing!" Jack vowed, releasing her to pace away, his fatherly pride burning visibly. "That cold, ruthless Viking beguiled you and seduced you, then carried you from your home, Corinna. I was remiss in my duty as a father—I should have found some way to intervene, to prevent that cursed marriage. But I swear I shall not make the same mistake again. I'm taking you home, where you belong."

"Well, you're not *my* father." Anne spoke up, fierce with indignation. "And how dare you presume to take such action upon my person? I shall not be dealt with like a wretched sack of flour! I demand that you turn straight around and set me back on Swedish soil this minute!"

"I shall not." Jack looked at Anne, then at Corrie, taken

aback by their anger. "The queen has sent me to bring you both home, and I intend to do that very thing."

"You have no right—" Anne shouted angrily.

"I have every right—a legal right!" Jack blustered, appalled by their stubborn resistance to what he saw as their salvation. "I have a writ from the queen to arrest the both of you. You left the country without permission," Jack declared, "and in the company of known enemies of the Crown. A treasonous offense."

"I left to live with my *husband,*" Corrie protested. "How can that possibly be treason against the queen? She would arrest me for following both the natural order and God's own law? For obeying both my sacred wedding vows and the longings of my heart?"

"When you are returned to England and to the queen, the charges will undoubtedly be stricken," Jack said doggedly.

"Returned . . . to the queen?" Corrie stared at her silver-templed father, feeling as if a great steel-clad hand had just closed around her heart, around her very life. "You've come all this way to return me to the queen?"

Rugar's words washed over her in chilled, sobering waves. Elizabeth had wanted her exclusively, he said; her company, her loyalty, her affections. She had gone so far as to warn others away from her "pet" when they came too close, and would stop at nothing to regain that which she deemed her rightful possession . . . even to having her "pet's" husband abducted on their wedding night. Now his charges against her were proven true; she'd ordered a bride stolen from her husband, a thousand miles away from the seat of her rightful power . . . to secure her property and suit her vengeful pleasure.

Corrie staggered to a chair. It was all true, every word, she realized with crushing anguish. The cuts and bruises on Rugar's face—the queen had inflicted them on him, the same as if she'd used her own hands. And now, because he'd taken something she insisted was hers, she'd declared him an enemy of the Crown and extended the long arm of her possession across the sea to reclaim it.

It was a killing realization, that Corrie had been beguiled and counted a possession, and was now treated like so much chattel. She'd believed in and defended the queen, had held the feelings and thoughts they had shared as a sacred trust. She'd made the queen perfect in her mind, just as she'd rendered Rugar flawless in her heart. And now that last bit of innocence, her unquestioning trust in her sovereign lady, was swept away. For the first time, she saw Elizabeth with eyes stripped of girlish awe; as a possessive, demanding mistress who guarded her ladies like a tyrant and jealously hoarded their love, attention, and loyalty.

She looked at Anne, who was now seated on the bunk, looking strangely bereft. Anne had felt the cruel bonds of the queen's possession and had tried to warn her. But Corrie had steadfastly refused to see.

Corrie turned to plead with her father. "Father, you cannot take me from my—"

But she stopped. The weight of the night's heartache and of her public embarrassment of Rugar crushed her heart, robbing her of the assurance to demand the right to stay at her husband's side. Even if she could persuade her father to take her back, would Rugar still want her?

Rugar returned to his house at dawn, his hair and clothes wet from the fine, freezing mist. He had begun to make peace with himself and was determined to make peace with Corrie as well. He had so much to tell her. He prayed he could make her understand the changes in him and that she would find it in her heart to forgive him and his wretched countrymen.

But when he bounded up the stairs past his red-eyed housekeeper and his hand-wringing steward, he found Torgne waiting in the parlor outside his chamber. He paused and scowled at Torgne's agonized expression, then rushed past him toward the chamber door, calling Corrie's name. Torgne restrained him in a fierce grip.

"She's not here, Rugar, she's gone." His voice was hoarse with pain. "They came for her . . . they've taken her back to England."

Rugar stared into Torgne's haunted eyes and felt the words spearing his heart. "The hell they have!" He wrenched away and stormed into his chamber.

It was true, devastatingly true. She was gone, taken. And in her place was a writ, signed by Elizabeth of England, against the freedom of Lady Corinna Huntington Kalisson and Baroness Anne Bosworth. He stared at the flamboyant signature, feeling pressure building in him. He'd underestimated Elizabeth yet again, her cunning, her ruthlessness . . . and the long arm of her retribution.

He stood by the bed, trembling, caught between anger and despair. His sweet Corrie, his beloved wife, had been taken from him. And he honestly didn't know if he had the right to try to bring her back to a land where she'd been scorned . . . or if she would even want to come.

Chapter Nineteen

The next day, Corrie stood by the railing at the stern of the ship, looking out over the ship's wake, watching the miles spread between her and Rugar. She recalled her thoughts on the way to Sweden. She'd been so filled with anticipation, so eager to see the world, to experience a new country and a new way of life, at Rugar's side and in his arms. She had been so determined to love his home, she had never once considered that his people might not feel the same about her.

It was one more experience in the ways of the wide world she had so eagerly sought. In truth, she had gotten her heart's desire. She had experienced love and passion and betrayal and joy and heartache. She had been married and abducted and carried to a foreign country, where she'd learned new customs, a new language, and a powerful, painful lesson on being a stranger in a foreign land. She had learned a great deal in an astonishingly short time. And she'd discovered that the world of wonders wasn't always so wonderful after all.

Sometime later, she went below and found Anne sitting in the chilled cabin, wrapped in a blanket. She looked up with reddened eyes and an odd, waiflike expression.

"It's not fair. Bess gets an itch, and the whole damned

world has to scratch. Well, what about when I get an itch?
Or you? What about our poor dreams and loves and desires?
Do they not matter at all?"

The wretchedness of Anne's tears and her disconsolate
state soon bore through Corrie's own misery. She hurried
to her cousin's side, then pulled back, confused. A few
weeks ago, Anne had been pitching furious at being abducted to Sweden. Now she was heartbroken at leaving?
Itches? She thought of how docile and sweet-natured Anne
had been of late. Someone had been scratching Anne's—?

"Anne!" Corrie stared at her. "Do you mean to say . . .
Torgne Sigurd? You and Torgne? Together?"

"You always were slow about these things, Cub." Anne
sniffed. "I'm mad about him. I know he seems proud and
stern and uncompromising. But inside he's the most tender,
giving, and loving man I've ever known." She sighed miserably. "I'm not the least bit ashamed that he shared my bed
every night we were in Stockholm."

"In Stockholm? Every night?" Corrie whispered.

"Twice a night, actually." Anne's lashes lowered, and
color bloomed in her fair cheeks as she confessed softly:
"Three times if I was especially . . . good with my Swedish."
She looked up, her lower lip aquiver. "I never expected to
love anybody again, Corrie. It's like it was with Bosworth,
only it's completely different, because Tor's completely different. And it's so much more precious to me now because
I know how rare it is to love so well. I was wrong, Corrie."
Tears poured down her cheeks. "It can happen *twice* in a
lifetime."

Corrie gathered her into a hug and let her cry it out,
wondering if there might someday be a second time for her
as well . . . or if there was such a thing as "twice" with the
same love.

They sat on the bunk, huddled together, sharing their
miseries in silence. Then Corrie released a shuddering sigh.

"Well, here we are. Abducted again. Aboard another moldy old ship. At least this time we have clothes."

The passage to England was exceedingly slow, often against icy head winds. It was mid-January before they finally docked in London. The city was damp and frigid—which also described the state of relations between Corrie and her father. For most of the voyage she wouldn't speak to him, would look at him only when it was unavoidable, and refused to be in the same cabin with him for more than a brief time. Her attitude did not improve upon learning that they were to go straight to Hampton Court Palace upon arriving. The queen had moved there from Whitehall at the turn of the year so that Whitehall could be cleaned and freshened.

Once inside the opulent Hampton Court, they were shown quickly into Elizabeth's presence. She greeted them with queenly pleasure. "Welcome home, Corinna, Anne. I trust your journey was not too taxing."

The taste of bile rose in the back of Corrie's throat, but she managed to keep her voice and gaze steady. "We are . . . well enough, Your Grace."

Elizabeth searched her countenance, the new, self-possessed womanly aura about her, and frowned. "Well, at least you are back where you belong," she declared with an imperial edge that forbade any other opinion.

Corrie lifted her eyes to the queen's and silently dissented.

New flint in Corrie's gaze resisted the steel of Elizabeth's, striking an unnerving spark between them. Elizabeth turned away, visibly disturbed, and made a show of examining some papers on her writing table. "It is clear you will need some time to recover after such an ordeal. I give you leave to go to Straffen with your father. And I shall send you, Baroness, to your father in Kent. Then you may both join me at court in the spring, after you've had time to . . . rest."

And repent, Corrie thought grimly as she curtseyed and withdrew.

Thus Corrie and Anne parted, one bound for Straffen in Hertford, the other for Kent. The roads to Hertford were frozen, and travel was reasonably swift, despite the cold. When they arrived at Straffen, Jack and Corrie were greeted with the news that just three days prior, Merrie Huntington had been forced to take to her bed for the final stage of a difficult pregnancy. Alarmed, they hurried to her bedside and found her strength and spirits exceedingly low. But the very sight of the two of them, whole and hale, worked a miracle in her. She managed to sit up and looked as if a huge weight had been lifted from her shoulders.

"I was so frightened for you. I'd had no word since your father left England to bring you home," Merrie whispered, stroking Corrie's face.

"Well, I'm home now and so is Father. And you must let us take good care of you from now on."

Corrie smiled and kissed her cheek, but Merrie, with a mother's special sense, detected the hurt that lay behind her determinedly cheerful face. When Corrie left them alone, Merrie took Jack's hands and pulled him onto the bed. "You've brought her home . . . but oh, Jack, she's so unhappy." She searched the darkness in his face and glimpsed the pain that lay in his heart. "Was he really so bad that you had to take her away from him?"

Jack looked at the loving faith in Merrie's eyes and was stunned to realize it was the same look Corrie had given that great, rangy Swede . . . the look of a heart freely and tenderly given, a love that had no conditions, no reservations. And he finally admitted he'd made a mistake.

Years ago, when others had contrived to separate him from Merrie, he'd have moved heaven and hell to return to her. No one had the right to part him from his lawfully wedded wife, he had declared vehemently. And now in the name of "protecting" his little daughter, he'd done to her what he himself would never have tolerated. He'd dragged her from her husband, ignoring her heartfelt pleas, to satisfy his own fatherly pride.

Now he could only hope the Swede was hardheaded, foolhardy, and possessive enough of his love to do the same thing he himself had done years ago—come and fight for her.

Corrie was engulfed by the affections of her nine-year-old sisters, Diana and Cynthia, and spent the rest of that first afternoon with them, listening to all their achievements and mischiefs, and meeting and approving their new pets, which included a motherless fawn adopted in their father's absence. Corrie hugged the little doe's neck and felt tears rising at the memory of another deer, one with fat little hooves and stubby antlers.

That first night was the worst. She retired to her old chamber, feeling out of place and out of time. Nothing in it was changed, which made it seem as if she'd never left, as if all the wonderful and terrible things that had happened to her were just dreams. Then, to one side, she saw her trunk, which had apparently been sent from Whitehall in her absence.

Kneeling beside it, she lifted the lid. Memories boiled up with the scent of the herbs used in packing her garments. Her red bodice lay atop her maiden clothes, and she took it out, hugging it to her, remembering. Then her gaze fell on a crushed ring of bright, multicolored ribbands. Her bridal crown. Maudie had apparently packed it up with all the rest of her possessions.

She cradled it lovingly in her hands, teary-eyed but smiling. Rugar. The queen had had him abducted, and he'd still managed to come to her that night with ribbands in his hands.

A new flame of hope flickered in her heart.

Currents of anger swirled in Rugar and Torgne's path as they strode forcefully through the cold stone halls of the palace in Stockholm. Their shoulders were rigid, their jaws were hard and stony, and their eyes burned like hot blue flames.

It was nearly a fortnight since Corrie had been taken from Rugar, and they had proved the worst two weeks of his life. He had spent long, sleepless nights tossing and turning in the bed they had shared, and endless, agonizing days pacing the chambers haunted by echoes of her vibrant spirit. He drank to numb the pain in his heart and found it only deepened his misery. It was little consolation to him that Torgne fared no better, pining for Anne. He was too disconsolate even to be shocked to learn that righteous, moralistic Torgne had taken Corrie's brazen, willful cousin to his bed.

Then, when his spirits were at low ebb, the final blow was struck. A trunk containing much of the clothing he'd ordered made for her was delivered to his house. Unsure what else to do with such valuables, Fru Nilsson ordered the trunk placed in his bedchamber. When he discovered it in the middle of the floor, he just stood staring at it for a long while, feeling the pull of her on his heart.

He sank to his knees beside it and lifted the lid. As his fingers stroked the rich garments, each texture recalled something about her—the satins her skin, the velvets her lips, the golden embroidery the sparkle of her eyes. He recalled the girlish joy with which she'd chosen them, and the wifely care with which she'd spent his coin.

Suddenly he could see her face clearly, smiling at him, loving him, forgiving him. The pain of his crushed heart was killing, terrifying; he wondered briefly if he was dying. But when it finally subsided, and he found himself still sitting on the floor of his chamber, alive, he staggered to his feet and looked down at those precious garments. And he knew he had to go to her. He had to give their love one more chance.

He and Torgne were shown into King Johan's council chamber, where Johan was conferring with a number of his advisors. Everyone in the chamber came to attention at the fierceness displayed by the usually genial count.

"My wife has been taken from my house . . . arrested on the orders of Elizabeth Tudor and carried to England," Rugar declared with a deep, ragged anger as he held out the writ to Johan. "And I want her back."

Shock spread through the chamber, then into the corridors and through the rest of the court. It wasn't long before the name "Corinna" was on nearly every tongue. The Count of Aelthar's little bride: the court began to recall how lovely she was and what a sweet countenance she had. It was monstrous of that wretched Elizabeth to steal her from her Swedish husband—and her newly adopted home!

"That wretched English whore," Johan ground out, smashing the writ on his writing table in anger. "I know Elizabeth. She's like a badger—all teeth and claws. I shall write a letter demanding your wife's release and return, but it won't bring her home."

"Then let me go after her myself," Rugar declared, leaning

across the writing table. "You made me an ambassador onc
Your Grace. Make me an ambassador again!"

Days turned into healing weeks and the weeks into or
month, which marched stolidly on toward two. Teasing hin
of spring—swelling buds and moist zephyrs—accompanie
the traditional late February thaw. The warmer weather an
bright sun stirred the countryside, and it was not lon
before Straffen received a visitor.

Anne Bosworth arrived in a flurry all the way from Ken
accompanied by two servants. She was as itchy and restles
as Corrie had ever seen her, and her tongue was razor-keen
But the warmth of Merrie and Jack's welcome soon melte
her brash mien, and as she let down her guard, strain an
unhappiness showed hauntingly behind it.

"Uncle Jack, you know how my father is," she sai
sighing. "I've had nothing but sermons and lectures f
nigh onto two months. I simply couldn't bear it anoth
minute."

Jack understood all too well. Merrie smiled generous
and insisted Anne have a long visit so she might get a
quainted with the niece she'd never had the pleasure
knowing.

Corrie was overjoyed to have Anne's company again ar
spent the entire first evening catching up on rumors
the latest court scandals and intrigues. After supping, the
retired to Anne's chamber and laughed, chatted, and gi
gled until the candles burned low. Then Anne sobered a
looked searchingly at Corrie.

"There's yet another scandal about to break at court."

"What is it?" Corrie frowned, sensing Anne's tension

"The Baroness Bosworth is breeding." When Corr
glanced, wide-eyed, at Anne's tightly laced stomach, An

made it clearer still. "I'm with child, Cub. I'm carrying Torgne's babe."

"Oh, Anne." Corrie reached for her hand. "I don't know what to say."

"Say you're happy for me, Cub." Her smile bore a trace of sadness. "For I cannot be unhappy that I shall have a babe to remind me of our loving. I have always wanted a child, and, bless his generous heart, Tor has given me one. But it will not be easy, Corrie. My father will certainly disown me, and who knows what Bess may do when she learns of it."

Anne was right. Elizabeth would undoubtedly see it as an injury to her queenly pride, and might well lash out viciously at Anne. The idea sent pure rebellion up Corrie's spine.

"Then you'll stay here with us," she resolved, squeezing Anne's hands tightly. "We'll have to tell my mother, and eventually my father. But they would never turn you out. You've a place here, Anne, as long as you wish it."

A crew of seamen jumped from a longboat into the surf along a rocky beach on England's Essex shore. They seized ropes and hauled the bow of the craft up onto the sand; then two tall figures in plain woolen cloaks vaulted over the sides onto the wet sand. While four large trunks, two saddles, and a number of other odd-shaped items were unloaded, the two passengers watched the vessel from which they'd come. First one horse, then another, was lowered over its side in a leather harness, released, and allowed to swim toward shore.

"Here they come!" Rugar stepped into the gentle surf and whistled and waved to the struggling horses, and soon the animals touched bottom and scrambled for footing in the shifting sands. When the horses were safely ashore and the baggage unloaded, the longboat pushed off, and Rugar and Torgne were left drying and saddling their mounts.

"We didn't have to bring all that." Torgne jerked his head at the pile of trunks and crates. "It will only slow us down."

"I paid good money for those clothes, and I don't intend to see them wasted. Besides, if we look like merchants, we'll draw less notice. It won't take long to find a cart; the captain said there's a village not far inland." Rugar flashed Torgne a grin as he hefted the saddle to his mount's back and reached for the girth. "A bit eager, are you?" When Torgne shot him a slitted gaze, Rugar laughed. For the past two months Torgne had moped about, smitten to the bone, plagued with miseries too deep for words, and now as they approached the end of their long journey, he was frantic to get on with it. Rugar shared all of his excitement, his longing . . . and his dread.

"Besides, I may need a peace offering," Rugar mused with nervous wit. "And with Anne of Bosworth, you may need a *bribe*."

The sun was warm and the air was cool one afternoon in early March, exactly the sort of weather to turn a country-bred woman's thoughts toward gardens. Corrie and Anne had gone out to Merrie's walled flower garden at the rear of the new wing of Straffen to assess the winter damage and do a bit of planning. The air was so pleasant, so filled with the promise of spring, that they sat down on a bench just to enjoy it. That was where Cynthia and Diana, Corrie's little sisters, found them.

"Corrie!" They nearly tripped over one another in their eagerness. "Corrie, she's out. Rosebud. You must help us find her before Father does," Cynthia cried.

"Prithee please!" Diana wailed. "He'll have her for stew meat if we don't get her in—that's what he always says!"

Corrie looked at their flushed, distraught faces and knew from experience that their dread was real . . . just as she knew that her father would never actually carry out his perennial threat to cook their pet fawn. She turned to Anne with a grave look. "Rosebud again. I'm the best deer-catcher around," she explained, "and I'd best go help them, or we could be eating their precious pet for supper for the next week."

Anne shuddered and waved her on to it with a sour face. "By all means, go and save us."

Diana and Cynthia dragged Corrie through the garden gate, across the rear yard, past the kitchens and buttery and dovecote, to a pen near the stables. They paused, looking at the open gate, and Corrie turned a narrowed gaze on her sisters.

"But we didn't leave it open! Truly we didn't!" they protested in unison.

"The fact remains, it's open." Corrie scowled and huffed with resignation. "From experience, I would say she has headed either for the cart path and the fields or into the woods near the road. You take the cart path; I know the woods best." She lifted her skirts and hurried for the little-used stone path which led around the north end of Straffen Manor.

The woods crowded near the path in several places, and she craned her neck to search the trees as she looked for the best place to cross through the brambles and shrubs. She was completely around the house, skirting the edge of the front entry court, when she caught a movement on the road which led past the woods to the front doors of Straffen Hall. She whirled, then melted with relief. Rosebud.

No sooner had she started for the little deer than she

slowed. Rosebud was wearing something on her back . . . something blue . . . azure blue. And yellow . . . the color of buttercups. Corrie froze, her gaze riveted to the animal as it regarded her suspiciously and lowered its head to take her scent.

Blue and gold fabric; a field and a cross. It was a flag, tied across Rosebud's back and now slipping slightly to one side. The sight seared a path from Corrie's eyes all the way into her heart, setting it afire in her breast. A Swedish flag? How could it be? Unless . . .

She looked frantically around the empty front court, at the woody front garden on the far side, then whirled to search the bare shrubs and trees behind her. Nothing seemed out of place; all was quiet, peaceful. With soothing murmurs and slow movements, she approached the deer and finally lunged and clamped an arm about the little beast's neck. Rosebud bucked and scrambled, and Corrie had to release her to keep from being trampled by sharp little hooves. But she had managed to grab the cloth and yank it off as Rosebud kicked at the air and ran harum-scarum for the woods. Corrie stared at the rectangle of blue and gold silk in her hands.

Rugar, she thought; it had to be! Her heart thudded as she pressed that silk banner to her breast. And he had to be nearby! But where?

Choosing the direction from which Rosebud had come, she lifted her skirts and ran toward the road and the woods that bordered it.

Rugar and Torgne stood in the cover of the great old trees, where woods and road met. They had traveled hard for the past three days, sleeping in the open and eating cold rations, avoiding inns as they slowly made their way across the countryside toward Straffen. It had been a long and perilous journey, and now that it was at an end, all they could do was wait to see if they would be welcomed or sent packing. The uncertainty and helplessness were excruciating for men used to taking action.

"I told you the deer was a bad idea," Torgne grumbled, staring at his feet. "I still have no feeling in half my toes." It had been his task to hold the doe while Rugar strapped the flag on its back.

"Corrie's the 'deer-catcher' hereabouts. When she finds the beast missing, she'll look for it, and when she sees the flag, she'll know we're nearby and come looking for us." Rugar defended his plan, though it was losing some of its appeal now that he realized all the things that could go wrong with it.

They had spent the morning spying out Straffen Manor, its arrangement and workings, hoping for a glimpse of Corrie and trying to decide on the best means of approach. If possible, Rugar wanted to see her alone first, to have time to talk with her before facing her angry father and whoever else might take exception to his presence. The waiting had been pure agony for him, seeing the home Corrie had described to him so vividly and feeling her presence so close . . . yet so far away. As they crept around in the woods, Rugar had spotted the pet deer in the pen by the stables and gotten the idea to use it to lure Corrie out to them.

Rugar suddenly stiffened, grabbing Torgne's arm as his eyes fixed on a spot of white, down the road, coming toward them.

Corrie ran slowly, searching the barren trees and brambles for some sign of him. Then, far ahead, just off the road, in the shelter of the woods, she glimpsed a movement, a shape . . . then a flash of something golden. She stopped, her chest heaving, her hands curled around fistfuls of skirts. He seemed to materialize out of the misty grays and dark hues of the damp woods, his broad shoulders cloaked in a muted color, his blond hair like a halo around his head. It was as if the longings of her heart created him from light and shadow as she watched.

She walked toward that vision, feeling awkward and slow, unable to keep up with her heart, which fluttered like a caged bird in her breast, eager to fly.

With each step he grew more real, and her hope soared. Her imagination would not have conjured the way the breeze playfully flipped up the collar of his cloak and molded the dark garment over the hard, diagonal ridge of the sword at his side. His long legs were spread. One hand was set at his belt, and the other rested on his sword hilt.

With each stride the familiar details of him became more distinct: the aquiline elegance of his features, the solidity of his square jaw, his light eyes, and the silky abandon of his wind-tousled hair. As she drew closer, she could make out more: the tension in his expression and in the set of his shoulders as he watched her come to him.

The urge to run straight into his arms was almost irresistible. But—a small, panicky voice whispered in her head—what if his arms didn't open to her? That wary impulse deepened as thoughts of the pained circumstances of their last moments together boiled up in her. Her joy at seeing him here, in England, was suddenly tempered by the knowledge that even though he'd crossed a sea to come to her, there were still barriers, in some ways more difficult obstacles, between them. She jolted to a stop twenty feet away, struggling for breath and squeezing her skirts into hopeless wads.

"Rugar." Her throat tightened around his name. "You came." Her eyes burned dryly; her hands ached to touch him. Everything in her yearned to cast reason, experience, and caution aside to hold him and to be held.

"I had to come, Corrie." His voice was full but tautly reined.

His gaze searched her as hers did him; she could feel it like a touch against her cheek. She wanted to curl around that caress, to absorb it into the hungry depths of her, to savor and tend it so that it would grow into the sweet intimacy of mind and body they had once shared.

"Why did you have to come?" she asked, holding her breath. Everything in her was straining against the bonds of wisdom and control as she prayed it would be the answer she needed to hear.

"You left some things in Sweden," he said with quiet emotion. "And I had to bring them to you."

Such unexpected words, spoken with such a tender edge, stirred confusion in her. He had come all this way to return her *things?*

"What could I have left in Sweden?" she asked. *Besides my heart.* She followed his gesture to the baggage cart amongst the trees.

"These clothes . . . that were made for you." He turned back and took a step closer. The glowing intensity of his eyes sent a quiver through her heart. He pushed back the edges of his cloak to reveal his simple woolen doublet, then opened his brown-clad arms and lifted them slowly, displaying them.

"And these arms."

At the ends of those arms, his big hands opened wide to her.

"And these hands."

The chaos in her senses suddenly stilled, and the tension binding her heart began to loosen. In calling up the tenderest moments of their wedding night, when he'd offered up the sundry parts of him to satisfy her curious heart, he conjured all of the passion and promise they had discovered that night . . . all the joys, pleasures, and caring that had balanced their troubles. She could scarcely breathe against the hope swelling in her chest.

"These eyes," he continued, letting the warmth in his heart rise into his gaze. "And these lips. They are yours, Corrie. I am returning them to you." His voice deepened, growing velvety, resonant with longing. "What use you will make of them, only you can say."

He stood there with his arms outstretched, his eyes shining with love for her . . . so generous, so brave. So vulnerable.

It was the greatest risk of Rugar's life . . . baring his heart, his pride, his whole being to her . . . offering himself totally, nothing withheld, nothing protected.

He had watched her run to him at first, then saw her slow as memories and old hurts bore in on her. But it was that first impulse, that heady burst of joy upon seeing him, in which he had desperately placed his trust. And it was the unquenched glow of feeling, deep within her jewel-clear eyes, as she settled breathlessly before him that gave him the courage to hazard all on such a brazen offer of self. He had once experienced the fullness of her love, had felt the depths of her longing for him, had sampled the largess of her forgiving heart. And he prayed that his selfishness and his people's scorn hadn't diminished the genuineness of her spirit . . . that rare willingness to give and to trust and to love which had made her so very precious to him.

For a long moment, neither spoke, neither breathed.

He had offered.

Now she accepted.

With first one step, then another, she plunged headlong into those strong arms, into the middle of that powerful male presence, and into the center of that vulnerable heart.

"Yes, I want them—all of them—everything!" she

declared into his wool-clad chest, while his arms clamped tightly, fiercely about her.

He shouted a triumphant laugh as he snatched her hard against him and lifted her off the ground, whirling her around and around with him in dizzy spirals that matched the love-drunken reeling of his heart. Only the threat of toppling over completely halted him. He staggered with her, then set her on her feet. His head lowered slowly toward her radiant face, and he claimed her mouth in an achingly sweet kiss.

As his great cloak swirled around them both, she rose onto her toes against him, opening to the soft wonder of his mouth on hers, sensing the purposefulness in his restraint and somehow understanding it. The stark tenderness of his lips on hers bespoke a new priority, the putting of love ahead of sensual need. Together they would hold desire at bay while caring and intimacy worked their magic . . . binding up the raveled strands of two hearts into one glorious tapestry of love that would stand the wear of time and the assaults of fortune.

He filled both her arms and her senses; hard to the touch, smelling of warmed wool and woodsmoke and the faint, piquant musk of his own maleness. And slowly he filled her heart; gentle and unhurried, careful of the tenderness unfolding between them again.

"I had to see you, Corrie," he said, giving her a last, soft brush on the lips before pressing his cheek against hers. "I've missed you so and I've worried so much about you. I walked the streets that night, all night . . . and when I came back the next morning and found you gone—found Elizabeth's damnable writ instead of you on our bed—it felt as if my whole world had been ripped from me."

She pushed back in his arms with her eyes glistening. She could see the truth of his words in the rings beneath his eyes and in his drawn features. She dragged her knuckles over his cheek, then turned her hand to caress him.

"The queen sent my father to bring us back. I tried to persuade him not to take us, but he was so furious, he wouldn't listen. And after what happened, I wasn't sure . . ." She looked away, reluctant to reveal her fear.

He somehow knew what she meant and sensed why it was so difficult to speak of it. It was the same fear that had tortured him these past weeks, through endless, lonely nights and across a thousand miles of icy seas. He delved deep into the very sinew of his male pride and spoke it for them both.

"I wasn't sure . . . you'd want to see me."

She looked into his eyes, into the bare feelings and aching question they contained. And she reached into the vulnerable recesses of her heart to answer it.

"Rugar, I love you," she whispered. "How could I not want to see you?"

And she realized that in answering his unspoken question, she'd answered her own.

"Corrie—my sweet, wonderful Corrie—I love you, too." In a burst of sheer male exuberance, he lifted her and swung her around again, laughing, drawing her into the sheer joy of his proclamation. "I love you . . . I love you . . ."

Each time he said it with more feeling and a bit less volume. As his voice quieted, his motion slowed . . . until they were standing still again, facing each other. Toe to toe, heart to heart.

In the sudden hush their hearts opened and touched with breathtaking intimacy.

"I've had a long time to think, Corrie, and I've learned some hard lessons of late. No countries, no people, no revenge, no pride . . . nothing is more important to me than loving you." He cradled her face in his hands. And he spoke the hard won wisdom of his stubborn heart in a desperate whisper that evoked echoes of the pain with which it had been bought.

"When I saw my people, the nobles of my country, tittering and sniggering, when I saw the way they judged you . . . I was too stunned, too angry to think clearly. I came within a hairsbreadth of calling them out, running them through, every last one of them. I trusted them to receive you, to make you welcome in the home and land I had cherished and defended. And they betrayed my trust in the cruelest way possible . . . by hurting you."

"Shhh, it's over now." She placed her fingers on his lips, but he collected them in his hand and kissed them.

"No, I have to tell you, Corrie, and you have to hear it." He stroked her cheek, her cap, her shoulder. "I was so proud of you for all your work at learning our language and our customs. I was so proud of how bright and learned and beautiful and good you are. And all they saw—all they wanted to see—was the foreign way you said their words and the awkward steps you made in a meaningless dance. They treated you like an ignorant . . . foreigner."

She felt anger rising in him and tried to allay it.

"But I *was* a foreigner. The 'Corrie' and the 'English' are inseparable in me, Rugar. I see that now. I tried to pretend it wasn't so, tried to become as Swedish as possible, to please you and them," she declared. "I didn't know enough about the world to realize they might resent my attempts at their language and my adoption of their ways. It was naive of me not to realize they would think of me as a foreigner." Her smile bore a hint of sadness. "It's just that nothing about you had ever seemed foreign to me."

"Nor were you ever a stranger to me," he said softly. "I think from the first I somehow recognized that you were the missing part of me, Corrie. You are the heart of me. I finally know what that means. And I'll not ever forget it."

He fitted their palms together and gently threaded his

fingers through hers, then curled them down over the back
of her hand. When her fingers instinctively did the same,
he smiled and stared at that simple but perfect symbol of
their joining.

"There is nothing more important than this, Corrie." He
squeezed her hand. "A man can love a country or a people,
a cause or an ideal . . . but they will not ever truly love him
in return. They may respect and obey him, may exploit and
consume him, may elect and even honor him. But in the still
of the night, the loneliness and anguish of a human heart
can only be touched and comforted by another human
heart. What nobility there is to be found in mankind is
found in loving . . . in the free giving of self to another . . .
in the tender companioning of another's struggles in life."

Tears rolled down her cheeks as she listened, as she absorbed that precious wisdom into her heart and let it work
its healing wonders within her.

"Can we start again, Corrie?" he asked. "Can we put all
this behind us and start again?"

A second chance. *Twice* with the same love. She didn't
even have to think.

"Yes—oh, yes!"

She threw her arms around his neck and pulled him
down to kiss her, molding her body tightly against him and
freeing the desire that had been held in check. The brightness of the day, the chill of the air, the trees around them,
all faded from her senses as her mind filled with the raw
pleasure of feeling his warm, vibrant body against hers.

They kissed and pressed, hands roaming, bodies rubbing, heat increasing. She burned to feel his hands on her
body, his weight on her breasts . . . the hard, pulsing length
of him deep within her. Desire licked up the back of her
throat, searing hot, demanding . . . now. . . Her knees weak-
ened, and she sagged in his arms.

Raising his head, he seemed a bit surprised to find they

were still at the edge of the barren woods, by the road. He drew back, blinking, recalling more.

"Please, Rugar," she whispered, dark-eyed, pulling him back to her. "It's been so long . . ."

"B-but Torgne—" He held her by the shoulders and looked around them. "Torgne is with me. He's—"

"Torgne came, too?" Corrie glanced about. Finding they were alone, she snuggled suggestively against him again. Her only thoughts were of having Rugar to herself. Suddenly she straightened. Lud! They were all but standing in the blessed road!

"Then come with me. We can use your cloak." She grabbed his hand to drag him further into the woods, but they went only a few yards before he dug in his heels and reeled her back to him. He kissed her hotly, a deep, bone-melting ravishment of a kiss that left her limp against him.

"It's too cold out here," he murmured, nuzzling her neck. "I want to peel you and . . . Is there anywhere we can go?"

"My chamber—" She stopped, feeling as if she'd been sluiced with cold water. Her chamber . . . her home . . . her family. Lud!—her father! The problems they faced widened like ripples in a pond. Suddenly the least of their problems was finding a bed for a hot, salty bout of loving.

"Rugar! My father . . . my family . . . *the queen*." From the look on his face, he was remembering those same formidable barriers. "We could slip away . . . leave right now." She pointed to the baggage cart. "I need not even pack!"

Rugar held her still and made her look at him as he studied her. He had meant to save this part for later, when the joy of their reunion made it easier to speak of. "Corrie, I know you have no reason to love Sweden, but it is where my home and estates are. And just now it seems the only place we can live together as man and wife. Will you come with me?"

"It would be a hard choice if I did not love you so," she

said quietly. "But I would rather live in Sweden with you than anywhere else in the world without you." When he expelled a deep, shuddering breath of relief, she smiled. "Now can we go? Straightaway, before—" But she halted, thinking of her mother and her sisters, of not seeing them again for a very long while.

Rugar scowled at her and at the temptation she presented him with. "No more slinking and skulking, Corrie Kalisson. I have to face your father and set things right. I don't want him coming after you again."

Corrie nodded. "But the queen would be furious to know you're in England, Rugar. She'd stop at nothing to punish you." Through his eyes she could see his mind working. Then he winced.

"Very well, then, we'll compromise. I'll face your father, and then we'll slink and skulk to avoid the queen."

The sun seemed to dawn in Corrie's face. She threaded their fingers together. Then she led him slowly toward her home.

Across the nearby field, hidden in a hedgerow, a pair of devious eyes had watched the reunion of count and countess and now narrowed as the pair strolled toward the front doors of Straffen Hall. After weeks of waiting, hiding in icy fields, lurking about in the raw winds and rains, the time had finally come. The Swede had come for his precious Huntington bride, just as the queen had expected he would. Morris Lombard crawled back into the shelter of the hedges and stretched the cramps from his scrawny frame. The comeuppance of the almighty Huntingtons was finally at hand!

Chapter Twenty

Torgne had retreated from the sight of Rugar and Corrie's meeting, moving far enough away to escape their voices. When he saw Corrie fly to Rugar's arms, he sighed raggedly and turned away to give them some privacy. It appeared Corrie had forgiven, and there was a good chance Rugar could make her forget as well. And now as Torgne stalked through the woods, the image of their embrace sent a fierce longing through him.

The first part of their mission was accomplished, and he was impatient to get on with the second part: searching out Anne's home so that he could ask her to marry him and come back to Sweden with him. Now he began to think: if Corrie agreed to go back to Sweden with Rugar, her disappearance might alert the queen and make it difficult for him to see Anne. Perhaps he should leave today . . . this afternoon.

He found himself at the edge of the woods, overlooking the rear yard of Straffen with its brick kitchens and buttery, its women's houses, cottages, and byres, and the deer pen they'd raided earlier. The little beast that had trampled his toes was now back in her place, he realized, and his awareness broadened to include several children hanging over the fence, fondling the creature and holding out wisps of dried hay to it. But there was another figure approaching . . . with a womanly sway and a head of tawny blond hair.

Anne. His heart all but stopped. Here! He stood frozen, watching her talk with the children, pet the fawn, then lift her skirts and turn to go. His aching eyes followed her familiar, blood-stirring curves toward what appeared to be a walled garden. Suddenly his feet were following, too. He slipped from tree to dovecote to the edge of the buttery. His heart pounded as he glanced around, praying no one would see him and sound an alarm. He sprinted across the open yard to the garden wall and slammed against it, then slid along the length of it and finally darted inside the open gate.

Anne was standing in the midst of the garden. He crept up behind her and slid his arms around her, pulling her wriggling form against him and cupping a hand over her mouth.

"Tysta!" he rasped breathlessly. "Be still, *skönhet,* and let me hold you."

Skönhet—"beauty." Tor's pet name for her. She went perfectly still in his arms, and when he released her mouth she gasped, "Tor?" She turned in his tight embrace to face him, looking stunned. "You're here? Faith, you're really here!" Then she lost not one more minute to wonder. Throwing her arms around his neck, she blistered his mouth with a joyful, soaring kiss.

He groaned and plunged into the lush, sultry depths of her mouth. His hands covered her possessively, reclaiming her, and she responded with sighs of deepening longing. They explored each other to the limits of both clothing and prudence. Only then did Anne pull back, gasping for breath, her eyes shining.

"How did you get here? What are you doing here?" she demanded, rubbing her thumbs over his kiss-swollen lips. "Oh, how I've missed you."

"I came with Rugar to get Corrie," he said, swallowing

against his rising anxiety. "And to get you." He searched her rosy face with a look of tortured hope. "I want you to come to Sweden with me, Anne. I want you to marry me."

"Ohhh—Tor—" She swayed on her feet, flushing hot, feeling suddenly light-headed. Inside she was a mass of conflicting joy and dread, wanting to see delight in his face when she told him about the babe, yet so deathly afraid she might encounter his stern conscience instead. She pulled away and tottered to the stone bench nearby.

"What is it, Anne?" Torgne followed her with weighted steps, dread rising. When she lifted her face, tears had filled her eyes.

"Before you say more, you must know . . . I . . . I'm with child."

His eyes flew wide, and he swayed on locked knees. "A b-babe. I—I never imagined . . ." He sank onto the bench beside her, his big hands limp in his lap.

She watched the look of profound shock on his face and felt her heart sink toward her knees. Any moment now, the proud, righteous Baron Sigurd would turn to her and demand to know how she could be sure it was his babe, then disclaim any part in the making of it. She shut out the heart-rending sight of his disbelief and made to rise, but his hand on her arm prevented her. He called her name softly. So very softly. She opened her aching eyes.

He was staring at her with a bewildered grin that grew broader and giddier with each passing instant. "I'm going to have you *and* a babe. I'm going to be a husband and a father! A babe . . . a new Sigurd . . . an heir! Oh, Anne!"

"Then you're not unhappy or embarrassed?" she asked, her voice a mere squeak as it squeezed past the lump in her throat.

"Embarrassed? I am purely mortified! I never considered there might be consequences from our . . . our . . ."

"Loving?" she supplied in a tone that asked the question that lay in her heart.

"Our *loving*," he answered, his fierce Nordic features softening remarkably. "Lud, yes, it was loving . . . it is *loving* that we make. And I do love you, Anne."

"And I love you, Tor."

He engulfed her in a great hug and held her fiercely against him, as if she were too precious to allow out of his arms for an instant. Moments later he stiffened with horror and set her back, searching her for evidence of damage. "I'm sorry, I didn't think . . . the babe . . . I must be careful with you now." The rueful cant to his grin was irresistible.

Anne's eyes glistened mischievously. "You really do have a number of things to learn about breeding women. And I can think of no better time to begin teaching you than the present." She took his head between her hands and kissed him breathless. And while he was still too stunned to resist, she pulled him to his feet and led him stealthily to the edge of the garden, to the side door of Straffen Hall, and up the servants' stairs to her chamber. Once inside, she bolted the door and rubbed, catlike, against him.

"Have you never heard that breeding women get strange cravings?" she purred. He shook his head, his eyes hot upon the laces she was loosening and the delectable breasts she would soon bare to him. "Well, we do. And mine, of late, has been for a big, juicy Swede . . ."

A maid in the hall outside could have sworn she heard a squeal coming from the baroness's chamber. But when she paused to listen, all was quiet, so she shrugged, picked up her pail, and told herself it was likely one of the cats . . . having caught something.

The master chamber of Straffen Hall was sun-dappled and quiet when Corrie and Rugar crept inside. Mercifully, the Great Hall of Straffen had been deserted, and they had climbed the stairs and gallery undetected. Rugar waited by the door, glancing around the vaulted chamber, while Corrie approached her mother's bedside.

Merrie Huntington was asleep. Corrie stood looking at the crinkles that worry and care had traced at the corners of her eyes and the lines that laughter had etched around her mouth. She had helped place those lines in her mother's face, Corrie realized, and when Merrie learned of her plans to go back to Sweden with Rugar, more worries would likely be added.

"Mother." Corrie shook her mother's shoulder, and Merrie started awake. Seeing Corrie, she smiled, relieved. "I've someone I want you to meet."

"Someone? Who . . ." Merrie struggled up behind the mound of her belly, and Corrie hurried to fluff and stack bolsters behind her. "Who is it?"

When Corrie beckoned, Rugar stole toward the great postered bed and came to stand next to her, taking her hands in his. "Mother, this is my husband, Rugar Kalisson."

"Your husband?" Merrie's eyes widened, and she struggled to sit straighter. Her gaze roamed the tall man garbed in traveling clothes, noting his vivid blue eyes, his broad, sensual mouth, and the aura of strength emanating from his uncommonly broad shoulders. She observed his courtly bow and heard the silky, deep rumble of his lightly accented voice as he expressed pleasure at meeting her, and fear of overtaxing her. In his clear eyes, she read the sincerity of his words.

"Mother, before you judge—you must please let me explain," Corrie began, as Rugar drew her protectively against his side.

"Hush, Corrie," Merrie said softly. "Just stand a moment and let me see the two of you together." Corrie bit her lip and looked up at Rugar, who reddened slightly and met her gaze with an unmistakable look of reassurance. That unspeaking exchange spoke volumes to Merrie about the rightness of their match. They were beautiful together . . . he, so strong and manly; she, so soft and womanly. There was a fierceness, an arrogance with which his features had been cast. But when his eyes swept Corrie, his face softened and became loving. It was all Merrie needed to see.

"Pray, sit with me a while, Rugar Kalisson." She pointed to a nearby chair. "Let me hear of you . . . and welcome you to my family."

A teary smile burst upon Corrie's face, and she hurried to circle her mother's shoulders with a soft hug. Then she settled on the edge of the bed, and Rugar drew the chair close and sat down.

The hours passed quickly. They spoke of homes and family ways and of the wedding Merrie had had to miss; sometimes laughing, sometimes sitting quietly, too filled with emotion to speak. As the afternoon wore on, Rugar's sage, lovely, and thoughtful mother-in-law charmed him to his very toes. There was no doubt, he decided wryly, from whom Corrie had taken her irresistible wit and charm. And Merrie Huntington smiled fondly at her son-in-law, thinking how like Jack he was, and how both men would probably be outraged to hear her say it.

When the shadows began to lengthen in the chamber, their precious time together came to an end. Merrie declared that Rugar should stay in Corrie's chamber until she'd had a chance to speak with Corrie's father about his presence. Reluctantly, Rugar agreed, and he and Corrie bade Merrie rest well and withdrew.

But they had no sooner opened the door and stepped through it than Jack Huntington rounded the top of the gallery stairs, headed for his chambers. He stopped dead, blocking their path, and reddened as he stared at Rugar.

"What in hell are you doing here?"

"I've come . . . to collect my wife, sir. I'm taking Corrie back with me," Rugar said evenly, watching the earl's fists hardening at his sides and sensing the coming fight.

"Father, please—" Corrie tried to put herself between them, but Rugar thrust her out of the way, back through the doorway.

"Jack—Jack, you must listen to them!" Merrie called out from her bed. "Don't do anything you'll regret—"

"Do you want her enough to fight for her, Swede?" Jack demanded fiercely.

"I have no wish to fight my wife's father, sir," Rugar declared. "But I will do what I must to protect and secure my wife!"

Jack stalked one step, then another, and Rugar held his ground—while grappling to restrain Corrie behind him. In a flash they were toe to toe, eye to eye—and a strangled cry rang out from the chamber.

"Ja-ack!"

Merrie stood in her bedgown and bare feet at the end of the bed, clutching the massive post and her bulging middle. Her pale face was contorted with pain. Jack whirled, horrified, and in a trice he and Corrie were rushing to Merrie's aid.

"Have you lost your senses—what are you doing?" Jack groaned, scooping her up into his arms and carrying her back to bed.

"Stopping you from"—Merrie gasped and groaned through her teeth—"doing something stupid. And having your baby. Oh, Jack—it's coming! Now!"

Rugar and Jack were banished to the Great Hall to wait, while the master chambers became a hive of inscrutable female activity. Rugar sat in the hall with his father-in-law, watching his anguish at the possibility of losing his beloved wife in childbed. Rugar thought of how he would feel if it were Corrie in that upper room, and a protective instinct surged through him. It was probably the same sort of feeling the earl had experienced when Corrie was born. And it didn't seem the sort of impulse to dim over time. His animosity toward the earl was dealt a killing blow.

"You know, of course, if this babe is a boy and lives," Jack said heavily, "he will take Corrie's place as my heir." There was regret in his expression as he looked at Rugar. "She will never be Countess of Straffen."

Rugar smiled. "I don't think she will mind. She is a countess already, and I've never known her to be greedy."

Those words, softly spoken, went straight to Jack Huntington's harried heart. In that bit of comfort and in the shared wretchedness of waiting, a peace was made between them.

Three interminably long hours later, Corrie descended the stairs into the Great Hall, where her father and husband and a goodly number of the servants sat in fearful suspense. Her father lunged to his feet, and a smile bloomed on her face as she hurried straight to him and took his outstretched hands.

"You've a son, Father. A new heir." The mixed emotions in his face as he received the news tugged at her heartstrings. "Congratulations, my lord earl," she said, kissing his cheek.

He engulfed her in a great hug, then shouted to the whole hall, "I've a son—it's a boy-child!" Amidst the servants' cheering, he went bounding up the stairs to see Merrie and the babe.

Not long afterward, Corrie led Rugar to her chamber. When the door had closed on them, she threw herself into his arms and kissed him as if she were starving and he were manna from heaven. The excitement of his return and the earthy and overwhelming experience of assisting with her brother's birth had made Corrie feel her femininity deeply, had kindled a hunger in her for the fullness of a woman's pleasures. Holding his mouth captive on hers, she led him toward the bed, working his ties and buttons as quickly as her trembling fingers would allow.

"How I've missed you," she murmured, dragging his doublet from him even as he fumbled with her bodice. "Come, show me what husbands are good for."

"I should think you'd seen quite enough of 'what husbands are good for' this day," he murmured, holding her tight against him and gazing wonderingly into her eyes.

"You are a troublesome lot." She smiled seductively as she untied his shirt and nuzzled the silky hair on his chest. "But you do have your compensations." The ties of his breeches went next, and they slid to the floor. "So . . . come and 'recompense' me." She raked his lower lip with her teeth. "Kisses . . . I want kisses."

In mere heartbeats, he had stripped the rest of her clothes from her, and bore her back onto the bed with a throaty, impatient growl. Trapping her beneath him, he showered dozens of short, noisy kisses all over her face and shoulders. A moment later, he paused on his elbows above her, panting.

"Enough?"

She narrowed her eyes to a sultry glare. "Not *English* kisses . . . I want *Swedish* kisses." When he looked confused, she scowled. "Don't tell me you've forgotten how."

"Can't remember a bit of it," he declared with a sly grin. "Perhaps you could . . . *teach me*."

Laughing, she rose immediately to the challenge, pushing him down onto the bed on his back and sliding atop him. When she sat up, astride his belly, the sight of his bare torso trapped between her naked thighs sent a quiver of excitement through her, and she wriggled in response.

Then, coming back to the business at hand, she lowered herself over his chest so that she was nose to nose with him.

"This is an English kiss." She laid a dry, smacking kiss on his cheek. "And this." Another quick, compulsory-feeling squish on the lips, and she paused for a bit of commentary. "You see? Brisk, robust, and juiceless. Thoroughly English."

"Hmmm," he murmured judgmentally. "And a Swedish kiss?"

"Now, mind closely—this first part is important." Wetting her lips provocatively, she leaned over his mouth. "Part your lips. A bit more. Ummm . . . very nice, milord." Tilting her head, she pressed her mouth to his and made wet, tantalizing circles over his lips. Then her tongue darted into his mouth and teased his to life, caressing it with long, sinuous strokes that generated tremors in the very core of him. His arms suddenly clamped around her, and he returned her kiss with voracious hunger. When she raised her head, minutes later, her eyes could scarcely focus.

"There you have it," she said hoarsely. "Slow, soul-jarring, and juicy. Thoroughly Swedish."

"It's nice to know you still think so highly of Sweden," he murmured thickly.

Her gaze finally righted on his passion-darkened face and roguish smile. "The marvelous thing about Swedish kisses is"—her eyes glowed—"they're not limited to lips."

It was a flagrantly wanton invitation. And he accepted it. In a trice she found herself on her back, trapped beneath his gloriously hard and heated body, being consumed by searing, openmouthed kisses; sharp, erotic nibbles; and tender, rousing suckles. Her earlobes, her throat, her breasts, the crooks of her elbows and waist, all were given exquisite, lingering attention that made her squirm and sigh and squeal. Then his mouth drifted to areas she had never considered particularly kissworthy . . . hipbones and knees and the sensitive flesh of her inner thighs . . .

"Oh, Rugar. Should you really . . . I never imagined that would feel so . . . Ohhh!"

"Lie still," he whispered, enforcing his command with masterful hands and subtle shifts of his body. "I think I'm finally getting the knack of it."

"You certainly are." She drew breath and shuddered. "Only . . . perhaps . . . a bit to the left? Ahhh . . . what marvelous lips you have, milord."

Fiery darts of pleasure slithered up her legs, then plunged inward and collected in the sensitive hollow of her woman's body. With eager hands, she returned his caresses and soon lured him between her thighs. Then with brazen roundings of her woman's mound against his hardened shaft, she enticed him into the creamy heat of her body and hissed softly as he parted her flesh with his and filled her.

It wasn't possible to rein passions so long denied and so deeply desired. They moved together, undulating in wild, changing rhythms, rolling and tossing in total abandonment . . . until their senses were filled to bursting and exploded. Wave upon wave of heat roared through them, dissolving their individual boundaries, mingling their senses, so that each experienced the other's deepest throes of pleasure. They rose and soared, spread on pleasure's hot winds.

Later, they lay entangled, deliciously exhausted, wrung of every drop of pleasure. "This feels so good," he murmured.

"Ummm . . . yes." She undulated slowly against him from his thighs up to his chest.

"I meant the bed," he said with a chuckle, then— "Owww!"—winced when she thwacked him on the shoulder. "Make no mistake, you feel marvelous, too, sweetness. It's just that, after nights of sleeping on the cold ground, listening to Torgne's doleful sighs and snoring—" He suddenly stilled. "Troll's Teeth! Torgne. I forgot all about him!"

Corrie's eyes flew wide. "And Anne!" She sat up quickly.

"Lud, Rugar, she's here and she's been pining for him terribly. She's—she's going to have his child." Rugar's jaw dropped. "I have to tell her he's here!" She rummaged about in the bedcovers for her smock and donned it, then ran to her wardrobe for a dressing gown. By the time she came back to the bed, Rugar had pulled on hose and breeches and was reaching for his shirt.

They flew down the hall and around the gallery to Anne's chambers in the far wing. Corrie tried the latch, found the door bolted, and banged on it. After an agonizing delay, the door swung open a bit, and Anne's glowing face appeared in the crack.

"Anne—Torgne's here!" Corrie gasped.

"He certainly is."

"Troth, I mean—" Corrie frowned, noticing Anne's docile-as-a-lamb smile. "You already know?"

"I found him wandering around . . . and . . . brought him home with me." She let the door swing open. Torgne sat on the edge of the bed, looking sheepish indeed as he fumbled with the ties of his shirt.

"I . . . ummm . . ." He lurched to his feet, reddening. "Anne has agreed to marry me." When Rugar laughed, he reddened even further.

Corrie hugged Anne, then drew back with an impish grin. "'Imagine wanting to marry a Swede,'" she quoted Anne's words back to her. "I guess it's true that some sins are their own punishment."

Anne blushed for the first time in years—and they all laughed.

At the first rays of dawn, just as the kitchens, work-houses, and cottages of the estate had begun to stir, a storm of horseflesh and armed soldiers descended on Straffen Hall. Scores of the queen's mounted guardsmen thundered down the road and across the open fields that sloped toward the manor house.

They surged around and against the hall in a destructive red tide, demanding entrance. Then, without waiting to be admitted, they rammed the front doors again and again to force passage. The time-tempered oak bar held long enough for the house to rouse to the noise of the assault. Jack came charging out of the master chamber, barefoot and with his shirt half on, but with his blade in his hand. From the gallery, he spotted his steward, Seabury, running into the hall below and called out, "Spread the alarm!" As the steward jolted to obey, the doors began to splinter with a series of sickening *cracks*. Jack raced for the stairs, bellowing, "Aelthar, Corrie—queensmen!" By the time he reached the hall below, red coats were squeezing through the breached doors, and he braced to meet them at the bottom of the stairs.

When Jack's bellow of warning reached Corrie's chamber, she and Rugar had already bolted from the bed and were frantically donning breeches and skirts and shoving into boots.

"They've found us out—we'll be arrested!" The anguish in her voice caused him to turn to her for just one instant. Love, pain, longing, anger were compressed into that one look, into that one powerful exchange of instant meaning. If they were taken, there was a good chance they would be parted forever.

"Not this time," Rugar growled, reaching for his sword. "Not without a damned fight!"

The door swung open and Rugar whirled, blade in hand, to find himself facing Straffen's red-faced steward. "Horses . . . I sent word to Chester . . ." Seabury panted. "If you can make it out the side door to the stables . . ."

They lurched into motion, but had scarcely cleared the doorway before a wave of queensmen crested the top of the stairs and forced Jack back along the gallery. Half a dozen guards, directed by a shout of "There they are!" appeared in the hallway to their left and came after them. Rugar and Seabury wheeled and met their charge full on.

Rugar lunged and thrust and slashed, over and over, meeting English steel with a ferocity that momentarily shocked his attackers. The queen's swordsmen fell back, and Rugar and Seabury pursued their advantage, forcing them back onto the gallery, where Jack Huntington had retreated and was being overwhelmed. Across the Great Hall, they could see Torgne engaged in fierce combat, and in the hall below queensmen grappled frantically with servants armed with sticks of firewood, stools, and fire irons.

When a blade tip darted in to slash the shirt above Rugar's shoulder, Corrie cried out his name and started to run to him.

"Go for the horses!" he shouted at her as he lunged and sank his blade into one of his opponents' shoulders. Instantly, two more guardsmen swarmed in to take the place of their fallen comrade. Whirling to gain purchase for a thrust, Rugar glimpsed her shocked hesitation and bellowed, "Go!"

His shout penetrated her panic and sent her down the hall at a dead run. She flew down the servants' stairs and out into the rear yard, where she was stopped in her tracks by a new wave of guardsmen dismounting to invade the rear door of the hall. She ducked around the corner and pressed against the wall, searching frantically for a clear route to the stables. Her heart thudded at the sight of Straffen's burly stableman, Chester, leading saddled horses out the stable door.

Ducking first to the cover of a shrub, she made it to the dovecote and eyed the seemingly endless distance across the open yard to the stables. Gathering both breath and courage, she made a mad dash—and was spotted. The sight of her running toward saddled horses galvanized a number of soldiers who had not yet dismounted, and they started after her. She could never make it in time; the horses were forfeit. "Chester—help!"

At her cry, Chester dropped the reins and ran toward her, dodging riders. "Lady Corrie—" He swept her up in a thick arm and carried her toward the garden and the safety of the house. "Get back inside!"

The butt end of a pike, swung from a pursuing horse, crashed into the back of Chester's head, and he went sprawling . . . but not before he managed to launch Corrie toward the side door. She stumbled and scrambled for footing, and glanced up to see half a dozen guardsmen bearing down on her. Spinning, she made it to the house just steps ahead of them and managed to close and bolt the door. Up the stairs and down the passage toward the Great Hall she flew, searching for Rugar.

The sheer number of guardsmen had overwhelmed Rugar, Jack, and Torgne. They had retreated to the far end of the gallery and appeared to be holding their own against the odds—until she appeared. A shrill male voice called out, "There she is!" and the guards along the gallery railing, between her and Rugar, turned to pursue her. She fled back down the hall, hair and petticoats flying—and ran smack into a contingent of soldiers that had broken down the door and followed her up the side stairs. There was no way out. They stalked and seized her, then hauled her, twisting and struggling, back to the gallery.

A small, wiry man in brown woolens—Morris Lombard— mounted the stairs behind the captain of the guardsmen and immediately took charge. "We have Lady Corinna!" he shouted across the hall. "Lay down your weapons, Swede, Straffen. You have no chance to escape and will only make

things worse for yourselves. And you wouldn't want . . .
Lady Corinna to come to any harm . . ."

Jack was the first to see her, captive in their relentless
hands, and the threat cut him to the quick. Then he recognized the voice of the man who spoke, and knew the threat
was genuine. Morris Lombard would love nothing better
than to inflict pain on a Huntington. The conflict slowed as
Jack disengaged and called to Rugar, "He means it, Aelthar.
He'll hurt her if we don't surrender." Then he called to his
servants and householders in the hall below to cease fighting and save themselves.

Rugar was the last to be taken. He fought on, spurred by
sheer anguish, and wounded yet another guardsman. But
when he caught a glimpse of Corrie standing on the far side
of the gallery with tears streaming down her face, he finally
admitted it was lost and disengaged. They seized him and
Torgne and Jack, and dragged them around the gallery
and downstairs to the Great Hall, where the turmoil was
slowly dying.

The household looked on in horror as Rugar and Torgne
were bound tightly and Morris Lombard strutted back and
forth, savoring his long-awaited victory. Jack lunged at him
and was caught back and given a chastening blow by the
guardsmen who held him.

"Don't try anything foolish, Huntington," Lombard
crowed, brandishing a parchment bearing a royal seal. "I
have a writ of arrest signed by the queen herself, and I am
empowered to add the name of any who would impede the
execution of the queen's justice. Your daughter's husband is
a foul, heathen rogue who must be brought to justice for abducting God-fearing English subjects, trespassing England's
sovereign borders, and conspiring against our queen."

"You cursed weasel—" Jack snarled. "You foul, putrefying piece of —"

"One more word, Huntington, and I shall add your name to the writ. Then where will your precious wife and daughters be?" Lombard sneered, stalking closer to Jack. "I've waited a long time for this. How does it feel to be on the receiving end, Huntington?" Then he turned and ordered his men to bring Lady Corinna and the baroness downstairs as well.

"My wife has done nothing—" Rugar strained against his bonds and received a blow to the ribs that doubled him over.

"She is included in the writ," Lombard proclaimed nastily, "as is Baroness Bosworth. They are to go to the palace. And *you*"—he punched a knotty finger at Rugar and Torgne— "go to the Tower."

As he was dragged toward the door, Rugar managed to gasp out something about credentials to Jack—before a hamlike fist silenced him. Shortly, he and Torgne were shoved into a commandeered farm cart, without coat or cover as protection from the elements, and were carried off toward the London Road.

Corrie was permitted enough time to gown herself and to pack a small bag. She'd had no parting from Rugar; no last embrace, no last word. She felt as if a piece of her had been ripped away. She moved as if in a fog, unseeing, unthinking, unable to believe it had all happened a second time. It was little comfort to her that Anne was soon deposited in the cart alongside her for the long ride to London. Behind her, through the wrecked doors of Straffen Hall, she could hear her father grappling with the soldiers who had been left behind to restrain him until they were safely away, and shouting to her that he would find some way to help.

Corrie and Anne were taken directly to Hampton Court Palace, outside London, and were locked in separate,

Spartan chambers. Two interminable days passed as Corrie sat in abject solitude, seeing no one but the guard who brought her food and water. She slowly realized that the isolation, silence, and endless waiting were deliberate . . . meant to make her frightened, as they had before, and penitential. She was expected to use her time to ponder and rue her wrongs against the queen—whatever they were supposed to be.

But Corrie Kalisson was no longer the naive little maid Elizabeth had bedazzled and brought to court for her own private amusement. She was a woman now, with a woman's heart fired and tempered by adversity. She did succumb to tears now and again, but instead of cowering and wringing her hands, she paced her small chamber for exercise and recited her favorite passages from Seneca to steady her mind. The long hours only clarified her thoughts and deepened her resolve to stand against her arrogant sovereign.

In all those hours, Rugar was constantly in her heart and in her most fervent prayers. What fate awaited him, she could only guess. But he had entered England, already wanted for a previous "abduction," with the clear intent of taking an English subject from the country without the queen's permission. It mattered not that his "victim" was his lawful wife and that she had wanted to go with him; Elizabeth could have her wretched legions of lawyers weave a net of falsehoods and half-truths to entrap St. Peter himself! And to every angry charge, to every bald accusation, Rugar would likely raise that stubborn chin of his and make matters that much worse for himself. He was a Swede, a foreigner, and disastrously proud of it. In her mind the prejudices he would face and the defiance he would display to an English tribunal grew appallingly clear.

On the third day, the guardsmen came for her, taking her by the arms and leading her through a maze of narrow corridors. They sullenly ignored her demands to know where she was being taken. As they proceeded, the corridors widened and arched, and the walls became plastered and the floors wooden. They mounted a set of ornately carved stairs, and their surroundings became all marble and tapestry and giltwork and carved wooden ceilings. Anxiety constricted Corrie's lungs.

There was no doubt; she was being taken to the queen.

She was ushered forcefully through a great set of double doors, into the Queen's Audience Chamber, and dragged forward under the stares of a number of councillors, court officers, and secretaries.

Elizabeth stood by a long, leaded window, staring out over the Thames with her hands clasped before her. She was clothed in pearl-crusted black velvet, with great fanlike headrails rising from her shoulders and a notable ruff and a number of strings of pearls down her bodice. "The Lady Corinna." One of her escorts said her name, then waited to be acknowledged. Slowly, Elizabeth turned to face Corrie, her face as stark as her black gown. After a long moment she waved her hand, and the guardsmen released Corrie and retreated just outside the door.

"Corinna." She came forward slowly, allowing her wide skirts to swish the floor with each step.

Corrie executed a stiff curtsey, then looked tightly around the chamber at the faces trained upon her. There was a noteworthy lack of scarlet robes, and there were no spectators or judicial bench. Elizabeth's pet dogs tussled near the hearth, and papers of state littered the great writing table, tended by secretaries. It was a tableau from the working life of a queen, a scene Corrie had glimpsed numerous times.

"Where is the tribunal, Your Grace? The one that is to hear the charges against me."

"There are no charges against you, Corinna," Elizabeth

said curtly. There was a subtle tightening around her mouth that bespoke irritation with Corrie's unexpected mien.

"If there are none, Your Grace, then why am I kept as a prisoner . . . confined to a small chamber, prohibited from seeing anyone, forbidden even to write a letter?"

"You are here as a witness."

"Against whom? My husband?" Corrie choked on a sudden roil of volatile emotions. Dearest Heaven—did they really expect to make her bear witness against Rugar?

"He carried off my subjects!" Elizabeth stalked closer and glared hotly at her. "He invaded my borders and flouted my sovereign authority and—"

"And stole your 'pet,'" Corrie said hoarsely, before she could bite it back.

Elizabeth's face filled with blotchy color beneath its layers of counterfeit youth. She whirled abruptly and shouted for all in the chamber to leave, instantly. There was a less-than-dignified scramble for the door as the echoes of her shrill order died in the polished chamber.

When the door had closed and they were alone, Elizabeth began to pace furiously, staring at the scarred floor. Anger was visible in every line of her imposing frame, anger so towering that it was impossible to see anything else in her. Corrie had dared much with her words, and she held her breath, waiting to learn if they would be counted as treason, too. Finally the queen stopped and advanced on her.

"He's lied to you about me, poisoned you against me— the barbarous wretch!" The flecks of fire in her eyes united into a blaze that would have charred a lesser soul. But Corrie stood her ground.

"He has never lied to me," she declared. "Not even when a lie would have made things easier between us." Corrie balled her trembling hands into fists at her sides to steady herself. "Any poison between you and me . . . is not of his doing."

Elizabeth's dark eyes now burned like dark coals. She stiffened, her eyes darting over Corrie, plumbing the new depths she glimpsed within her. Then she whirled and retreated behind the writing table, near the window. Corrie choked on inward tears and swallowed hard to clear her throat.

"You had my husband abducted on my wedding night. And when he escaped and came to me anyway, you had him abducted a second time." She lurched to the writing table, grasping the edge for support. "Then he came for me and took me to his home . . . and you sent my father and that cursed Lombard to bring me back to England. You've taken me from my husband's side twice, battered him, and arrested me." Her expression, like her voice, was raw with pain.

"Why . . . why would you do such things to me? What have I done that was so terrible?" she whispered.

"It has naught to do with you." Elizabeth turned on her, vibrating with tangled emotion. "It's him . . . he's the one who schemed and connived, beguiled you and stole you from me."

"It has everything to do with me, can you not see that? I'm not a pet or a curiosity or a thing to be possessed—or *stolen*. I'm a woman, a flesh-and-blood being, with a mind and dreams and desires of my own, and a heart that beats and loves . . . and sometimes breaks. He did not steal me. I gave myself to him, out of love."

The pain evident in Corrie's delicate face somehow unleashed Elizabeth's own. For one brief moment she stood outside the trappings of rank power, a woman of great personal force . . . and pathos.

"I loved you as a bit of my own heart," Elizabeth said, her voice hushed and filled with mingled hurt and anger. "I gave you my favor, my protection, my confidence. And you betrayed me!"

"I never betrayed you, Your Grace." Tears ran down Corrie's cheeks. "I loved and trusted you in all things. I adored you as my sovereign lady, my guide, my friend. I was always loyal to you, even as I learned to love my lord husband." She leaned across the writing table. "Can you truly believe that because I chose to love him, I had no love left for you? The heart is not a basket, Your Grace, which when its contents are parceled out is merely empty." She reached deep into her heart for the tatters of the love she had once borne for her beloved queen.

"One love does not replace another in the human heart. The heart merely enlarges to make more room."

Elizabeth's eyes shimmered and her chin quivered as she stared at the light in Corrie's countenance. Each word convicted her; each bit of wisdom grated with unexpected sharpness on a conscience so often eclipsed by the worldly necessities of rank and statecraft that it had atrophied. She silently recoiled from that discomfort, retreating into the safety of her queenly persona.

"I refused to believe you had a hand in abducting Rugar, refused to believe you would ever behave so vengefully . . . until you abducted me forcibly from his side," Corrie went on, desperate to say what lay in her heart and heedless of the disparity of their rank and power. "You once told me the Almighty entrusted the virtue of loyalty to women. Then what of queens? Do they not share that precious womanly trust?"

Elizabeth flinched and paled as Corrie's tacit charge against her loyalty struck.

"Enough!" Seizing her voluminous skirts in trembling hands, she rushed toward the door, shouting furiously, "Guards! Guards!" When they came bursting into the chamber, pikes poised defensively, she pointed to Corrie. "Remove her—take her back to her chambers, immediately!"

Minutes later, Corrie sank down on the narrow bed in her barren chamber and gave way to full sobs. It was her one chance to be heard . . . and she'd thrown caution to the wind and accused Elizabeth instead of placating her and pleading for Rugar's safety. She'd been so caught up, she hadn't even learned what the queen planned for them. If their doom hadn't already been decreed, she realized, her own reckless behavior just now had likely sealed it.

Chapter Twenty-One

Early that afternoon, William Cecil, Lord Burghley, hurried toward the Audience Chamber of Hampton Court as quickly as his aging legs would carry him. His long, august face was grimly set, his eyes as dark as his customarily somber garments. In all his long and sometimes perilous years of advising Elizabeth, he had learned that when she took the bit firmly in her mouth and set her head, there was no turning her from her course, however disastrous. And in the matter of Lady Corinna and the Swede, her chosen course had been disastrous from the very start.

Jack Huntington strode at Cecil's side, his countenance equally bleak. He had hurried from Straffen straight to Elizabeth's trusted Secretary, knowing he could influence the queen, if anyone could. When the queen's guardsmen withdrew from Straffen, Jack had searched Rugar's belongings and found the pouch containing royal documents among his personal effects. But as important as those precious documents were, he knew that Elizabeth was capable of striking them all aside without a qualm if they ran counter to her will. He depended heavily upon Cecil's power of persuasion with Elizabeth. It might prove Corrie's only hope.

As they approached the guarded doors, Cecil paused to instruct Jack. "Let me speak for the both of us. And whatever she says or does to provoke you, hold both your temper and your tongue. Your son-in-law's head may depend upon it."

Elizabeth sat in a huge, carved chair near the hearth, brooding, her elbow on the chair arm and her chin propped on a fist. One look at Cecil's taut expression, the sheaf of documents in his hands, and his companion, and she knew instantly what this interview was about.

"If I had known you were bringing him"—she flung a finger at Jack while addressing Cecil—"I'd have refused to see you. If you've come to intercede for the Swede or to plead for Corinna, save your breath. I'll hear none of it."

Cecil bowed, drawing Jack down with him. "Your Grace, if you will stop your ears, then prithee, at least open your eyes . . . upon these." He held out the small stack of documents. "They are the count's credentials, and letters of support from Swedish nobles."

"I'll not touch the cursed things!"

"He is a *full ambassador,* Your Grace," Cecil said evenly, undeterred.

"He is a rogue, a foul seducer, and a trespasser!" she insisted.

"But he is a *credentialed* rogue, foul seducer, and trespasser," Cecil argued with some exasperation. "You cannot ignore the urgings of a fellow monarch in this matter . . . particularly the rogue's monarch." He paused for emphasis. "Especially since he has written you a letter."

"A letter?" she bit out, her body snapping forward. She took the sealed letter Cecil held out to her and visibly contemplated tossing it into the nearby flames, before ripping open the seal and perusing it. Her face reddened as she read, her eyes narrowed and sparked, and her thin mouth drew into a single line.

"Damn and blast!" she roared, lurching from her chair to pace back and forth, staring at the parchment. "He begs me to intervene with the gell's father, to see her restored to her husband and, in time, to the Swedish court—where she has many admirers, himself included!" She halted and flung the letter down onto her chair and paced away, rubbing her hands together. The letter clearly disturbed her for a number of reasons, not the least of which was the way it revealed that Rugar Kalisson enjoyed a special place in his king's affections.

"What am I expected to do—just throw down my borders and allow any knave or thief or pretender to come and carry off whatever part of my kingdom he fancies?" she raged.

"With all respect, Your Grace, he did not carry off any part of your kingdom except one woman . . . and her his lawful wife," Cecil reasoned.

"I want the insolent wretch punished—made an example to all who counter my will!"

Cecil settled a canny gaze upon his mistress. Through her protests, he heard the keening wail of wounded pride. It was not the breach of the borders of her nation that infuriated Elizabeth; it was the violation of the boundaries of her personal gravity, dignity, and emotions. Such an injury, while beyond the scope of law, was grave indeed to a ruling monarch and required retribution.

"Then fit the punishment to the offense," Cecil proposed with a stroke of diplomatic brilliance. "He trespassed your borders and offended English sovereignty . . . then make him pay homage to it. Give him the chance to redeem himself . . . by pledging fealty and service to England. And to yourself."

"God's Teeth—do you honestly imagine he would—" But Elizabeth halted, and a calculating glint quickly replaced the scorn in her expressive eyes. The idea seized her imagination. It would be an interesting test of his vaunted male conceit and his insufferable Swedish pride to put that very choice before him . . . while Corinna looked on. He must bow the knee and pledge loyalty to her and to England, or forfeit his marriage and his life with the wife he claimed to love, to spend years in the Tower. An icy smile spread over her face. The idea appealed to every part of her.

"Troth, Cecil . . . what would I do without you? An excellent solution. I shall send to the Tower immediately for the Swede and his jackanapes of a friend." She turned on Jack Huntington with a fierce and queenly smile. "Never let it be said that Elizabeth dealt unjustly, even with those who dealt treacherously with her."

"You are a very fount of mercy, Your Grace," Jack said with a solemn look which scarcely covered his dread.

Rugar and Torgne were taken separately from their cells in the Tower of London to small chambers at Hampton Court Palace, where they were permitted to bathe and given a change of garments. Stony silence greeted each of their demands to know why they'd been summoned, and in that disconcerting quiet, each read a grim portent.

As soon as he was washed and clothed, Rugar was taken, under close guard, through several corridors, outside, and across a large court overseen by a great clock. A trial, that was Rugar's guess, and without time and recourse to lawyers to prepare a case. He was led up a great set of stairs into the grand public chambers of the palace, where he glimpsed the familiar faces of men associated primarily with Elizabeth's governance. He was led into the Audience Chamber, which contained a number of milling councillors, court officers, and a few lords and ladies.

The entire hall was constructed to focus attention on the great gilded chair on a single-stepped dais, where Elizabeth sat, clad in stark black and white, conferring with her somber advisors.

At the forefront of the lords, near the queen, stood Corrie's father, his wrists clasped tightly before him and his bearing grave. Rugar felt the earl's eyes upon him as he was brought forward, and those eyes seemed to plead with Rugar. But for what? he thought grimly, searching the chamber for some hint of what was afoot. Judicial robes were conspicuous by their absence, and there was no table or bench; the trappings of a trial were missing altogether. Had he been called here for sentencing . . . to hear himself declared guilty and condemned to forfeit his freedom—or even his head? Kings and queens seldom bothered with such formalities, he knew. They simply issued a warrant and had the deed done—keeping the gore out of sight and out of mind, both for their own conscience' sake and to forestall any sympathy for the condemned.

As he was thrust forward to stand before the throne, flanked on each side by a pair of guardsmen, Torgne was brought in under equally close guard and was halted slightly behind and beside Rugar, but facing him, so that Rugar could see his grim expression. They managed to exchange speaking looks. They had weathered much together, and each was comforted by the other's presence. Then Rugar raised his head . . . and saw Corrie being escorted into the chamber from a side door.

He felt stunned and air-starved, as if he'd fallen down a well. She was garbed in black velvet, with only small ruffs at her neck and wrists to soften the starkness of her garments, and she wore a white silk cap overlaid with a black and silver French hood. It was the sort of gown she had worn when he first knew her, simple and uncontrived, the very expression of her inner self. Her face was pale, and her large, jewellike eyes bore traces of sleeplessness beneath them as they searched him with undisguised longing.

He wanted to go to her, to gather her into his arms, just for a moment.

Corrie was brought to stand twenty feet from the man she loved and constrained to only look at him. She, too, had been summoned without a word of explanation or warning, and she, too, had dreaded what she would find. Now relief went through her at the sight of him whole and hale, followed by near anguish at the sight of him captive and constrained. He was so tall and noble and proud, and because of his love for her, so doomed. They had undoubtedly been brought here to have their fate announced, but in her heart she already knew their lot; the queen, deeply wounded and vengeful, was set to destroy them. And the queen's angry pride—Corrie gazed miserably about her at the august personages Elizabeth had assembled—demanded an audience for her vengeance.

A herald called the chamber to attention, and the Lord Chamberlain himself stepped forward in the hushed company to unroll a document and read the charges against Rugar. The text was glowering and pretentious. Every experienced ear detected in the charges Elizabeth's personal tone and syntax; clearly, she had dictated them herself.

". . . did breach the trust of crown and nation to unlawfully, and with malice, abduct loyal English subjects from their rightful home . . . to wit: Lady Corinna Huntington Kalisson and Baroness Anne of Bosworth . . ."

Corrie's heart thudded painfully as she stared at Rugar; then she dragged her eyes to the queen, who leaned to one side on the arm of the chair, her dark, unreadable eyes penetrating in their scrutiny of Rugar.

". . . did willingly and knowingly enter the sovereign reaches of the English realm without clear passage, and with the foul intent to steal the persons aforenamed and to defy and to injure the English crown . . ."

It was a harrowing list. Rugar heard in each charge a

knell against his freedom, perhaps against his very life. When he glanced at Corrie, the tears rising in her eyes were torture to him. In that moment he would have given any-thing—*anything*—to go back to that late November night when he'd been caught with her, or to that first glimpse of her on the dais at the tournament. If only he could undo some part of it . . . purge the driving lust for revenge that had brought them both such pain.

All fell silent as the Lord Chamberlain finished and stepped back to the edge of the dais. Elizabeth straight-ened, laid her hands regally over the arms of her chair, and regarded Rugar with cool disdain.

"You have heard the complaints against you. You have set your head and your hand against me, Aelthar. More than once. You were a foreigner in my country, admitted to my presence under the grace extended to your lord and sover-eign. You were sent to serve him . . . and served your own purposes instead. Against my expressed wishes, you courted and beguiled a woman of my own chambers, and compro-mised her." There was a murmur around the chamber at that. "And when I permitted you to marry to save her name, you betrayed my generosity by stealing from the country like a thief—abducting her and carrying her abroad without my knowledge or consent! And to make matters worse, you carried off another lady of my chambers, unrelated to you."

She rose with vehement, queenly gravity and stepped down from the dais. "I have legal recourse against you. I have it in my power to sign a warrant this instant"—she gestured as if stroking broadly with a pen—"and imprison you for life—or even render you shorter by the head!" Her eyes narrowed on Rugar's tightly controlled expression, as if searching for some sign of quailing. Finding none, she raised her head to regard him speculatively in the breathless silence.

"But to imprison or behead you serves no purpose but

vengeance . . . and God knows, I am not a vengeful woman. I have witnessed your skill at arms and the pride and loyalty with which you wield them in Sweden's name. Your allegiance to your native land has carried you to great lengths." Her eyes sought his. "It would be a foul waste of such nobility to have you mired away in the Tower for the rest of your stubborn life. I would instead—as the Almighty did with Joseph in the land of Egypt—bring good out of the evil that has been done. I would turn your arm and your skill and your loyalty to better purpose."

She stalked a step closer. "I offer you a chance—*one chance*—to redeem yourself and salvage the life you have so recklessly hazarded in breaching English sovereignty and defying the royal will." She paused, savoring the flicker of shock she glimpsed beneath his controlled mien. And she delivered her final thrust.

"You must kneel in homage to both England and myself . . . and swear before God to pledge both your loyalty and your service to England and to me."

The words fell with the force of a war hammer in Rugar's mind. He almost staggered. A wave of shocked murmurs ran through the councillors and court officers, and he heard Corrie gasp.

Elizabeth would give him his life, his marriage, his future—Rugar scrambled mentally—for an oath of loyalty to her and to the country he'd spent half his lifetime loathing. In all his deepest fear and dread he had never imagined being presented with such a choice. She demanded his honor, his loyalty to Sweden as the price of his future. His ribs seemed to contract violently around his heart and lungs; he could scarcely breathe.

When he looked into her canny, piercing eyes, he realized she had read him true and fully understood the conflict such an offer would generate in him. He could have his loyalty to Corrie and a life with her, or his knightly oath of honor and his loyalty to Sweden; she was forcing him to choose. The turmoil such a choice bred within him was massive, crushing . . . exactly as she had intended it to be.

Dragging his eyes from Elizabeth, he turned them first on Torgne, whose look of shared pain neither condoned nor condemned. It was Rugar's decision, that look said. And then, as if unable to bear the sight of Rugar's dilemma, Torgne lowered his eyes. Rugar's gaze flew to Corrie, who watched him through a veil of tears, hurting visibly for him. She wanted him desperately but, true to her loving nature, would not plead with him to abandon honor and the other love of his heart. It was his choice, the love shining through her tears said eloquently, and she would love him, no matter which he chose.

Rugar was acutely alone. And yet the fate of several lives lay upon his broad shoulders.

Elizabeth had watched Rugar's gaze fly to Corrie and seen Corrie's pained and loving expression. She intercepted Corrie's gaze and leveled a speaking look upon her former pet. See where a man's loyalties will lead him, that gaze declared. And prepare to rue your wretched choice of him, for he will never choose you, a woman, over his honor, his vow of loyalty to something loftier . . . his country.

Corrie understood the retribution that was intended upon herself in this offer of clemency and closed her eyes and lowered her head.

Rugar stiffened, his mind racing, his heart thudding. The hard lessons of recent months reared their heads through the tempest raging in his core. His betrayed love for his homeland . . . the futility and destructiveness of revenge . . . the equity of human nature, which knew no national bounds . . . the character of true loyalty . . . the value of a healing and unconditional love.

His own words to Corrie came back to him: there was nothing—no country, no people, no king, no pride—nothing more important to him than loving her. Seeing her injured, he had faced the truth about the flaws in his people and in himself. Seeing her forgiveness, he had learned the marvel of the human heart. Seeing her goodness, he had yearned to be a better, more noble man himself. She had opened new worlds to him, taught him with her innocence and the sweet nobility of her love. She had put her faith in him . . . and he must be worthy of it.

The storm raging in him slowly quieted. He had spoken truthfully; his love for Corrie mattered more than anything in his life. And he must find a way to serve that love . . . in all honor.

Every eye in the chamber was trained hard upon him. Scarcely a breath was taken or released. Rugar stepped forward, his hands clenched at his sides, and every heart stopped.

He went down on his knees before Elizabeth in the raging silence.

"I, Rugar Kalisson, Count of Aelthar"—his voice rang deep and clear—"do hereby swear before God to bear faith and fealty to the English state and to Elizabeth, her sovereign queen . . . just as I am loyal and faithful to the land of my birth. And I swear to uphold and to serve England and Elizabeth, her queen, in every interest and endeavor, with all my strength and might and purpose . . . even as I have sworn to uphold Sweden and Johan, her king."

Silence fell with his last words. After a moment's shocked silence, a commotion broke out among the lords and witnesses. He had fulfilled Elizabeth's conditions . . . but added his own. He had sworn to uphold England . . . but only as he did Sweden. Had he salvaged his freedom with such an oath, or not?

"You dare to place another country beside England in your oath, Swede? A divided loyalty is no loyalty at all!"

Elizabeth declared hotly, infuriated by his ploy and by his unexpected choice in her test of loyalty.

"Years ago I took a knightly oath to Sweden, to love and uphold and defend her. What was given was given. I cannot renounce or withdraw that oath. I can only pledge myself to England and to you as my queen as well. I shall love and serve England . . . I shall honor and serve Elizabeth as my queen, as you have required. But I cannot denounce or deny the oath I once made to the country of my birth."

Elizabeth reddened visibly; her eyes crackled with fires of indignation. Her first impulse was to cut off the rogue's wretched head! But then she was never one to act on her first instinct—or sometimes even her second. She turned aside to pace and stopped short, finding herself facing Corrie's tear-filled eyes. In those liquid depths was a hope, a faith that reminded her of former days . . . of a precious innocence she had claimed briefly and then lost to another. Those eyes spoke to her of all the nobility and higher principles they had witnessed in her queenly heart. Rugar had chosen Corrie and England, and those eyes pleaded for Elizabeth to honor that choice. She whirled away, then paced back, staring down at Rugar.

Behind her hard look, Rugar glimpsed a wavering will and spoke to it. "I was sent as Johan's ambassador, to serve you. Pray allow me to be your ambassador as well . . . to help bring the English and Swedish courts closer together." In a final act of fealty, he bowed his head to her.

"You will make England your home, your principal seat?" she demanded in a choked voice.

Rugar's head snapped up. "I will."

"You will further English interests and serve English purposes, even with the Swedish court if necessary?"

"I shall, as God will give me grace to do," he said solemnly.

Elizabeth stared at him for a long, scintillant moment,

searching the earnestness in his face, the emotion embedded in his eyes. Her angular hauteur softened briefly as she stepped closer.

"Do you love her so?"

Her poignant words carried no further than Rugar and his guards. But she did not wait for his answer; she already knew it. She lifted her skirts and strode back to her great chair.

"Rise, Aelthar . . . new Englishman . . . redeemed rogue and miscreant." When he was again on his feet, she sat down on her chair with dramatic flair. "You are henceforth my loyal subject. And within the bounds of that broad and merciful grace, you are free to go."

For a while Rugar just stood, disbelieving his eyes and ears. *Free to go.* Then his tension suddenly melted.

"Your Grace." He made a deep and reverent bow, then turned immediately to Corrie, who met him halfway and slid into his arms with a joyful sob of relief.

His eyes closed. His jaw clenched against the tidal wave of emotion surging inside. At that moment, he held his entire world in the circle of his arms.

Suddenly Jack Huntington was beside them, clapping Rugar on the shoulder and prying Corrie from his possessive embrace to give her a hug. The Lord Chamberlain himself came down from the dais to offer Rugar a hand of welcome, and the chamber erupted with noisy relief. Only one heart in the chamber was left unmoved by the sight of Corrie and Rugar's reunion; Morris Lombard stood by the side door in his new legal robes, furious at the outcome of the queen's test—and of that indominable "Huntington luck."

In the midst of it all, Corrie pulled away and approached the throne. Elizabeth's aloofness was forced and haunting. Of all present, Corrie understood best what this act of queenly grace had cost Elizabeth in personal terms. Whatever Elizabeth's faults as a woman or a friend, Corrie realized, she was peerless in her role as monarch. She sank onto her knees before her former mistress. When she raised her head, her face was shining with gratitude and with something even more important: a restored bit of faith in her sovereign queen.

"Thank you, Your Grace."

Elizabeth met her jewel-clear eyes one last time and nodded.

By the time Corrie and Rugar reached the doors, they were engulfed in a full storm of excitement and congratulations. Rugar lifted her in a fierce hug and whirled her around and around, laughing through the emotion that clogged his throat.

"Free—" Corrie choked out, hugging him as if she'd never let him go. "We're free!"

"And home," he said thickly, gazing into her glowing face. "We're home."

As they made their way through the human gauntlet of goodwill outside the Audience Chamber, Corrie turned a smile over her shoulder and caught a glimpse of Torgne being ushered before Elizabeth. "Torgne!" she gasped, pulling Rugar to a halt.

"Troll's teeth—I forgot all about him!"

They hurried back to stand behind him as Elizabeth sat eyeing his tall, taciturn form with blatant skepticism. "I'm not sure I fancy redeeming *two* Swedes in one afternoon," she said caustically. When he reddened and stiffened, she sighed heavily. "Nor do I fancy having that long, gloomy face impaled upon the Tower gates." There was a murmur among the onlookers as she added, "I don't suppose you would like to be an Englishman as well . . ."

Torgne crimsoned in stoic Swedish silence.

"I supposed not. Well, I cannot just let you go, you . . . rogue's apprentice." Elizabeth propped her chin upon her fist.

"If I may be so bold as to offer assistance, Your Grace." Rugar stepped to the side, bowed, then braved Elizabeth's surprise to stand forth between them. "If I may suggest a fitting punishment for a Swede who has demonstrated less-than-perfect respect for England . . ."

Elizabeth narrowed her eyes on him and said suspiciously, "You may."

"Make him take an English bride, Your Grace," he suggested with great drama. "Someone who will outwit and outtalk and utterly dazzle and befuddle him. Someone who will spend him blind as a beggar . . . and make him old before his time."

Elizabeth snorted a most unladylike laugh. "'Od's Teeth, Aelthar, you do have a devious mind. Be warned, I shall watch to see it is always used in my service." She paused, eyeing Torgne, considering it, then turned back to Rugar. "Unless I miss my guess, you have a candidate for his comeuppance already in mind."

"Anne, Baroness Bosworth, Your Grace." Rugar laid the name before her with a respectful nod.

"I might have guessed." She turned to Torgne, thinking of the pair together. Flirtatious, sharp-tongued Anne of Bosworth and this priggish, long-faced Swede . . . God only knew how they would get on.

"I would be pleased to help negotiate the marriage, Your Grace," Rugar offered earnestly, "as someone with both English and Swedish interests dear to heart."

"See it done, then!" Elizabeth smacked her palm down on the arm of the chair. She leaned forward and impaled Torgne's shocked form with her sardonic stare. "And may God have mercy upon your soul."

As Rugar and Corrie collected Torgne and hurried

toward the doors, William Cecil stepped to the side of Elizabeth's great chair and followed her gaze to the handsome pair and their friend. He heard her heavy sigh as she watched the threesome pause outside the doors to joyfully embrace each other.

"A most queenly bit of justice, Ma'am," he murmured.

"It was indeed. But then, Cecil, I am *always* queenly."

In the corridor, Torgne whooped and threw his arms around both Corrie and Rugar, thanking Rugar for suggesting his "punishment." Corrie laughed through more tears and flung her arms around Torgne while Rugar grabbed his hand and pumped his arm in vigorous congratulations. Then the earl clapped his shoulder and offered to lay on a huge wedding celebration at Straffen, a gesture Torgne was pleased to accept.

As the earl led them off toward the ladies' apartments to free Anne and give her the wonderful news, Torgne's great, beaming smile came under a cloud, and he pulled back on Rugar's arm.

"Do you really think she'll spend me blind?"

Corrie laughed. Rugar roared.

Epilogue

One month later, the hall and grounds of Straffen Manor overflowed with guests and rang with merry toasts and gay celebrations of the various wonders and passages of life. Noble families from the entire county had come to enjoy Straffen's famous hospitality and to shake off the doldrums of the fading winter. Noteworthy among the guests was Baron Henry Huntington, Jack Huntington's dour eldest brother and Anne's father, who had come to be reunited with the earl after more than two decades of estrangement.

The first day of feasting celebrated the marriage of Baron Torgne Sigurd and Baroness Anne of Bosworth, and their recent purchase of an estate not far from Corrie and Rugar's holdings in Essex. The second day feted the five-month-old marriage of Corrie and Rugar, and the new home they had just been granted as part of Corrie's revised wedding settlement. And the third day's merriment centered on the christening of Corrie's infant brother, the new heir of the earldom of Straffen.

But three successive days of energetic games and dancing and sporting, and three successive nights of determined feasting, had gradually taken their toll. By the end of the third day, most of the guests had taken either to their horses or to their makeshift beds in and about Straffen Hall, leaving the family mostly to itself. Jack and Merrie Huntington, both pairs of newlyweddeds, Anne's father and mother, and the good bishop who had presided over the festivities lolled pleasantly about the huge table in the Great Hall, enjoying the calm and the mellowness of kinship.

"He's a fine strapping boy, your lordship." Henry Huntington raised one final goblet to his younger brother. "And a most interesting name, Roarke Huntington. How came you to choose it?"

Jack looked down the great table at his wife, Merrie, whose adoring gaze, after nearly twenty years, still had the power to warm his heart. "'Twas Merrie's notion to give the boy an uncommon name, one well fitted to a 'strong ruler.' I trow he'll grow into it"—he grinned proudly—"for he rules the roost hereabouts already."

There was laughter at that, and Rugar pulled Corrie close against his side and smiled down into her upturned face. With a hint of mischief, he raised his gaze to Torgne and Anne, who sat across the table from them, cuddled like folk wedded only two days, which was exactly what they were. "And you, Torgne and Anne, have you given thought to what you'll name *your* firstborn?"

Corrie pinched Rugar on a sensitive spot on his inner thigh beneath the table, making him flinch privately, and Torgne and Anne turned to glare at him. They had gone to some lengths to keep news of Anne's impending motherhood a secret from her stern and moralistic father. But Rugar could scarcely resist giving Torgne a prod now and again, after having endured years of his self-righteous abstinence.

"Of course, there is plenty of time," Henry said, turning to his new son-in-law. "But if you were to have a son . . . well, is your heart set on calling him Torgne?"

"Certainly not." Torgne forced his gaze away from Rugar

and smiled at his father-in-law. "I've always had a great urge to call my first son Heimdall."

Anne's eyes slowly widened, and she sat away from him. *"Heimdall?"*

"In Norse legend, he is the guardian of the rainbow," Torgne informed her. "He had senses so keen he could hear the grasses growing."

Anne's tawny eyes narrowed as she realized he was serious. "You want our son to have ears so big he can hear grass growing? And pray, what would you name our daughter?"

"Well . . . I've always fancied Huldagard."

"Huldagard?" She nearly strangled.

Torgne cast a bewildered look about the table, seeking support. "What's wrong with Huldagard? I have an aunt named Huldagard . . ."

Anne rose to her feet with a womanly glint in her gaze. "I can see this is a matter that may take some . . . negotiation. And there's no better time to begin than right now. We bid you good evening." She pulled Torgne to his feet and to the stairs. And as they faded from sight along the gallery, his thickening voice floated back to them. "Yes, well, I suppose we could give it a bit more thought . . ."

Rugar laughed, thinking of the sort of negotiations Anne had in mind. "They shall probably name him James."

Sometime later, things grew quiet around the table as each reflected on the week's events. Then Rugar's voice, deep and rich with feeling, nudged aside the silence.

"I don't know when I've felt so at peace," he mused. "I'd forgotten what it was like to have a family around me. My parents both died years ago, and Torgne is the closest thing I've ever had to a brother. This last month has been precious indeed. It will almost seem a shame to leave for our own house."

"Not to me," Corrie said. "I can scarcely wait to be in

our very own home." She caught the flicker of sadness in Merrie's face and reached across the table to reassure her. "We won't be far, just over in Essex. And our house is large and has such a pleasant, sunny aspect. When Rugar and I go to Sweden for a visit in the fall, I intend to bring back a number of those lovely weavings and hangings the Swedes love so. They're so bright and warm. Oh, they have the most wonderful little earthen stoves—you'd love them, Mother." She turned to Rugar, her face alight with excitement. "Like the ones in your house in Stockholm . . . recall how warm and delightful they were? Well, I mean to install them in every chamber, and I—"

But Rugar's fingers against her lips stopped her. "Faith— she's determined to import half of Sweden!" he complained good-naturedly. "She's become a better ambassador for my homeland than I am." But the softness in his expression spoke of pride at her forgiving attitude toward his home and people. She insisted on accompanying him back to Sweden so that she might see his ancestral home and learn more of his countrymen's ways, vowing that this time she would know what to expect, her Swedish would be better, and she would be prepared. Now he shook his head and drew her affectionately against his side.

She was still in love with the world, after all it had done to disappoint her. And for that stubborn and precious bit of wonder in her soul, he would always be grateful.

It wasn't long before Corrie and Rugar wound their way upstairs to their chambers, arm in arm, eyes warm and glow-ing. When the maid withdrew and the door closed behind them, he pulled her into his arms and nuzzled her temple.

"I love you, my little English wench. And it's because I love you that I have to confess: those little stoves you love . . . they're not strictly Swedish. I got them in Hamburg the last time I was there."

"And it's because I love you, my lord, that I'm going to always think of them as Swedish anyway."

He caught her lips in a sweetly rousing kiss that soon drove all thoughts of Sweden and stoves straight from her mind. She shifted her body against his, and he moaned approval and began to work the laces of her bodice. She shivered as he peeled her elegant blue watered silk from her shoulders and slid his mouth across the shoulder he was baring by small, tantalizing increments.

"You were a wicked, wicked boy this evening, almost giving Anne and Torgne's secret away," she said with sultry desire rising in her voice. He pulled her bodice from her, then stared hotly at her thinly clad breasts. She took his hands and placed them there, then drew his gaze into hers.

"And you know what happens to wicked boys, don't you?"

When he shook his head and raised his eyes to hers, she laughed. The full, throaty sound was pure seduction.

"They usually get exactly what they want."

He scooped her up into his arms and carried her to the bed with a heated and adoring smile.

"Then I must be wicked indeed," he murmured, sinking into the softness of her embrace. "For I have everything my heart could desire."

Author's Note

I hope you enjoyed the story of Corrie Huntington and her handsome Swede. Corrie and Rugar, Anne and Torgne . . . my goal was to make them stride as boldly and irresistibly into your imagination as they did into mine.

One of the challenges in writing this book was the portrayal of Elizabeth I as history shows her to have been in mid-life: brilliant, vain, and full of astonishing energy, strength of will, and charisma. An unmarried queen in a time when women were considered morally and intellectually inferior—and thus "unfit to rule"—she defied tradition, convention, and the will of her nobles and advisors to preside single-handedly over England's rise as a major power in Europe.

Despite the power she wielded and the public adulation she received, hers was a lonely and difficult course. The demands of her roles as a woman and queen were often at odds. Her overblown masculine manners and equally exaggerated attempts at feminine coquetry made her the target of derision—even among her personal attendants. It is recorded in letters and diaries that her ladies "did mock and play at being her in her absence," one taking her part while the others played the parts of overheated swains, hapless servants, or court ladies who ran afoul of her vanity or temper. Thus, as fantastic as it seems, the events at the orgy Corrie and Anne attended had historical precedent!

Other aspects of the story were drawn from history as well. Elizabeth's possessiveness with the ladies of her chambers is well documented. She considered it a desertion from duty—a disloyalty bordering on treason—if one of her ladies wished to marry. Those who married secretly were sometimes imprisoned in the Tower—the famous Sir Walter Raleigh suffered just such a fate. Many of her ladies preferred to "burn"—with both passion and resentment— instead. Such arrogant control over others' personal lives seems cruel by modern standards, but the English monarchs had deemed it their right to control the marriage of their nobles for centuries. Elizabeth simply exercised that right with more obvious personal motives than others.

Also historical are the disdainful attitude the English court displayed toward the manners and customs of Sweden, and the "hierarchy of refinement" Anne delineates in the story. Like most prejudices, English contempt for the Swedish court ignored the facts. In Sweden, as in England, the nobility had worked hard at adopting prevailing Continental standards for dress, manners, and culture. With increased trade and commerce among countries came an exchange of goods and ideas, which had spread a similar standard of refinement all over the Continent. There were probably greater cultural differences between the English nobles and their own peasantry than there were between English and Swedish nobles of the day.

Rugar's traumatic experiences in England also have a basis in fact: in the first several years of Elizabeth's reign, delegations from Sweden paid earnest suit to her on behalf of Prince Erik . . . and were treated disgracefully by Elizabeth and her English court.

Thus, Corrie and Rugar's story could have actually happened! An innocent young girl, claimed by her sovereign and taken to court, and a handsome Swede, bent on a very personal bit of revenge against a vain and possessive queen. I'd like to think that Corrie and Rugar went on to improve relations between their two countries—while filling their house with dark-haired sons and titan-haired daughters, and with love and laughter. And I'd like to think that Corrie's baby brother, Roarke Huntington, grew up to be a handsome, incorrigibly charming rake . . . who kept the aged Elizabeth entertained in the final years of her reign, and found himself embroiled with an irresistible and unscrupulous minx with the last name of Lombard.

Happy reading!

Read on for a preview of
New York Times bestselling author
Betina Krahn's next romance,

ANYONE BUT A DUKE

On sale in December 2019!

Prologue

London, January 1896

"Our family has never had much luck with dukes," Elizabeth Bumgarten declared, smoothing her already impeccable skirts and staring out the window of the darkened carriage into the chilled winter night.

"He's not a duke," Sarah Bumgarten countered her mother's observation, sitting straighter so as not to crumple her costly blue satin. "He's an earl. A new one at that . . . three months . . . mostly spent in Italy garnering family support and alliances." She smiled, thinking of his handsome face and irreverent wit. "But he's finally home."

"I am only saying, he could have found time in his busy schedule to call on you." Her mother sniffed. "In London for days and not even a word."

"He is now responsible for his family's businesses." Sarah thought of his previous devil-may-care attitude toward those weighty concerns. No doubt it was a huge adjustment for him to have to contend constantly with managers, ledgers, and lawyers. "I'm certain that after tonight you'll be complaining that his lordship is always underfoot."

She glanced down at her smartly gloved hands and the

package they held. She couldn't wait to see him open the birthday present she had chosen.

"At least he's not a duke," her mother muttered. "One in the family is quite enough."

Sarah half expected her mother to recount the unfortunate way that her son-in-law had become the Duke of Meridian . . . his older brother Arthur had died abroad, under unknown circumstances. It was just one of several unfortunate happenings involving their family and men of ducal rank. It was almost enough to put Elizabeth off noblemen altogether. Except, of course, that she had one more daughter to see married. And for once, Sarah found herself in sympathy with her mother's fondest hopes.

Last season, Terrence Tyrell had talked and teased, walked and waltzed with her under the gaze of London society, raising both eyebrows and expectations. Then, just over three months ago, he'd inherited the title of Earl of Kelling and was whisked away to Italy by the family elders. Now he was back and was undoubtedly expected to settle down, take a wife, and produce an heir. What better time than the first ball of the season to take the next prescribed step in the life of a nobleman?

Before he left London he had dropped hints that the family council would meet in Florence, and he made references to the exquisite ring that every earl's bride had worn. Tonight could be the night. If he proposed, by next Monday the *Times* would share the news with all of England, and her mother would be over the moon with delight.

The grand Palladian style mansion glowed with candlelight reflected by gilt furnishings, French satin, and family jewels. No garish gas light or nouveau electrics would intrude on this grand gathering. They paused in the doorway as their names were announced and Sarah took a deep breath. Her mother's hand on her elbow reminded her of decorum's demands, but she couldn't help scanning the faces, looking for *him* as they moved forward.

She had to greet their host and hostess, the Earl of Sunderland and his countess, Lady Maribel, and then to acknowledge sundry others of rank and precedence before she would be free to join him. It was the first major social event of an exceptionally early season and, coincidentally, his birthday. She held the flat, ribbon-wrapped box at her side, now wishing she had waited to give it to him . . . or at least had chosen less conspicuous wrappings.

Smiles, Continental kisses, and handshakes distracted her as she paid duty to all the proper people. Mercifully, her mother absorbed most of the attention, answering queries about married daughters and a forthcoming grandchild. She managed to steal away and enter the ballroom proper, smoothing her rich blue gown and her long kidskin gloves.

Heads turned and whispers began as she made her way around the room, scanning the glittering crowd until she spotted him.

It would be crass, under so many searching eyes, to rush to his side. She had to let him come to her. As she paused to exchange greetings with an older couple she had met before, he turned slowly toward her.

That dark hair, those aquiline features, that easy smile . . . were attached by an arm to a dark-haired woman in a pale yellow gown. She was a sloe-eyed beauty with olive skin and a demure smile that seemed oddly knowing, almost amused. As the pair turned, his gaze swept across the ballroom and passed over Sarah without the slightest glint of recognition.

She stood with leaden limbs and a racing heart as one of the earl's boisterous dark-haired companions pointed to her and asked the earl something. He turned with a half-smile and replied in Italian before escorting the woman on his arm across the ballroom toward her.

"There you are," he said a bit too loudly, before speaking in what she recognized as Italian to his voluptuous companion. "*Mi amore, vi presento* Signorina Sarah Bumgarten." The woman said something in a dry tone that sounded like "*Sono, in effetti, incantata*" to her, which might have meant "enchanted" or "eat grass, you cow" in her language. He nodded before turning to Sarah. "My dear girl, I would have you meet Signorina Ava Marie Lombardi, of Florence . . . soon to be my countess."

Words—always her obliging servants—utterly failed her.

She looked between them and forced a brittle smile to hide the fact that her heart was shattering into a million pieces. She managed a sociable lie about the pleasure of making the woman's acquaintance, and watched helplessly as Terrence's Italian bride turned to him and said something that set the Italians around them smirking. She caught two words that were appallingly similar in English: *dollaro* and *principessa*.

She backed a step and brought her hands up defensively—realizing too late that they held the gift she had brought.

"Ahhh." The Lombardi creature pounced on that mistake with icy amusement, focusing on that pretty blue paper and brilliant yellow bow. *"E cosi per lui? Eri una **bambina** tanto dolce."*

Bambina. She had read enough of Dante and other Italian classics to know she had just been called a child. When she looked up in disbelief and caught Terrence's gaze, he quickly looked away. He might be uncomfortable, but he clearly did not value her enough to intervene in such rude and degrading treatment.

She glanced away, only to find a quarter of the ballroom watching that unthinkable exchange. Standing at the front of the onlookers was her mother, and the horror on Elizabeth's face jolted her wits back into action.

"I believe you have mistaken me for someone else," she said, throwing the gift on the floor near his feet and hearing the satisfying tinkle of breaking glass. "I am not now, nor have I ever been a 'sweet child.' And it appears that I have mistaken you, sir," she looked at the earl through a prism of hot tears, "for a gentleman of character and worth."

She turned on her heel and strode for the door, spine straight and head held high, ignoring the slither of gossip trailing her through the crowd.

Moments later, as she donned her wrap near the front doors and prepared to leave, her mother came rushing down the stairs from the ballroom to pull her aside.

"What did that beast say to you?" she demanded.

"Nothing I shouldn't have seen coming," she answered bitterly.

"Where are you going? You cannot run from this, Sarah. You must stay and hold your head up and brave it through. The Richardsons are here and the Muellers and the Spencers. They will see us through."

She pulled the hood of her cloak up over her hair and looked around the grand entry hall, watching the faces of the people staring at them while pretending not to stare.

"I don't want to be seen through. I don't want to have to bow and scrape and pretend I give a flying fig about these awful people. They think I'm odd and eccentric because I read so many books and help stray animals and study medicine and agriculture. Well, they can all bloody well die on the privy, for all I care."

As she turned to the door, her mother grabbed her wrist and held her until Sarah turned a scalding look on her. She loosened her grip and then, reading the pain and fury in her daughter's gaze, released her.

"Wait, I'll get my cloak—"

"No. You stay and gut it out with the Spencers and

Richardsons and Muellers." Banked tears finally slipped down her cheeks. "You'll want a life here after I've gone."

"Gone? What are you talking about? Where are you going?"

"*Anywhere*," Sarah forced the words past the constriction in her throat, "*but London*."

Chapter One

The English countryside, June 1896

"Blasted animal," Sarah Bumgarten muttered as she strode down the tree-lined country lane. She had started this search near the main house, and ventured farther and farther—until she now found herself almost to the village, still on foot and in unsuitable shoes. It was an exceptionally warm day for early June and she was annoyed to have to spend it looking for her dog when there was so much to be done at Betancourt. Every footfall of her shoes on the gravel of the road sounded like teeth grinding.

Consarned dog. She pushed her hair back from her face. *Running off to hell and gone, again.* The last two times, she had found him in Betany terrifying the locals. Nero was more dog than most of the villagers had ever seen . . . Irish wolfhound with a bit of heft that probably came from a mastiff somewhere in the line. He was tall and gray and had red-brown eyes as bright as copper pennies. He was stunning. And intimidating. And he had a grin that could melt an iceberg. All of which had combined to lure her into rescuing him from London's mean streets. She had no idea how an Irish wolfhound pup came to be running free in

London's West End, but she wasn't one to pass up a hungry, frightened animal when it came her way.

It wasn't long before the Iron Penny Inn and Tavern came into view. The rambling stone and half-timber structure had served as the social center of the village of Betany for generations. If anyone had seen Nero in the vicinity, it would be Bascom, the sturdy, taciturn innkeeper. He kept an eye on the village as well as his own property. If he hadn't seen Nero, there was a good chance she could get him or his son William to help her search.

Raucous male voices and harsh laughter from the far side of the tavern caught her ear as she approached the inn. That low, wicked rumble was punctuated by a yelp of surprise . . . anger . . . pain.

Damn and blast!

"Bascom!" she shouted as she ran past the open tavern door. "Bascom, I need help!"

A dog was in trouble, and she would have bet her best riding boots which dog it would be. Her heart gave a furious thump as another yelp and then some snarling reached her.

Around the corner, in the side yard of the Iron Penny, four men surrounded her wolfhound. Nero was growling and showing teeth as he crouched defensively and looked for a way out. But the men were steadily closing the gaps between them, hefting rocks and taking turns taunting Nero. As she caught her breath, one of the four lobbed a rock at her dog, who dodged, but only into the path of another missile hurled at him. He yelped and shrank for an instant, then came back growling and baring teeth.

She bolted toward the fray, yelling, "Stop! This instant!"

The men turned on her, surprised—by her appearance as much as her demand. She had dressed for a day of visiting the local vicar and a few tradesmen; a yellow cotton day dress printed with blue flowers, made with French blue piping, and satin ribbon laced through the bodice. She had

meant to present a ladylike appearance to the people of
Betany—to reassure them that someone was upholding
Betancourt standards. However, her hair was down and
windblown—she hadn't had time to put it up when house-
maid Mazie stumbled up the stairs to tell her that Nero was
missing again.

"Well . . . look wot we got 'ere," one of the men said,
turning to her with an ugly grin filled with dark gaps and
yellowed teeth.

"That's my dog." Her anxiety rose as two of the others
closed on Nero. "You leave him alone!"

"Ooh, hear that? *Orders*. We got us a duchess, boys," another, taller fellow declared before giving an enormous
belch. Fumes from spent liquor wafted her direction as he
made a sloppy bow of deference.

Drunk, she realized. At this hour of the morning.

"Yer mutt near took my leg off when I went out back to
take a piss," the farthest wretch snarled, glaring at Nero as
he removed his belt. "He needs teachin'." He drew back
with the strap and found his arm stopped—held. His wrist
was caught in the grip of a man with long hair, hands like
iron bands, and eyes filled with heat like forge flames.

"Lemme go." He turned and swung at the stranger with
his free hand, but his ale-sodden reflexes were no match
for the stranger's quickness. The blow was deflected and
the next minute, the stranger's fist slammed into his gut
and all hell broke loose.

The wretch nearest Sarah lunged for her and she
slammed a fist straight into the middle of his face. There
was a crunching sound and a howl that might have come
from her as pain shot up her hand and arm. Suddenly there
was a storm of scuffling and growling and the sound of
fists smacking flesh all around the tavern yard.

She got in several solid kicks and at least one more good
face punch before a shotgun blast jarred the scene and the

frantic conflict froze. Bascom charged into their midst, his formidable double barrel shotgun leveled at the miscreants.

"I told you lot to get out," he ordered. "You ain't welcome in my tavern nor the rest o' Betany." He gave the closest fellow—the one cradling a bloody face—a shove.

"She broke my damned nose!" the rogue howled, stumbling to the side.

"Out. Now." Bascom stalked closer and shoved again, harder. "Pick up yer friends, an' clear out."

For a moment it looked as if he might turn on Bascom, but instead he looked past the innkeeper to Sarah with eyes burning.

"Ye'll be sorry, *Duchess*. You an' yer mangy mutt."

Sarah's heart hammered. She gulped a breath as the ruffian stumbled over to his closest comrade, helped him to his feet and braced him upright as they staggered off together. She looked around to find Nero sitting primly between two figures sprawled and motionless on the ground.

Behind him stood a man in shirtsleeves, vest, and riding breeches with his booted legs spread and his arms crossed. His hair was long enough to brush his shoulders and his face was sun-bronzed. But his eyes—for a moment, across that space, she could have sworn there were white-hot sparks in his eyes. She looked away and blinked to clear her vision. When she looked back, he had turned and was disappearing down the bend in the village road.

Trembling, she turned to Bascom.

"Who are those men?"

"The same lot wot's been around this past month or two. Always trouble. Drunk half the time, fightin' the other half. Tearin' up shops and market stalls. Jus' plain mean, the lot of 'em."

"Ugh." She made a face and stuck out her tongue. "I think I might have bit one of them. I have an awful taste in my—" She headed straight for the pump at the nearby trough, gave the handle a few pumps and flushed her mouth out with cool water. Looking up, she found Bascom cradling his gun and watching her with a wry expression.

"Well, Lord knows where they've been," she said defensively.

He chuckled and gave her injured hand a nod.

"Better see to that."

She winced as she gave her throbbing fingers a couple of exploratory touches that made her draw a sharp breath. "Nothing seems broken. A soak in some Epsom salts and some willow bark tea will fix it up."

"You know best. Jimmy Donnert tells one-and-all how you saved his arm after he got it broke in the thresher." He frowned as he watched her wrap her hand in a handkerchief. "But, now, will ye take a bit o' advice and chain up that beast o' yours?"

She cradled her injured hand against her middle, reluctantly considering that advice and wishing there were another alternative. She looked around for Nero, and caught sight of his rump escaping around the corner of the tavern.

Annoyance ignited to full anger as she took off after him. Bascom wasn't far behind as she raced to catch Nero. The dog ran pell-mell to the rustic stable behind the inn that served the guests' horses. She lifted her skirts and ran faster, muttering between breaths when she saw him dart inside the shed-like stable. She stepped inside and found it darker than expected and she had to pause a moment to let her eyes adjust. She called for Nero, but there was no response.

In a far corner, she found him braced in a guarding stance—body taut, ears up—beside one of the empty stalls. He watched her approach with a wariness he had never displayed toward her before.

"What the devil?" She moved cautiously forward. She knew Nero wouldn't harm her, but clearly he intended to keep them from—

She stopped beside the stall. There was something dark on the straw . . . another dog. Something beside it was squirming. Soft mews reached her.

Puppies.

In the stall lay a female dog with a young litter, no more than a week or two old. Sarah grinned and gave Nero a stroke down his back as she edged past him, into the stall. At her gentle touch he relaxed visibly, then hurried to the mother dog and nosed her as if assuring her that this human meant no harm to her and her babies.

The mother lifted her nose to Nero's muzzle in acceptance of his presence. It struck Sarah as she watched her troublesome pet settle beside the female's head that this was what Nero had been doing these last few days: visiting this dog and her puppies. There was probably only one reason he would do so.

"You rascal," she muttered as she bent to look at the little ones. Their eyes were just open and their bellies bulged as they rooted for more milk. They were mostly black or gray, like their parents, and it was hard to say which parent they would favor as they grew. A soft chuckle made her look up. Bascom was leaning against a roof post, wagging his head and grinning.

"Looks like yer boy's got hisself a family."

"Looks like."

"That's a sheep dog—one o' them Borderland collies. From up north country. Ain't much work for a sheep dog if there ain't no sheep."

Sarah scowled. "No sheep? The farmers up there are selling off their flocks?"

He nodded and frowned. "These are bad times, milady. Not much work and lot of mischief goin' on. Strangers ramblin' here and yon. It's got so ye don't know who to trust."

A flash of memory brought one specific stranger's face to mind: the man with the sparks in his eyes. She recalled a blur of motion and the sound of struggle behind her while she was dealing out a nose-breaker. After Bascom's warning shot, there were two bodies on the ground and the man stood over them, chest heaving, as he watched her. He wasn't part of the group that had abused her dog—he'd somehow rendered two of the wretches unconscious.

"That other man—the one with the long hair and steely eyes—who is he?" she asked Bascom.

"No idea," Bascom said on a heavy breath. "Like I said, lots o' strangers about in these parts."

She took in that response and then looked back at the dogs. Nero was licking the mother dog's ears and muzzle with surprising tenderness. "Any guess where we might find her owner?"

"Aw, she's a stray. Some sheep herder couldn't feed her no more, so he turned her out . . . or she run off."

She nodded at his logic.

"Well, I can't have Nero coming here to see her every day and getting into trouble." She pursed one corner of her mouth. "I'll send young Eddie back with the pony cart to pick them up and bring them to Betancourt."

She looked down at the now sated and drowsy puppies.

"We always have room for a few more babies at Betancourt." She smiled in spite of the pain throbbing in her fingers. "I can't wait to get my hands on them."

Connect with Us

Visit us online at
KensingtonBooks.com
to read more from your favorite authors, see books
by series, view reading group guides, and more.

for sneak peeks, chances to win books and prize packs,
and to share your thoughts with other readers.

facebook.com/kensingtonpublishing
twitter.com/kensingtonbooks

Tell us what you think!

To share your thoughts, submit a review,
or sign up for our eNewsletters, please visit:
KensingtonBooks.com/TellUs.